D0891776

LOST AMERICAN FICTION

Edited by Matthew J. Bruccoli

The title for this series, Lost American Fiction, is unsatisfactory. A more accurate series title would be "Forgotten American Works of Fiction That Deserve a New Public"—which states the rationale for reprinting these titles. No claim is made that we are resuscitating lost masterpieces, although the first work in the series, Edith Summers Kelley's *Weeds*, may qualify. We are simply reprinting some works that are worth rereading because they are now social documents (*Dry Martini*) or literary documents (*The Professors Like Vodka*). It isn't that simple, for Southern Illinois University Press is a scholarly publisher; and we do have serious ambitions for the series. We expect that these titles will revive some books and authors from undeserved obscurity, and that the series will therefore plug some of the holes in American literary history. Of course, we hope to find an occasional lost masterpiece.

Although *The Devil's Hand* is a previously unpublished novel, it belongs in this series. Edith Summers Kelley wrote it in 1924—following *Weeds*—but was unable to find a publisher. Since the rediscovery of *Weeds* resulted from its republication here, it is singularly appropriate for Mrs. Kelley's second novel to be introduced as the fourth volume in this series fifty years after it was written.

M. J. B.

A novel by

Edith Summers Kelley

The Devil's Hand

With an Afterword by

Matthew J. Bruccoli

And A Postscript by

Patrick Kelley

SOUTHERN ILLINOIS
UNIVERSITY PRESS
Carbondale and Edwardsville

Feffer & Simons, Inc.
London and Amsterdam

Library of Congress Cataloging in Publication Data
Kelley, Edith Summers.
The devil's hand.
(Lost American fiction)
I. Title.
PZ3.K2868De [PS3521.E4117] 813'.5'2 74-10552
ISBN 0-8093-0675-1

Printed in the United States of America
Designed by Gary Gore

The Devil's Hand

CHAPTER 1

THE TRAIN pulled endlessly across flat stretches of deserted corn and wheat fields lying dank and dreary under a sullen November sky. Stark farmhouses slipped by and slatternly outbuildings and deep-rutted miry roads and barbed-wire fences and long windbreaks of scraggy, leafless trees. The small towns through which the line of cars swept without slacking speed looked all alike: the same shed-like stations, the same clusters of drably weatherboarded houses, the same prim little churches, the same mud-spattered cars and farm wagons, the same handcarts piled with trunks and suitcases, the same leather-faced drivers in caps, mackinaws and rubber boots.

It was hard to believe that each one of these dismal little towns, whizzed by and left behind in a second, formed the whole environment of hundreds of human beings, that under the roofs of these few drably weatherboarded houses lay all their ambitions, their loves, their jealousies, their angers, their despairs, everything that made up their lives. Looking out of the window at the meager shifting things, Rhoda Malone felt settling upon her a cold, dull depression. Her spirit faltered under this bird's-eye view of life which made people appear so small and wretched, the business of their lives so mean and trifling, so undeviatingly the same, as if they were a swarm of ants scurrying hither and thither with no apparent purpose, each one carrying a morsel identical in size and shape. Clammier and heavier the depression settled upon her.

In this mood her features took on a pinched look that made her seem older than her twenty-nine years. Her blue-gray eyes, the only arresting feature in a thin Celtic face, seemed to reach out, search and question. As they gazed out of the window they looked very deep and mournful. Her mouth, a sensitive, thin-lipped mouth, drooped a little at the corners. When it drooped in that almost childishly pathetic way one could discern about it fine lines of unchildish disillusion, of weariness and faltering of spirit.

A long stop at Newton, Kansas, the view from the train dismal and dispiriting, nothing to be seen but grim angles of gaunt buildings, tracks, freight cars and a dreary length of cluttered station platform gray and dripping under a late afternoon drizzle. When at last the train clanked and swayed out of the station it was the same thing all over again: the same stark farmhouse and slatternly outbuildings, the same deep-rutted miry roads and barbed-wire fences, the same windbreaks of scraggy leafless trees, the same dismal little human burrows.

Gradually the country changed to rolling, and now she began to see here and there strongly braced wooden fences set up to save the track from being drifted under by the great blind blizzards of winter.

Her eyes fell upon a slow-moving farm wagon, the wheels halfway up to the hubs in mud, the horses with bowed heads and straining haunches, the driver's shoulders hunched under his mackinaw, his cap pulled down and collar turned up against the rain.

"Where is he going I wonder," she said aloud, but more to herself than her companion.

The woman beside her cast a half glance out of the window.

"Why home of course to his chores and his eggs and bacon," she answered in a matter-of-fact voice.

At that moment it seemed to Rhoda Malone impossible that the man could be on his way to such a safe and prosaic place as home or to such cheerful and commonplace things as chores and eggs and bacon. With his hunched shoulders, his horses with sagging heads and his half-mired wagon he seemed to be moving forward inevitably to that distant place where the dull sky bent to the dull earth. When he got there he would fall off, horses, wagon and all, into an immensity of gray, vast and terrible, and that would be the end of him forever. The fancy numbed and chilled her, she felt her hands and feet cold and clammy and an icy weight sat at the pit of her stomach.

Her companion took an apple from a paper sack in the rack, pared and quartered it methodically with a penknife drawn from a mannish vest pocket and ate it with bored relish.

"Good Lord, I'll be glad when we can shake a leg again," she sighed, and clasping her hands behind her head, yawned and stretched to relieve her fatigue.

She was a woman apparently in the early thirties, not bad looking in a large featured, masculine way, with keen, alert gray eyes under black brows. Her straight bobbed hair curved forward on her cheek as straight bobbed hair has a way of doing. Trimmed very short it thrust into view her mature neck which was too thick. She wore a suit of gray mixture, neat and practical with plenty of pockets, and looked like an efficient business woman which indeed she was.

Rhoda Malone sat looking out of the window at the blurred and darkening landscape until the lights were switched on and the country outside turned black and her own face looked back at her spectrally from the glass. That night in her hot cindery-smelling upper berth she tossed to and fro for a long time thinking drearily how far she was from her home in Philadelphia, her people and her friends, the office where she worked, all the homely, familiar places that hitherto had bounded her life. The jarring clank, clank, that formed an overtone to the prolonged roar of the train, seemed like a hammer beating the dull ache of her head into acute pain. She wished desperately that she had never listened to Kate Baxter. She was penetrated through and through with homesickness, loneliness, a dread of the unknown future, an undefined sense of loss and futility. At last in the cool of the early hours she fell asleep.

She opened her eyes to a pervasive light that crept in beneath the drawn blind and filled her niche with soft radiance. As she pressed the snap of the blind it flew up with a jerk and she sat spellbound before her first vision of the West.

It was the sky, the all-pervading sky that made her catch her breath. It was pure, limitless, tingling with subdued but infinite light. Its serene blueness penetrated everything. It arched over a world that seemed to stretch away forever into a blue, unending distance of hope, joy, romance, unbounded zest of life.

The ground near the track was level, but not far away it rose into a half-dozen cone-like peaks with snow on their tops. Not far away it seemed to Rhoda Malone, and yet as the train swept on it did not pass them. They stood there in the middle distance motionless, white-tipped, draped sumptuously in blue and purple veils.

A faint blush of frailest pink touched the snowy peak of the highest mountain. It deepened, sprang to the others, spread downward and changed the blue and purple veils to gossamers of gold and rose and misty pearl. It raced over the farstretching prairie grass and outlined the hummocks and low places with light and shadow. It illumined the still, blue serenity of that great sky. The sun of the West had risen.

Rhoda Malone could contain herself no longer, she uttered a shrill, piercing, half-stifled little scream of excitement and delight.

"For the love of Mike, what's biting you?" came drowsily from the berth below.

"Oh Kate, look out of the window. Isn't it tremendous and glorious? We're there."

She heard Kate's blind spring upward.

"The dickens we're there. Do you think we could raise alfalfa on that prairie-dog land? We've got a good three days and two nights to run yet."

"I didn't mean we've got to the Valley, silly. But we're in the West. Isn't it—oh isn't it just RIPPING!"

"Well I'm glad you think you're going to like it, and I hope you won't change your mind. You seemed a bit off your feed last night." There was a note of genuine if grudging satisfaction in the matter-of-fact voice from the berth below.

"Like it? I'm going to LOVE it!"

"Case of love at first sight, eh?"

In the dressing room, washed and refreshed and brushing out her long brown hair over her blue crepe kimono with machine embroidered daisies climbing up the back on stems a yard long, she was voluble and ecstatic as a child. One could not see now the fine lines about her mouth, and with her eyes glowing and her thin cheeks flushed with excitement she looked girlish and charming. When they got out for coffee and rolls at their first Fred Harvey restaurant, so Spanish, so sun-steeped, her ebullient gaiety attracted the attention of a horse-faced travelling salesman who had got on at Chicago and was now for the first time aware of her existence, so immersed had she been during his brief absences from the smoking car in daily papers and gaudy magazines.

"Western air's gone to that girl's head," he remarked to the stoutish, worldly-wise-looking woman with whom he had struck up an acquaintance.

Rhoda overheard him, threw him a smile and laughed with gay abandon.

The train bell rang and they were off again. To Kate Baxter who had made a trip to the West before, and who looked askance at heights and depths of emotion, the change from Kansas to New Mexico in November was nothing more than agreeable. To Rhoda it was the entrance into a new world. She could not take her eyes from the window. Absorbedly she watched as they swept through prairie land fringed by distant mountains, the prairie grass growing every mile scantier and drier, being replaced by growing things that she had never seen before, gray sagebrush, dark, scraggy greasewood and angular cacti. Eagerly she looked out to the far horizons, wonderingly she peered down into the deep, perpendicular canyons cut into the erosive clay soil by the fierce downpours of the desert.

She was filled with delight at sight of the sun-steeped Spanish stations with red tiled roofs and bright flowers against the stucco walls and dark-skinned men in big hats lounging in the sunshine. These dark people began to get on the train at the stations: men in sombreros and blue overalls, dumpy women with black shawls over their heads and big-eyed children clinging to their skirts, the little girls with great manes of coarse black hair. They were strange, silent people, reposeful and self-contained. Rhoda eyed them curiously.

Gradually the sagebrush was passed and the greasewood. The clay ground cracked and eroded by sun and water merged into a softer, sandy looking soil, cacti sprang everywhere from the arid earth and they were in the desert.

Night fell and found them still passing through the great waterless country. Rhoda Malone's eyes, timid but searching, travelled out into the terrible spaces of that weird region, drawn by the fascination of a seemingly endless array of spiteful, extravagant phantoms. Their gray-green color changed to black in the deepening twilight, they stretched out gesticulating arms, at the same time beckoned and threatened: grim giants, witches in wild disarray, gibbets to hang men on, great pillars set up for some fiendish sacrifice.

In whatever way she looked they were there, always different, always the same. She marvelled to think how dauntless must have been the men who ventured forth on foot and on mule-back to lay out a path for the railroad across this pathless waste. How terrible to stray from that path, to wander alone through interminable stretches peopled by these fiendish hordes. Ever and ever the track stretched forward into the narrow cleft of clearing; ever and ever the telegraph lines hugged its side, close, close that neither be lost in the terrific wilderness. Shot forward at breathless speed along the one slender thread that traversed this vast No Man's Land of mystery, the people about Rhoda chatted, yawned, ate and slept as if they were on their own front porches.

When morning dawned the desert was left behind and they were winding upward through mountains, not such mountains as Rhoda Malone had known, the wooded hills of Pennsylvania, but towering masses of jagged rock without a scrap of vegetation, piled one upon the other in some tremendous upheaval of eons ago, yet looking as clean, as new, as sharp on the edges as if the great earthquake had happened yesterday. Sometimes the train wormed its way so closely between high walls of rock that she had to crane her neck to see the sky. The two engines panted hard. Sometimes peering ahead she could glimpse them crawling perilously along a narrow ledge hewn into the face of the mountain. When the view opened there were long vistas of these many-shaped and many-colored rock piles, gigantic and inhospitable. Colors such as she had never seen in a landscape before, sulphurous yellows and saffrons and intense brick reds stood out blatantly in jagged outlines against the bluest sky that she had ever seen. Looking at these savage colors, these bold outlines, she caught her breath with a sense of exaltation as though she heard a blare of trumpets and found herself leaping forward in answer, fired magically with a zest and daring of which she had never dreamed.

She had hoped that they would reach Needles while it was

yet daylight. But the early falling November night had closed down before they steamed into the town, and peer as she might she could not see the Colorado, that great river that brought down from the snows of the North the water which was to make for her and Kate in the Imperial Valley a semi-tropical paradise.

They alighted on the station platform of Colton, California, in a sparkling blue dawn. They would have a long wait there before taking the train for Imperial Valley. It was good to be able to stretch one's legs, to breathe clean air free from the smell of soft-coal smoke. Walking uncertainly and feeling still the motion of the train vibrating through their bodies, Rhoda Malone and her companion drew in deep, satisfying breaths of this crisp morning air.

They ate ham and eggs and drank coffee from thick cups in a smeary little stationside restaurant. It seemed strange to Rhoda Malone that after this long exciting leap across the continent, after great plains, deserts and mountains, vast, lonely solitudes, the wonders of new skies and strange peoples, a vision of a world gigantic and inspiring, they should be sitting here eating the same vapid and spongy bread, the same doubtful ham and more than doubtful eggs, sipping the same muddy coffee out of the same thick cups from the hands of the same indifferent and dirty shirt-sleeved waiter that they would have met with in any smeary little stationside restaurant in Pennsylvania.

But outside the too familiar restaurant, Fairyland once more closed about her. In a little park that lay between the street and the railroad station palms waved their long green fronds, roses bloomed and strange flowers flaunted their brilliance in the strong sunshine. Rhoda Malone was fascinated by the great shaggy trunks of the palms and the fringe of dead branches below the green, awed by the majesty of the palm avenues. Wandering down a street she gasped with delight when she saw her first orange tree. There were oranges on it too, lots of them, some green some yellow, and they lay scattered on the ground under the tree as though they were of no more account than cider apples on the fringe of some old pasture. In the gardens they glimpsed lemon trees and staunch little glossy-leaved shrubs burdened with the weight of heavy clusters of grapefruit. Flowers were everywhere, blossoming shrubs and gorgeous vines that climbed up the trunks of palms and over the roofs of houses. There were fine-tooth-combed lawns, parkings planted with palms, immaculate concrete walks, charming little stucco houses gleaming from the foliage. Everything was washed, combed and in order; the very street pavement looked as clean as a bathtub. A lovely immaculate Fairyland, but there was no Prince Charming anywhere in sight.

It was not Sunday, but a Sabbath stillness hung in the air. They walked for blocks without meeting a living creature. No human being, no tail-wagging dog, no horse profaning the impeccable concrete, not even a motor car. When Rhoda Malone had calmed from her first excitement at seeing palms, orange trees and great vines that covered whole houses with purple bloom she noticed with wonder this dead calm. It seemed indeed a sleeping princess town under the spell of the bad fairy.

"Oh it's lovely; but where are the people, Kate?"

Kate shrugged her tailored shoulders.

"Inside, I suppose, running an eye over the morning paper, or maybe not up yet."

"But doesn't anybody come out to go to work or anything?"

"Work? Nobody works here."

"But how do they get their living?"

"They got it before they came here. The people that live here are retired people; most of them are old and lots of them are sick. These Southern California towns are dead burgs, but there's lots of money in 'em."

"It won't be like this in the Valley?"

"Oh Lord no."

On their way back to the business section, a string of elaborately appointed and very high-priced stores, they met one stout dowager all in white tottering along on high-heeled shoes, one elderly couple, frail and sick looking, and one Airedale dog. They were glad when their train at last pulled out of Colton.

The desert again and, hiding under dust-laden palms, strange little desert towns that seemed to have no excuse for existence. At Indio a long stop amid intense mid-afternoon heat. After Indio again the desert.

The driest desert that they had yet passed through, and always it kept getting drier. Mesquite disappeared and greasewood and even cacti until at last there was nothing but fine white sand drifting, drifting under a strong wind. The men who had been lounging and smoking on the outdoor platform came in and closed the double doors; passengers pulled down the windows and drew the blinds. Still the fine, penetrating sand drifted into the coach, settled on the plush seats, the suitcases, the bags of lunch, the passengers' hair and hands and clothes, irritated the nostrils, roughened everything with grit. From the windows there was nothing to be seen but driving sand that spattered like hail against the glass. To Kate and Rhoda the heat was almost unbearable; in its stifling clutch they sagged, wilted, felt as if the very life juices were being wrung from their pores. Yet they noticed that most of the other occupants of the car seemed not greatly incommoded.

Toward sundown the wind ceased and the doors and windows were opened again, admitting a cool breeze singularly sweet with refreshment. The people in the car shook and brushed themselves, dusted off their belongings, went into the lavatory and washed away the grit from their hands and faces. The train was now sliding downward, always downward through the length of a narrow valley hemmed in on both sides by mountains. In the light of the setting sun these great piles of barren rock stood draped in soft veils of purple and amethyst and saffron and rose, the colors shifting and magically interweaving as though the harsh, bold outlines lay softened under a rain of opal dust. Above them rose an evening sky ethereally delicate and pure. At their base, mile after mile along the length of the valley nothing but blond drifts of sand delicately smoothed, fluted, curved and spiralled by the fingers of the wind. No slightest breath disturbed the pure tranquility of the treacherous defile so lately fierce with sand and wild with wind. It was like a land in a trance. Always the train kept sliding downward, downward. It was like a place in an Arabian Nights tale, a savage, inhuman place transfigured with sinister beauty.

A sliver of blue, strange in the desert, slit the blond sand beneath the base of the right-hand mountain range, then widened into a lake, a long, narrow, shining lake reflecting the delicate blue and rose of the evening sky. For miles and miles the train skirted its shore. Rhoda thrilled with excitement. She knew that this desert-fringed lake must be the Salton Sea, formed by the Colorado when it had broken its dam and rushed through the Valley to settle in this lowest basin. She knew that she was more than two hundred and fifty feet below the level of the sea and that she was about to enter the strange new country for which she was bound, itself in long-past ages a part of the sea bed, the land that the Indians had called the hollow of God's hand.

The twilight was thickening fast. She strained her eyes out of the window hoping to catch a glimpse of the first houses, the first cultivated fields blossoming out of this most savage and arid of deserts. A strange sight it must be. But the night closed down over lonely and unbroken stretches of sand. It was only when she saw electric lights twinkle out of the darkness that she knew she had come once more into a land tamed and bridled to man's will. The train began to stop at stations that had formerly been for her names upon an eagerly scanned map. People got on and off. She looked at these people eagerly, curiously. They were Valley people, they lived here far below the level of the sea in this deep hollow of God's hand. At last the guard trumpeted "El Centro."

CHAPTER 2

THEY AWOKE next morning to the hysterical ringing of a telephone bell, a sound of water running, doors slamming, feet scurrying and pounding along bare, sounding-board passages, somebody hammering, and above all this two voices, male and female, raised in heated argument.

"Now listen here, Myrtle, this is past the limit. You can't quit me cold on an hour's notice; I won't stand for it."

"I can't, can't I? Well you just tell me what law says I can't. I'm goin' an' I'd just like to see you stop me." The voice was high-pitched, strident and strongly nasal.

"See here, you're tryin' to play a dirty trick an' you know it. You know the house's jammed an' I'm shorthanded. If you leave me now you leave me in a awful hole."

"I don't give a darn what kind of a hole I leave you in. My sister's took sick an' I'm leavin' to take care of her an' I'd like to see you or anybody else stop me."

"Now listen, Myrtle, be reasonable. Stay on to the end of the week an' I'll give you an extra five-spot."

"Not on your tintype. You think money'll do anything, don't you?"

"Well I'll make it ten if you'll stay till Sunday night."

"No siree, not if you offered me a hundred. My mind's made up an' I'm goin'."

"Oh well then for God's sake go an' go to Hell."

"You'd better look out, Mister Rumsell, how you talk to a lady. I don't have to listen to langridge like that out of any man's mouth."

A door slammed with vicious violence and the male voice was heard again addressed to another person.

"Holy mackerel, this help problem'll have me in the undertaker's parlor yet. Her sister sick! Dollars to doughnuts she never had a sister. Call up Judd's agency and see if he's got any girls. Of course he hasn't, damn him."

"Rhoda, what kind of a joint have we struck?"

Kate yawned, stretched luxuriously and put her feet out on the pocket-handkerchief-size rag rug beside the bed. Rhoda who had already risen was going about in her kimono examining the strange room.

They had come to the "Palace Rooming House" from motives of economy. The night before they had been too tired to do anything but bathe and go to bed. The bathroom had had the usual appointments and the hot baths had been grateful and satisfying. Now with the refreshment of a long sleep and the stimulation of novelty they felt born again.

"You may well ask what kind of a joint, Kate. There's newspaper spread out on the washstand. The pitcher's got a big chunk broken out of the spout. The dresser's a packing case draped in cheesecloth and one of the pillowslips is made of two flour sacks sewed together. You can still read the print."

Kate verified the truth of these statements with a sweeping glance. "Well it's the great free West ain't it?" she laughed and began to dress. "Anyway it's better than the coats and coats of decorous inherited dirt I've run into in many a furnished room back East."

"And Kate there isn't a sign of glass in the window—only this."

She pulled at a rope and a big white canvas awning flew up leaving open more than half of one side of their room and letting in a flood of sunlight. It revealed a bare beaten space of ground, a tin can dump, a prowling cat and the clean pine boards of some newly erected buildings. From outside came sounds of hammering, sawing, whistling and the buzz and rumble of motor car traffic.

As they dressed they heard the occupant of the next room, separated from them by the thinnest of wallboard partitions, get out of bed, go through his various toilet operations, snap his suitcase shut and depart. They were happy even to gleefulness, laughed over the discrepancies of the room and as they packed their suitcases eagerly discussed their plans for the future. They stopped to pay their reckoning in the office which was also the front porch and with their suitcases in hand left the Palace Rooming House forever.

When they had checked their suitcases at the station and eaten breakfast in a slapdash cafeteria full of steam and clattering dishes they set out to see the town.

El Centro was a town of only six thousand, but its business district gave the impression of being that of a much larger place. There were cars everywhere; they lined the business streets solidly and stood parked beside the humblest shanties: exclusive sedans and dignified touring cars and rakish sport models; runabouts, coupés, deliveries, ponderous double-wheeled trucks and saucy little bugs in gaudy colors; Fords with the ephemeral first gloss still undimmed, Fords with disembowelled upholstery and bodies eaten through with rust. They started in luxurious salesrooms glittering with plate glass and ended on the ragged fringe of the town where in more than one unsightly cemetery the rusty skeletons of dead cars lay in great lugubrious scrapheaps. Everywhere cars, cars and again cars.

The streets were thronged with people, most of them men. A few wore the conventional business suit and the others were in overalls, riding breeches of khaki or corduroy and leather or canvas leggings. Soldiers' clothes were much in evidence, not because the wearers were ex-soldiers but because the army store offered these garments for sale very cheap. Cowboys strode by under big hats and Mexicans loafed and loitered, their gaudy shirts making bright splashes of color. Here and there a little brown Japanese in a white paper hat trotted with the crowd; and twice they came upon a group of Hindus in conversation at a street corner, the younger men shaved and dressed like Americans, the older bearded and wearing the turbans, the smocks and sashes of their race.

"Aren't they good looking, Kate, and picturesque?" Rhoda whispered excitedly to her companion.

"Humph, not so far as I can see," answered Kate. "All these dark people look dirty to me, and I wouldn't be afraid to bet they are too."

Their way along these business streets led through the length of a perpetual arcade, for the solid-looking stuccoed business blocks were built with the upper stories extending to the outer edge of the sidewalk and supported by arches like those of the old Spanish missions. This gave shade and coolness and made of the outer sun-filled street a constantly recurring series of framed pictures. Rhoda was charmed.

The stores seemed to be mostly restaurants, pool rooms, tobacco stores, motion picture theatres and real estate offices, the windows of the latter full of placards and decorated with grapefruits, bunches of dates and heads of kaffir corn. Through the open doors of these offices they glimpsed men in earnest conversation and caught snatches of their talk: "Five thousand dollars," "Eighty acres on the shares," "Forty acres of the best soil in Meloland," "Three hundred dollars an acre," "Seven thousand dollars handles it." It was all about acres and dollars, acres and dollars. They were intensely interested and deeply excited. This was the sort of talk they had come to listen to.

They read eagerly the placards in the windows. These told about tracts of eighty acres, of forty acres, of a hundred and sixty acres, of three hundred and twenty acres for sale or for rent. Only here and there was there a baby tract of twenty acres. There was alfalfa land, cotton land, grapefruit orchards, grape vineyards, land plowed and ridged all ready for cantaloupes or lettuce. All of it was the best of land and a great bargain.

Kate made as if to go into one of these places but checked herself.

"Let's pass it up," she said, "until we get the hang of things a little better and find us a place to roost. We don't want to have to go back to the Palace."

The lodging place which after long search they secured in a shabby corner of that greatly overcrowded town was a section of a long shed-like building built of glistening new pine boards. There were two of these long sheds with a twelve foot alley between. The carpenters were still working busily on the ends of them, but up to the very squares and levels they were teeming with life. The apartment which they rented had just been vacated by the carpenters and sweet-smelling shavings lay scattered over the floors. It consisted of two small rooms and contained a roughly built pine table, a set of shelves to be used as a cupboard, an oil stove, a double bed with a bright new mattress on it, a flimsy secondhand bureau with a face-distorting glass and two or three rickety chairs. Their landlord brought them on a wheelbarrow the rest of the furnishings: some sheets and cheap comforters, three ten-cent store knives and forks and a motley assortment of dishes and kitchen utensils picked up at the secondhand store. He was a cheerful, obliging young man with face and neck burned brick red and hair bleached white by the Valley sun. When he was not installing new tenants he was busy building a bright new pine walk down the middle of the alley and little bright new pine walks leading from it to the several doors of the apartments. As he worked he whistled and sometimes broke into song.

"Gotta get this job done before it rains," he explained to Rhoda who had come out to draw a bucket of water from the faucet in the alley which supplied all the apartments.

"Rains!" she echoed and looked at him in amazement and

then upward at the cloudless expanse of blue. "I thought it never rained here."

"Don't you believe it. When it rains it rains cats an' little dogs, an' what it does to this here 'dobe is some wicked work, an' the 'dobe wouldn't do a thing to them nice shiny kicks o' yours. It's hell out in the country when it rains; traffic has to lay down except on the paved roads, there's simply nothin' doin' till the mud dries up."

Rhoda liked this young man immensely. He was so healthy and happy, so cheerful and friendly. When their baggage came he helped the expressman to install it. A little later he came dragging two rustic arm chairs which looked as though they had spent most of their lives on the sidewalk outside a commercial hotel.

"I just stepped over to the secondhand store an' picked up these two chairs," he explained. "You'll set more easy in 'em. Anything you find you need an' haven't got why just holler for me. This is my first try at the apartment house business an' I ain't always sure I've done the correct thing."

The new tenants found that there was some truth in this last remark. In the miscellaneous assortment of dishes and cooking utensils which their landlord had brought to them they found three pressed glass butter dishes, an old-fashioned cruet stand, a waffle iron, a tuning fork and several large platters. But there were only three plates and of the two cups one was without a handle. They made shift to get along however with what had been provided and did not trouble him for any additional furnishings with the exception of a broom.

That evening after a snack dinner in their new apartment they strolled out to take a look at the externals of El Centro's night life. The sky above the little shacks was deep and velvety and the stars hung low in the warm air like little golden lamps. They skirted the autocamp ground, a place touched with charm and mystery by the darkness and exotic with the stately lift of palms and the drooping lace of pepper trees. The lighted tents shone through the gloom with a diffused roseate glow like gigantic Chinese lanterns. A bonfire of some belated diner sent up dancing red flames that lighted in gipsy fashion the tree trunks and foliage. The shadows were black and mysterious.

The sounds that came from the camp ground were less romantic: a baby crying, a woman telling her husband in shrill tones what she thought of him, somebody trying to start a tired Ford.

They passed through a poorly lighted street of mean and sinister-looking little shops that belched forth odors of onion, garlic and chili peppers. Chinamen shuffled along the sidewalk and Mexicans hung in the doorways. Inside men of dark skins and black hair lounged about pool tables or munched sandwiches and swilled coffee from indestructible cups. Their mustaches were long and fierce looking, their hats tremendous; they were all that the motion pictures had represented.

In the business district the streets were thronged and the store windows brightly lighted. Pool rooms, movie theatres, barber shops and soda fountains were doing a rushing business. The women as they passed looked much alike; it was hard to distinguish between street walkers and high school girls because the use of the rouge pot and lipstick gave them all the same general appearance.

At a street corner they came upon a religious open-air meeting and paused on the outer fringe of the circle of listeners. A fat woman with run-over heels was talking excitedly in a high-pitched, febrile voice.

"And I want to say to you tonight—dear brothers and sisters—what God has done for me—praise His blessed name."

After each phrase she gasped and took breath. She kept going on and on and always these same expressions kept falling from her lips: "Bless his name," "Glory to Jesus," "And I want to say to you tonight." From the little circle around her came groans, murmurs, exclamations: "Glory,"

"Praise Him," "Hallelujah," "Praise His name," "Blessed Lord," "Glory."

At last she stopped and they swung into a hymn.

"Glory hallelujah, I'm on my way to Jesus,
Travelling along, travelling along."

A big Negro sprang with the lightness of a panther into the middle of the circle, his eyes and teeth glistening, his whole face aglow with joyful enthusiasm.

"Ah dear brudders an' sisters, how happy happy happy we are, happy in Jesus, happy in Jesus!"

His voice was rich and mellow, spontaneous too, like the bubble of a mountain spring. What he said had no meaning to Rhoda any more than the words of the woman who had preceded him, but the sound of his voice filled her with a sense of richness and joyous abandon as if he were a fountain brimmed full and running over. As he sang the praises of the faith that had filled his soul with bliss, she scanned with interest the little circle of enthusiasts about him. Skimpy creatures, most of them, with warped features and shabby clothes, they looked as if the hope of Paradise was indeed all that life held for them. Her eyes were particularly drawn by a very short woman no longer young, whose pinched face showed grotesquely small under a big coarse sailor hat. She wore a flimsy white shirtwaist, a cheap black skirt, and her small feet looked smaller still in little short-vamped shoes, ridiculous little shoes several years out of style, which she had probably bought for ninety-eight cents at some rummage sale. During the rhapsodies of the Negro this woman swayed to and fro with closed eyes; a smile played upon her lips.

All at once while Rhoda was looking at some other members of the circle she felt her hand grasped by a thin clammy little claw. Instinctively she made to pull her hand away, but the thin, clammy little claw closed more tightly on it. The little woman in the big sailor hat and the foolish, short-vamped shoes had edged around to her and was looking up into her face with appealing gray eyes.

"Are you saved, sister? Are you happy in Jesus? Have you been washed in the blood?"

Rhoda felt embarrassed, ashamed and angry. She had been brought up a Catholic, but it was a long time since she had been to Mass or confession, and since the war she had not been able to believe in God. She felt with annoyance that whether or not she had any religion was not this stranger's business. With a determined effort she pulled her hand away and plucked at Kate's sleeve.

"Come on, let's get out of here."

They went on down the street.

At the next corner but one they came upon another evangelist. He was a fine strapping fellow dressed as a cowboy and dangling with picturesque trimmings and accessories which Rhoda felt sure no cowboy off the stage had ever worn. At his feet lay an enormous Mexican saddle. It was a warm night and he was perspiring freely from the zeal with which he described the evil ways of life that had been his before he found religion. As he bellowed stentoriously about the shameless manner in which he had drunk, gambled, frequented the haunts of fallen women, scattered money to the four winds, a circle of admiring young men and boys stood about him, their tongues fairly hanging out.

What a strange preacher, Rhoda thought, and why did he preach? Could it be for vanity? And indeed he did look dashing and manly in his high-heeled boots and spurs, his plaid shirt, his wide, high-crowned sombrero. When he took off the sombrero to lead his listeners in prayer she noticed his haircut was a good one and his head well shaped, the line of the back of the neck strong and beautiful. His hands fascinated her; she was absorbed in watching the way the large, square-tipped fingers played with a rawhide thong and she would have continued to stand there watching them if Kate had not jerked her sleeve.

"Oh come on," she snorted, "why the dickens do we stand here listening to this dressed-up baby."

CHAPTER 3

IT SEEMED strange that anybody should die here where life was so new, so brisk, so busy. But one of the old men who lived across the alley had been found dead in his bed. They had taken him at once in a long wicker box set crosswise on the back of a Ford touring car to the undertaker's establishment and there the funeral was held the next day. Returning from this funeral Rhoda found that his apartment had already been rented to another old man. As she went about peeling potatoes and washing lettuce for the evening meal Rhoda could not help thinking about this old man and how quickly he had disappeared from the earth. Only two days ago he had been sitting there in front of his door smoking his pipe and peering dim-sightedly into his newspaper, with a big bunch of dates ripening on the sunny wall beside him. When she went out into the alley to draw a bucket of water he had called her over to him, given her a handful of dates and talked to her about the fortune that he had made and lost in mining, about the orange orchard that had kept him poor for years and about how next month he was going up into Riverside County to a mine that he still owned and of which he expected great things. Now he was lying dead under the ground and there was another old man in his place.

As she stood frying steak over the oil stove she thought of the funeral. She recalled the mechanical singing hired by the undertaker, the hurried hollow sermon preached by a pimply young man who must have only recently emerged from his theological school, the handful of idlers who had dropped in from the sultry street to listen. At the cemetery the undertaker had provided himself in advance with a half-dozen pebbles, and when the minister came to "Dust to dust, ashes to ashes," he had flicked them into the grave with a bored, perfunctory gesture. If they had only dug a hole and buried the old man simply, without the mock solemn singing, the sham sermon, the lame attitudinizing, it would not have seemed half so raw and crude. And now already there was somebody else in his place.

There were several of these solitary old men in the long shed across the alley, which was divided into tiny one-room apartments. Of a morning they sunned themselves before their doors with pipe and newspaper, like old groundhogs at the entrance of their burrows. They wore work shirts and baggy trousers held up by suspenders that had been mended with string; and the grizzled hair grew at will down the backs of their seamy old necks. Their hands were warped, trembly and swollen-veined. They had pet cats, canaries, parrots and heavy, old-fashioned watch chains from which hung a treasured nugget or a gold piece of fifty years ago. Glancing through their open doorways one glimpsed a roughly made bed covered with gray blanket or patched quilt, an oil stove set upon a soap box, a table, a trunk and a chair. In their better days these old desert rats had been cowboys, ranchers, prospectors, miners, soldiers of fortune. They were feeble now, dumpy and commonplace-looking for the most part; but here and there among them was an erect, broad-shouldered figure, a long, drooping mustache, a keen eye, a rakish swashbuckler hat, that seemed to have strayed out of one of Bret Harte's stories, a bit frazzled to be sure and travel dusty from the long journey, but with more than a little left of the old gallant recklessness. Now that they were wheezy with asthma or crippled with rheumatism they spent all the time that they could get anybody to listen to them in telling stories about the times they had seen and the fortunes they had made and lost in the good old days that were gone forever.

They were not niggardly with their advice either. Sagely, solemnly and stentoriously they warned these adventurous young women against undue haste in buying land, against the tricks of real estate sharks, against 'dobe, black alkali and waterlogged land. They discussed with them at great length and in minute detail the relative advantage of raising cotton, alfalfa, kaffir corn, grapefruit, of vineyarding and dairying. Each and every one of them was an authority on all of these activities. Never once was one of these old men heard to say, "I don't know." It was bewildering to the tenderfoot girls how much these old western wiseacres knew and could communicate. At night their minds seethed with the heavy clutter of knowledge accumulated during the day.

In the camp ground at the end of the alley where auto tramps of all ages and stages of trampishness cooked their meals, washed their clothes and tinkered their cars, there was also much freely proffered advice to be had and in addition all sorts of lore brought in fresh from the road: the grape and apricot picking at Fresno, the orange picking in Riverside County, the good roads, the bad roads, the towns that had good camp grounds, the towns that gave the traveller a raw deal and the towns where it was impossible to get a job. Among these shabby people who chatted, loafed and worked together, advised and helped each other by day and not infrequently stole from each other by night there stirred a warm sense of fellowship: the mutual helpfulness of the poor and the light-hearted camaraderie of the tramp and gipsy.

In the apartment next to them lived a widow from Arkansas who did washing and ironing assisted somewhat reluctantly by the two daughters who were big enough to work. She was wizened, her hair drawn tight and her skin the color of leather, out of which her eyes shone strangely bright and blue. When she talked the listener's eye was fascinated by the play of the cords in her skinny neck. She looked frail but was in reality powerful before the washtub and inured to its rigors. Through the thin board partition her nasal Arkansas drawl could be heard as she unendingly scolded her daughters for not doing their share of the work. The two girls were skimpy and awkward, with blank, stupid faces; but Rhoda noted that they had lovers who came to see them nearly every night. Four younger children ran loose in the alley.

A woman with a baby on her arm and a two-year-old child clutching her skirt was always trailing up and down the alley on her way to and from the water faucet or the toilet or the clothesline. She had a skinny, flat-chested figure and her face and hair were the same color, a blanched drab like the alley dust. The neighbors said that she was here for her asthma and that her husband had lately gone off and left her without giving warning or leaving trace.

In the evening the washwoman's young ones, with children from the camp ground and the neighboring shacks played at tag and hide-and-seek in the alley, filling it with laughter, the swish of skirts and the patter of feet. After they had been called in it was not long before darkened windows and a gentle sound of snoring told that most of the old soldiers of fortune had gone to bed. It was about ten o'clock when the washwoman's daughters and their sweethearts came back from the walk or the movie show and said good-night with prolonged sniggering and banter. After that, if one of the younger children didn't have the toothache or the earache, quiet would settle down; and the girls, tired from the excitements of the day—the new information gleaned, the new ranches visited, the giddy rides in realtors' autos along the dusty roads—were glad to go to bed.

A strange country, and Rhoda could not make up her mind whether she loved or hated it. She did not quite know what she had expected, but she had not expected this. Once free from the walls of the town, whizzing along in the auto of some solicitous real estate broker, one could see it all at a glance: a long valley, flat as a table, hemmed in on every side by barren mountains, crossed and re-crossed by ditches big and little through which flowed tawny water. Trees too along the ditches: tall, mournful eucalypti and white-skinned cottonwoods and the trailing abundant lace of pepper trees. Everywhere long rectangular fields of deep green alfalfa, of lettuce just planted for the winter crop, of cotton shrivelled and dead with the cotton pickers plucking the white fluff and stuffing it into long sacks that hung from their shoulders, of abandoned land that was once more sprouting gray-green desert weeds, rising into hillocks, going back to the desert from which it had come. Here and there in the corners of these long rectangular fields scrubby little houses patched together out of scantlings, canvas and mosquito netting and flanked by dusty cattle corrals, muddy settling tanks, outdoor toilets, milkhouses and chicken runs. In the towns it was not hard to believe that the Imperial Valley was prosperous; but looking at these sordid and lonely little huts one wondered and doubted. In this dull plain of wide, dust-deep roads, muddy canals, box-like shanties and fields laid out with mathematical precision there was nothing that Rhoda had learned to associate with the words "country" and "farm." She thought of her uncle's place in Pennsylvania where she had always spent her two weeks of summer vacation, of the old Dutch house nestled under the hill with its steep roof and stone fireplace, of a winding lane edged by zigzag fences that were overgrown with woodbine, poison ivy and blackberry vines, of a brook that trickled down from the hill and wound its way among mosses and the trunks of trees, of sunny, sweet-smelling pastures edged with gnarled old apple trees, of tall hickories and maples and little roads grown up with grass and fringed with wild flowers. Here there were none of these things, no beauty, no charm as she had known beauty and charm.

And yet the strange place beckoned to her with a compelling fascination. The far, mountain-fringed horizons lured her eyes and from the great blue tent the warm fingers of the sun stretched down and probed her flesh, caressing her very bones. Eagerly, gratefully, she soaked up the strong sunshine.

At night before she went to sleep she saw passing before her closed eyes the minutiae of this curious land: a snowy mountain of cotton in the midst of a scraggy, picked-over cotton field, a pink oleander tree smothered in bloom, a Mexican in a magenta shirt and a great hat, riding a donkey that seemed scarcely bigger than himself, cattle chewing their cud in the shade of eucalyptus trees along a ditch, a house on wheels by the roadside with children wiggling their bare toes in the dust and a woman hanging out clothes to dry on a wire fence, date palms burdened with heavy clusters of fruit, a turbaned and bearded Hindu sitting motionless on a ditch bank looking like an idol carved out of black jade and old ivory. And always as a background for these shifting pictures the intense blue of the desert sky.

They had been recommended to a Mr. McCumber, a man who was working up a law practice and handling real estate on the side. The general opinion seemed to be that this man was honest, and looking into his straightforward gray eyes even Kate could not doubt it. One day he whirled them down toward the Mexican border and stopped before two tall sentinel palms that flanked a gate. Looking up the driveway they saw a squat little brown house that stood some distance back from the dusty road surrounded by alfalfa fields.

"Now if you ladies want a sure enough good buy you can't beat this," he said as he pushed open the gate. "Twenty acres, all in alfalfa, not a better stand in the whole Valley and not a better piece of land anywhere. You can pay for the place while it's in alfalfa, and when you get tired of running alfalfa you can put it into grapefruit or Thompson seedless grapes and in three or four years make it worth a thousand dollars an acre. You know the saying: 'Keep a grapefruit orchard four years and it'll keep you for life.' At four hundred dollars an acre you won't find a better investment."

"Are you sure it isn't waterlogged?" ventured Rhoda timidly.

"Waterlogged! I should say not." The look that he cast at her made her feel like an ignoramus and a simpleton. But it was not so much his pity for her ignorance as his indifference that made her cringe. She felt that as a "prospect" he was willing to give her his time and attention, but as a person she had no existence for him.

"Just look at that stand of alfalfa," he went on, "you can't grow anything like that on waterlogged land. That's the beauty of buying a ranch with the crop on it; you can see just what it'll produce. When I came here from Omaha five years ago with a friend they saw my friend coming and stuck him with a black alkali ranch that wiped him out clean. They had it all plowed up ready to plant and it looked like the richest kind of loam. It took him the best part of a year and most of the money he had to find out that it wouldn't grow a darned thing. At the end of that time he turned it back to them to sell to some other poor boob. Lord knows how many they've sold it to since then. Now I don't handle that sort of thing. I try to do a self-respecting business and I don't deal in anything but land that I know will deliver the goods. Sometimes I make out where fellows who think they're a lot sharper fall down, because I'm getting a reputation in the Valley for doing a straight business. Anyway the last thing I'd do would be to sell two women a gold brick."

"Don't think you have to discriminate in our favor just because we're women," answered Kate with a laugh that had a touch of acerbity. "We're able to take care of ourselves."

They strolled about looking over the place. The little one-roomed house had a wide screened porch and an overhanging roof that took away some of the packing-box effect. Its sun-bleached redwood was lustrous in the sunshine like tobacco colored silk. At the back was a ramada thatched with arrowweed and shaded by a grapevine. Chinaberry trees stood about the house; they were leafless now and looked skimpy, but Mr. McCumber assured them that they would give ample shade in summer. The watering hole was overhung by a big cottonwood and along one side of the twenty acres ran a fringe of eucalyptus trees. After stark shanties, many of them set treeless under a blazing sun, this little place seemed all comfort and beauty. It was good land too, there could be little doubt about that with such a crop of alfalfa on it, and it was the size they wanted.

After they got home they sat up far into the night talking and figuring it over. They had been searching for over three weeks and this was by far the best that they had found. By the end of the week they had talked it over with the old-timers across the alley and the camp-ground people and Kate had negotiated the price down to three hundred and twenty-five dollars an acre. On Saturday they closed the deal, paying two thousand dollars down, the mortgage to accrue interest at the rate of ten per cent.

"But it's an exorbitant interest, Kate, away out of all reason," objected Rhoda. "I know it's the regular interest here, but how do people ever manage to pay it? And are you sure we'll be able to meet the payments?"

"Of course we will. This isn't Pennsylvania you know. Around home if the farmers make enough out of their crops to keep the table spread and pay the taxes and the interest on the mortgage they think they're doing fine. But farming here isn't the penny pinching game that it is back East. If it was we wouldn't be here. The ranchers here handle real money and aren't afraid to spend a dollar. Anybody might as well be dead as skimping and pigging along the way they do back on those old eastern farms."

The days were a fever of hurry and excitement up to the time of their departure for the ranch. They fine-tooth-combed the two secondhand stores looking for furniture, dishes and kitchen utensils. Kate too poked about after all sorts of farming implements and tools: Hoes, rakes, shovels, a post hole digger, a brace and bit, a pipe wrench, a wire cutter, some of them things of which Rhoda had never heard. She was awed by her companion's technical knowledge. Kate too became acquainted with a horse and mule dealer and bought from him a team of mules and a second-hand farm wagon.

"But how'll we get them out to the ranch?" inquired Rhoda anxiously.

"Why I'll drive them of course, silly."

She started early on the morning of their moving day. The patriarchs of the alley and the camp-ground crowd stood about to see her off and give last words of warning and advice. Dressed in a man's shirt, a brand new pair of overalls, the largest the store had in stock, and an old slouch hat pulled over one eye she swaggered in her joy at emancipation from skirts.

"Gee, this is the life," she chortled as she climbed onto the seat. "I'll get some groceries before I leave town, Rhoda, and a five gallon oil can, and I'll be there long before you. Goodbye all, wish me luck."

She waved her hand as she drove off in a cloud of dust, and the old desert rats and camp-ground loiterers set up one of those weak and faltering cheers that leave everybody looking foolish and feeling like an imbecile.

Rhoda went back into the apartment. She was amazed at and envious of the temerity of her friend. To drive off alone behind strange mules along strange roads into a strange new country seemed to her an extraordinary feat of courage. She wished ardently that she was able to do things like that; she wished that during the war she had not stuck to her stuffy office routine but had gone out like Kate and driven a truck and in summer hired herself out on a farm and learned to drive horses, pitch hay and do all sorts of bold physical things with the sun and the wind for her companions. Ever since that unforgettable morning when the sleeper blind had snapped upward and revealed to her the great sky and the limitless stretches of the West she had felt constantly within her a restless, driving urge to do something, be something different from anything she had ever been or done before. She found herself enjoying this new life with a keen zest and a sense of freedom such as she had never known; and yet at the same time she was agitated and disquieted by many things. There were moments when she found herself almost giving way to wild impulses to do and say the most extraordinary and outrageous things. Almost she seemed a stranger to the woman she had been. She wondered at herself, sometimes looked into the glass to see if there was any change in her appearance, but saw only the same slim, rather pale features, the same questioning eyes, the same demure mouth with sometimes just a flicker of a whimsical little smile stirring one corner.

She spent the morning packing the suitcases and setting the apartment in order ready to be turned back to its owner. The furniture, tools and trunks had already gone by truck; and in the afternoon Mr. McCumber was to take her and the suitcases in his car.

About noon as she was sitting at the table sipping a cup of tea and eating some leftovers from breakfast she was surprised to see the patch of sunlight on the floor grow dim and blur into shadow. At the same time a strong gust of wind swept down the alley whirling a cloud of dust. She looked out and saw the sky a pale, uniform gray. Another gust drove sharp grit into her eyes and nostrils.

"It's one o' them gol durned sandstorms," quavered the old fellow across the way as he folded up his newspaper and hoisted his rheumatic old bones out of the chair. "Best shet yer winders up good an' tight."

She closed the door, let down the canvas over the holes that were called windows and in the diffused twilight thus induced went on with her packing, wondering where Kate was by this time.

She expected Mr. McCumber and was all ready for him by two o'clock, but he did not come. Half past two and still no car. Three o'clock, half past three, and she listened in vain for the honk of a horn. To pass the time she read columns and columns of an old Sunday newspaper that had been spread out on one of the shelves: all about the adventures of a beautiful Russian countess fleeing before the Bolshevists, about why brunettes make better wives than blondes and why red-headed girls have bow legs. Then a column of somebody's advice to the lovelorn and something about why you ought to always wear your birthstone and how to be beautiful though forty. The wind was still blowing a gale and driving fine sand and dust into the flimsy shack. Everything was covered with it. Tired of waiting and straining her eyes in the dim light, she went out and paid a round of goodbye visits to the neighbors who had also closed up as much as they could against the storm. It was half past four when she came back, gritty and windblown. She carried out the suitcases, locked the door and delivered the key over to the brick-red young proprietor who was busy building a set of shelves in one of the unfinished apartments. He grasped her hand warmly.

"Well Miss Malone, I sure hope you an' your pal does good. If you hit any snag an' want somebody to put you wise just run over an' see me when you're in town gettin' your groceries. I was raised on an alfalfa ranch in Oklahoma. If you got any more friends comin' on an' they want a place to light while they're lookin' around I'll be mighty obliged if you'll say a good word for the Eureka Apartments. I wanta get a nice class a people in here like you ladies, not a bunch a dirty bums. Well so long an' good luck."

Rhoda assured him that she would not forget to recommend the Eureka and went out and sat on her already dust covered suitcases at the end of the alley with her back to the wind. At last Mr. McCumber arrived with a perfunctory excuse and apology.

In a few moments they had passed beyond the town's outer fringe of shanties and were speeding along the wide, straight road which on clear days ran to the horizon. Now the flying dust blotted out all but a few yards of it and the full force of the wind struck them squarely. Rhoda pulled down her hat, turned up her collar and closed her eyes against the dust and wind. For a moment there flitted across her mind a vision of the driver she had seen from the train near Newton, Kansas, his cap down and collar up against the rain; and with it came a sense of that numb dreariness with which she had gazed at him. It passed however at once, because she had her own affairs to think about. She wondered if Kate had arrived safely and if she had been sure to remember the kerosene and the matches. When from time to time she opened her eyes she marvelled at the cool hardihood with which her companion steered the car into that impenetrable wall of dust. As he drove he talked to her about methods of irrigation, about date growing, about the great future before the Valley, about the laziness and shiftlessness of Hindus and the industry of Japs. She knew that he was only making conversation for the sake of politeness. Every time they bounced over the little risings that marked the crossings of the water ditches she caught her breath.

Once when the car had gone up one of these little risings it wavered and seemed to sway. She looked down in alarm at the yellow water swirling beneath and saw how perilously close they were to the edge, with no railing between. Her heart jumped into her throat. She was reassured by a matter-of-fact voice.

"God damn those cursed mules! This is the third time in a week I've run into 'em. If that good-for-nothing Texan don't keep his fences fixed I'll notify the pound man on him. For two cents I'd knock one into the ditch."

Raising her eyes from the sliding water she saw that they were in the midst of a drove of mules. Their moving heads, rumps, flanks surged forward out of the dense cloud of dust kicked up by their hoofs. Cautiously the car moved forward into them and Rhoda breathed more easily when the swirling yellow water was left behind. The mules stared at the intruding car with lazy impudence, laying back their long ears. With the utmost reluctance they moved out of its way.

"Excuse me, Miss Malone, for using bad language, but it sure gets a man's goat when he runs into a bunch like that."

At the top of another ditch crossing the car stopped suddenly with a scream of brakes and Rhoda was thrown violently forward.

"Hey there, look out where you're going," came in an angry growl as a big car broke from the cloud of dust and almost locked wheels with them. Both cars backed and Rhoda looked anxiously over the side to see how near they came to backing into the water.

"Look out yourself," answered the real estate broker gruffly, "and keep to your own side of the road."

Then he went on talking to Rhoda about alfalfa raising as though nothing had happened.

He was a well-set-up man somewhere in the thirties, rather inclined to pudginess, but with a wholesome face browned by exposure and large, calm hands. Rhoda particularly admired the calm, strong looking hands that lay so capably on the wheel. Brushing elbows with him her mind began to wander into strange and devious paths and she was thankful that he could not look into it and read her thoughts.

At last they reached the pair of sentinel palms and passed up the short driveway to the house.

Not a sign of Kate or the wagon or the mules. Everything bare and empty under the whipping of the wind. Rhoda felt her heart clutched by a terrible fear.

"Why I—I was sure she'd be here by now," she faltered.

"What time did she leave?" asked Mr. McCumber, a serious expression on his face. The serious expression was caused by his fear of being late for his appointment at Calexico; but Rhoda misconstrued it and her heart was gripped more tightly in an icy clutch.

"Before nine o'clock this morning."

"Well of course ordinarily she'd be here long ago; but in a storm like this there's no telling. She's probably strayed from the right road and maybe gone miles out of her way. Of course somebody'll put her right again, but in the meantime it's tough on her and tough on you."

"You don't think–"

"Certainly I don't think. Of course she'll be all right and she's likely to be along any minute. But just the same I don't like to leave you here alone because she may be delayed longer than we think. I've got a rather important date at Calexico at six-thirty." He hesitated for a moment. "Suppose you come along with me and we'll get something to eat in town and I'll bring you back later in the evening. How's that?"

She felt acutely his desire to be rid of the situation, his complete lack of interest in her as a woman and even as an individual. She shrank from being left alone in this empty shack in this strange, lonely place with the night fast coming on. She felt lost and forlorn.

"No thank you." She forced herself to smile and found that she felt better when she did so. "I'll just wait here and I'm sure she won't be long in coming. I can be getting things straightened out a bit. There are no bears or mountain lions I suppose."

She smiled again with that whimsical little flicker of one side of the mouth.

"No, nothing fiercer than a gopher snake or a Johnny owl. Still I hate to go off and leave you before she comes. It looks callous–and if I didn't have that appointment–"

"Oh you don't need to feel that way at all. I'll be perfectly all right."

"Well I'm glad you're not a 'fraid cat." She could feel his sense of relief that he did not have to wait around or take her with him. "If you feel like looking up the neighbors there's some I think not so far away in that direction." He pointed south. "I don't know whether they're Japs, Hindus or white people, but anyway I'm sure they'll treat you ladies on the level. If any of them ever try to get the best of you in any way just let me know. Sometimes we have to put these foreign fellows in their places. Well, so long, and I hope she gets here soon."

She felt how glad he was to be gone and was relieved and dismayed when his car chugged down the driveway. She sat down on the pile of suitcases which he had placed on the porch, all her show of assurance vanished, and began to cry.

After a little while she dabbed her eyes with her handkerchief and got up to go into the house. The door was locked and she remembered that Kate had the key.

There was nothing to do then but sit and wait till she came. She had hoped to shorten the time by busying herself with unpacking. Then she realized that even if she could get into the house her time of unpacking would be short, for it was fast growing dark and she had neither matches nor kerosene. She sat down on the pile of suitcases and gazed dolefully into the deepening twilight. Then, unable to sit still any longer, she wandered down the driveway to the gate and strained her eyes in the direction from which Kate would come, trying to peer into the cloud of dust, listening for the rumble of the wagon.

But there was nothing there, nothing but the sharp, driving dust and the wind that wound her skirts about her legs and lashed her cheeks with loosened wisps of hair. From the other side of the road came a constant roaring and rushing and she knew that it must be the water of a big main ditch pouring through the gates. For a long time she walked up and down, up and down through the thick, powdery dust of the road which rose above the tops of her oxfords. When at last feeling desperately tired she went back to sit on the porch it had grown so dark that she had to grope for the screen door. With a weary sigh she sank down again on the suitcases.

But she could not stay there. In a few moments she was

out again and down at the gate, pacing restlessly back and forth, back and forth, in the thick dust. The night was growing chilly; she shivered and buttoned her coat about her throat. She felt cold through and through, not so much from the wind and the night chill as from dismal thoughts and gloomy forebodings. Why had she left everything, her family, her friends, the safe security of her home, and come away into this bleak, bare, inhuman land, putting her savings of ten years into a venture beside which almost any sort of gambling would be safe and prudent? What could have induced her to do such an outlandish thing, an act at variance with the habits of her whole life? Here she was with a woman who until recently had been nothing more than an acquaintance, three thousand miles from home in a strange, desert land among strange houses and strange trees and strange dark-skinned people with ways utterly foreign to hers, queer silent people from Mexico, from Japan, from India. She recalled the remark of the real estate broker: "I don't know if they're Japs, Hindus or white people." She strained her eyes into the darkness to try to catch a glimmer of a light, but through the driving dust nothing could be seen. She listened and could hear no human sound, nothing but the rush and roar of the ditchwater and from time to time a thin, mournful cry on two notes, more like the ghost of a cry, an uncanny sound.

Up and down, up and down, up and down. Hemmed in by the thick darkness, there was nothing that reached her senses but the sharp, driving sand, the whipping of the wind, the thick, soft dust underfoot, the rush and roar of the ditchwater and at irregular intervals this one thin, mournful ghost of a cry.

As time wore on, her discomfort and loneliness, her fears and regrets were lost in a growing anxiety for Kate. At first she had expected at every moment to hear the rumble of the approaching wagon; but now the silence had endured so long that it seemed as though it would never be broken.

What could have happened to her? At this moment she might be driving along some road in the pitch darkness, miles away and headed in another direction. Or she might not be driving at all. Rhoda remembered how perilously in some places the roads skirted the ditches, how recklessly great automobiles dashed along the roads and over the ditch bridges. How easily there might have occurred a terrible accident. And again, in this strange country of dark, alien men, what might not have happened? In spite of her exhaustion her step quickened with anxiety. She chafed at the restriction that held her helpless: No light, no telephone, no means of moving. If Kate did not come she knew that she would have to pace up and down there in the road until the late December dawn.

Suddenly she thought she heard a voice and stood still, tense with attention. For a long time she stood listening but could hear nothing but the rush and roar of the ditchwater. Heavy with disappointment she again began her restless pacing.

At last she thought she saw a glimmer of light. Yes, this time it was not a fancy; the light came nearer, a small, reddish speck. Then all at once out of the darkness Kate's voice: "Hey there, Jack, you keep in the road will you, you long-eared son of a gun."

The sound of this cheerful, matter-of-fact voice speaking with such placid casualness to an erring mule instantly dispelled all Rhoda's gloom. She was no longer even tired as she ran forward toward the light and the sound.

"Hello there, Kate."

"For the love of Mike is that you, Rhoda, and am I really here at last? I feel as if I'd driven a thousand miles. Three times I got off the road and once I went five miles out of my way, and back there on the main highway every car tried its best to hit me. Every time I'd take a ditch I was sure I was going to run into one. I've been between "Oh Lord" and "Thank God" ever since this darned sandstorm blew up.

And it was a good thing I bought this lantern and had it filled with kerosene or I wouldn't have been able to move a foot after night fell. And besides that I haven't had a bite to eat since breakfast."

There was intense weariness in her voice and jubilant satisfaction.

Rhoda felt like throwing her arms about her friend's neck, but she knew that such a thing would offend Kate's undemonstrative nature so she contented herself with telling her own tale of woe.

By the light of the lantern they unloaded the things from the wagon and Kate unharnessed and fed the mules. When she came to water them she found that the horsepond and the settling tank were both dry. They had forgotten about opening the ditches and the mules would have to go thirsty till morning. Rhoda went down to the big main ditch with the lantern and a bucket to draw water for themselves. The unsettled water was thick with mud, tawny as Father Tiber himself. The coffee that she made with it tasted of the mud and she remembered having seen a dead sheep float down one of the ditches that day; but she was too hungry and thirsty to let either the mud or the sheep spoil her supper. When they had drunk the coffee and eaten enormously of fried ham and eggs they unpacked some bedding and spread it on the cots. Kate slipped under her pillow the loaded automatic which all day she had been carrying in her overalls pocket and the two women, only partly undressed and neither washed nor combed, pulled up the covers and fell dead asleep.

CHAPTER 4

ON A morning in late February a woman in soldier's clothes walked up and down between a road and a ditch bank beside a water gate waiting for the zanjero, the man who rides about all day measuring out irrigation water to the ranchers on his circuit. The woman was rather slight and somewhat above the medium height and her figure displayed by the soldier's breeches and leggings looked supple and strong. She walked with a springy step and sometimes broke into a run and raced with a young collie that hung at her heels. Her khaki shirt, open at the throat and rolled to the elbow, showed neck and arms browned to a pale tobacco color and a healthy glow shone through the tan of her cheeks. Her dark bobbed hair unconfined by a hat was ruffled a little by the slight morning breeze. It was Rhoda Malone after three months of Valley ranch life. In this elastic girl who looked not more than twenty-five there was little resemblance to the rather pinched woman in a decent tailored suit over a respectable corset, a firmly anchored hat and a pair of gasoline-cleaned gloves whom the real estate broker had set down there scarcely three months before. It was more than a change of clothes and of health, it seemed almost a change of personality.

Rhoda pranced up and down and frolicked with the dog in precisely the same spot where three months before she had plodded to and fro in the darkness through a swirling sandstorm. She remembered how alien the place had seemed that night, how bleak, lonely and inhospitable. Now it was home, safe, familiar and friendly. It had seemed that night that there could be no human being for miles around; and all the time, just across the road beyond the ditch in the little brown cookhouse shack had been the Japanese truck grower and his dowdy little Japanese wife and the four little roly-poly Japanese children whom she could now see playing under the eucalyptus trees. The ditch bank was so high that it had hidden the light of their windows.

A thin cry, a mournful, plaintive little two-note cry. It was the same cry that then had seemed so wild and ghostly; but now she knew that it was only a Johnny owl. Her eyes travelled over long carpets of deep green alfalfa, great stretches of young cotton and endless rows of lettuce which little groups of Japs and Mexicans were cutting and packing into glistening new crates. Far away beyond the lettuce field a range of mountains fringed the horizon. Much nearer than this range a single cone-like peak lifted itself from the flat earth, its jagged surface boldly outlined with the light and shadow by the newly risen sun. Mount Signal, the guardian of the Valley. It was springtime now, warmer than a Pennsylvania June, and the irresistible upward gush of new life was everywhere. Along the ditch bank the shooting arrowweed spread a tender green mist and underfoot lusty new life was creeping swiftly over last year's Bermuda grass. Under the deep sky whose intense blueness seemed to pierce and suffuse everything the air was quick with sunshine and the singing of meadow larks.

A Mexican came by driving a sorrel mule and leading a bay. He rode lazily, carelessly, beautifully as Mexicans do. The feet of the mules made no noise in the soft dust of the road. He took no notice of Rhoda but passed on along the wide gray roadway at the end of which another range of mountains lifted jagged, sun-illumined and deep-shadowed sides against the sky. Two Hindus chugged past on a motorcycle, one wearing a slouch hat, the other a turban. Neither of them even glanced at Rhoda. A ponderous truck loaded to toppling with crates of lettuce lumbered along on its way to Calexico, driven by a little Jap who looked no larger than a child. A whole spring wagonload of Mexicans cantered by, the women and children in hard bright pinks, salmons and magentas, tempered by black head shawls. A Jap wearing a white Japanese paper hat came and sat down on the bridge over the sliding yellow water and began figuring with a stub of a pencil in a small notebook. He nodded to Rhoda, smiled and went on with his figuring.

All at once the bright air was cleft by a strong and impatient halloo.

"Hey, Rhoda, Rhoda, what the devil?"

The Jap moved his head slightly, smiled to himself and went back into his notebook.

Rhoda made a trumpet of her hands about her mouth and shouted back.

"Hello Kate, watcha want?"

"Say, hasn't that zanjero come yet?"

"Not yet, but it's past his time."

"I'll say it's past his time. Hurry up here as soon as he comes, I'm all ready to stack."

He came at last in an old Ford runabout, bringing a cloud of dust with him, a wizened but jolly old man with a stiff leg.

"Well how's ranchin' today?" he rallied Rhoda. "Still like it better'n keepin' books, eh?"

"I should say I did. Can we have a foot of water tomorrow morning?"

"You bet." He made an entry in a notebook. "It'll come on tomorrow about nine o'clock. That suit all right, eh?"

"Yes, that'll be all right."

"You gals 'ud better pick yuh out a brace o' husbands so you c'n have them do the irrigatin'."

He sniggered and looked at her with little twinkling gray eyes.

"Oh we don't need any husbands."

As she turned away the Jap got up and approached the zanjero with his order for water.

As she was about to go in at her own gate she started suddenly and almost uttered a cry. She had almost run into a man who had come silently along the roadside path behind the arrowweeds. He took a step backward and touched his hat with a half-apologetic gesture. She saw then that he was a Hindu.

"You live here?" he asked, inclining his head sidewise in the direction of the house.

"Yes," she answered with a slight catch of the breath.

"You have alfalfa hay to sell?"

"We have hay stacked in the field. We haven't sold any yet."

"You will sell some?"

"I—I don't know. I couldn't sell any without seeing my partner. If you'll come up to the house I'll speak to her about it."

He made a motion of acquiescence and started to follow her. A motor car came along the road; and above the purr of the engine the voices of the occupants were clearly audible.

"Who owns that nice little place with the palms at the gate?"

"Oh a couple of old maids have that place. I sold it to 'em three, four months ago. I haven't seen 'em since. Must run in and see how they're makin' out. Nowadays women that can't get married'll stick their fingers into most any kind of a pie."

Her cheeks flushed a deep, resentful pink. "A couple of old maids indeed, all ticketed and shelved!" She cast a furtive glance at the man behind her to see if he had heard, but his face was quite noncommittal. Once or twice she slackened her pace to give him an opportunity to catch up with her, but he remained always a foot or two behind. Kate was in the corral unharnessing the mules from the hayrake and Rhoda left the stranger under the ramada while she went to consult her.

"Kate, there's a man here wants to buy some hay from us."

Kate glanced in the direction of the ramada. "A Hindu? Tell him no. We don't want to have anything to do with the Hindus."

"But Kate, why not? We might as well sell some of the hay loose and save the cost of baling. And everybody says the price is going to go down instead of up."

They argued it back and forth and at last Kate gave in.

"Oh well have it your own way," she condescended and sauntered toward the ramada.

While she was negotiating the sale Rhoda, standing in the background pretending to be busy sorting out heads of lettuce for the chickens, looked at the man curiously. Riding breeches, leather puttees, a soft hat, an old sun-faded coat that drew across his broad shoulders. Under the hat a handsome, shaven face, full but not coarse lips which never smiled, and the luminous dark eyes of his race. She found herself fascinated by his hands: long, slim, dark hands, flexible, reposeful and self-contained. She could not imagine them ever clenching in anger or fluttering in panic or twitching awkwardly in embarrassment. She had never seen hands which radiated such complete self-possession.

When he had concluded his business he touched his hat gravely and turned away. Rhoda became aware with a little flutter of the heart that it was toward her and not Kate that he had looked when he touched his hat. A flush surged into her cheeks.

Kate too had noticed it.

"Why honest to goodness, woman, I declare you're blushing. Do you mean to tell me it was that dirty Hindu who made your cheeks pink up?"

"What nonsense! Of course I'm not blushing. But I wish you wouldn't call everybody 'dirty' just because they're not Americans."

Kate shrugged her shoulders with exasperating indifference and went back to the corral.

When next day the Hindu came for the hay he brought another Hindu with him. Rhoda, who was driving the mower, stole furtive glances at this man from under her wide straw hat and asked herself if she had not been transported into some tale of the Arabian Nights. High on the stack, in vivid outline against the intense sky, the white turban, the long black beard, the sulphur yellow smock, loose trousers and floating sash made a picture wholly exotic. With unbelievable strength and agility he handled the pitchfork, and she could not help thinking of a devil in hell.

When on its round of the field the mower passed close to the stack she could see clearly the dark, inscrutable features, the play of the brown-skinned muscles, the bare feet and the mat of black hair on the open chest. She shivered as if some presence subtly hung near her. The shiver was cold yet half pleasurable, like the shivers of children listening to ghost stories in the dark. For relief, a relief which she was not quite sure she wanted, she looked toward her acquaintance of yesterday who by contrast seemed almost Western. His coat was off and he was pitching hay too, with perhaps as much strength but no such tiger-like agility as his companion. She shrewdly surmised that he was not exerting himself as much as he might and was thus managing to let the other fellow do most of the work. As she continued to watch she became quite sure of this. Yes, by contrast he was almost Western—and yet? She began to amuse her fancy by taking away from him the clothes he wore and putting on him a long black beard, a white turban, a sulphur yellow smock, open over the chest, a floating sash and full Eastern trousers. Would he then be as exotic, as wholly from the Arabian Nights as the man beside him? No, she could not believe that he would. There was a difference. And yet she liked to tell herself that they were both jungle animals. What was the difference? Ah, it was this: her friend of yesterday was a lion—he had tawny lion's eyes, mild and thoughtful; and the agile giant in the turban was a tiger—a "tagger" she used to call it when she was a little girl. Somehow a "tagger" seemed a lot fiercer than a tiger. Neither the lion or the tiger took any notice of her. Kate stood bossing the job.

When the men and the towering load of hay were gone the alfalfa field seemed lonely and colorless.

So far she and Kate had made few acquaintances among the neighbors. The Japanese dairyman down the road treated them with reserved civility; the Japanese truck grower just over the ditch was just as civil and just as reserved. When they went to his place, as did many of the other neighbors, to get cull lettuce heads for themselves and their chickens he told them to help themselves to all they wanted and went on about his business. His wife was nearly always inside busy with the babies. The Hindu cotton raisers kept to themselves. The Mexican field hands who worked in the lettuce and cotton passed them on the roads silently or with a mere grunt of greeting.

To Kate this seemed right and natural; she took it for granted that these dark people should have nothing to say to the white and assumed toward them, even when she was asking for favors, a bullying air of superiority which made Rhoda feel ashamed for her.

A widow with three children, a woman still under thirty, was their only American near neighbor. Her husband had died only a few months before and she was desperately lonely, surrounded as she was by silent and alien Japs and Hindus. In her joy at acquiring neighbors not only her own race but of her own sex and stage of life she fairly threw herself into the arms of Kate and Rhoda. Almost every evening she came to see them, bringing the three little orphans, quarrelsome and cantankerous brats who as the evening wore on fell asleep on chairs and couches and had to be shaken and scolded into consciousness for the walk home. Every other Sunday she invited the girls to dinner and on the alternate Sundays they had her and the children. She was clumsily made, a slatternly woman exceedingly nervous and excitable, with stringy, dust-colored hair that was always working loose and hanging about her face in wisps. Her name was Ruby Peterson.

On these evening visits Ruby talked about how her husband had liked fried cabbage and his beefsteak rare, about the good money they had made during the war and the swell tailored suits she had been able to buy, about what she had had for dinner that day and what she was planning to have tomorrow, about Mildred's bad cold and Juanita's new dress and the way Melvin wore his shoes out in the toes, about her strong suspicion that the Jap to whom she now leased her forty acres was giving her the worst of the deal. It never seemed to occur to her that her listeners might not be as interested in these things as she was herself.

One Sunday when they went to Ruby's for dinner she met them at the door of her redwood shack in a smeary kimono, her hair straggling about her face, a dishrag in one hand and a long butcher knife in the other. Inside the phonograph was racing madly through a galumphing jazz record.

"Come in girls, if you can get in for dirt. Say, I'm just so excited I don't know what to do. I haven't got my dinner half ready nor my house half redd up. I just can't seem to put my mind on anything. I start out to do a thing and then forget all about it an' go to doin' somethin' else. I'm like that when somethin' good happens or somethin' bad or when I get mad at somebody. Now then, Melvin, you quit teasin' Juanita an' leave her have the doll buggy, an' Juanita you shut up your bawlin'. A person can't hear theirselves think. You know when I feel blue I set the phonograph to goin' an' it cheers me up an' when I feel good I set it to goin' an' feel just grand. I don't see how folks got along in the days when they didn't have phonographs. Well, what do you think? The Pruetts are comin' back."

"The Pruetts? Who are they?"

For a moment the widow looked surprised and taken aback that there should be anybody who had not heard of the Pruetts. Her own immediate circle was so all in all to her that it was hard for her to realize that it did not embrace the universe.

"Well yes of course you girls wasn't here when they left. The Pruetts owns Umasawa's place; he'd had it leased four years now an' his lease is up next month an' the Pruetts is comin' back on the place. Oh it'll be just grand to have white neighbors again, an' such good neighbors. The Pruetts is the grandest people. Mrs. Pruett's been just like a mother to me. Melvin, if you don't leave off teasin' Juanita an' makin' her cry I'll take the switch to you. Believe me, I have my hands full with them young ones now their poor father's gone. He knew how to make 'em mind; he didn't even have to raise his voice."

She sighed and went to stirring something furiously over the oil stove. The record had run its triumphant course and was buzzing and scraping raucously in the last groove. She let it buzz and scrape until she had stirred her stewed chicken and thickened the gravy, drained and vigorously mashed her potatoes. Then she stopped it, wound the phonograph as though she had a spite against it and set going a jaunty foxtrot. All her movements were rapid, spasmodic, immensely expenditive of energy but curiously lacking in precision. She darted here, careened there, reprimanded the children, all to very little purpose. All the time she perspired freely, mopped her face with her apron, pushed back her stringy wisps of hair and panted with the heat.

In the meantime Kate had set the table and Rhoda, who was attracted to children, however spoiled and naughty, had wheedled the three young Petersons into having their hands and faces washed. The girls knew that it was only in this way that the meal could be gotten on the table at anything like the usual time, and they preferred to do something rather than offer themselves up idle and helpless victims to the uncompromising jazz, the screams of the children and the shrill reprimands of the mother. At last the dinner was on the table and when the young Petersons had been served and the dispute had been settled as to which child's turn it was to eat the neck comparative peace reigned.

A strange country, Rhoda thought, and a strange household, with squalor and exotic luxury linked arm in arm. The table was laid on the screened porch which served alike as kitchen and dining room. Outside the wire screening palms and pepper trees made a tropical tracery against the deep blue of the sky. Beyond, green fields drowned in sunshine, long lines of stately eucalyptus trees and the distant mountains, a view for a prince's table. The immediate foreground, the widow's dooryard, was less beautiful. It's bare, beaten surface was scattered with trash: sticks, scraps of paper, old tires and inner tubes, rusted license plates, broken playthings and shrivelled grapefruit rinds. At pitching distance from the back door a frowsy pile of rusted cans, gaping and battered, betrayed the widow as a canned goods housekeeper.

On the oilcloth-covered table the dishes were few and coarse and none too carefully washed; yet they contained in addition to the Sunday stewed chicken and mashed potatoes, ripe tomatoes, fresh from the vines, the crispest and whitest of lettuce and the juciest and sweetest of grapefruit. The widow, who had been living in the Valley since she was nine years old, had small regard for these rich men's winter delicacies that cost her nothing and scraped them lavishly to the hogs and chickens.

It gave Rhoda a curious feeling of emancipation this juxtaposition of squalor and luxury that she found on every side in this strange new country, a feeling that she had been born again into a new and utterly different life, a life of new ways, new values, new standards. Something deeply seated in her nature responded joyfully to this urge toward a less trammelled existence. She found herself falling in love with this country, its ugliness as well as its beauties. Expanding like a flower in its unaccustomed winter warmth and sunshine, she reached upward toward the sun and bright sky, yet did not feel like scorning the earth from which she sprang.

She had been brought up in a home rather skimpy but decent, a home commonplace, clean and orderly, like millions of other American homes, a home where the beds were changed with clockwork regularity and the meals always on time and the cooking always the same, a home of no surprises. At seventeen she had left high school to go into an office; and because she had been an intelligent and faithful worker she had remained in the same office for twelve years. Her life up to the age of twenty-nine. Some obscure prompting, the restless bubbling of some secret spring deep in her being, had led her, a quiet, refined almost prim girl, to be attracted to Kate Baxter, to her mannish ways, her vulgarity, her profanity, had caused her to lend an ear to Kate's bold schemes for a freer existence and at length brought her here to this new land, this new life. She was born again and she was glad.

During the succeeding weeks she thought often about the Pruetts, wondering what they would be like, anticipating their coming. She felt constantly growing within her a strong urge toward her kind, a desire to talk, to laugh, to have people to dinner, to see familiar faces when she went to town and stop and chat with people on the street. Wistfully she followed with her eyes the Japs, the Hindus, the Mexican field hands who passed every day along the road or came to the water gate to leave their orders with the zanjero, hopeless of ever bridging the gulf of race which separated them but wondering curiously what had been their lives before they came here and what were their lives now, what they thought about, what they hoped for. With the Pruetts it would be different; they were her own kind, there would be no blank walls of racial difference.

When the Pruetts arrived all three families at once became intimates, Sunday dinners in each other's homes, frequent visitors, lenders and borrowers. Pa Pruett turned out to be a spare, bald, active little man, formerly a country lawyer, who at dinner sucked his teeth and made puns. Aside from these ornaments of conversation, the one thing he talked about was money and how to make it. The two boys were pimply-faced, spindling youths in the middle teens, bashful and awkward. Ma Pruett left no doubt that she was the driving force of the family. "The woman should lead," was one of her most frequent remarks. In practice she was not content to lead, but also pushed.

She was an angular woman, energetic, strong minded and pious. She came from Indiana and from New England progenitors. She had inherited from these forbears the New England figure and the long Boston jaw. She managed her own family affairs and was willing and indeed anxious to manage the family affairs of others. She clashed with Kate from the very start.

"If that human pile driver thinks she's going to railroad us into attending Christian Endeavor and farm center meetings she's got another guess coming," Kate fumed to Rhoda on their way home from the first Sunday dinner at the Pruetts'.

"Oh she's not so bad," placated Rhoda, "she means well."

"You bet she means well. She's got the exact variety of well-meaning nosiness that riles me most. Now the old man's different; he seems a real nice sort."

"You like him because you feel pretty sure you could boss him," answered Rhoda with a wicked little smile.

CHAPTER 5

As SPRING advanced and the heat of the sun grew daily stronger the girls slipped into hot weather ways of living. They moved the table, the oil stove and all the cooking paraphernalia onto the porch, leaving their one room nothing but a storehouse for trunks and clothes. Under the north east corner of the ramada where a grape vine was beginning to spread its broad leaves and the shade of arrowweed thatch and overhanging chinaberry trees was heaviest they kept the water filter dripping into the olla, the big earthenware water jar, with all its beauty of line smothered in a swathing of wet gunny sacks. As the days grew warmer they discarded underwear, stockings and at last even shoes. When they went to work in the field they put on the shoes against the sharp cockleburrs and on their heads, big straw hats with pointed crowns. The alfalfa was growing incredibly fast now and had to be cut and stacked about once a month, and on cutting and stacking days they got up when it was just beginning to grow light and started work before the sun rose. After the sun was up it grew almost at once desperately hot and the perspiration ran from their bodies in streams. At noon they took a long siesta, drank lemonade and ate cantaloupes. Into the cool gloom of the porch overhung by the black shade of chinaberry trees the mellowing cantaloupes shed a delicious aroma. About the middle of the afternoon they went out again into what seemed the hottest part of the day and worked as long as there was light. When they came in they were dog tired, ready for a bath which they took by throwing water over each other in the washtub, and in spite of the heat ravenous with hunger.

When they went to town, which since the advent of the heat Kate had christened "Hell's Center," to sell their eggs and buy their groceries they found that there was no coolness to be had from the swift motion of a car. Instead a hot, dry wind like a blast from an oven struck them in the face, the hard sun on the white road almost blinded them and when another car passed it left them powdered with dust.

Scattered over the sun-baked fields to right and to left the Mexicans were picking cantaloupes. Not in the cool of the morning or the cool of the evening, but all day long under the searing sun these dark, silent figures moved about plucking the heavy melons, stuffing them into big sacks and carrying the full sacks to the sheds where the more fortunate packers worked in the shade.

"I wonder," Rhoda said to Kate as they chugged past one of these melon fields, "when the rich people back East eat those melons if they ever think how much those poor fellows have to sweat to produce them?"

"Well you eat them yourself all the time don't you? Seems to me you're about as nimble a little melon eater as I ever knew—and you don't have to pay anything for 'em either."

"Yes, but that's different."

"No it ain't."

In town, in spite of electric fans and sprinkled water, the streets and stores were heavy with heat and people went about languidly and had little to say. There were not many cars now and they were all parked in shady spots. Everybody who was able to leave the Valley had "gone out."

While Kate exchanged the eggs for groceries Rhoda usually went to the Public Library and took out books to read during the heat of the day. These novels were mostly of western setting because she was interested in the West and wanted to read all she could about it. She found in them however a West which had few points of resemblance to the West that she was learning to know. They were, with few exceptions, very much alike. There was always a manly and courageous hero, a beautiful heroine of spotless and quite unassailable virtue, a villain or several villains and a set of circumstances which made it well-nigh impossible for the hero and heroine to marry and live happily ever after. This set of circumstances involved many desperately entangled situations out of which there seemed no happy outcome possible. Rhoda soon learned however that it was foolish to work up any excitement about these entanglements, because as surely as the book arrived at a close it would bring complete felicity to the hero and heroine, the only people whose welfare mattered in the least. She soon wearied of these books and stopped getting them. Kate missed them.

"Why don't you get out any more library books?" she inquired.

"I got tired of them. They all seem so silly; the people in them and the things that happen are not a bit like real life."

"Real life? I should say not. What the devil do we want to read about real life for? Haven't we got enough of it and ain't it too damn real? When I read I like to read something exciting and romantic with lots of thrills and adventures in it like *When a Man's a Man*. What do you want to read about anyway? Do you want to read about stacking hay and cleaning ditches and stopping gopher roles and scouring water filters and ollas and cooking and washing dishes and wiping the sweat out of your eyes? Haven't you got enough of these things without reading about them?"

"I don't want especially to read about those particular things; but I like to read about people who seem real and about what they do and think and how they feel about all sorts of things."

"Humph, a fat lot of entertainment in that. I like a book where there's something doing."

The daily paper which was left every afternoon in their mail box down by the water gate told of happenings quite different from those which occurred in the western novels. It did not tell about women's club meetings and teas and lodge activities and Chamber of Commerce dinners and church entertainments in the Valley towns because all these activities were suspended for the summer, the participators being far away in mountain or seashore resorts. Indeed during these summer months it did not tell very much of anything. Sometimes however cattle disappeared from a man's pasture and nobody knew where they went to. Sometimes a drunken or jealous Mexican beat his wife or stabbed her and the long strong arm of the law took him up by the scruff of the neck and set him down in jail. Automobiles were held up by bandits and automobiles going too fast turned over or ran into each other. Illicit stills were "knocked over" and the operators fined, or jailed if they couldn't pay the fine. Women were suing for divorce, most of them because their husbands spent too much time and money in Mexicali just over the border. Houses of people out of the Valley for the summer were looted right and left. Rhoda read the newspaper accounts of these doings a little wistfully.

The routine of alfalfa raising was becoming a bit dull and with the heat, onerous and exhausting. She was beginning to long for a break in the monotony and something to think about. She wished she knew some of these people who were getting divorces or having accidents or making moonshine or beating or stabbing or stealing or being stolen from.

In the cool of evening when the work was done, the supper over and the dishes washed, she sat on the porch in a nightgown amid the aroma of melons, smoking a meditative cigaret and looking out toward the road where, beyond the gray-green screen of arrowweed, silent figures barely seen passed like shadows. They were for the most part only Mexican field hands who went by afoot along the road, humble and simple people returning wearily from their long day's work under the cruel sun; but behind the screen of arrowweed which changed with the swift-falling twilight from sage green to gray and from gray to black they seemed to her fancy to flit by furtively and stealthily like villains in a melodrama, like phantoms, like spirits. She had a feeling that all about her, to the very edge of the little ranch, there stirred a strange and alien life, a life silent, inscrutable and apart. She had small hope of ever bridging the gulf that lay between that life and hers, yet it allured, tantalized, beckoned with silent, provocative finger.

The Hindus did not come back to buy more hay.

While June was still young the hot weather regime had become a long-established thing and it was hard to realize that days had ever been cool. One hot Sunday in early June when the girls went to the Pruetts' for dinner they found there a visitor.

"My brother, the Reverend Mr. Spicer," proudly introduced Mrs. Pruett.

She might have omitted the "Reverend" for although the visitor was dripping with the heat and without socks, coat or collar, he shed about him so strong an atmosphere of clerical dignity that it was impossible to mistake his calling.

He gave the girls a comprehensive glance in which Rhoda sensed a shadow of disapproval as it slid past their bobbed hair.

"Well, well, happy indeed to meet you, young ladies," he said in a voice which visualized for them a pulpit and stained glass windows. "My sister here tells me that you are two enterprising farmerettes who have come to make your fortune out of the land in this great Imperial Valley."

"The fortune part of it looks a bit distant," answered Kate, "and we don't seem to be moving fast enough to raise much dust. We're lucky just now if we can pay our taxes and water bills."

"Oh well the rest will doubtless come in good time, in good time. Rome was not built in a day."

While the girls were helping Mrs. Pruett put the dinner on the table the Reverend Spicer ran his eye over a newspaper.

"I note here," he said in his deeply resonant, clerical voice, "that an unfortunate man shot himself because his wife had bobbed her hair. Think how terribly remorseful that woman must have felt when she saw her husband lying cold in the coffin."

"Perhaps she went lighter without both the hair and the husband," suggested Kate brightly.

He disdained to notice this flippant remark, but went on as from the pulpit stand.

"It may astonish you to know that I do not lay the blame on women for their present-day unsightly and immodest attire. The root of the evil lies deeper than mere feminine vanity. It lies in the silk shirt and the soft collar. When men began to discard the stiff collar and the starched bosom and with them that propriety and dignity which were one of the strongest bulwarks of society it was not to be wondered at that the members of the weaker sex should allow themselves to slip into such frivolities as low necks, short skirts, rolled stockings and the like."

Kate, behind the Reverend Spicer's back, made such a mock solemn face for Rhoda's benefit that she had a hard time to keep her features in order.

"Indeed I wouldn't let them off that easy," barked Mrs. Pruett. "The blame lays with them an' not with the men an' there'd otta be a law to keep shameless hussies from wearin' skirts up to their knees."

When they were seated at the table before the inevitable stewed chicken and flanking vegetables the Reverend Spicer was moved to remark: "It seems to me sad that in this fruitful valley, so rich and productive, under the drooping pepper tree and the spreading palm that there should be so little of the religious life. My sister tells me that there are no churches here except in the towns. The little country church of our childhood days, with its spire pointing silently to Heaven, which formed the religious and social center for its rural district is not to be found here. It is a great pity."

"It is that," sighed Mrs. Pruett. "There'd otta be a law that puts a church every so many miles same as a schoolhouse."

Everybody else was too busy with chicken to have any opinion on this subject.

"The church is neglecting here a great opportunity," went on the Reverend Spicer, after a successful onslaught on a second joint. "At great expense we send our missionaries into Japan and India and neglect these Japanese and Hindus who are here in our very midst. These Mexicans who were taught the Christian faith by the early Franciscan fathers—not of course that I am an upholder of Catholicism—these Mexicans are allowed to slump back into the mire of ignorance and animalism. It is a shame that such conditions should be allowed to prevail in a portion of this enlightened Christian country."

"Well I don't know about that," deliberated Kate. "I'm very doubtful if the Christian religion would make any difference in the way these people act. Matter of fact it seems to me they act just a little more Christian than most Christians. And how many Christians work at the job of being Christians anyway? Who's done all the swindling that's been done in the Valley, the profiteering, the selling of bad lands, the duping of greenhorns, the foreclosing of mortgages? Why Christians of course."

"But these Japs and Hindus are making money hand over fist," put in Mr. Pruett.

"Well is it a sin to make money? It's what we're all trying to do isn't it? They pay their way and make their money by hard work and good management. Especially the Japs. I can't say I'm fond of either Japs or Hindus, but I believe in giving the Devil his due. We're jealous of them, that's all. If Americans were willing to work as hard and live on as little as Japs they'd make money out of lettuce and cantaloupes too. But they don't like to work hard, so they make it out of trickery and swindling."

"Well I dunno," put in Ruby. "They say Japs are honest, but my ranch don't seem to do good since I leased it to the Japs like it did when Ed was alive. Of course I ain't sure Morokawa's holdin' out on me, but—"

"They're all bad enough in this Godless Valley, heathens and Christians alike," proclaimed Mrs. Pruett, as she helped Ruby's eldest to more chicken. "Everybody racin' like mad for the money an' thinkin' of nothin' else. An' it ain't no better in the other parts of Californy either. We didn't find it no diff'rent the four years we was out. I don't know what the world's comin' to."

"It is not by his actions that a man is judged," announced the Reverend Spicer. "A man may obey all the laws of man and yet be bound straight for Hell if he has not been washed in the cleansing blood of the Lamb. It is this simple old-fashioned message that I feel bound to spread abroad in this benighted district."

By this time the chicken stage of the dinner had been passed and halved cantaloupes were set upon the table. The

Reverend Spicer dug his spoon into one and a smile of ineffable satisfaction spread over his perspiring features as the delicious morsel melted in his mouth.

"Why my goodness, Ella, this is the most delicately flavored melon that I ever tasted in my life. Are there more where this came from?"

"Plenty," answered his sister. "The Jap gives us all we want to carry away. You see they can't ship only the perfect ones; if they ain't just right in shape or have even a little scar or sunburn they have to discard 'em."

"And the discarded ones go to feed the hogs, the chickens, and the neighbors," supplemented Kate.

The Reverend Spicer did not take offense at this classification; he was too happy with the melon. After he had eaten four halves he was in the best of humors, and while the women cleared the table and washed the dishes and Mr. Pruett and the boys were out attending to the irrigation water he entertained Ruby's children with tales of his adventures as a boy, his prowess as a hunter, fisher, slingshot maker and collector of beetles and butterflies.

The whole of the next week he spent in driving over the hot, dusty roads in the Pruett's car inviting Japs, Hindus, Mexicans, Americans, everybody in the neighborhood proprietors and field hands alike, to come on Sunday afternoon to listen to the Word of the Lord at the Pruett's. He was determined, he said, to do his share to spread the good tidings of great joy.

When Sunday afternoon arrived Kate could not be persuaded to go. It was the hottest day of the year so far and she sat draped in a thin muslin kimono in a rocking chair from which she had removed all cushions, her bare feet, fat and not very sightly feet, extended on another chair; on the table beside her a pile of old magazines, three melons, a pitcher of lemonade and a glass. From this position and environment she refused to stir.

"Do come, Kate. I'm afraid they'll be awfully offended if you don't," urged Rhoda.

"No sir, you can't pry me from this spot," Kate said firmly. "I'm here till chicken feeding time just as stationary as the boy on the burning deck. If that old geezer wants to know why I'm not there, tell him I can't stand people who go around trying to do good to others. What they have to give away, you'll notice, is always something that nobody wants."

She knew Kate well enough to know that further persuasion would be useless, so she went by herself, bumpety-bump over the chuck holes in the old third-hand Ford which Kate had taught her to drive. It was only a few hundred yards to the Pruetts' place, but it was too hot and dusty to walk. On the way she called for Ruby and the children.

"I don't believe there's a hell," said Ruby as they drove along, the hot, dry wind smiting their faces. "I think the dead just lays in the grave till the last day and then only the ones that done right in this life is called up to meet their loved ones." She sighed, thinking of her husband.

"I'm sure I don't know," answered Rhoda. "Nobody really knows what comes after death. You mustn't let yourself grieve, Ruby."

"I try not to," answered Ruby with another heavy sigh.

At the meeting, besides Rhoda, the Petersons and the Pruett family there was only Mrs. Sasaki, the wife of the Japanese truck grower, a little dumpy creature with a pretty face, who trotted rather than walked, her four doll-like children, all dressed in holiday best, and an old barefooted Mexican in patched overalls and a green-and-pink plaid shirt. The Reverend Spicer's jaw sagged with disappointment and he kept looking along the road for the crowds that did not come; but the smallness of his audience did not cause him to shorten his sermon. It dragged on interminably into the hot, late hours of the afternoon. The shade of the pepper tree under which they sat grew more and more inadequate against the ever encroaching rays of the sun; the backless campstools became instruments of torture. The children squirmed and wriggled, grew each moment more restless and hard to keep in their seats. The youngest Peterson and the youngest Sasaki fell asleep in the hot laps of their respective mothers; and still the Reverend Spicer meandered along about what an important parental duty it was to have little children instructed in the Holy Word and how the whole hope of the future lay in the hands of these little ones who were entrusted to our charge. All unmindful of their importance and their great mission, the unfortunate children shifted and squirmed more and more uneasily, drew pictures in the dust with their bare toes, twirled their moist handkerchiefs into grotesque, long-legged mannikins, pulled at their mothers' clothes and begged in impatient whispers for release. Rhoda's heart ached for the miserable young things forced to sit through the long, intensely hot afternoon. The Pruett boys helped to pass the time by unobtrusively whittling at sticks and the stoical little Japs stood it better than Ruby's children. Mrs. Sasaki too remained outwardly calm. But there was a frantic look in Ruby's eye and her brood was on the very brink of open revolt when at last the Reverend Spicer drew his exhortation to a close and led them into the singing of "Jesus bids us shine," which he bellowed forth in a deep and stentorious bass.

After the hymn was finished he distributed leaflets on which was printed a poem signed with the name of the Reverend Henry Spicer.

"Take good care of these papers, little ones," he admonished, "and when you are old you can show them to your grandchildren and tell them that you knew the author."

"My, I hope he won't talk so long next Sunday," sighed Ruby on the way home, while Melvin busied himself making a paper dart out of his poem. "I'm glad enough to go to the meetin's; I've thought a good deal about religion an' such things since Ed died, an' I do think it's a shame to let children grow up like little heathens. But it's too much to expect them to sit there nearly three mortal hours on a day like this. Melvin and Juanita have got my arms just pinched black and blue, an' I dunno what I'd a done if Mildred hadn't slept through most of it."

The next Sunday the old Mexican was not there, neither was Mrs. Sasaki nor the four young Sasakis; and Rhoda felt that she was not believed when she told for the second time her lie that Kate was not feeling very well. Fortunately the discourse had to be cut short because three hogs broke out of their pen and into a field of kaffir corn. The Pruett boys chased hogs with more fervor than they had ever shown before in their lives.

"Gosh I'm gettin' to hate them old prayer meetin's," confided Ruby on the way home. "I was tickled to death when the pigs got out. I'd quit comin' only Mrs. Pruett's always been awful good to me an' I hate to offend her. An' then you know the Pruetts is somehow the sort of people you feel you don't dare to go agin. They're not just folks like you an' me; but they're so good it seems like they must be always in the right, an' if you do anything that's agin them you gotta be in the wrong. It's awful hard on the children too. I'm sure I dunno what to do."

When they reached Ruby's place there was a strange car drawn up in front of the door, a bright blue bug with white trimmings and a flippant little fringed top. She got out quickly and hurriedly helped the children to scramble out of the back seat, looking flustered and excited. She did not ask Rhoda to come in.

The next Sunday she was almost as restless as her youngsters. She seemed on pins and needles, twisted her handkerchief between her moist hands, dabbed at the beads of perspiration on her face and kept glancing half expectantly, half apprehensively toward the road. Whenever she heard the sound of a car she started as if one of the big red desert ants that crawled about in the dust had bitten her. She was wearing a new apricot colored dress of some sheer material and in spite of the heat she looked unusually young and fresh. Rhoda thought that if she had only brushed and not frizzed her stringy hair she would be quite pretty.

When at last the hateful tedium of the long sermon was over and they went out to get into Rhoda's car they saw a blue bug with white trimmings standing at a discreet distance down the road. Ruby motioned frantically to the blue bug to retire.

"It's a friend of mine," she explained. "He works in that auto repair shop just out of Calexico. I told him for sure not to come anywheres near the Pruetts' place; an' just to be o'nery he said he didn't care nothing about the Pruetts an' he'd come anyway an' fetch me home, an' just for that he can turn around an' go back where he came from."

When they reached Ruby's house the blue bug was drawn up in front.

On the following Thursday, as Kate and Rhoda were walking along the street in El Centro, a blue bug with white trimmings and a fringed canopy flashed by them and in it Ruby gay in a pink muslin dress, her cheeks berouged, her long green Woolworth earrings swinging in the breeze made by the swiftly moving car. About the saucy little car and the swinging of the green earrings there seemed to Rhoda a holiday air of festive abandon that somehow made her feel a little sad for herself. Later they ran upon Ruby in the grocery store and she told Rhoda in a half-hesitant, half-defiant way not to call for her on Sunday because she wasn't going to the prayer meeting.

Rhoda felt rather tired that day and a little sickish at the stomach from the heat, so she sat in the back seat of the car while Kate finished up the errands. As she lay back watching languidly the people who passed on the sidewalk she happened to notice a man who sat smoking a cigaret at the wheel of a big car parked at her left. The shirt he wore was sun-bleached and drew across the shoulders and there seemed something familiar about his back; she noticed too that he smoked in a peculiar fashion. Watching more closely she saw that the cigaret never touched his lips; instead he made a funnel with his hand and drew the smoke by suction without actual contact. When he turned his head a little she saw that he was the Hindu to whom they had sold the hay. As she eyed him narrowly she became aware that he too was watching the passing dribble of humanity. There was something deeply reposeful, something sophisticated and calmly appraisive about his easy sidewise slouch and the indifferent turns of the head with which he followed the movements of the passers-by. She had an intuition that this was a man who had passed through many places and cast a thoughtful and critical eye upon many kinds of people. It seemed to her that she too had learned much about people since coming to the Valley, that her eyes had been opened and her perceptions sharpened. What did he think of these passers-by she wondered as, following the movements of his head, she let her glance fall where his fell; and as she continued to follow his eyes she passed into one of the strangest experiences of her life.

It had not been her habit to look at people critically or narrowly; she had been accustomed to take them as a matter of course as she had taken everything else that life had offered her. She had little experience upon which to base standards of any kind and she was not naturally inclined to sit in judgment. But it seemed to her that since coming to the Valley she had begun to look at people more narrowly, that she was growing to understand better the springs that moved them. And now in some strange, intuitive way she found herself looking at these passing people with cool, detached appraisal as if she were the Hindu who slouched there smoking negligently in the big battered car. She saw pool room loiterers with coarse mouths and blotchy faces and she knew that these young men were rotten before they were ripe, diseased in body and mind and without hope for the future. She saw old derelicts with bleary eyes and dragging steps and knew that they had spent their lives in pursuit of something which they had not found or found only to lose again and that their enfeebled minds fumbled about in the past. Women of all ages passed by in knee-short skirts and outrageously high-heeled shoes. Sometimes a slim young girl tripped gracefully enough, but mostly they waddled, tottered, plunged, limped painfully or minced along with precise little steps which bespoke tight shoes, a tight, hard mind and unalterable convictions based upon fleeting externals. She saw painted women pass and knew by the hard, indifferent stare in their eyes that they were professional harlots, protected in part at least by the harlot's armor of callousness. She saw other painted women pass and knew that they were not harlots but for the most part weak, fluttering and sensual. She saw sleek, well-dressed men with white hands and fat, shaven necks and knew they were pampered, gluttonous and full of money lust. Everywhere she looked she saw stupidity, cunning, greed, blank apathy, disillusion and despair. As she looked at the hard, dead faces of these people, the awkwardness and angularities of their warped bodies, their pampered fatness, their silly pretensions put on under the delusion that good clothes can cover naked coarseness and ignorance she felt herself pervaded with a sense of restlessness, of confusion, of futility, of cruel greed for something worthless and empty, of intense and desperately selfish striving for something not worth striving for.

"Rhoda, for Pete's sake what's the matter? You look as white as a ghost."

She came to herself trembling all over, feeling weak as though her body were flowing away from her like water. Kate was stuffing the packages into the back seat beside her.

"Oh I'm all right," she faltered, making an effort to pull herself together, "just a little bit frazzled by the heat."

At the sound of Kate's voice the Hindu turned his head and touched his hat to her. Then he caught sight of Rhoda in the back seat and smiled. It was the first time that she had seen Hindu lips smile. A gleam of white teeth, a sense of something warm, dark, pervasive and sensual. It was only a flash and his head was turned back to its old position. Kate cranked the car, jumped into the driver's seat, banged the door shut and backed out recklessly into the traffic.

CHAPTER 6

THE NEXT Sunday Ruby and her three little ones were not at the meeting.

"What's went with Ruby an' the children?" demanded Mrs. Pruett of Rhoda in a manner which was more than a little inquisitorial.

"I'm sure I don't know," answered Rhoda looking as innocent as she could, which was very innocent indeed. "On Thursday when I saw her in Zapp's grocery she told me she wouldn't be able to come and not to call for her."

The following Wednesday in the cool of the evening Mr. and Mrs. Pruett came over to pay a visit to the girls and incidentally to borrow a post hole digger. Rhoda had just time to throw a kimono over her nightgown and hide the cigarets and the telltale ashtrays. She had never smoked till she came to the Valley, but now she enjoyed a cigaret as much as Kate. Kate, in pink striped pajamas, refused to make any change in her costume.

As Rhoda looked at Mrs. Pruett in the straight-backed chair which she had chosen in preference to a rocker, she could not help admiring the strength of character which enabled her in the midst of this demoralizing heat to preserve the prim starchiness and modest petticoatedness of a New England spinster on a chilly Sabbath afternoon. It was not that she was greatly starched or unduly petticoated, but in her decent checked bungalow apron she somehow managed to give the appearance of being both.

The Pruetts had brought with them the welcome news that the Reverend Spicer had departed the day before for a cooler climate. They also brought a large, dead-ripe and well-chilled watermelon. They had all been sitting on the porch for a half hour or so enjoying the deliciousness of cold watermelon, and by Rhoda's count Mr. Pruett had already made five puns, but Mrs. Pruett had said only once that there'd otta be a law, when they heard the sound of a passing car, a male voice in rallying tones and a prolonged female giggle.

"Joy riders," said Kate, shooting a melon seed from her lips to her plate.

"Yes, an' it's the like of them that's responsible for most all the accidents," proclaimed Mrs. Pruett. "There'd otta be a law forbiddin' young people from courtin' in ottymobiles. They turn the roads into reg'lar death traps for all the rest of us. Such recklessness is sinful, an' if I had anything to do with the makin'—"

She broke off, paralyzed with amazement. Out of the bursts of laughter, the giggles and sniggers, a sentence had emerged: "Say, Roy, now you just quit that," and she had unmistakeably recognized Ruby's voice.

"Well!" she exploded with an emphatic outgo of breath, and sat rigid. Her whole reaction, a Gargantuan reaction, was expressed in that one word and the explosive blast of breath. Pa Pruett shifted his knees uneasily, tried to look disapproving and succeeded only in looking interested. Kate continued to eat watermelon with undiminished relish and Rhoda, to help cover the embarrassment of the situation, began gathering up the rinds.

All at once it became apparent to her apprehensive ear that the worst was about to happen. The car had turned in at their gate and was coming up the driveway. The next moment Ruby burst in upon them flushed and giggling followed by a well-set-up young man in a porous undershirt and a pair of khaki riding breeches.

Her jaw dropped when she saw Mrs. Pruett, who had risen in self-righteous majesty, and there was a moment of dreadful silence broken only by slight noises which indicated that Kate was still eating watermelon.

"Mr. Pruett," she announced at last after what seemed to Rhoda an interminable period of suspense, "Mr. Pruett, I blush with shame to think that I'm a woman. Come."

She sailed out, and her husband, after a coy and embarrassed glance around, slipped into her wake.

Ruby waited till she heard the little whining noises which indicated that the engine was being started. Then she burst forth.

"Gosh what an old hen! If she thinks she's goin' to keep on bossin' me an' tellin' me every move to make she's mighty mistaken. I don't care if she did learn me how to make caramel puddin' an' cut out dress patterns. I've took that sort of thing off her long enough an' I don't have to take it off anybody. I guess I'm old enough to be my own boss."

She tossed her head with a great show of defiance.

"Have a piece of melon, Ruby. And you, Mr.–?"

"Oh yes, excuse me. Meet my friend, Mr. Purdy."

The young man acknowledged the introduction with an embarrassed grin, accepted a large section of watermelon and ate with healthy relish. As they continued to eat melon they fell into talk about the things which interest Valley people: about grapefruit growing and dairying and the last drop in the price of alfalfa, but principally about the heat, which was the all-absorbing topic of the moment. Ruby, her cheeks blazing, took little part in the conversation but interjected into it from time to time remarks of a peculiar irrelevance.

"We got only fourteen dollars a ton for our last alfalfa, and just over in San Diego they retail it for twice that. At fourteen dollars it won't do more than pay the water bill. Do you think alfalfa's going to go up or down, Mr. Purdy?"

"Yes, an' if that old cat thinks she's got me under her thumb, she's got another guess comin'."

"They say it went to a hundred and fifteen in Brawley yesterday afternoon."

"And a hundred and twenty at the Salton Sea."

"That's nothing to back in 1913. I've seen it hang around a hundred and thirty."

"She'd better leave me be, that's all I gotta say."

"Which grapes do you think pay the best, Mr. Purdy, the Malaga or the Thompson Seedless?"

"Well now they say the Thompson Seedless—"

"I've put up with her all I'm goin' to, so there. I guess I got a right to have a little fun while I'm alive same as other folks. I'm gonna be a long time dead."

"They say alkali land will grow beets when it won't grow anything else."

"Yeh, the gover'ments been gettin' some o' the returned soldiers to put in beets on alkali land. I haven't heard yet how it's panned out."

"No siree, no more prayer meetin's for mine. I guess there ain't no law that says I can't put in my time to suit myself."

When they had gone and Rhoda was clearing away the ruins of the watermelon, she said abruptly: "A nice spectacle of herself Mrs. Pruett made tonight."

"Yes, the old girl sure knows her own mind too well," agreed Kate. "But Ruby ought to be ashamed of herself too—her husband not dead six months."

"Why do you say she should be ashamed of herself? Perhaps she should. But how can you or I or Mrs. Pruett or any outsider say she ought to be ashamed of herself? What do we know about it?"

"Well all I know is I saw that dinky blue bug of his, fringed top and all, standing out in front of her place at two o'clock in the morning last Monday when I came back from turning off the water."

"Well, what if you did?"

Kate looked up in surprise from the farm journal in which she was reading how best to get rid of chicken lice and mites.

"Why, Rhoda Malone, do you think it's right for her to have that fellow in the house all night—and her husband hardly cold in the grave?"

"I don't say it's right—or wrong. I say it's Ruby's own business—not yours nor mine nor Mrs. Pruett's. I think Ruby has a right to do what she likes with her life regardless of what you or I or Mrs. Pruett think she ought or ought not to do with it."

Kate shrugged one shoulder indifferently.

"She can go right ahead; she certainly won't meet with any opposition from this quarter."

She returned to the article on chicken lice and mites and all the fascinating ways in which to deprive them of their lives.

Rhoda had lighted a cigaret and sat in a low rocking chair looking out through the hot darkness at the blurred stars and the drooping black outlines of the eucalyptus trees along the ditch bank. She could not put Ruby and the events of the evening out of her mind. She felt restless, excited, eager to talk, and wished she had somebody there instead of Kate, somebody who would take the other side with heat and vigor and so stimulate her to say what she thought or rather what she felt. She was filled with astonishment and wonder at her own sudden and determined championship of Ruby. It was not that she liked or admired Ruby; she felt for her at best nothing more than pity and half-condescending tolerance. And because she and Ruby were both of Irish descent she had even felt a little degraded by a lurking sense of kinship, as a refined Jew regards with more than alien horror the gluttonies and gaucheries of his race. Moreover she could not remember ever before having given such a subject a moment's thought. It had not occurred to her to question things as they were in this matter or in any other. All her life she had accepted established things as taken for granted. Yet now that she was faced with a concrete instance, she found that her mind had made itself up clearly, definitely, even belligerently in opposition to all existing standards. She puffed at first excitedly, then slowly and meditatively, looking out through the hot darkness at the tall, black trees and wondering at herself.

Kate got up, stretched her arms above her head and yawned.

"Well there's one poor boob in this dugout that's gonna hit the hay. How 'bout you?"

"I think I'll smoke another cigaret," answered Rhoda.

CHAPTER 7

So FAR the heat though intense had been bearable and the nights cool enough for sleep. But now August laid a hot, clammy hand over the Valley and its tortured inhabitants gasped for breath. There was no visiting any more and one went to town only in the very early morning or what was called by courtesy the "cool" of the evening. Through the hottest hours of the day the girls drooped limply on cushionless chairs, fanned and mopped their faces, fought off the flies that swarmed in despite of all their patching of the rusted screens, took the broom every hour or so and swept from the porch floor the big red desert ants that bit so viciously, paced about restlessly, made nervous by the sticky heat. From time to time they made more lemonade from the lukewarm water in the olla or went out to the ramada and standing in one of the washtubs poured water over each other. They were languid and irritable; headachy and squeamish at the stomach. It was too hot to read, too hot to write a letter, too hot even to think. The fierce glare of the burning day seemed to last unbearably long.

When at last the afternoon declined and the sun sank into a burning saffron smudge behind the fringe of arrowweed and the dark eucalyptus trees it was still hot and breathless, but the nerve-straining glare was gone. As the dull, hot colors of the short afterglow smouldered into ashes, a few dim stars appeared and the night drew a close mantle over the sweltering earth. Through the twilight they sat at the table sipping cold coffee which was the only thing that tasted good. The Valley delicacies, lettuce and tomatoes and cantaloupes were gone, and these things which a few weeks ago had been plentiful as water were now exorbitantly high priced in the stores. The bread was doughy and tasteless, the butter a little pool of oil. When it grew dark they did not light the lamp because of the heat that it would make and because millions of little black gnats would come instantly through the screening and swarm over everything. Instead they lay down on their cots and tossed restlessly until from sheer exhaustion they fell asleep.

In the early morning there was a brief period when the world awoke refreshed and jubilant; then it wilted like a morning glory in the pitiless clutch of the sun.

On days when they had to work in the alfalfa they set the alarm clock for two. Rhoda dreaded these days. She had overcome to some extent her fear of the big heavy-hoofed mules and had learned to drive the mower and rake. Often the landscape swam before her eyes and the seething heat rose and threatened to choke her, but she managed to keep her seat and guide the mules. It was the stacking that she dreaded most. She was afraid of the gaunt wooden arms of the great stacker, afraid of the taut cable which she always imagined was going to snap and fling a terrible steel death whip through the air and she was glad that she was not expert enough as a driver to gee and haw and back the mules at the stacker. Kate, who laughed at her silly fears, did this part of the work, and it was Rhoda's job to climb by means of a ladder to the top of the stack and with a hay fork level off the top after each unloading of alfalfa. The work of forking hay on top of a high stack in the full glare of the Valley August sun was the most strenuous and exhausting thing that Rhoda had ever attempted. She literally poured with perspiration and constantly dabbed at her eyes to keep the sweat from blinding her. The particles of hay crept like live things down her neck, up the legs of her overalls and the sleeves of her shirt and added maddeningly to the irritation of the acrid sweat. The loose hay into which she sank knee deep seemed to draw the heat, which rose about her in suffocating billows. Often she thought about the two Hindus she had seen pitching hay. How easy and graceful they had been, how utterly masters of the situation. They had not struggled and floundered and gasped like her. How satisfying it must be to be strong and competent, to do everything with ease.

When she felt that she could not stand the heat any longer, that everything was going to go black if she stayed there another moment, she slid down the ladder to the bottom of the shady side of the stack and drank great gulps of water from a canteen which they kept there wrapped in a wet gunny sack. When she went up the ladder again it always seemed hotter than ever, hotter than she could possibly stand; yet she managed to stand it for a few unloadings. Then she would have to go down again.

One very sultry morning they had worked longer than usual to try to finish the field, and Rhoda in her anxiety to hurry the work had stayed a long time on top of the stack. Just as she felt that she was at the end of her rope and must go down at once the relentless arms of the stacker dumped a fresh load of hay. She stepped back hurriedly to avoid being buried under it and the impish flying particles rained about her and all over her. To get to the ladder she would have to wade through or fork away part of the hill of hay which had just been dumped. As she looked at the hay obstructing her path she realized with a wild, panicky sense of helplessness that she had waited too long, that she had no strength left to wade through the hay or to fork it away, that the heat was rising up around her in dense billows and was going to smother her. If only she had a drink of water! She tried to call Kate but her tongue felt like flannel in her mouth. A wave of nausea swept over her. She had a vision invading her eyelids of a brilliant blue sky over which a black curtain was suddenly dropped. Then she knew nothing more.

When she came to herself she was at the bottom of the stack and Mrs. Pruett was bathing her face. The first thing she noticed was that the heat had caused Mrs. Pruett's glasses to irritate the bridge of her nose; it was swollen and red and the nosepiece of the glasses was swathed in cotton wool. Beside her Kate was cracking ice and when she tried to sit up she saw Mr. Pruett in the distance leading the mules away to their much needed rest and shade. The Pruett car was drawn up nearby.

"There now, you're feeling better, dear?" questioned Mrs. Pruett.

"For the Lord's sake don't you ever do a thing like that again," admonished Kate. "The three of us had a perfect devil of a time to slide you down that ladder. Haven't I told you again and again to dive for the ladder when you felt like fainting and faint down below? Here, Mrs. Pruett, put this ice at the back of her neck. Lucky thing you people had some ice. We poor boobs can't afford to take ice and we certainly can't afford to buy an ice box to put it in."

When she was able to get into the car and they had driven back to the house she lay on her cot, her head surrounded by ice packs, while Mrs. Pruett fanned away the flies and bathed her face and wrists. She felt as weak as water, nauseated and acutely miserable. The cot was horribly hot and there was not a breath of air.

"That work's too hard for Rhody," said Mrs. Pruett, wiping the trickling perspiration from her own face and glancing at Kate with no very friendly eye. "She ain't staout like you, Miss Baxter, an' she tries to do more'n she's able."

Kate cast at Mrs. Pruett's back a look which said in strong language that she was able to manage her own affairs and had not asked for advice. All unaware of the look, Mrs. Pruett went on.

"What you girls'd otta do is to git you a few caows an' use your land for pasture. Lettin' the caows eat it off is a heap easier'n cuttin' an' stackin'. The both of you could soon learn to milk, an' milkin' an' separatin' is somethin' a woman kin do most as well as any man. I think there'd be more profit in it too, the way the price of alfalfy hay's been droppin' lately."

"That's fine an' dandy, Mrs. Pruett; but to buy cows and a separator and the rest of the equipment you need for a dairy takes money, and Rhoda and I'll be lucky if we can pay our taxes and interest this year. The water assessments and water bills alone keep our pockets nearly flat and everybody says money's getting tighter every day and the banks are shutting down on their loans."

"Yes that's so; but Mr. Pruett an' I been talkin' it over, an' if you girls have a mind to go into caows we wouldn't mind lettin' you have mebbe fifteen hundred to make a start. The caows 'ud stand good fer it an' of course they'd be havin' calves right along an' you'd have young heifers comin' on an' soon you'd have a nice little dairy. Mr. Pruett an' I has a little money to spare; we done good when we was here before, an' the Jap paid us good rent the four years we was away, so we wouldn't mind givin' you a little help."

Kate's face was a study of mingled expressions.

"That's mighty good of you, Mrs. Pruett, to make such an offer," she said in a changed tone. "Rhoda and I will have to talk it over."

"Wasn't that awfully good of Mrs. Pruett to offer to lend us money?" said Rhoda when she was gone.

"Well, decent enough of the old girl of course—and yet I don't know. She wants to lend us money because she wants to railroad us into doing something she's picked out for us and because she's taken a fancy to you. Notice the way she always calls you "Rhody" and me "Miss Baxter" bless her old heart. Besides it's really a mighty good investment; she takes practically no risk and gets ten per cent on her money instead of four."

It seemed to Rhoda a rather hard way of looking at it.

As time went on and the price of alfalfa hay kept dropping it grew more and more apparent that they would have to do something more than raise alfalfa to pay for their place. In the paper they often saw advertisements for milkers. They began to scan it every day looking for a job in their neighborhood and every afternoon at milking time they went over to the Pruetts' and practiced milking on the Pruett cows.

Through these intensely hot days they sweltered even at the evening milking. The cows, brought up from the pasture at half past five, came panting, their tongues hanging out, their rumps swarmed over with flies, their sweaty flanks exhaling a damp, sickening heat. Pestered by the flies, they flicked their tails and shifted their hind legs restlessly. Rhoda was afraid of them at first but she soon found that they were gentle beasts suffering from the heat like herself and like her, restless and irritable.

One evening as they were leaving the Pruett corral after milking, Mr. Pruett said to Kate: "Say, seeing that you girls are going to Calexico tomorrow, I wonder if you'd mind doing a little errand for me. It won't take you over half a mile out of your way."

"Sure thing, dad," answered Kate. "Where to?"

"To those Hindu fellows who raise cotton and kaffir corn just below you. Their shack is a quarter of a mile to the left of the first water gate below your place, the gate just outside the Jap's. Tell that fellow—I don't know his name, but he's the one who bought hay from you and he seems to be the boss of the bunch—tell him I want to get some kaffir corn and if he's got any to sell to stop in here next time he comes by and see me about it. Talkin' about Hindus, that Hindu that shot the Mexican girl up in Brawley 's been sentenced to hang. Good 'nuf for him, too."

The next morning while Rhoda was doing up the housework Kate went out to clean the little ditch which fed their settling tank with water. She stayed too long in the sun and when she came in she had a splitting heat headache.

"Good Lord, I won't be able to go to town today," she groaned, sipping black coffee at noon. "You'll have to take those chickens yourself, Rhoda; I promised them for sure for Friday."

Rhoda had to crate the chickens by herself too, so she was late in getting started on the trip, and the sun was setting by the time she reached the Hindus' place on her way back from Calexico. A little distance back from the road two tent houses stood beside a group of pepper trees and under the pepper trees four Hindus sat smoking cigarets. A few yards away over a campfire another Hindu in a yellow smock and white turban was frying cakes that looked like Mexican tortillas. Peering more closely she saw that his combined stove and frying pan was a big disc from a disc plow, a circular piece of steel about a yard across. It was almost covered with the browning cakes which he tossed as dexterously as any Child's Restaurant cook. The others, squatting tailor fashion on the ground, looked before them in grave silence; it seemed to Rhoda as if they had never spoken in their lives and never would. The setting sun reached long, hot, copper-colored fingers across the ground and touched the lacy branches of the pepper trees, the blue smoke wreaths from the cigarets, the white turbans, the black beards, the dark, slumbrous faces. Once more Rhoda had the illusion of being transported into the Arabian Nights.

As she got out of the car a man rose from the group and came toward her and she saw that he was the one who had bought the hay. Less picturesque than the others, his clothing consisted of a perforated undershirt and a pair of khaki trousers. She gave him Mr. Pruett's message.

"All right," he answered, throwing down the stub of his cigaret. "I will come and see him."

Then he stood statuesque and impassive waiting for her to turn away. If he had been dressed in the most correct of clothing he could not have been more gravely and distantly courteous, more completely self-possessed. She wanted to say something more, but for her life she could think of nothing than would not sound silly, trivial and trumped-up. Before his grave composure she felt like a foolish moth fluttering in a lamp chimney. She turned awkwardly back to the car.

Then, standing so that her body screened her fruitless efforts, she was deliberately unable to crank it.

When she had half turned the handle a few times she stood up and looked back at the Hindu who had rejoined the group under the pepper trees. He rose and came toward her once more. Her face was scarlet and she hated herself.

CHAPTER 8

EARLIER IN the summer they had had an opportunity to buy cheap from the Jap, Umasawa, who had moved over into Mexico, the kaffir corn on a twenty acre field which adjoined their ranch. A couple of Mexicans loafed into their dooryard one day looking for work, and as the heads of kaffir corn were ripe and ready to gather, Kate hired them at so much an acre to cut the field. She was an unashamed and persistent bargainer and managed to get them for a considerably smaller sum than they had first asked.

They went to work and every day for many long, burning days they came early in the morning and worked as long as there was light. All day under the pitiless August sun they moved slowly but steadily and persistently up and down, up and down the endless rows. In the coolest corner of the ramada the thermometer climbed every day to a hundred and ten, a hundred and fifteen, sometimes even a hundred and twenty. If the same thermometer had been laid out in the sun where the Mexicans worked it would have risen till it broke the glass. Yet there where the thermometer would have burst with heat the two blue-shirted figures moved up and down, up and down with dogged patience. From their sweating shoulders hung big gunny sacks into which they stuffed the heads of corn as they cut them from the stalks. Long before the sacks were full they were dragging down the shoulders under that August sun in the breathless heat that seethed between the rows of tall, suffocating corn. Rhoda knew what the work was like; she and Kate had tried it for a few hours one day hoping that they would be able to save money by doing it themselves. "You'll find you won't make a go of it," Mr. Pruett had warned them. "Corn cuttin's only fit work for Mexicans." They had found that he was right. Besides the intolerable heat and closeness they had been driven frantic by the sharp chaff that was shed from the corn and like a million vicious little devils armed with invisible forks attacked their shuddering flesh already irritated to rawness by the heat and sweat.

These few hours had been enough to make them decide to hire Mexicans.

At noon the two men ate their lunch in the field under whatever shade they could find and several times a day came up and filled their battered old canteen with lukewarm, unfiltered water from the settling tank which lay seething in the full glare of the sun. The first time that Rhoda happened to see them doing this she insisted on giving them filtered water from the olla. They stared at her with amazed eyes which showed that this was a new experience for them. Several times after that she carried them out to the field cold tea or coffee which they swallowed in a few gulps, handing back their cups with a grunt of thanks.

When evening came they trudged away into the twilight going God knows where.

Once at dusk when the two women had just dumped a last load from the stacker, the Mexicans lounged up to them. There was something purposeful and expectant about their slouch.

"You fellows finished?" queried Kate in the loud, patronizing voice which she always used when talking to foreigners.

"Yes we all finish," answered their spokesman, taking a cigaret from his mouth and blowing a succession of rings.

He was a handsome half-breed, tall and muscular, with fierce black mustaches like those of a villain in an old-fashioned melodrama, his Spanish blood showing itself in the height and modelling of the brow and the finer lines of the mouth and nostrils. His companion, swarthy, thick-set and low-browed, a pure Indian to all appearances, hung a little behind him.

Kate took a step or two toward the two men.

"Now look here, you fellows, I happen to know you're not finished. I went over the field last evening on purpose and I know there was more corn left uncut than you could possibly cut in a day. Did you cut that corner over by the Hindus' cotton?"

There was a moment of hesitation during which the two men exchanged glances. At last the half-breed said hesitatingly: "No we not cut that. It not worth cut—not worth cut at all—only for fodder."

"That's just it. It's not for you to say whether it's worth cutting or not. You agreed to cut the whole field for so much an acre. When you get it all done I'll pay you and not before."

The two men shifted uneasily.

"We cut already more twenty acre the way I step it off."

"That's all right. You didn't say a word about it's being more than twenty acres before you started. You said it was twenty acres and you'd cut it for so much an acre."

Rhoda had slipped down from the top of the stack and was standing in the deep shadow listening with growing apprehension as she watched the little group: Kate in her big overalls, her feet belligerently wide apart, the two Mexicans somber and hulking, all around them long, darkening fields, rows of trees deepening from gray to black and the great ring of the horizon swiftly melting into shadow.

In his swarthy hand the half-breed held a knife which Kate had loaned him because it was stronger and sharper than his own, a big pruning knife with a broad, curved blade, a sinister-looking thing. Its sharply whetted steel reflecting the last light from the west gleamed out of the surrounding darkness. Why, Rhoda asked herself, did he carry it open, seeing that it was a clasp knife? Was it by design or only by accident that he had neglected to close it? A prickly chill ran up her spine to the base of her brain.

"We want money tonight." The words sounded in Rhoda's ears ominously significant. She felt her head beginning to swim.

"Well you won't get it tonight. You'll get it tomorrow noon after you finish cutting that corn."

There was a long brooding silence.

How could Kate stand there so nonchalantly and face him with that gleaming knife in his hand? And how tall and powerful he was, how thick-set and strong the other fellow. How easy it would be for them to overpower first Kate and then her, cut their throats and go up to the house and take what money they could find. She felt she wouldn't altogether blame them either.

At last the half-breed spoke: "We no come tomorrow."

"What's the reason you can't come tomorrow?"

"Because," he hesitated, groping for words to express his meaning, "we all worked out—we through with job—we go on—we no come back."

"Well you'd better think that over and decide to come back if you want your money."

Another long, ominous silence.

And if they killed her and Kate there beside the hay stack what clue would there be to trace them by? Nobody knew that these men were cutting corn for them; nobody knew their names nor where they camped nor anything about them. They might kill them and ransack the house and walk away and never be suspected. For days perhaps nobody would even know that anything had occurred, and by that time the men could be far below the Mexican border. Not that it would make any difference to her and Kate whether they made their escape or not.

Every moment it was growing darker and the figures were becoming more and more blurred into the surrounding shadows. There was no one within sight or hearing—everything still as the grave—not even the murmur of a distant car. Confusedly she tried to think what she ought to do. Should she step up and try to induce Kate to pay them? Or should she make an attempt to slip away and bring help? But if she did what might happen in the meantime?

Suddenly the half-breed made a movement with the hand that held the knife. She gasped, half started forward and was about to rush to Kate's rescue when she saw just in time to avoid making a fool of herself that he had merely extended a finger of his long, powerful hand along the back of the knife blade and with a strong, precise movement of that finger snapped it shut. This done he held it out to Kate in his open palm and turned away.

It was a gesture of only a moment; but never in her life had she seen anything so eloquent, so replete with the pure essence of drama. In the stretching out of the open palm, the almost imperceptible shrug, the resigned turning away into the darkness he had said all that he could not put into words with a beauty, a simplicity, a finality that left nothing wanting. For that moment at least the gesture completely satisfied his soul and the soul of his race; for that brief moment a barrier was lifted and she knew him and was at one with him. In another instant the two silent, somber figures had merged into the darkness.

"Well I'll be damned!" ejaculated Kate gaping after them, her jaw dropped for sheer amazement. "If a Mexican can't be seven different kinds of a damned fool I'll eat my hat."

"Do you think they'll come back tomorrow?"

She shrugged indifferently. "Search me."

"But Kate, with all your bullying and laying down the law, you were wrong and he was right. You know as well as I do that they've a lot more than earned their money, and you know that patch over by the Hindus' cotton isn't worth cutting."

"I don't care, I'm not going to have two Mexican loafers tell me where I get off. They said they'd cut the whole field and they've got to do it before they get their money."

"And Kate, how could you stand up there and talk to him like that when he had that open knife in his hand? I was beginning to be awfully afraid he was going to use it."

Kate drew a long, thin whistle expressive of sudden illumination. "By George I never even thought of it. Fact is I was so mad about their not finishing the corn that I never even noticed the knife till he shut it up and held it out to me. I guess you're pretty nearly right; they might have pulled off anything they liked here and got away with it, and I wouldn't put it past them either. It was rather a lucky thing for us the mood didn't happen to hit them that way."

It had grown so dark that they could hardly see to unhitch the mules. As they went about doing their evening chores Rhoda found herself speaking in hushed tones, starting at noises and glancing sidewise into the shadows. There was no telling after all at what moment the Mexicans might change their minds and come back for their money.

When they had eaten supper and Rhoda had washed the dishes, she spread out the daily paper for a few moments under the lamp. The first headline that caught her eye was

"MEXICAN RUNS AMUCK; KNIFES THREE." Continuing to skim the headlines she read of houses looted, cars held up by bandits, cattle stolen, a service station entered and robbed, a Chinaman shot dead in his own grocery store by a masked bandit.

"What a dreadful lot of crime in the paper," she said to Kate, "there must be a wave of it passing over the Valley."

The heat and the swarms of black gnats were becoming unbearable, so she blew out the light. A twig crackled just outside the porch. She started and peered apprehensively into the darkness. It was only Rowdy the dog changing his sleeping quarters.

"For the Lord's sake don't go getting the fidgets," rallied Kate. "Nobody could come near the place without our knowing it. Rowdy would give the alarm while they were a quarter of a mile away."

After their first few nights on the ranch it had never occurred to them to be afraid. But tonight before she went to bed Rhoda latched the screen door of the porch and felt grateful for even this frail protection. As she was doing so she heard a click behind her and glancing about saw Kate dropping cartridges into the chambers of the automatic which ever since shortly after their arrival had lain empty and forgotten in a drawer.

However, aside from rather uneasy slumbers, the night passed as peacefully as every other night since they had come to the ranch. As they were sitting over their toast and coffee in the brief deliciousness of the early morning the two Mexicans appeared at the screen door of the porch.

"Well you fellows decided to come back, eh?" said Kate in the voice which she reserved for foreigners. "Want the knife again?"

"Yeh, we cut that piece you say," answered the half-breed, looking a little ashamed, a little sheepish. His companion hulked behind him like a dog waiting for his master.

Kate went to get the knife and incidentally slipped the

automatic from under her pillow into the pocket of her overalls.

"Come back at noon and you'll get your money," she said, handing him the knife. The men filled their canteen at the settling tank and plodded away toward the cornfield.

About eleven o'clock they were back, breathing hard and dripping with sweat.

"All finished?" inquired Kate.

"Yeh, all finish."

She went into the house and got the money, at the same time slipping the automatic again into her pocket, came out and counted the bills into his hand.

"That all right? Satisfactory?"

"Yeh, that all right." He turned to the other man and counted out his share of the money; then the two walked away with a step which by contrast with their usual slouch was almost alert.

"Straight as a bee toward Mexicali," commented Kate, glancing after their southward moving figures, "and like enough to spend every cent of it before tomorrow morning. Isn't that a Mexican for you?"

"Well they earned it, and I suppose they'll have some fun spending it," said Rhoda.

Secretly she felt a little envious of the two Mexicans. After all was it so great a foolishness to spend all the money on one glorious spree? Did not some wise little bird whisper to them that that way lay their one chance of a few moments of joy? This morning they had been in hideous bondage; this afternoon they would be kings.

What a dreary thing monotony, she thought, as she went about the tasks of the day.

A half hour or so after the men had gone Kate slapped her thigh, taken by a sudden thought.

"Drat that Mexican! He never gave me back my knife. It was a hell of a good knife too. I've a notion to hop into the car and go after him."

"Oh don't, Kate, let him keep it. Don't have any more trouble with him."

Kate hummed and hawed for a while as if she had been a real man, and finally allowed herself to be dissuaded.

That night the newspaper seemed to Rhoda more than usually full of accounts of crime. A man who kept a service station in Heber, a genial fellow from whom they had often bought gas, had been robbed on his way home, not a hundred yards from his service station at half past seven in the evening. A man walking along the highroad down near Calexico had been held up in broad daylight, knocked on the head and left for dead. These things happening to people whom she knew, people only a mile or two away, cried to her from the printed page. She thought of the swarms of men who were wandering about looking for work. The hot darkness beyond the porch seemed full of mysterious, lurking dangers; every least sound out of that darkness filled her with apprehension. When Rowdy, lying out under the chinaberry trees, stirred in his sleep and gave a low growl followed by a short, sharp bark as if at a stranger's distant approach she started up and peered out toward the gate, trying to see through the darkness. The dog had merely been dreaming and did not bark again. The cries of the Johnny owls, made thin and mournful by distance, did not disturb her; but when one wheeled and uttered its hysterical screech close to the porch she started nervously and almost cried out herself. Kate ridiculed her foolish fancies; but she noticed that when Kate went to bed she again slipped the automatic under her pillow.

Lying uncovered on her cot, for the heat made even a sheet unbearable, Rhoda could not help thinking of the two Mexicans and how easily they might have killed her and Kate. The danger from them was over of course, she told herself. They had been paid their money and were now miles away carousing in Mexicali. Probably they would never be seen in that part of the Valley again. And yet in spite of all attempts to reassure herself, she was full of flutter and heart-quake. One thing, the rapid panting of a tractor not far off, helped to calm her. It was reassuring to know that there was somebody working on a night shift not far away. She dozed, started nervously from her sleep, then dozed again; at last fell into deeper slumber.

All at once she sat up in bed, startled awake by a growl from the dog, a low, guttural, ominous growl. Her throat tightened with panic and she felt as if some thing had gripped her vital organs and held them in a relentless clutch. The dog was not dreaming this time; she could hear him sniffing about through the grass and weeds. She strained her ears but could hear nothing, not even the tractor; except for the dog everything was sunk in that tranced hush that settles down upon the earth between midnight and dawn.

"Kate," she called in a husky whisper. A gentle snore was her only answer. How could anybody be such a sound sleeper?

"Kate, wake up, the dog's growling."

"What, dog growling? Well tell him to shut up. It's like enough a stray cat or a gopher snake."

Suddenly the dog broke from growls into staccato barks, then growled again more fiercely than before. Rhoda was sure it was no mere stray cat or gopher snake. All at once he bounded forth into the darkness with a furious burst of savage yelps such as only a strange human scent at night can excite in a watchdog. Kate got up hurriedly and struck a match.

"Oh Kate, for goodness sake don't light a lamp."

"I will too. If I'm gonna shoot anybody I wanta see who it is first."

A wave of acute terror surged over Rhoda and in its grip she fled into the stifling inner room and crawled under the couch. Her hiding place was thick with dust and densely threaded with cobwebs and even in her panic of fear she remembered with a touch of shame that she had not swept under there for months. Over the pounding of the blood in her ears and temples she could hear Kate pulling on her overalls, lighting the lamp and calling the dog who circled back toward the house then darted forth again, savage and furious, into the darkness. It seemed hours that she crouched there listening to the dog barking, to Kate moving about opening and shutting the screen door, asking "Who's there?" and scolding the dog. At last she heard the voice of a stranger and instantly reassured she crawled sheepishly out from under the couch. She could not hear what he said, but she knew beyond a shadow of a doubt that the owner of that voice would not do violence to anybody. As she fumbled for a pair of overalls and tried to shake and claw the dust and cobwebs out of her hair, she heard Kate say: "Well for the love of Mike, man, what got you into this condition?"

Then she slipped back unobtrusively onto the porch.

A man in a work shirt and overalls had fallen into a chair by the screen door, his arms limp, his head sagged forward, his hair matted and face streaming with blood. In the dim, reddish light of the little lamp he was a ghastly sight.

"Sorry–to intrude," he mumbled brokenly through a badly cut lip. "Couple fellows back there–I say all right, we all eat lunch–share and share alike. One stiff pulled a knife–other guy had big fists–"

His voice trailed away, his head fell forward again upon his breast and they thought for a moment that he had fainted. They got him as far as Rhoda's cot, heated water and washed his wounds which were many but not deep and poured them full of peroxide. While they were working over him he fell into a deep sleep.

In the morning the stranger seemed quite himself again, although he looked worse than the night before because swelling and discoloration had set in. One eye was black and blue, one side of the nose and the opposite side of the jaw swollen to twice the normal size. The upper lip had been bruised and was puffed out hideously. To these disfigurements were added several other cuts and discolored bruises. But through the swollen grotesqueness of this distorted face Rhoda discerned something fine and charming. She saw it still more clearly when he spoke.

"What sort of a mess have you been mixed up in?" demanded Kate, scrambling eggs over the oil stove.

"Nothing nearly so exciting or romantic as you probably imagine," he answered, with that weird distortion of the features which Rhoda knew was an alluring smile. "No lady was in the least concerned in it, nor was I in any way a hero. Quite the contrary in fact."

"In that case you won't tell the truth," predicted Kate.

"Haven't I made a pretty good beginning at truthtelling by admitting that I was no hero? This was all that happened. I was driving a night tractor for old man Badders, the old scallawag who owns that big tract on the highway just south of the Jap's melon patch. He's rushing work on the tract and running two shifts. A little after midnight I stopped the tractor and went over to eat my lunch; and there under the eucalyptus tree where I'd left it I found two boes eating it up as merrily as one usually eats stolen provender. I went up to them and suggested that they let me in on it because after all it was my lunch and a long time till morning. One of the fellows took this suggestion in such ill part that he poked me one in the eye. The other fellow must have been cornfed, because he had his jackknife open and was cutting up my sandwiches into neat little squares before he swallowed them. When you do that it's a pretty good sign that you've come straight from the soil. When this fellow saw his pal paste me in the eye he lit into me with the knife and there was a general free-for-all. It didn't last long because, as I'm not a brave man, I legged it as soon as I could make my getaway. I suppose I ought not to admit it, especially before ladies, but discretion always did seem to me the better part."

How grotesque his smile was, and how charming it would have been if his lip hadn't been swollen.

"How did you happen to come here?" asked Rhoda, scraping burnt spots from the toast and arranging it on a plate.

"One of the punches I got must have stunned me. I found myself wandering about without the least idea where I was or the tractor or my shanty or anything. At last I heard a dog bark, then a little after that I saw a light and I made for the light. This Valley grows on me; it's a country of surprises."

"How surprises?" queried Rhoda.

"Oh, all sorts of surprises, delightful and otherwise: fellows who eat your midnight lunch and bite the hand that feeds them; ladies in overalls and bare feet who take you in and wash your wounds as the good Pantagruel rescued Panurge. I like the combination of ladies, overalls and bare feet. You'll hardly find it anywhere else. I like feet when they've gone bare a long time and are nice and slim and brown."

Rhoda looked down at her own feet. Yes, they were slim and brown. She colored a little.

He had been going about straightening his bed, wiping last night's dishes, helping to set the table in a deft, experienced and thoroughly at-home manner. Kate followed his movements with a look combined of admiration and despisal.

"You're not like most males, who sit and wait for the food to drop into their mouths," she commented.

"It's all in what the occasion demands," he replied. "Put the human male in a lumber camp, a mining shack or a dugout and he takes care of his wants; but lead him back into the home with the wife and daughters and he becomes as helpless as a fledgling. And yet it isn't so much because he's ashamed of knowing how to keep house as it is just ordinary common dog laziness of which we males have all got a heavy, or shall I say a blessed heritage."

They were at the table now, the coffee and eggs steaming, the toast crunching between their teeth. The morning air, full of the fresh scent of newly irrigated fields was for this brief hour deliciously cool, clear and stimulating. Obliquely across the corner of the porch the newly risen sun cast a broad golden band. The stranger, sipping his coffee, looked out across the sun-flooded fields to the distant mountains.

"The thing that makes it hard to pull up stakes out of this hot Valley," he said, his eyes wandering from the mountains to the russet tops of the eucalyptus trees, "is that it hasn't any walls. Almost everywhere you go, no matter how much you may otherwise live in the open, you sleep behind walls and you eat behind walls."

"But sleeping porches are all the rage everywhere," said Kate.

"Sleeping porches!" He spat the words from him disdainfully. "The devil take sleeping porches. I mean a place like this, really open, with lots of sky and long fields and mountains. I can hardly imagine a more luxurious meal than this."

"Well you bet your favorite silver dollar I can," said Kate, stirred to ardor by the mention of food. "It's been so fiendish hot lately and so disagreeable to go to town that we two women have eaten eggs till we're ashamed to look a hen in the face. A chop or a chunk of steak would look about a thousand per cent better to me than a whole crate of eggs."

He laughed as gaily as a child. "I'll remember that," he said, "when I come again. You're going to ask me to come again, aren't you?"

Kate looked a little annoyed and pretended to be busy with a fresh supply of toast.

"Of course we want you to come again," Rhoda hastened to say, "but don't be surprised if my partner puts you to work."

"Oh that won't deter me; the only time I hate work is when I earn my living by it."

"A queer fish that, full of gas and blarney," said Kate after their guest had gone. "He talks as if he'd been to school. I wonder how he comes to be driving a tractor."

"I'm sure his face is handsome when it's not all blackened and swollen."

"Handsome is as handsome does," said Kate drily.

"Well he hasn't done anything yet that isn't handsome, has he?"

"No, but there's something mighty queer about him."

When they went to the Pruetts' to borrow a doubletree they told them about their adventure of the night before.

"Is he a guy kinda good lookin' but sissyfied?" inquired Cliff Doble, a young fellow who was doing a few days' work for the Pruetts.

"Well he didn't have much looks when I saw him last," answered Kate.

"Of course he's good looking," put in Rhoda impatiently. "And he had on the same kind of clothes as the rest of us, a khaki shirt and blue overalls; only there was something refined—"

She caught herself up, afraid of wounding the feelings of these good people. She need have had no fear.

"I think I know the guy," said Cliff, with an air of condescending superiority. "No fightin' blood in him. Just like him to let a couple of boes eat up his lunch. Fella seems able-bodied, but he's damn lazy an' shiftless. He's some kind of a nut too, hangs out over there back a Beasley's place in a little old shack made a melon crates. Works a week an loafs a month. I kinda think mebbe he's in with a bunch a fellas that's makin' booze. But I dunno. If he ain't, he's nuts to hang out there all alone like he does."

"That must be Andy Blake you're talkin' about," said Mrs. Pruett, "he helped Mr. Pruett bring home some cattle from a sale here a while back. But if he's in with folks like that he'd otta be watched an' brought to account," she went on severely. "Moonshiners an' bootleggers is comin' to be the biggest curse o' this country. There'd otta be a law—"

"But Ma, there is a law," interrupted Mr. Pruett, winking slily in the direction of Kate and Rhoda. "Ain't you never heard of the Volstead Act?"

"Don't try to be smart. Of course I know there's a law; but what use is it if it ain't enforced? The whole thing is a shame an' a disgrace an' had otta be put a stop to."

A few days later when the girls came back from irrigating through the hot saffron of the August twilight they found the man to whom they had played good Samaritan sitting on the back doorstep. The cat had clawed the paper of a package which he had thrown on the ground beside him and was chewing vigorously on an end of meat. Her jaws had to be pried apart before she could be separated from her prey.

"Why did you let her get at it?" demanded Kate.

"I—I really didn't notice her; I got to thinking about something else. Anyway she hasn't eaten much of it."

"This is no place for woolgatherers," she admonished, as she cut away the end of meat that the cat had mangled.

"All right, put me to the test and see if I'm a woolgatherer. Give me a job and let me prove that I can clean ditch, milk cows, water horses, shovel manure or fix up the place in the fence where the colt got out as well as any Texas ranch hand in the Valley."

"You can peel potatoes," directed Kate. "That's your punishment for letting the cat get at the meat."

He peeled potatoes with the expert hand of a scullion. Kate fried the steak, Rhoda set the table and made a lettuce salad and they sat down in the hot thick twilight to eat. Kate, soothed into a good humor by the excellent steak, rallied their guest about the damage done to his beauty, about his housewifely ways, about all the little traits which had already signalled him out in her mind as "queer." She made in fact all the crude and obvious remarks that popped into her head, exercising to the full the right of the female to be impertinent to the male. To these unsubtle attacks he replied with sprightly good humor, devoting a large part of his attention to the steak and potatoes. In the dim half-light Rhoda studied the stranger's face. It was still badly discolored, but the swellings had gone down leaving it normal in shape. It was not a very young face; even through the dusk she could discern lines about the eyes and mouth that made her think him well over thirty. The brow was wide and high, the features fairly regular, the chin a bit weak, weaker than she liked in a man. The great charm of the face lay in its smile. There was a half-breed grocer boy at the store where they dealt in El Centro who had a smile very like it: bland, childlike serenity made piquant by a subtle gipsy charm. In that town where among the stores and offices few people ever stretched their mouths in anything but a professional smirk this smile had completely captivated Rhoda. The smile across the table was not so purely bland and serene; there were fine lines about the mouth that gave it subtleties of expression unknown to the half-breed lad, but the general character was the same.

After dinner they sipped their cold coffee, smoked and chatted, looking out across the ditch's fringe of arrowweed to where beyond the long, level stretch the sunset's last bars of saffron and dull red fell to ashes into the hot darkness. Rhoda had said little during the meal and as the evening passed her silences grew longer. A growing sense of frustration and annoyance pricked her mind into irritability. Why did Kate say such obvious and asinine things and make such a fool of herself? Why couldn't she see that he was barely tolerating her? She had even called him "Handy Andy!" How could people be like that and not see that they were boring other people to death? She was as bad as Mr. Pruett.

She could talk to him, she knew she could, if only Kate was not there doing the bull-in-the-china-shop act. Why was it that when you had a chance at something you really wanted there was always something in the way?

"And how's the work on the tractor coming on?" asked Kate.

"The tractor? Oh I've ditched that job. I got tired of it. Night work's not bad for a while but it soon gets to be a bore."

"And what are you going to do now?"

"Oh I dunno. Loaf for a while I guess till the hot weather eases up."

She looked at him with penetrating severity.

"You won't make much headway sailing that tack."

"I don't expect to," he answered genially.

"Queer duck as I ever ran into," she opined after he was gone. "He seems healthy enough and not exactly lazy either. I wonder what's the reason he doesn't want to work?"

"But Kate anyone can easily see that driving a tractor and work like that isn't the sort of thing he ought to be doing."

"Well then why the dickens doesn't he get into something else? And why does he swelter here through the hottest part of the year when he's footloose to go where he likes? A smart, sleek looking young fellow like him with an education oughtn't to have any trouble getting a responsible position with some good business firm."

"Maybe he doesn't like business."

"Oh LIKE," in a tone of boundless disdain. "Who ever likes anything they have to do for a living? Do I like to pitch hay with the sun so hot it bursts the thermometer? No I don't. But I do it so as to try to get somewhere. Tell you what I think: he's making booze or handling it, like a lot of these other idle young sports, and he works for a while now and then as a blind. They say there's good money in it too. I wouldn't mind going into it myself if I knew the ropes; but don't whisper them words to Ma Pruett."

That night there was a slight, delicious coolness in the air, a faint but grateful promise of the relaxing of the heat. It soothed Rhoda's raw nerves, and as she sat on the porch smoking and looking out into the warm darkness she fell into a brown study thinking of her childhood, of her youth, of dreams she had dreamed and flimsy little romances that had troubled her heart and come to nothing. Her vagrant thoughts fluttered hither and thither like a butterfly over the poor blossoms of her past. She recalled the house that had been her home all her life till she had come to the

Valley, a good enough house it had seemed then, but now so stuffy, narrow, chilly and dark. She wondered that she had ever been able to breathe in those cramped, sunless rooms. She saw again the skimpy hallway, the worn stair carpet, the lace-curtained parlor, the dining room with its thin slit of a window looking out onto a narrow alleyway between brick walls. A dreary place and one she felt that she could never return to, but full of tender memories of youth.

She thought about her school days and her old schoolmates, remembering how a group of them used to loiter home together on sunny spring afternoons chattering and laughing and thinking it a huge joke to push each other into the entranceways of cigar stores and barber shops. She remembered her first silk petticoat and her first party dress and a pink chiffon summer hat that had been very becoming. She remembered a young man who had walked home with her from the office a few times and once taken her to the theatre.

There was another young man whom she had met at a picnic, a blond fellow with smiling blue eyes. He had walked with her down a lovely forest path and they had talked about all sorts of things. And when the picnic broke up he had asked for her address and for permission to call. But he had never called.

She remembered best of all a "pick-up" in the park. She thrilled again at the recollection of that exciting adventure. She had been sitting on a bench and he had come and sat down on the other end of the bench and she had covertly eyed his feet and legs thinking them very slim and elegant. Then when she had ventured to take just a peep at his face she had discovered that he was merry-eyed and that he was looking at her and she had smiled because she couldn't help it. Encouraged by the smile he had moved nearer and started up a conversation and it was not long before he had told her that he was in his second year in college and that he had not made up his mind yet whether he was going to be a painter or a violinist. He had been full of boyish chatter about books and music and pictures, all the alluring things of life. Twice after that he had met her by appointment in the park—ah the thrill of those clandestine meetings—and they had gone off on long, delightful walks together. Then he had been called away by the death of his father and she had never seen him again.

This was her pansy bed of memory, a poor flower patch perhaps, but her own and transfigured for her by the subtle glamor and the faint perfume that hovers over memories of youth.

Which one of these men would she have continued to encourage, she asked herself. And because she was in a mood for frankness, a mood not always hers, the answer came quite readily and naturally—any one. But it was of the pick-up that she thought most lingeringly.

He was just such a boy as Andy Blake must have been at that age. If her life were a book Andy Blake would be the pick-up brought back to her by the miraculous hand of fate. Did such things ever really happen?

What a long time since she had stopped to think of those old days.

CHAPTER 9

A WEEK, two weeks passed and nothing happened to break the monotony of the daily routine. Then one afternoon when Rhoda was returning on foot from an errand to the Pruetts', she came to a sudden determination to do something that for two weeks she had been nursing a secret longing to do. Instead of going on to the crossing of the main road she turned off onto a narrow path that ran beside a small ditch under a row of cottonwoods and eucalypti. Narrow paths under trees were rare things in the Valley. It seemed fitting and natural that the place where he lived should be reached by one of these instead of by the wide, bleak, dusty roads that ran before the houses of ordinary people. She hurried, for she did not want any questions from Kate as to why she was late in getting back; but she was breathless with something more than haste when she paused at the first glimpse of a drooping pepper tree and beside it what looked at first like a pile of old melon crates. Venturing to approach a little nearer she saw that the melon crates were arranged to form a house, that there was a large hole for a door and a smaller hole for a window. A camp cot covered by an army blanket stood outside against the wall. She hesitated, picked up a dry twig and broke it noisily. There was no sound from within. She came a little nearer, making her footsteps crackle over the dry cottonwood twigs and the shed bark of eucalypti. Still no sign of life. At last she made bold to edge toward the door and peer inside. There was nobody there, and she stepped in and looked about her.

The sun, now nearly to the horizon, stretched prying red fingers through the holes in the melon crates and laid them obliquely upon a rusty oil stove, a chair, a packing case that served as a cupboard and another packing case with one side knocked out which did duty as a table. There was no feeling of sordidness about the little room; it was not particularly clean or orderly, yet somehow it breathed an atmosphere of cleanliness, order and ascetic simplicity such as she imagined would benignly suffuse the cell of some wise and holy anchorite. One shaft of fire lay across the backs of a few pocket-size books set upon a rough shelf and brought out the greens and browns and russets of the bindings, with here and there the pure gleam of a golden title.

What kind of books did he read, she wondered, and took one from the shelf. It was in the Greek language and she could make nothing of it except that it was by Aristophanes.

She put it back and took down another. Her heart gave a leap of pleasure and her lips fell apart in a smile as she opened this book. She fluttered the pages eagerly, searching for and finding familiar things. She had had two years of German in high school, enough to recognize and be able to read "Du Schönes Fischermädchen," and "Du bist wie eine Blume." As she turned the pages, skimming here and lingering there, the sun slowly shifted one burning finger and laid it across her face bringing out the red of eager, sensitive lips.

"Auf Flügeln des Gesanges
  Herzliebchen trag ich dich fort,
Fort nach den Fluren des Ganges;
  Dort weiss ich den Schönsten Ort."

How easy it would be with his help, if he were only so minded, to fly away with him on wings of song, away from everything that was sordid and petty into a world that nobody else in the Valley knew anything about. There they two would be alone in a world all their own.

Gently, lingeringly, she set the book back in its place on the shelf and took down another. As she fluttered the pages her eye was caught by a phrase in a little poem, "We may be happy yet," and she paused and read it through.

"When you are very old at evening
  You'll sit and spin beside the fire and say,
Humming my songs, 'Ah well, ah well-a-day,
  When I was young of me did Ronsard sing.'
None of your maidens that doth hear the thing,
  Albeit with her weary task foredone,
But wakens at my name and calls it one
  Blest to be held in long remembering.

I shall be low beneath the earth and laid
  On sleep, a phantom in the myrtle shade,

While you beside the fire, a grandam gray,
My love, your pride, remember and regret;
Ah love me, love! we may be happy yet
And gather roses while 't is called today."

Silently the sun withdrew his red fingers and left the little room suffused in a golden glow. She stood aureoled like a saint in a niche. About her thoughts too hung a nimbus of dreams, a mist penetrated with the colors of rose and flame. "Of me did Ronsard sing." She said it over softly to herself. To have a poet for a lover, that must be something very wonderful, something that surely no woman however proud and beautiful could allow to pass her by. If such a man should come to love her, were it only for a month, for a week, for a day, she would have that memory always to cherish in her heart. It would be something to keep—

She looked up with a swift, startled movement, then shrank together in disappointment and dismay. There in the doorway stood a half-breed girl, handsome, insolent looking, a salmon colored skirt hanging about thick ankles, a red handkerchief tied over black hair. She made an inarticulate sound of astonishment, muttered a word or two in her own language and disappeared.

Rhoda put the book back hurriedly and fled from the hateful place.

They had been having a great deal of trouble lately with the irrigation water. Their ranch was watered not from the main ditch at their gate but by a smaller ditch which passed a half mile or so beyond the back end of their place. Often this ditch did not contain enough water for the lands that it was supposed to irrigate and always it was undependable. Sometimes the water would come with a good flow when the zanjero turned it on, and perhaps a few hours later it would be only a dribble. Kate stormed and blustered about having to pay for water and not getting it.

"I'll bet it's those damn Hindus up the line," she said one morning when she came back disgusted from an almost dry ditch. "Everybody says there's nothing like a Hindu for stealing water. I've half a mind to go down and have a look at their water gate. If it wasn't so hellish hot I would."

A few days later when it was Rhoda's turn to attend to the water she found the ditch again nearly dry. No water at all for the thirsty alfalfa roots. She looked southward in the direction from which the water came and her eyes rested upon the clump of pepper trees and the two Hindu tent houses. They were a mile away but over the level country the distance looked scarcely half a mile. She turned and walked southward along the ditch bank.

When she reached the Hindus' water gate she found it up, the ditch still nearly dry, no signs of water on the Hindus' cotton. She stood irresolutely looking in the direction of the pepper trees and tent houses a quarter of a mile to the west.

An unlovely old hermit who lived in a shanty on the other side of the ditch was sitting smoking his pipe in front of the hole that he called his door.

"You lookin' fer the Hindus, missus?" he called across the ditch in a cracked high-pitched voice.

"Y–yes," she hesitated.

"Tain't no use yer goin' there, you won't find none of 'em to hum. The hull lot lit out fer Mexicali a half hour ago, all piled in that big car. I reckon Hindus likes a good time same's the rest o' the fellers. He he he!"

He leered at her significantly with his rheumy old eyes. She turned away full of disgust.

That evening as she and Kate sat at the table in the sultry twilight sipping cold coffee, she said abruptly: "Do you know Kate we've been living for three quarters of a year within four miles of Mexican soil and haven't once set foot on it yet."

"Well I guess we haven't missed much. Everybody says so," munched Kate.

"Perhaps not. But I'd like to go over and see for myself. Tomorrow when we take the rest of the chickens to that Calexico butcher let's go across and have a little look around Mexicali."

The next day, after they had disposed of their chickens, Rhoda reminded Kate of her wish to see Mexicali. Kate protested grumblingly while she allowed herself to be persuaded to turn the car southward. In a few moments they came to a place where a large sign, "International Boundary," spanned the roadway and turnstiles blocked the sidewalks on both sides. A pompous and gorgeously uniformed Mexican guard glanced them over casually and motioned to them with lordly indifference to pass on out of his sight. With one chug of the engine they had left Calexico, California, and were in Mexicali, Mexico. Instantly they found themselves in a town foreign to all the best American traditions.

Here there were no cement pavements, no dressed display windows behind glittering plate glass, no processions of cars, no busy crowds, no noise, no bustle, no excitement. Wide, aimless beaten spaces like Gargantuan cowpaths took the place of streets. Along these cowpath streets Chinese shops with narrow, second-story balconies, saloons, lazy little fruit stands, more Chinese shops and more saloons. A great hideous casino, blazoned as "The Owl," in outer appearance a cross between a gas tank and a barn. Fringing these in haphazard fashion, scattered little houses of redwood or adobe some with bright flower patches about them, others set sordidly in bare, beaten yards scattered with rubbish. Long skinny cats, drowsing dogs, little naked children.

The people who loitered through these streets from house to shop, from shop to saloon, the doorway-leaners and kerb-sitters, were silent, dark-skinned people. Big-hatted Mexicans in blue overalls sat in rows on the shaded parts of the kerbs, hung in doorways, lounged in relaxed groups at the street corners. Fat Mexican women with clumsy ankles waddled hither and thither. Slinky Chinamen in smocks, slippers and flapping drawers slipped in and out of the shops, passed here and there swiftly and silently like shadows. The streets were hot, sun-steeped, drowsy and dusty. Over all there hovered a sense of timeless leisure.

They drove out of the town for a few miles into a savage, adobe country, rugged and vast and heat-smitten, with only here and there a few small watered spots. Tawny desert ground sun-baked and blistered, little tawny houses that seemed mere upheavals of the earth, scraps of desert vegetations warped and gray, these stretched away to a chain of rock-piled mountains, the same mountains that they could see from their porch at home, lonely, barren mountains indifferent to man.

They turned and drove back to Mexicali over bumpy roads deep in hot dust, a searing wind in their faces. By the roadside lay a dead horse stinking horribly.

"It seems to me," said Rhoda glancing about, "that Mexicans must either hate work for its own sake or else they've made up their minds that they won't get anything they really want by working. I wonder which it is—or maybe it's both."

"Lazy, shiftless lot," commented Kate in disgust. "They say there's some pretty nice tracts a bit further down, but they're all in the hands of Americans."

"Perhaps that's one reason the Mexicans don't work. Perhaps they know that if they got anything the Americans would take it away from them."

Coming back through Mexicali they skirted the wide and deep gorge that had been cut into the erosive clay soil by the flood waters of the Colorado when in the early days of the Valley that unruly river had broken bounds and rushed downward through the land it had made habitable to the Salton Sea, taking houses and farms with it. Rhoda shuddered as she looked into this great gaping hole and saw how close the river had come to washing away the whole town. There had been grave fears of flood only two months ago;

for weeks the paper had kept the ranchers posted on the height of the river, the frantic work at the levees. She was glad that when she had been reading those reports she had had no picture of this terrible gulf before her mind's eye.

A smell no longer allowed publicity in the United States, a pungent, maltish odor delicious on a hot day, floated out from the saloon doors.

"Well seeing we're here I suppose we may as well have a drink," suggested Kate.

"Shall we? Do you think it's all right for women to go in?"

"I don't give a damn whether it's all right or not; I'm gonna have a beer."

She stopped the car in front of a saloon and led the way. Rhoda followed hesitatingly.

The barkeeper did not even glance curiously at them as he handed them their drinks over the beer-slopped mahogany bar. Apparently he was used to seeing women in his place. To their parched tongues and wilted bodies the weak, bad beer was deliciously refreshing.

The place was empty except for two hunched-over Mexicans playing cards in a corner. But while they stood sipping their beer a man and a woman came in, a handsome Spanish-looking young fellow and a girl with a heavy face, white as chalk from powder, and full, sensual lips outlined in screaming scarlet. Her sleazy black dress, quite sleeveless and cut very low in the neck, made her look rather more than naked. She ordered a whiskey straight. They caught snatches of her conversation.

"Did yuh glim the fat coot that's all off on top? They say he's lousy with coin. Some nifty gas wagon he's got too."

The young man, speaking in a more restrained voice, said something to her in which there was mention of somebody named Loretta. He pronounced it as the Spanish do, separating the t's.

"All right, she'd better go slow an' not try to put none o' that stuff off on me or I'll spit in her eye."

Her companion shrugged his shoulders, smiled, said something in a low voice.

"Aw shut up an' quit kiddin' me Joe, yuh dirty bum."

It was women like this then that the Hindus had gone to visit, Rhoda thought as they drove homeward. She knew that the little town of Mexicali, so sleepy by day, woke to feverish activity by night, that it was full of big, shiny cars, full of Japs, Chinamen, Hindus, full of field hands, ranchers and sleek American business men. It was women such as this who drew them there. What difference anyway? What business was it of hers? No business, only—

There flashed across her mind a vision of a handsome, insolent face, a slatternly, salmon colored skirt hanging about thick ankles, a red handkerchief tied over black hair.

She gave a dispirited little lift of the shoulders. Her slender hands drooped mournfully in her lap. She felt miserable, dull and lonely like a child who sees all the others go gaily off to a picnic and is left alone for all day in a chilly, dismal house.

It was Rhoda's turn to attend to the water. She woke in the very early morning even before the alarm clock rang. It was still quite dark and utterly quiet too, yet she sensed everywhere the stirring of myriads of small, powerful, restless forces that told her that the dawning was at hand. She lay looking up at the stars and wondering how without seeing or hearing she could sense these forces when suddenly with an unholy clatter the alarm clock rang. She grabbed it, smothered it under her pillow and dozed off to sleep again.

She was awakened by Kate's voice.

"Say, Rhoda, don't go letting on you don't know it's your turn to tend to that water."

She hated to come to herself, for since the alarm clock rang she had been dreaming a lovely dream, one of those ineffable dreams which transport the dreamer into a sort of intimately personal fairyland where everything is touched with mystery and charm yet nothing seems unnatural no matter how miraculous. She was standing on a dark, water-lapped wharf buying a ticket, darkness everywhere and about her only the soft monotonous sound of water lapping, lapping at invisible piles. As the ticket agent handed her the ticket he leaned forward and kissed her in the darkness. It was only a light butterfly kiss, a mere brushing of wings. It seemed natural and to be expected and at the same time delightfully surprising. As she passed on enfolded in the soft, murmurous sound of lapping water she took the kiss with her.

She was standing under a dark arch on the edge of the dark pier, dark water lapping against the piles below her feet. The stirring of countless small forces, unseen, unheard, told her that the morning was not far off. Lifting her eyes she saw dimly the black hulk of a ferryboat coming toward her across the dark water. As the black hulk moved nearer, the sky slowly whitened, the water rippled to silver, a breeze blew in her face and lifting her eyes again she saw the sky a delicate morning blue flecked with little clouds of purest gold. The boat came alongside the pier, she stepped aboard and at once it swung out again into the dawn. As she paced the deck she saw that she was approaching a white and green city which rose steeply from the water's edge. Fringing the sea on each side of the city ran a long line of rocky cliffs strangely like the Mexican mountains to the south of them. Like the Mexican mountains too their jagged sides were cut sharply into deep shadow and high relief by the morning sun. The sea was deep blue now, the light breeze fluttering and bouyant. All the time she was carrying ecstatically the ticket agent's kiss. She felt gay, free and light like a disembodied spirit.

A man, who seemed to be the only other passenger on the ferryboat, came toward her, and as he approached she saw that his features were swollen and discolored. But as he passed he flung her a charming smile, frank and boyish. She was not disappointed that he had not stopped to talk with her because she knew that on his round of the deck she would soon meet him again. But when next he came near his features were neither swollen nor discolored; they were long, slim, Oriental features calm as if chiselled from ivory. And he passed without a shadow of a smile, only a look, a steady, pervasive look from calm, Oriental eyes. But she felt sure that when she met him again his face would be swollen and discolored and he would have the smile again. Next time she would stop him, she would take hold of his hand—

Then she heard Kate's voice, but still she would not come to herself. In a warm, delicious daze between sleeping and waking she clung lovingly to the dream, thrust out soft, eager tentacles to hold it when it seemed to be escaping over the rim of consciousness. It was a precious thing and she wanted to keep it; she wanted to see if—

"Rhoda, get up, drat you, you've foxed long enough. If that water isn't shut off pretty pronto we'll have some scalded alfalfa."

Reluctantly she came back to reality and pulled on her shirt and overalls.

Light was breaking as she passed out through the dooryard and the cattle corral, an irrigating shovel over her shoulder. One by one the hens, still dazed and sleepy, fluttered down from the chinaberry trees. The cat uncurled herself from a gunny sack, stretched, yawned and looked about her. On the top of the shaggy arrowweed thatch over the milkhouse ramada the five turkeys stirred in their sleep, stretched their long necks and preened their feathers, their big bodies black against soft gray like a Japanese print. On every hand she felt the soft, insistent stirring of life.

At the water gate she found the ditch again nearly dry. She looked toward the cluster of pepper trees and the two tent houses, hesitated for a moment, then walked southward along the ditch bank.

There was a delicious freshness in the clear, still air. How big the delft blue sky, how big the world, how far, how far to the horizon. And now from every point of that far horizon came the crowing of countless roosters. Mellowed and blended by distance, the music was like that of some great universal orchestra, with here and there the solo notes of a nearer clarion call in bold and clear vibration above the chorus. From everywhere all around the great ring of the horizon the unending chant arose. Upward pushing and irresistible as young life, it surged stronger and stronger, a mighty and triumphant pean of pagan joy to greet the birth of a new day.

Rhoda walked along the ditch bank with the same light, disembodied feeling that she had had in her dream, the feeling that comes to people who rise and go out under the sky before the dawn. She felt exultant, gay and adventurous and as if she were being carried forward on the billows of that vast chorus. In her nostrils were damp, fresh odors from the irrigated lands. When she lifted her eyes she saw the great sky, deep, pure, serene, waiting for its lord the sun.

He came and turned the tops of the eucalyptus trees a warm russet, then sent long shadows across the fields of cotton and alfalfa, brought out in jagged shadow and relief the mountains to the south, startled the half-dreaming world full awake as with a trumpet blast, and the flower of the day was full blown.

When Rhoda reached the Hindus' water gate she found what she had half expected, yet was shocked and at the same time rather pleased to find, the water gate down and all the water in the ditch flowing onto the Hindus' cotton and kaffir corn. She stood irresolute, uncertain what to do next.

At a little distance a man was driving a disc harrow over a piece of land from which the early kaffir corn had been harvested. He looked in her direction once or twice, then as she continued to stand at the gate, he stopped the mules, got down from his seat and came toward her. She recognized him as the man before whom she had already made a fool of herself and began to tremble, wondering what she would say. He came up with an easy, muscular slouch, negligent and self-possessed.

"You wish to speak to me?"

"I—yes. I—I," she colored furiously. "There isn't any water in our ditch and we're supposed to have water last night and today."

For answer he walked over and raised the gate, letting the water pour through.

"Surely you shall have water," he said coming back toward her. "If I had known you had it ordered I would not have let down the gate."

She had been summoning all her courage and now she said with a tremendous show of boldness: "But you had no right to let the gate entirely down. Surely you had not ordered all the water in the ditch."

For the first time in her life she heard a Hindu laugh. It was a laugh she did not like to hear; indulgent, patronizing, almost sneering. It made her shrivel and feel foolish.

"I had no right? Perhaps so. If everybody did only what they had a right to do your country and all countries would be quite different. Many times we order water, we pay for water and somebody further up the ditch takes it all and we get none or only a dribble. Just the same we have to pay. So when water comes down and we need water we take all we can. So does everybody else, but the Americans always say, 'Oh yes, it is the Hindus that steal the water.' They are not worse perhaps than the rest of us, only they are more hypocrites. It is all—how do you call it—a game of grab, like so many other games in your country. You understand, do you not?"

She hated him for the indulgent, superior way in which he spoke to her, like a father explaining to his child a sum in arithmetic.

"Thank you for lifting the gate," was all she could think of to say.

"I shall always lift it when you tell me," he answered with

a gallant smile in which she detected just a shadow of a sneer.

"Thank you," she said and turned away abruptly.

When she had gone a few steps she was irresistibly impelled to turn around. He was standing just as she had left him, looking after her. She walked back to him.

"Yes?"

There was something hideously self-possessed about the monosyllable, something coldly sneering and appraisive. She stood before him like a fly impaled on a needle.

"I just wanted to say that we'll be using water till tomorrow morning."

"Very well, I will see that it is not stopped here."

She turned away more abruptly than the first time.

Kate was scrambling eggs over the oil stove when she returned. "How was the water?" she asked.

"A good flow. But it took me a long time to change the ditches; everything seemed to be stopped up and there were an awful lot of big gopher holes. We'll have to be doing something about those gophers."

That evening as she went about working with the water she looked often along the empty stretch of ditch bank and often she paused with her foot on the shovel listening to the silence. As the night came on she lighted her lantern, thinking how far the little tip of flame could be seen, "like a good deed in a naughty world." She shivered in the slight chill that fell with the shadows, laughed a little to herself in the enfolding darkness. But nobody came.

It was later than usual when she came up across fields to the house. She had put the lantern out. At the back of the cattle corral she softly set the lantern down and slid away through the darkness. There was no light in the house. Kate must have gone to bed.

The light of a shaded lamp on Ruby Peterson's living porch cast a diffused glow into the surrounding night. The little house radiant with yellow light that streamed through black palm and pepper tree looked romantic and beautiful enough to be the abode of a prince in exile or the retreat of a pair of lovers who had fled from the world. A shadow moved across the light. It was only Ruby hastily washing up the dishes that all day long according to her habit she had left piled in the sink. But it ought to have been a prince—or a lover. The stars hung low and golden in the warm darkness.

She passed on lightly, stealthily, a moving shadow under the shadow of the eucalyptus trees. The ditchwater slid by without a sound.

Far ahead she saw a little light burning and she walked toward the light silently, stealthily. As she drew nearer the light became more than a mere point and streamed out through pepper boughs and the spaces between the slats of old melon crates.

She paused, listened intently, then slunk back from the path and crouched down under a tent of drooping eucalyptus boughs. No it was not a footstep, only a cow on the other side of the fence, but she was afraid to go back into the path. From the eucalyptus tent where she sat with her knees drawn up under her sharp little chin she could still see the melon-crate house with the golden light pouring out between the slats. What was he doing in there? Was he sitting alone reading from a little green or brown book? Or was she with him? If she could be quite sure that he was alone she would go and knock at the door, she told herself, knowing all too well that she would never dare. She imagined herself giving a little tap on the melon crates and he coming to the door with no look of surprise but only welcome and drawing her inside and the two of them sitting down under the lamp and reading together:

"When I was young of me did Ronsard sing."

All of a sudden the light went out.

It seemed very lonely in the darkness; there was nothing

to look at any more and she got up and wandered aimlessly homeward, feeling vague and empty. As she walked she found herself thinking again of her school days, her early girlhood and the men who might have been her lovers.

Somehow there drifted into her head out of nowhere a few notes of a song, oddly familiar notes, yet so strange that they seemed as if they had been dropped by a fairy out of the air. A single little musical phrase, yet it came haloed by a haunting charm, a tantalizing allurement, a faint perfume like the breath from some long-closed chest of delicate and lovely things. Over and over again she crooned it to herself, fascinated by its subtle suggestion of beauty and strangeness. She sent forth blind feelers into the past, reaching out for more of it; and quite suddenly, as if again dropped out of the air, a few more notes of the song floated into her mind. They fell upon her spirit softly and restlessly like butterfly wings, and as she hummed the few notes to herself she reached back into the dark storehouse of her memory for more. When they came it seemed again as if the fairy had dropped them, a delicate surprise, out of the air. Bit by bit more and more of the song came back to her with memories of young dreams and fancies that had lain buried under years of office routine and the drab monotony of family life. She groped about in her memory but could not stabilize these dreams and fancies, could not pin them to any definite period of her girlhood.

Then quite unexpectedly she remembered exactly where she had heard the song. It was the young man she had picked up in the park who had hummed it one afternoon when they had gone off into the country on a long tramp. She remembered now as if it had been yesterday his careless stride along the old road through the woods and how he had stuffed his cap into his pocket and let the wind play with the brown strands of his hair.

CHAPTER 10

SHE WONDERED at herself that she was not unhappy, that she was not disappointed because she had not had the courage to go up and give a little tap on the melon crates. Instead she found it pleasant to wait, to nurse the idea that some day perhaps she would, to watch for him, though he still delayed to come, to hope that some happy accident would once more throw them together, to secretly turn over in her mind ways of bringing about that happy accident. As she went through the routine tasks of the morning, washing the dishes, sweeping the floor, scrubbing out the slimy olla and scouring the soapstone water filter, she trembled with the hope that perhaps that very day she would overtake him on the road and give him a lift in the car, that she would meet him on the ditch bank when she was waiting for the zanjero or see him on the street in El Centro. All day long, whether she drove the mower or stacked hay or shovelled dirt into gopher holes or stood on the sharp, treacherous V while Kate profanely urged the mules forward at the unspeakably filthy task of ditch cleaning, she found herself wondering where he was, what he was doing, whom he was talking to, what he was thinking about. In these thoughts there lay for her a secret happiness that made her cheeks warmly colored, her eyes full of depth and clear shadow.

She gave attention to her appearance and her clothes, for she could never tell when she might meet him. One day when she was on the street in El Centro dressed in her best and feeling more than usually adventurous and gay it occurred to her to go in and pay a little visit to Mr. McCumber, the agent who had sold them their place. He rose from his desk as she entered, and she knew by the expression of his face that he did not recognize her. She beamed upon him with frankly flirtatious eyes and the most charming smile of which she was capable.

"Don't you remember me, Mr. McCumber? My name is Malone."

"Well well well, of course it's Miss Malone. How stupid of me." He set a chair for her in his best manner. "Well I will say, Miss Malone, the Valley hasn't done you a bit of harm, nor the hot season either. Say, I've been intending all the time to run down there and see how you folks are getting on, but somehow I haven't got around to it yet."

She knew in her simple blue muslin dress and wide straw hat she was looking disconcertingly fresh and pretty; and with keen zest she sensed her power to project an aura in which he was flustered, bewildered and taken by storm. She sat chatting with him only a few moments, just long enough to carry off the palm of victory, and left him transfixed with a parting smile.

"That'll teach him to call me an old maid," she told herself with a little triumphant pout and that whimsical lift of one corner of the mouth.

On the pavement just outside she almost ran into a tall man in a khaki shirt and riding breeches. Sparkling with gaiety and flushed with triumph she drew back and looked up smilingly into a pair of tawny, Oriental eyes.

"Good morning, Mr.—I don't know what it is, but it's probably got Singh on the end."

He smiled. "You are quite right, it has a Singh on the end."

"What does Singh mean?"

He drew a little more toward the inner edge of the pavement so that they would be out of the stream of traffic.

"It would take a long time to tell you that; but in a word it means that we do not go with the crowd. We are—you have a word for it—nonconformists."

"I think I like nonconformists."

"I am glad you like nonconformists."

"I didn't mean to say I liked them, I said I thought I might like them."

"I am glad you are disposed to learn to like nonconformists."

He smiled again and fixed her with a boldly provocative gaze. She looked down at the toe of her slipper and pretended to be dubious, then flashed him sidewise her most coquettish glance.

"Maybe after all they wouldn't improve on acquaintance."

"It is well to have the experimental mind. All things are found through experiment."

Yes, he was very handsome, very handsome indeed. She fluttered him another sidewise glance, not venturing to meet with too much frankness his boldly provocative eyes.

"Oh but some experiments are so unsuccessful."

"However unsuccessful, they still teach."

He ran his eye slowly, appraisingly along her length from the toe of her shoe to her wide hat.

"I see you do not come to town dressed like a field hand. You are very gay today like a blue butterfly."

"Rhoda, for Pete's sake, I've been looking everywhere for you. Did you get the meat—and the soup bone for the dog? Howdy, Mr.—ah. Oh say, by the way, did you have any fault to find with that hay we sold you?"

Over his lips there flitted just the merest shadow of an indulgent sneer.

"Certainly I have no fault to find with the hay you sold me."

"Well, some old geezer over near Calexico complained that it was full of water grass, and I told him, which was the truth, that it didn't have a quarter as much water grass as most Valley hay. But there's no pleasing some people."

"Your alfalfa is doing well? You will be watering again soon?"

"Again? How do you mean?"

Rhoda's quick glance of panic and warning was not lost upon him.

"I only wished to know because lately the water has been short. I do not wish to be watering when you water because there is not enough."

"Next Thursday I guess we'll water. Come on Rhoda, I'm nearly starved.—What were you talking to that Hindu about anyway?"

"Oh he just stopped to ask me if I knew whether Mr. Pruett would want any more kaffir corn this month. And say, Kate, eggs have dropped another three cents. Isn't that a shame we can't get anything for our eggs! And over in San Diego people are paying forty cents a dozen for them. Why can't we send them direct to San Diego?"

"Oh we haven't enough to make it worth while; we've just got to take what they give us and say nothing."

In the late long rays of the setting sun she went about working with the water, pulling out and resetting the tampoons, closing the entrance to this ditch and opening that, shovelling away oozy accumulations of silt, then exhausted and breathless leaning on her shovel handle and watching the sluggish yellow water as it crawled along the ditches which she had opened for it. It was fascinating to watch these slow streams creep like live things, feel their way gingerly, then plunge with a sudden rush into depressions, swirl, eddy, wash deeper beds for themselves, widen and narrow to fit their channels like baby Colorados. She had grown somewhat thinner with the hot weather and as she sloshed about in her high rubber boots through the mud and water, turning the current here, stopping it there, lifting out big shovelfuls of silt, the level rays of the sun threw into sharp shadow and relief her pointed Celtic face in which the eyes smouldered dark, brooding and mournful. A prosaic occupation, a new, raw land bare and open to the sky with neither charm nor mystery, a woman, all her life a sapped tool of routine, void of experience and shut away from the life of the spirit. Yet this might have been the face and these the eyes of Kathleen ni Houlihan glimpsed through an Irish twilight.

Crossing one of the lands she spied two little doves snuggled together in their nest on the ground. The water was only a few feet from them and before long would creep up and drown them. She took them up nest and all and set them on the top of a border, wondering if the mother bird would find them. How silly of doves to make their nests on the ground and in full sight. Why didn't nature take better care of them?

As she shovelled and as she leaned on the shovel handle she kept thinking that all the time he was so near her and yet so far away. It was nearly a month now since she had seen him and yet he was living there less than a mile from her. What was he doing at that moment? Was he in the melon-crate house with the long fingers of the sun falling across him as he sat reading in one of those little books? Was he all alone or was she with him, the girl in the salmon colored skirt?

Someone came up behind her as she was tugging at a big sheet-iron tampoon trying to raise it from the imbedding ooze. His approach had been silent and unseen behind the screen of arroweed that fringed the ditch.

"It is sunk in too deep for you to pull out," he said in a low, vibrant voice. She started erect her cheeks flushing hotly as a pair of slim brown hands took hold of the tampoon and pulled at it without success.

"Let me show you. Where is your shovel?"

He took the shovel from her hand and lifted away big dripping loads of silt from both sides of the tampoon, then raised it easily with one pull.

"Now show me where it should be put in again."

She led the way to the place where she wanted the ditch closed and watched with admiration the muscular ease with which he pushed the heavy iron sheet into the ground and banked up the ends with big shovelfuls of mud, saying all the time never a word. The sun had set and in the clear, uniform light the distant mountains, the lines of trees and ditch borders of arrowweed stood out distinct and fine like etchings. Not a sound stirred the brooding air; it was like a land in a trance.

"How many acres of cotton have you?" she asked to be saying something.

"Myself and my partners together have five hundred and fifty acres. If cotton is a good price we will make much money. I must build up the break in that border for you, already the water is beginning to leak through. And you must stop up the gopher holes more tightly, tramp them down like this. But I see that your feet are too little."

"Where did you learn to speak such good English?"

"Oh nearly all my life I have spoken English: first in India in the service of the British government, then in London, in New York, in South America, and at last here. I am what you call a rolling stone. You too who have come here where everything is quite new, you have wished to be a little adventurous also?"

"Yes—perhaps. We wanted something new, something different, a change from what we had been doing all our lives."

He leaned on the shovel handle and smiled slightly, showing his white teeth, then lighted a cigaret and blew a quick puff into the evening air.

"You smoke?"

"Yes."

He pulled one forward from the bunch and proffered her his package, lighted the cigaret for her and watched the match drift down the little ditch.

"It is the only way," he said, turning on her intently and gravely his dark, luminous eyes. "Nothing lasts long. You are in a place for a while; it becomes tame and stale, today is just like yesterday and tomorrow will be just like today. Your thought becomes tired and dull; you are dead, though you still breathe. Then if you are wise you leave that place and go where it is different so that you can live again. Life is for such a little while it is a shame to waste it in doing the same thing over and over again, like a horse on a treadmill."

"But a plant takes root where it grows, and if you move it it suffers and perhaps dies."

"Ah it is a good thing we are not plants," he answered with one of his flashes of white teeth. "Some women perhaps are plants, but we men should not like to be plants. You too are not a plant? You must from time to time have something new, something different so that you can live?"

"I don't know," she answered humbly, "I hadn't thought about it. I'm afraid you know a great deal more than I."

He laughed an unpleasant laugh.

"Then you are not like most of the people here. They think they know oh so much and we dark-skinned people know nothing. They put us in the same class with what they call 'niggers' whom they despise greatly. I am not then a dog in your eyes?"

"Oh no," she answered, looking at him with wide, earnest eyes like a child.

"Then perhaps you will let me come and help you when you water. The work is too hard for you; you are not big and strong like your friend."

"Oh I am stronger than you think," she said gaily, and taking the shovel from his hand began to show him what big loads she could lift from the ditch bed. He stood watching her silent, impassive, a slight, half cynical smile on his face, dark behind the glowing tip of his cigaret. As she glanced at him over her shoulder her coquettishness trailed off into a weak, fluttering sense of helplessness like a moth in a lamp chimney. Why did he stand there like a statue? Why didn't he move or say something? Why didn't he go home?

"See," she said, pausing in her work and trying to speak offhandedly, "I'm stronger than you thought."

"Yes," he answered, "you are a little stronger than I thought," and took one step nearer.

"You are so very strong, will you not show me how strongly and firmly you can stop this big gopher hole here at my feet?"

He did not move away from the gopher hole, and as she dug the spade into the ground the magnetism of his body enveloped her like incense. Away in the distance the headlights of a passing car gleamed for a moment, a clear jewel in the deep blue twilight. Suddenly she found herself wondering if there was a light in the melon-crate house streaming out through the slats and the pepper boughs, if he was sitting in there reading or eating something that he had cooked on the rusty oil stove. But perhaps the melon-crate house was dark and he was walking behind the arrowweed hedge with his arm about the girl in the salmon colored skirt. She could see the folds of the skirt flapping against her thick ankles.

The shovel and the wet silt seemed all at once desperately heavy. There was a buzzing in her ears and the ground seemed to be slipping away from under her feet. When she glanced around she saw that he was standing very close behind her, his arms folded over his chest. She hated him because he would not move. He only stood and waited.

"See," he said in a quiet, measured voice, "you are not quite so strong as you thought; so you will let me help you, will you not?"

An arm reached around from behind. A brown hand, slim and strong, closed over hers on the shovel handle. With an all-compelling, irresistible motion, as if borne forward on a great wave of the sea, she turned and threw herself into his arms and found—oh so easily—his lips with hers.

CHAPTER 11

WITH AUTUMN came the chrysanthemums. In the spring Mrs. Sasaki the Jap truck raiser's dowdy little wife had given Rhoda the roots and she had set them out with the meticulous care of the tyro gardener. All her life she had cherished a hankering for a flower garden. Now as the buds began to break she seized every odd moment to be with her plants, pulling out the weeds, chopping the ground about the roots, nipping off the too-numerous buds so that the flowers would be larger, peering eagerly to see which was going to be the white, the red, the bronze. Slowly at first, then with bewildering swiftness the flowers opened into a shimmering blaze of color gorgeous in the strong sunshine.

The time that she liked best to wander among them was after sunset when through the thickening gloom the hot ambers, the bright yellows, the frail pinks and delicate whites, the rich velvet reds seemed to glow intensely with an inner light. Then as she walked among these miracles of color splashed everywhere in shaggy petals she often bent and lifted the faces of the flowers to hers, inhaled their spicy autumn fragrance feeling with delicious vagueness that they were very intimately hers, that they had been created out of nothing to surround her with enchantment in this her hour.

One evening she had lingered a long time among her flowers, lingered while the sunset had flung a hoop of fire about the whole horizon, then withdrawn it slowly, leaving clear apple green that merged into luminous depths of blue. As she lingered she was thinking of tawny Oriental eyes, brown hands slim and strong—

She heard a step behind her and turning saw someone

whom she had hoped that she would never see again. He wore no hat and his shirt lay open at the throat. His old khaki trousers hung from his belt like bags; but she could not help discerning supple grace under the careless clothes.

> "Not God, in gardens when the eve is cool?
> Nay, but I have a sign,
> I'm very sure God walks in mine."

He looked at her with that charming, bland smile. She was smitten with sharp pain, smothered in surging confusion and could think of nothing to say.

"At this time of day they seem to shine with their own light, don't they."

"Yes they're lovely," she managed to stammer out.

"It's strange isn't it how this desert twilight closes about one—like black velvet curtains fringed with wine color. Have you ever noticed how it creeps up stealthily about you and then all at once throws a black veil over your eyes?"

"Rhoda, have the hens been fed?" Kate called irritably, and they went to the house.

He had brought with him good things to eat, but to Rhoda everything tasted like cotton wool and she could only trifle with the things on her plate. The talk drifted and dragged and if it had not been for Kate's clodhopper sallies would have trailed away into nothing. How stupid he must think her. She was filled with relief and misery, with solace and heartache, when shortly after the meal was over he went away. She sensed that he had a feeling that it would be a long time before he came back again.

Later that night she forgot him in the arms of another.

"Why are they always asking for married milkers?" asked Rhoda one day as she was running her eyes down the newspaper's list of advertisements. "What difference does it make whether a milker is married or not?"

"A great deal," answered Kate. "What they usually want and try to get when they advertise for a married milker is two milkers for the price of one."

"There's a married milker wanted on the Crosby ranch. You know that big place with the porches all around down toward Calexico. It can't be more than three miles from here."

Kate came and peered over her shoulder at the advertisement.

"Well," she deliberated, "it mightn't be a bad idea, seeing we're not experts, to get a job for a while as a married milker."

The next morning they drove over to the Crosby ranch.

Beyond the Crosby milking corral at a safe distance from the flies stood a big square house surrounded on all sides by wide, leisurely porches. There was no lawn or flower garden about the house, only the beaten ground and fringing soft dust that was to be found about all the Valley shanties; but orange and grapefruit trees were heavy with fruit and about the house clustered riotous and perpetual bloom of white, pink and scarlet oleanders.

"Quite a fancy dugout," said Kate drily as she shut off the engine.

"Hadn't we better go around to the back?" faltered Rhoda as she followed Kate up the driveway.

"Not on your tintype."

A stout woman in a clean bungalow apron came to the door. She had large mild blue eyes and a benign expression. Kate stated their errand.

"Yes, just come in. We did advertise for a milker. We thought if we could get a man and his wife—"

They sat down on the sunny porch amid a medley of old-fashioned sofas and rocking chairs submerged in cushions: chintz cushions, patchwork cushions, embroidered cushions, stamped leather cushions. In one corner a Morris chair with worn and flattened cushions surrounded by a footstool, smoking stand and a small table on which stood a lamp suggested that the head of the house was a man who liked his comfort.

"Well well, and so you girls are farming here and all by yourselves. A neighbor of mine was telling me about you just the other day. Well I declare! And you've come all the way from Philadelphia! I do think it's wonderful what young women are doing nowadays—not of course that I approve of all the lengths that some of the new women go to. When I was a girl back in Missouri some families considered even teaching not quite nice. But it's altogether different nowadays and so much better and wholesomer, don't you think?"

"If you hire us, how many cows would we be expected to milk, and what do you pay for the job?" demanded Kate with more than ordinary bluntness.

Rhoda was embarrassed by her partner's method of attack. She sat staring straight at a colored print of baby chicks over the frame of which actual chicken wire had been stretched and tacked.

Mrs. Crosby's face underwent that change of expression which comes to stingy people at the mention of money. There was a withdrawing into herself, a hardening of the mild blue eyes and a subtle sharpening of all the features.

"Well," she said in an altered tone, "we did have a man and his wife for eighty dollars. Of course they were Mexicans, but they were fine milkers. You know, I suppose, that a first-class milker is supposed to milk about twenty-five cows. But we've found that they hardly ever do and so we generally try to get a man and his wife."

"We couldn't possibly consider it for under a hundred," said Kate shortly.

"Well I don't know. I'll have to speak to my husband about it. I can let you know by mail tomorrow if you'll just write down the number of your box on this paper."

Having dismissed the subject of money, she was again all affability. She insisted upon showing them her garden and pressed upon them oranges, pomegranates, a paper sack full of late figs, string beans and heads of lettuce. As with most women brought up in the country, her stinginess did not extend to food. When at last they drove off she stood by the roadside and waved her handkerchief after them as if they had been old friends.

"Not such a bad old girl," commented Kate when they were out of hearing, "but I bet she keeps a tight hold on the purse strings. Did you see her close up like a clam when I mentioned wages? Hand me one of those pomegranates to sample; I've never tasted a pomegranate in my life."

She bit into the pomegranate and retreated abruptly, her teeth on edge.

"Good Lord, it's sour as a lemon—and all seeds. I thought from all the holler in the Bible about pomegranates that they were something on the end of a stick. Gimme a couple of those figs to take the taste outa my mouth."

She threw away the disappointing fruit and it lay burst open by the roadside, a lovely splash of Holy Grail color.

The next afternoon they found in their mail box a note from Mrs. Crosby accepting them as milkers at a hundred dollars a month and inviting them to dinner on the following Sunday.

The first few weeks of milking were a torture. Their fingers cramped and stiffened into aching rigidity. Their wrists and arms swelled to the size of two and throbbed day and night with a dull, distressful pain. They bathed them, soaked them in hot water, wrapped them in bandages dipped in vinegar, complained to each other unceasingly, decided a dozen times to give up the job; but when they considered their financial situation thought better of it and went back next milking time. At last they had their reward; gradually the torture lessened, the cramp went out of their fingers and the pain and swelling out of their wrists and arms. By the end of six weeks they were milkers, rapid, hard-sinewed, proud of their new achievement, each easily able to milk her fifteen cows morning and evening.

They got up at three o'clock, swallowed a hasty breakfast and by four were at the Crosby corral ready to begin work. From four to seven they milked steadily and after that went home and did their own work. In the middle of the day they took a short siesta. From four to seven in the evening they were again in the corral. When they got home they did up their evening chores, cooked their supper, washed the dishes and went to bed. A hard and long day, but not unbearably hard or long to those who have been inured to its rigors.

The days were not hard nor long to Rhoda. She carried through them on a triumphant wave of stimulation. She had a life of her own now, a life secretly fretted by half-stifled misgivings and regrets, but nevertheless a life rich, full and inspiring, full of dreams and visions, a life of which the material details of existence were mere incidentals. To screen this life from the prying eyes of others and especially of Kate, she had become the most adroit of liars.

The Doble family, who lived in a slatternly shack provided by the Crosbys, were their milking companions. Chester Doble, a long, stringy Texan with lank black hair, former rancher, cowboy and horse breaker, was taciturn and bilious looking. He had a melancholy face, but when he opened his mouth it was usually to say something drily humorous. He chewed and spat tobacco without ceasing. His wife too was long and stringy, with straight, clay-colored hair and the leathery skin of the Southwest. She wore a pair of old, slapping canvas shoes and a dirty cotton wrapper and chewed gum as constantly as her husband did tobacco and much more vigorously. When she went to town she put on high-heeled slippers and a mail-order skirt and coat in which she looked rather worse than in the wrapper.

The son, Clifford, aged seventeen, was conveniently unable to milk. He said it cramped his hands and he couldn't get over the cramp. He had a magnificent pair of shoulders and long, muscular arms like a gorilla and he walked with a step light and lithe like a panther's. He spent a good deal of his time about the pool rooms of Calexico. Already he was called "Kid" Doble and was going to make a name for himself in the ring or know why not. Willetta Doble was an overgrown, stupid girl of twelve, her heavy torso supported by enormous legs. With her great hams of hands she could milk eight cows morning and night. Junie, aged eight, could milk only four.

Rhoda fell in love with Junie. She was a homely little thing; her nose was pug and all her blunt features covered with big dark brown freckles; but she had such scampering feet, such eager bright blue eyes and such a ready, bubbling laugh that it seemed as if the very soul of gaiety had found a home in her stocky little body.

There had been other Dobles, but they had died or gone to earn their living somewhere else.

Under the arrowweed thatch of the long ramada these milkers milked between seventy and eighty cows morning and evening. The sun rose upon them at their work and striking through the fantastically drooping branches of thickly planted eucalyptus trees threw into mottled shadow and relief the slender tree trunks, the shining buckets and cans, the group of great-uddered, patient cows and the milkers at their flanks. They sat upon one-legged stools which were strapped to their bodies. From time to time a milker moved from one cow to another or when his bucket was full carried it to one of the big cans, the leg of his milking stool sticking out ridiculously behind. When Junie and Willetta were not quarreling about some matter of immense importance to themselves and of no importance whatever to anybody else, Junie sang in a shrill treble monotonous old ballads of Texas that she had learned from her father and mother or little songs picked up at school. If Cliff had been able to get up in time he moved about with lithe panther steps marshalling the cattle, driving off the ones that had been milked and bringing on the others, straining the milk into the cans and wheeling them on a hand truck to the milkhouse where soon the big separator would be put into buzzing motion to take out the cream. After this was all over and the heavy, rattling creamery truck had taken away the precious cream which had cost so much labor, the skim milk was fed to the hogs and chickens. It was Mrs. Doble's enviable job to wash the innumerable greasy-coated parts of the separator. They were many-sized and many-shaped, these parts, and full of all sorts of pockets and corners where souring cream could lodge. But they had to be all washed spic and span and rinsed and sunned and the milkhouse scrubbed out, for you could never know at what moment the creamery inspector would pounce down upon you. Aside from the milking this was the only part of Mrs. Doble's routine which she performed with thoroughness. She took a housewifely pride in the cleanness of her milkhouse floor, the shininess of her buckets and separator parts; but the Doble shack, which had nothing but the beaten earth for floor, was greased and grimy with long-accumulated dirt. Just before mealtime she wielded the can-opener with vigorous movements of her bony right hand, slapped chuck steak or broke eggs into the frying pan; and when the dishes were washed sat on the doorstep apathetically waiting for the next milking time.

In the evening they all milked steadily through the lengthening of the shadows and when the sun dropped below the horizon it left them still at the cows' flanks with the fiery desert sunset burning itself out beyond black tree trunks. As autumn advanced and the swift twilight became shorter, night was upon them almost immediately after the sun had set, and the work was finished by lantern light.

For Rhoda there was a heady stimulation in these rapid jolts over the chuck holes in the gray mystery of the early dawn, the cool crisp air blowing in her face and the gradual reshaping of the world. As she sat at the milking she delighted to feel the first rays of the sun touching her with lover-like fingers, lapping and enfolding her with warmth and brightness. She loved the evenings too, the winy desert sunset burning beyond black tree trunks, the stealthy creeping of the dark across long, level stretches, the tingling desert chill that fell at twilight out of the clear sky. In these mysterious dawns, these swiftly darkening chilly evenings there was something that stirred in her blood a tremulous response, perhaps because that blood had come to her from the veins of Irish peasants who had risen before dawn for the plowing and the planting and at the end of the long day plodded homeward through shadowy lanes, fearful of the banshee.

Under the pretext of attending to the water she stole at strange, delightful hours to the ditch bank to meet her lover, her heart fluttering with a tremulous joy. Often she thought with a passing ripple of pity of the people about her who lived only to work to eat and to sleep and who even now were glad to be asleep in their beds. Poor creatures, how little they had to live for.

Sometimes, too, in the hot blaze of noonday they met behind a feathery screen of arrowweed and lingered in the strong sunshine, pacing the path beside the ditch while he talked to her of strange and distant places: of Delhi and Calcutta, the great roaring city of London and the silent cattle ranges of Argentina. She listened with eyes wide and wondering like a child's.

They saw very little of the Pruetts or the Petersons any more. Mrs. Pruett had resumed her activities of four years ago; she belonged to the Ladies' Aid, the Woman's Missionary Society, the Farm Center, the Dorcas Society and the Society for the Improvement of the Condition of the Poor, and devoted a great deal of time and energy to the work of these organizations. Ruby was too much occupied with her new lover to have time for the neighbors.

One afternoon, however, as Rhoda was raking up the litter

in the dooryard she glanced up and saw Ruby coming along the driveway. The three children straggled behind, pushing and pulling one another. The dog came sniffing at their heels and at the tail of the procession a pet pig which Ruby had raised by hand and for which she felt so much affection that she refused to have it butchered.

She had come to borrow sugar and coffee to last her till she went to town next day. She seemed strangely absent-minded, had nothing to say and stayed only long enough for decency, departing as she had come, her retinue strung out behind her in the same order. Rhoda wondered what was the matter.

She found out a few days later when she went over to Ruby's to ask if she was finished with the food chopper. Before she got to the house she heard the sound of the phonograph going furiously, the continuous blowing of an auto horn and then the shrill voice of Ruby admonishing Melvin to get out of the car and leave the horn alone.

"My goodness, Rhoda, I'm ashamed to have you see my house, but come in. I haven't done a thing but play the phonograph all morning."

There had been a sandstorm the day before and the thick, gritty coat that it always left behind was still on Ruby's floor, shelves and furniture. The breakfast dishes in frowsy disarray still cluttered the table, the beds were unmade and children's clothes and toys lay everywhere. In the midst of this, Ruby, her eyes swollen and red, threw herself down into a chair and sighed heavily. Outside in the yard around the swing and the see-saw board the children laughed, cried and wrangled.

"Have you ever had any real bad troubles, Rhoda?"

Rhoda smiled with a tinge of embarrassment. She knew that if she had she would never confide them to Ruby.

"Why, no very terrible troubles, Ruby." She hesitated, "Why do you ask?"

Ruby had been sitting plucking nervously with her

stubby, work-coarsened hands at a hole in her bungalow apron. For answer she suddenly raised her hands to her face and burst into tears.

Rhoda wished that she was anywhere else; but she went and laid her hand on Ruby's stringy, mouse-colored hair.

"Why, Ruby, what's the matter? It can't be anything so very bad. It's your nerves that are all unstrung."

"Yes it *is* so very bad," she blubbered tremulously. "It's the worst thing that could happen. Roy's gone."

Rhoda, taken aback, did not know what to say.

"And now of course nobody won't think right of me any more. They'll all say I'm a bad woman an' look at me sideways when I go in town; an' I don't think that's right, 'cause it wasn't my fault he took it in his head to go off, an' me all fixed to marry him any minute he asked me."

"I'm sure it won't make any difference with me, Ruby, or with Kate. You mustn't let yourself care what other people think."

"Oh but I can't help caring. I didn't care a bit while I had Roy with me; but now he's gone I care like anything."

She began to sob again.

"He went last Thursday afternoon on the four-ten train," she went on, as though the exact time of his departure had some momentous significance. "He'd been actin' queer an' hardly comin' to see me for a couple a weeks. He's gone away up in Ventura County, his old boss told me yesterday, an' he never even let on to me he was fixin' to go."

She buried her face in her hands and burst into another storm of sobbing.

"Well Ruby, if he didn't want to stay you wouldn't want to make him stay, would you?"

"No–no," admitted Ruby with a vague note of surprised speculation, as if this was something she had not thought of before. "But Rhoda, after I got to goin' with Roy I had such high plans. I thought all along we'd get married an' when the Jap's lease was up Roy'd take over the place an' put cows on it like Ed had, an' we'd go once a week to the show an' get the mortgage paid off an' maybe get a new car after a while. Oh I tell you Rhoda my plans was high, but really they wasn't selfish plans, even if I did figger a little about a new suit. I was thinkin' all along what I'd do for the children, how I'd put Juanita in music, an' when they got past the grades we'd leave 'em go to high school. An' now I can't do a single thing only keep their stomachs fed an' send 'em through the grades. Oh I did have my heart on havin' Juanita learn to play.—An' Rhoda he was so nice an' jolly an' I really did think I loved him; but I don't love him a bit now he's up an' left. An' if I ever get a chance to do him a dirty turn you bet I won't let no grass grow under my feet."

By a determined effort of will Rhoda restrained an almost unrestrainable desire to laugh, composed her face and comforted Ruby as best she could. On the way home however she felt no inclination to laugh, but walked slowly and soberly feeling very sad and heavyhearted for Ruby. She had forgotten all about asking for the food grinder.

CHAPTER 12

WHEN THE cotton market opened that year it was found that there was no cotton market. The whole Valley dropped its jaw aghast; the great crop which had been mainly responsible for its wartime prosperity had slumped to nothing. During the war the cry had been for cotton, more cotton, always more cotton, and the Valley had responded nobly and greedily to the big prices offered. Now the war was over and there was to be no further need for cotton. People were going to go naked or wear silk or fine linen or clothe themselves in the skins of beasts—anything but cotton. "Overproduction," the cotton planters heard shouted at them from every side. They looked soberly at their far-stretching acres of snowy fluff burst from the bolls and wondered if the price would cover the cost of picking. Some of them decided to take the chance and called in a band of Mexican laborers, others shrugged their shoulders and left it as it stood, while the field laborers whom they would have hired searched in vain for jobs. People rushed to take their money out of the banks, fearing that they were about to close their doors. The ranchers who had not put in cotton that year congratulated themselves on their own foresight and felt that they had been especially watched over by Providence, just as when a big liner sinks the people who had intended to sail on her but didn't are firmly convinced that God had held them individually in the hollow of His hand.

Everywhere people talked about nothing but the cotton slump. In the banks, the stores, the autocamp grounds, the packing sheds and milking corrals it was the one topic of conversation. But with all the buzz of talk about the slump there was little surmising as to the cause of it. "Overproduction," "War's over," repeated parrotwise on every hand was enough to satisfy most people; and for the most part the losers took their losses lightly and bravely enough, like the pioneers and gamblers that they were.

In the Crosby corral at milking time the slump was talked threadbare.

"We're up a hell of a tree now," Kate said gloomily to Chester Doble. "We paid three hundred and twenty-five dollars an acre for our place and now we wouldn't get a hundred and fifty for it. We've got to either lose every cent we put into it or go ahead and pay off that double price with ten per cent interest to boot. A nice mess this farming game gets you into."

"Yaas, I reckon if people knew the ranchin' game before they went into it they'd go into plasterin' or preachin' instead," opined Chester Doble, thoughtfully stroking his long chin which seemed to have always just about two weeks' growth of beard on it and running his tongue over his decayed stumps of teeth. "It's the same with everything else as with cotton; all they need to do to jew the rancher down to a starvation price is to holler 'overproduction.' But when he comes to buy him some clothes they don't whisper no sech word into his ear. You gals wait till you go to the store to git yerselves shirts an' overalls made outa the cotton that's sellin' this year fer less'n the cost o' pickin'. You'll find you won't buy em' no whit cheaper. Matter o' fact, 'cept fer this little flicker o' war prosperity, I can't see but what the rancher's a-goin' to hev it harder'n he used to, an' he hain't never had no bed o' roses—not in my lifetime anyways. I bin in cotton, off an' on, all my life, an' I've knowed a heap o' grief along o' cotton. When I was a boy an' a young feller I worked in the cotton back in Texas along with all the rest o' the fam'ly, little an' big, an' we all sho'ly did work hard. It's one o' them crops like terbaccer that runs thirteen months to the year an' keeps the hull fam'ly a-hoppin'; an' we didn't git no fancy price fer that cotton. But in them days when dad come to buy a pair o' overalls they didn't cost him on'y but four bits; an' a yard o' calico didn't set maw back on'y but a nickel. In them days there used to be some connection between what a rancher got fer his crops an' what he had to buy to keep his fam'ly. But from now on there hain't a-goin' to be no sech connection an' jes' you wait an' see."

"It's a judgment on the hull Valley," declared Mrs. Pruett at Sunday dinner, "for the way it's been a-goin' on these wartime years. 'Easy come, easy go' is a true sayin', an' sech extravagance as there's been here since prices went up is somethin' the world hain't never seen. It's the days of Sodom an' Gomorrah all over agin an' worse, an' I can't see why there hain't laws made to stop it. Wimmin smokin' cigarets an' paintin' their faces an' exposin' their bosoms an' wearin' skirts up to their knees. Young folks drinkin' an' carousin' an' tearin' back an' forth over the country in ottymobiles—an' old folks too for the matter o' that. It used to be only men, but now it's men an' wimmin alike, that don't never seem to know when they're past the age fer carryin' on. It's a mercy some worse fate ain't happened to 'em afore this; an' there's many that's comin' to think it's the beginnin' o' the days when the Lord'll come in his wrath to judge the quick an' the dead."

The slump hit poor Ruby Peterson terribly hard. Her husband had worked heroically to pay for his forty acres; but the children had been expensive and Ruby in her slipshod Irish slavey fashion had been wasteful and extravagant. She had been content with a two-room shack and packing cases instead of furniture, had been willing to do without most of the things that in longer-settled communities are considered the necessities of life. But wartime prosperity had gone to her head and she had insisted upon some of its luxuries: sirloin steaks and lamb chops, fruits and vegetables out of season, summer silk dresses for the little girls and the latest-fashion foibles for herself. When "Ed" had died of overwork and getting hot too often he had left the ranch still heavily mortgaged. This year the whole forty acres were in cotton and there would be nothing—absolutely nothing—nothing to live on, nothing to pay the taxes, the water bills, the water assessments, nothing to pay even the interest on the mortgage. Inevitably she would have to give up the ranch.

Every night when she went to bed she cried her eyes out thinking of the dreadful fix she was in, half convinced that it was a punishment for the way she had carried on with Roy. By day she went about her work unkept and slatternly, her mouth drooping in sullen lines, eyes red and nose swollen with weeping, absentmindedly putting salt into the prunes and sugar in the boiling potatoes. When the children annoyed her she turned upon them with a viciousness that made them scurry away and hide behind the old dismantled milkhouse.

"Anyway," she said to Rhoda between bursts of sobs, "I ain't a-goin' to give up my babies. Folks comes here an' gives me all sorts of advice an' mostly they says send the children to a home, an' anybody that tells me that ain't my friend anymore—Melvin you go outside to blow that whistle. Good Lord, I think sometimes these young ones'll drive me crazy. I'm a-goin' to keep my children with me no matter what comes, an' if I have to work my fingers to the naked bone."

"It's a judgment on her for the way she's acted," said Mrs. Pruett, setting her thin lips grimly. "Them that sows the wind reaps the whirlwind. The things an' things I've done for Ruby Peterson an' her young ones—an' then to have her turn into a shameful woman! Well my hands is washed, I got no more to say; but I do think there'd otta be a law that'ud make her put them young ones in a respectable home. Anybody knows she ain't fit to bring 'em up. A woman that carries on the way she did an' her husband not dead six months can't have the natcheral feelin's of a mother."

Rhoda's first thought had been of her lover and the losses that he would sustain, but when she spoke to him about it he seemed not greatly perturbed.

"Yes," he said, with a slight shrug and a slighter gesture of the hands, "it is bad—bad for us—bad for all. But we cannot have the good luck always."

But a week later, down by the ditch bank, he said abruptly as they were about to part. "I am going away in a few days. I shall not see you again."

She looked at him with startled, incredulous eyes. Her heart seemed to have stopped beating.

"Not again? Never?" she managed to falter out.

"I am afraid never," he said gently. "The cotton is not worth picking and there is nothing here for me any more. I think that for perhaps many years it will not be worth while to raise cotton here."

"And where are you going?" She could hardly form the

words because her mouth felt so stiff. They sounded in her ears as if somebody else had said them.

"To Argentina. I have a friend there who is in the importing business. Perhaps I shall go in partnership with him. Perhaps not. Who knows where I shall be this time next year."

She was afraid to trust herself to speak.

"I feel sad to go," he went on, turning full upon her his tawny, luminous eyes. "But what can I do? It is life and it is fate."

They stood in silence for a long time.

"See," he said at last, and following the line of his long pointing forefinger she saw two eucalyptus leaves, little dun-colored daggers, floating down the sluggish water of the ditch. They drifted together, touched, then swam apart. One was caught in a little eddy which carried it toward the bank where it was stopped by a tangle of Bermuda grass. The other sailed on down the ditch.

"They are like you and me," he said with a slight, sad gesture of indifference. "We drift where fate will have us go. I cannot feel angry at fate which has led me if only for a little while to you. While I live I shall remember you as something—how shall I say—some flower not white but pale colored and of a perfume faint as if from far off. I shall think of you like that."

He was looking at her intently. She shivered and he saw the shiver pass over her.

"You are cold," he said. "You must go. Goodbye."

He made no movement to kiss or to embrace her, but held out gravely, respectfully his slim, dark hand.

"It is best that we should not meet again; it is easier that way."

"Goodbye, I shall think of you too," was all she could say, as they clasped hands.

He touched his hat and was gone.

Through the days that followed she went about feeling

stunned and bruised, yet with a deep underlying sense of calm and acquiescence that seemed to her the parting gift of the man who had been her lover. Always before her eyes she saw his slight, sad gesture of indifference, heard in her ears the gentle, mellow tones of his voice saying, "It is life and it is fate." In response to that gesture and those words something had risen out of her own nature, something that upheld her, bruised and stunned as she was, in the midst of calm serenity. In this mood she looked often across the long, level reaches that stretched on every side to the wide horizon and up into the deep desert sky, feeling that in this place nature too was large, calm and serene.

One morning near the end of milking time she heard Kate call from her cow's flank to Cliff who had just come into the corral and was marshalling the cows.

"Well Cliff old man, how did you come out in the boxing match in Mexicali last night?"

"On top of course," crowed Cliff. "Third round. I could a cleaned him up in the first, but I let him play along. Had to give the fellers lookin' on somethin' for their money. An awful crowd down there. Say, I saw that Hindu in the "Owl," the one that bought hay from you. Say he was pickled to the ears, an' him an' a bunch of other Hindus throwin' their coin on the tables like water, havin' one grand last bust. Him an' his pals has throwed up their lease an' is leavin' the Valley today. Last I saw of him he couldn't stand up no more an' was sittin' on a bench with a skirt in each arm. Some sporty lookin' chickens they was too."

Rhoda's heart contracted with a sharp pang, then when the stab was gone hung heavy and cold. Cliff's picture had been a vivid one, and to mate it a companion picture flashed before her mind: a girl in a doorway, a salmon colored skirt hanging about thick ankles, a red handkerchief tied over black hair. As her strong fingers mechanically squeezed the milk from the cow's teats she leaned her head against its side and looked off vacantly into space, her mind a prey to painful and confused thoughts that groped through darkness, fumbling blindly to discover the secret of the strange ways of men.

CHAPTER 13

In the middle of a December night it began to rain. The slanting shower beat in upon Kate and Rhoda and they had to get up and drag their damp cots and bedding into the room. In the morning the downpour was driving heavily before a strong cold wind. They made their usual hasty lamplit breakfast, put on extra old coats against the rain and with the lighted lantern went out and started the car. They had not gone twenty feet before they were hopelessly mired.

"It's no use," said Kate shortly. "The Doble's 'll have to put on some extra steam and get along without us." They went back to the house.

"I wonder what those Mexicans'll do that were camped down by the ditch bank," Rhoda said. "They didn't have a single thing to cover them, not a tent nor anything, only a rickety wagon and a skinny old mule. And they had a little baby only a few months old. I noticed it when we passed there yesterday."

"It looks like they're outa luck," said Kate, slipping on an old dressing gown for extra warmth.

All day the heavy, slanting rain fell. In old coats, irrigating boots and dripping slouch hats they went about their morning chores of caring for the stock, then scurried back and tried to make themselves warm and dry in the house.

But there was no warmth and no dryness there. After they had burned in the little sheet-iron stove their newspapers and the few scraps of wood left in the bottom of the box there was nothing more to burn, for outside everything that they could have used for fuel was soaked with rain. The driving rain seeped in through the cracks and made dark, fantastic blotches on the redwood boards. From three leaks in the roof three steady drip-drip-drips spattered to the floor, making three pools of water. They moved the beds away from beneath these leaks and put buckets to catch the drip, then sat huddled in sweaters and coats trying to keep warm.

"Gosh," complained Kate, "for a place to feel the cold give me the semitropics. And only yesterday about this time I looked at the thermometer and it stood at seventy-six."

Rhoda picked up a magazine and tried to read. She wondered if those Mexicans were still down there on the ditch bank and what they had done with the baby. Kate, growing restless, made candy, ate enormously of it and complained of feeling rotten. At last, driven by cold, dampness and ennui, they both went to bed and stayed there till evening chore time.

The next morning it was still raining. When Rhoda went down to the box at the gate to see if the mail carrier had been by she found it empty. The air, usually vibrant with the purr of near and distant motor cars, was still as the Sahara. A little later they saw from the window the creamery collector go by in a big wagon drawn by four horses. Other horses and wagons began to appear on the road, but never a car. The rain slackened to a drizzle.

For four days it rained and drizzled. Sometimes it stopped for a few hours only to begin again. The corral was a stinking, slippery morass, unspeakably filthy. Everywhere the flat, clay ground had absorbed all the water that it could hold and the rest lay in tawny puddles. Their whole dooryard was a shallow lake through which at chore time they sloshed in the big rubber boots that they wore when irrigating.

Kate, who had unearthed a pile of old magazines, read

and munched candy for hours together. Rhoda too tried to read, but could find nothing that would hold her attention. The printed words seemed utterly without meaning or coherence. Besides, Kate had established herself at the one window, the only place where it was light enough to read with ease. The overhanging roof cast a deep shadow into the room and in the stagnant and cluttered twilight Rhoda shivered in the draught that came through the cracks as she sat smoking cigaret after cigaret, flicking the ash and throwing the butts down the wide cracks between the boards of the floor, looking up at the little white wooly spiders' nests that dotted the rafters.

Her thoughts too were a twilit limbo of vague dreams and broodings, troubled memories and speculations that ended nowhere. Obsessed by unanswered whys, gray doubts and baffling uncertainties, she was gloomy company for herself.

From time to time she peered through the window toward the place on the ditch bank where the Mexicans had been camped and seeing no sign of them concluded that they had gone away and found shelter somewhere. But on the morning of the fourth day she caught sight of their mule between the eucalyptus trunks, his ears laid back disconsolately under the beating shower.

In the afternoon the rain stopped and with it the wind that drove the rain. Rhoda put on a soldier's coat and a slouch hat, and in the gray mist that now hung over the land picked her way down to the gate, skirting the deep mud of the driveway. From the gate she could plainly see the Mexicans' mule, looking a little less doleful now that the rain had stopped beating on him; and from a spot near him gray-blue spirals of smoke rose into the still air.

Approaching, she found a fire burning briskly, with old blankets and clothes stretched near it on eucalyptus boughs to dry. A woman was stirring a pot on a grating set over the fire, a boy about three was running about and at a little distance a man was chopping up eucalyptus boughs.

"Have you been here since it began to rain?" she asked, going up to the woman.

The Mexican woman smiled, nodded her head several times and said something in her own language, then smiled again and made with her hands little movements of apology as if to say she was sorry she could not speak the lady's language.

"Where is your baby?" Rhoda made with her hands a span indicating the baby's length and the woman evidently understood for she led the way to where under the wagon a hole had been scooped out of the ground with an overhanging projection of earth. Under this shelter, which was large enough for all four to huddle in, the baby slept peacefully, only its little head visible among the frayed blankets. Rhoda smiled goodbye to the woman and passed on.

They were not so stupid after all, these Mexican people, she mused. They knew how to protect themselves from the rain, how to make and keep a fire with wet wood, how to keep a little baby dry and warm through four days of downpour.

She wandered on along the footpath under the eucalyptus trees, glad of the soft, fresh air, the wide, peace-breathing quiet after the fretful clutter of the house. In the gray calm the eucalyptus trees hung black and mournful, motionless as trees of stone. Beneath their sorrowfully drooping branches their dead leaves and scattered bark rustled faintly under her feet. All the hectic life of the Valley, the roll and rattle of great, double-wheeled trucks, the pounding of excited engines, the quick panting of tractors, had been put to rest by the rain. The insect pipings at her feet only made the brooding silence more great and dumb. A little flock of kildees flitted about her on tip-tilted wings, circled close to the ground, alighted and circled again, uttering their plaintive plover cries. A Johnny owl rose silently on balanced, earth-colored wings, sailed a little distance and sank again into the ground.

She did not lift her eyes to the distant mountains hung with heavy mists, to the long, flat fields, the tawny ditch and wide, bleak road. She kept them on the black tree trunks, with gray and purple shadows between, on the sodden path strewn with leaves. These were things intimate and familiar, things she had always known. For the first time since she had come to this new land she felt at home and herself.

Looking back she recalled such days as this, pensive autumn days when she had wandered by herself in some little park or suburban lane, days of quiet, gray skies and leaves that rustled underfoot and insect pipings and the whirr of wings.

Now again such a day.

It came over her that amid the hot, strong sunshine, the sharp lights and shadows, the long horizons, the torrid days and desert-cold nights of this country of vast distances and bold extremes she had been living a charmed life, a life not hers nor in any way in keeping with her nature. Looking back over the past few months she saw herself pass before her own eyes like an actor on some weird exotic stage. There was no third dimension to that alien figure that moved from black shadow to bold sunlight under fierce sapphire skies. It was as remote, as impalpable as a dream, a creature to be looked at from afar and wondered at. She had nothing in common with that stranger. But here, closed in by this gray stillness, was walking she herself, Rhoda Malone, who lived in a narrow city-house, who got up at seven and hurried away to the office, who copied letters all day and at evening went home and had her dinner, then helped with the dishes, read a story in a magazine, mended the hole under the arm of her waist, sponged her blue serge skirt and went to bed.

Out of the all-enfolding grayness, the subdued earth tones, the pensive autumnal silence broken only by faint pipings and the restless whirr of wings there slid into her soul a gentle melancholy, a diffused sadness. She felt herself merge into the landscape and become one with it, earthy-toned, subdued and silent.

Loitering homeward by the way she had come, she came again upon the Mexican camp and found it deserted. There was nothing left but the hole in the ground and the embers of the fire, from which came a penetrating smell of burnt feathers. Kicking into these embers she found them soft and cloggy, as though the wet feathers of several chickens had been dumped upon the fire.

I won't say anything about it to Kate, she thought. If I do, she'll swear the chickens were ours, and she'll never stop talking about it. Ten to one they were ours too.

CHAPTER 14

CHRISTMAS AGAIN and she must do some shopping whether she felt like it or not. She must send some little gifts back home and get some trifles for the Doble girls and some toys for Ruby's children. In the hot, noonday sunshine she wandered along the street, her arms already full of little packages, looking into the windows at the tinsel and evergreens, the imitation frost and snow. She was so tired—always these days she was so tired.

She soon wearied of the windows under their glittering white powder and let her eyes wander to the faces of the people in the street. A tall Mexican stalked by in the crowd, bronze skin stretched taut over the bony structure of his melancholy, high-cheeked face. His eyes seemed to be looking far far away into some remote distance. At a street corner two old Spaniards, well tailored and immaculate, stood talking with animation in their own language. One was stout and commonplace but the other was lean, erect and distinguished looking. His black eyes, full of snap and sparkle, were the eyes of a young man; but they were arched by white eyebrows and his close-clipped mustache was white. He must have been a devil of a fellow in his gay youth, she thought. And now that it was all over did he have many regrets or had he forgotten? Surely he must have forgotten or he could not laugh so unconcernedly. How could the old have anything to laugh about?

An ex-soldier, both legs gone, was wheeling himself about on a wooden stand fitted with wheels. He was a good-looking lad, and as he stopped to chat with another young man she saw on his upturned face a merry and roguish smile and heard his voice as vibrant with youth as that of any sound young man. At first she had felt only vague pity for the cripple; but with the smile and the voice a sharp horror seized her and she hurried away trying to banish the vision from her memory. Where did it come from, the invincible spirit that made that smile possible, that allowed the old who had been gay and adventurous to laugh, that put brooding calmness into the eyes of the bony Mexican. She felt none of it in herself.

"Now now, Miss Malone, not so fast. Aren't you going to stop and say howdy to an old friend?"

A large, pleasant feeling hand took firm hold upon hers and she found herself looking into the shrewd gray eyes of Mr. McCumber.

She remembered the last time they had met and the foolish little triumph that she had achieved. She had not given a thought to it since. She felt no slightest inclination to coquetry now and only smiled because she felt that a smile was expected.

"Every day I've been planning to run out and see how you girls are getting along out there. But you know how it is these busy days; a man's time isn't his own and the very thing he most wants to do is the thing he can't seem to get around to. But you'll see me out there before long. I've a good deal of experience here in the Valley and I want to give you whatever help I can."

She became aware that he was still holding her hand and drew it away.

"You'll find us at home only in the middle of the day. We're milking a string of cows now for Mr. Crosby down near Calexico. Perhaps you know him."

"Crosby? Of course I know him—decent old scout. And so you girls have learned to milk. Well say, we've got to hand it to you that you've got pluck."

"People can learn to do all sorts of things when they have to," she answered with a little smile and made a movement to pass on.

"Well it shows you're good sports all right. I'll get out there some day soon, and if there's anything I can do—"

She let the crowd edge her away and thinking of toys for Ruby's children allowed herself to be caught in the stream of women who were pouring into the ten-cent store.

Pushed this way and jostled that, she eddied with the crowd from counter to counter looking at coarse muslin handkerchiefs whose embroidered corners were temptingly displayed in little flat boxes, at pink Celluloid photograph frames, pin-cushions, imitation lacquer trays and boxes, pink and blue stationery, wooden horses, wooly dogs, Celluloid ducks and brightly painted rubber balls. Bewildered by the dumbly surging crowds, the ever-present glitter of tinsel and tree ornaments and the indomitable strains of jazz records beating upon the stale air like an African war dance, she lost all idea of what she had come to buy, all hope of ever getting waited on, and drifted aimlessly here and there with a wide-eyed, hypnotized stare.

Floorwalkers hired for the rush season scurried about looking important, carried orders from one part of the building to another, got into sharp-toned disputes with sales-girls, watched to see if the customers stole anything. The girls behind the counters were flushed or pale with ex-haustion, irritable or indifferent. A few of them were pretty. Most of them were young and when they rested the hopeful look would come back into their eyes. But there were ageing women among them with hard, set faces and permanently disillusioned eyes. The worn, gray-white faces of these women above the piles of gorgeous trumpery drew Rhoda's eyes with a fascination that she tried to throw off.

To get away from them she fell to watching a very pretty girl who was enjoying a flirtation over the counter with a stalwart, sun-browned young fellow in corduroy riding breeches and a big cowboy hat. She was on duty in the hardware department, which was not so crowded as the other parts of the store. Rouge, lipstick, powder and curling irons, all greatly over applied had not been able to hide her natural beauty and charm. The curves of her slim body revealed by a simple black slip were dainty and exquisite and her arms bare almost to the shoulder were white, fine-skinned and perfect in shape. She had a bewitching little blonde face. The young man lingered, bought more nails and washers, priced the door hinges, the hocks, the screw-eyes, met her glance across the counter with the frank, gay, provocative eyes of charmed and eager youth. It was a lovely little idyll.

Presently the girl noticed Rhoda watching them. She shrugged her pretty shoulders and made a small disdainful grimace with her beautiful painted mouth. Rhoda turned quickly away ashamed of having been caught spying.

As she turned she faced herself in one of those ever-present mirrors which confront the unwary shopper in every store and use no euphemisms in telling her just how old, how gray-haired, how ill-attired, how over-fat or over-thin she has become. Rhoda looked into a pale, stary-eyed face with dark circles under the eyes and a mouth that drooped at the corners. It was not at all the face that had looked at her from the glass on that morning when she had gone into Mr. McCumber's office. She had come to the age then when a woman is young one day and old the next. From that it would be only a step to the age when she is always old. She peered again at the pale, stary-eyed face. There was a pinched, thin-lipped look about the mouth, a sharpness about the chin. It came over her suddenly that when she grew older she would have that haggish look.

The greatest crush was around the Christmas cards. Young women with tight little helmets and the slender silhouette of the fashion, older women with sagging figures and queer hats: fat women, scrawny women, high-heeled women, flat-footed women, skinny women, great-hipped women, lopsided women, women with bangs, with false teeth, with run-over heels, with shell-rimmed glasses, with bobbed hair, with bulging bosoms, with dangling ear-rings, with stubby, work-hardened hands, reached over each other's shoulders, under each other's arms, constantly clutching, pawing and fumbling these missives of Christmas cheer. They picked up one, glanced at its lighted candle or sprig of holly, laid it down, picked up another, read the legend under its star of Bethlehem and laid it down, picked up another, looked at its gaudy sprawl of poinsettias and put it in the other hand. Finally by an unknown process of selection they collected six, then did not rest till they had given them to the harrassed girl with a nickel and received them back in an envelope. There was no talk, no laughter, every face absorbed and serious even to sternness.

At Rhoda's side a salesgirl and a floorwalker were having a harsh-voiced dispute over a display of gold tinsel which should have been strung this way and had been strung that way. Behind a counter a sleek fat man, perhaps the owner, was giving directions to a youth on a stepladder how to loop up a string of Christmas tree ornaments. They were all so intent, so busy, so important—and about what?

Rhoda was carried on from the Christmas card counter past a towering stack of cardboard boxes big and little pasted over with red and green holly paper. Another dense crowd of women were fingering these, turning them over and over in their scrubby hands, setting them back, taking down a larger or a smaller one. Past the tissue paper, the tinsel, the

Christmas tree ornaments, the toy balloons and Celluloid dolls to the jewelry department where unbelievably long strings of beads of all sizes and colors made a gaudy curtain through which the electric light glittered and scintillated in hard reds and greens, blues and ambers. Here temptingly spread out under electric light bulbs the glass and brass "novelty" jewelry made a brave showing: fifteen-cent rings, ten-cent brooches, scarf pins, barrettes and bracelets. A half-breed girl with a voluptuous figure and a pretty, insolent face was standing before a mirror adjusting a pair of dangling ear-rings of rose-colored glass. Against her satiny, copper-colored cheeks the outrageous ornaments looked bewitching and flauntingly barbaric. A quick pain stung Rhoda. She looked the second time. No she did not think it was the same girl.

Again she found herself being drawn with the crowd toward the back of the store, this time past mountains of virulent-looking Christmas candy, with red and white barber's pole canes strung on strings above them, past jumping jacks, building blocks, climbing monkeys, squeaking rubber dolls, wooden wagons and tin automobiles. In her passivity she was jostled into the pointed elbows of skinny women, the bulging hips and rumps of fat women, the sharp angles of packages that protruded from the holes in fishnet shopping bags crammed to capacity. Whichever way she looked her vision was blocked by hair: long hair, bobbed hair, frizzled hair, straight hair, blonde hair, dark hair, tight little buns of gray hair and the abundant, lusterless, nit-infested tresses of the Mexican women. The tag ends of all this hair straggled in stringy wisps over blotchy necks, scrawny necks, yellow necks, wrinkled necks, fat creasy necks. In the dead, stale air a stuffy smell of long-worn clothes and unwashed humans grew momently denser. The straggling hair, the stringy and creasy necks, the sharp elbows, the great bulbous hips and rumps, the many-angled shopping bags, the bulging bosoms surged in upon her from every side. The dead air, the vile human smell pressed down upon her like a suffocating blanket. With a sudden wild sense of panic, a feeling that she must have room, that she must have air to breathe, she looked about her for a way to escape.

Her eyes fell upon a little girl towed along in the wake of her mother. The child's face was raised to the glittering tinsel, the bright ornaments, the holly wreaths, the dangling dolls and balls and jumping jacks with an expression starry-eyed and ecstatic. Looking at the child Rhoda remembered it all; the delicious anticipation, the excitement, the thrill, the joy, the wonder that had been for her in the Christmases of long ago. Could it be that it was here still, here in this horrible ten-cent store amid this gaudy mass of useless trumpery, crowded by these work-worn, frowsy, evil-smelling people, overhung by this stale, dead air? Christmas! The sound had power to breathe magic, like the enchanted words "picture book" which she could never think of without a sense of something rare, glamorous and alluring. How silly she was; of course it was not the Christmas season that had changed or the stores or the people or the things they bought. It was herself who was growing old, weary and disillusioned. She remembered how when she was a little girl she had eyes only for children, and when she grew older the world was peopled with young men and maidens. If she were a child she would only look at the tinsel and toys, seeing in them all the old rapturous glamor. If she were a young girl she would recognize in the passing crowd only the signs of youth: the fresh cheeks, the smooth necks, the dream-filled eyes, the stalwartness, the gaiety and the hope. They were there still, but not for her. Now all she could see were the marks left by sordid lives meanly plodded through, by creeping age, dullness and indifference.

It was all a joke then, a grim, humorless joke that life had played upon her and all these other dingy, ageing people. It was all a great hoax, a delusion, a sham. What was this thing called life for her and for all these others? The grind of the struggle for existence, which ended only with existence itself. And to make that grind endurable the pursuit of an ever vanishing will-o'-the-wisp. In childhood the will-o'-the-wisp danced only a little distance away and there were moments when one almost grasped it. In youth it withdrew itself, grew more beautiful and strange, more orioled with charm and magic. Then as the years passed it gradually lost its magical halo and receded further and further into the distance until at last there was nothing left but a faint and fitful gleam that perhaps was only a memory. What remained was the grind, the dull routine, the grim, unlovely facts of existence. These alone were real.

In the course of her aimless drifting she passed once more by the hardware counter where the sun-browned young man in corduroys still leaned over the counter pretending to buy tacks and brads. Two young girls brushed by her in the crowd, a charming glimpse of bright hair, soft contours and beaming eyes, chattering and laughing in the gay and intimate camaraderie of youth. Their silvery giggles penetrated to her ears above the nasal wails of a broken-winded tenor whining out of the phonograph, "You broke my heart to pass the time away." A little boy, a mere baby carried in his mother's arms, reached up and grasped a glittering scrap of tinsel which he bore away in his chubby hand with an expression of rapture. Perhaps these things, the glances of lovers, the gaiety of schoolgirls, the delight of a baby with a handful of tinsel had more right after all to be considered realities than tawdry display, glittering emptiness, the greed of shopkeepers, the weariness of salesgirls, the dull stupidity of sordid, slow-surging throngs.

Or perhaps they were all nothing but a dream, a fantasy, the beautiful and the ugly alike, and herself a dream woman moving among dreams.

There was something steadying about the thought, something calm, broad and sustaining. Over her emptiness, her sense of loss and futility this feeling of the unreality of all things rose like a softly enveloping mist. Under its hypnotic spell she looked out at the densely surging throngs with unfocused eyes, like one whose sight is failing and who sees only the great masses, the large outlines. These great masses, these large outlines removed themselves from her, became vague and shadowy as if seen through drug-dilated pupils. They and all that they contained were nothing but a dream. She herself was a dream. With a rapt, unseeing look like that of a sleepwalker she passed out of the store and into the crowded street, wandering a shadow among shadows.

Mr. McCumber in the act of leave-taking stood outside the door of the little ranch house, his hat in his hand, the early afternoon sun reflected from his sleek, fair hair. His new car, a fawn colored sports model, stood waiting for him in the driveway.

"A spin!" Kate sniffed her scorn. "Say maybe you think we don't do any spinning on our own account. We spin over to the Crosbys' twice a day to milk, making twelve miles in all seven days a week. Spinning with us isn't exactly a novelty."

His crestfallen expression lasted only a moment.

"Oh but we won't just spin. We'll go some places of course. You'll come won't you?"

"Well I don't know. We're pretty tired when we get home from milking."

"That's just the reason you ought to go. A little change will do you both good."

"Why does the son of a gun come around now after a year's past and offer to teach us how to farm?" she grumbled to Rhoda after he was gone. "In the first few months when he might have put us wise to a thing or two we didn't see hide nor hair of him; and now that we know all the ropes he comes around taking up our time."

"Oh well, I suppose we'll have to go. We didn't say we wouldn't."

"I didn't say I would either."

But when Thursday evening came she got out a clean waist and her old Philadelphia business suit. The prospect of a little outing didn't look so bad after all. Rhoda's one overwhelming desire at the end of the long day was to crawl into bed, and as she scrubbed at her hands she wished devoutly that she had never gone into Mr. McCumber's office. Such hands! Brush as she might she could not get all the dirt out from under the nails. The skin too was rough and red and broken by sore hangnails. On one wrist there was a jagged, festering scratch made by a piece of rusty fence wire and in one thumb a long redwood splinter that she had tried in vain to get out. She dedicated one short sigh to the memory of the time when she had been rather proud of her slim white hands.

But when she found herself bowling along over the road buoyed up by soft cushions and resilient springs she felt rested and refreshed and glad that she had come. It was the first time, she reflected, that she had been out for the evening since she had come to the ranch. How long ago was that? A full year and more.

"Well what's the good word? Where shall we go?" asked Mr. McCumber.

"I don't know. To Mexicali?" ventured Rhoda.

"N–no, not Mexicali. I hardly think you girls would care for Mexicali."

"Let's go to El Centro and take in a show," suggested Kate. "They say there's a pretty good movie house there. Rhoda and I haven't been to a show for over a year."

"Gee what a dull life you girls must lead out there on that lonesome little ranch."

"Oh not so dull. The gophers and one thing and another keep it pretty lively for us."

It seemed strange to be in a town at night. The pepper

and palm trees, black against the darkly luminous sky or outlined in bright green by the electric lamps, seemed artificial and exotic, like the stage setting of some drama laid in the tropics. After them the long arcades and brightly lighted windows of the business streets, the same old circle of religious enthusiasts praising God at a corner, the same scraggy little fringe of listeners, the same clerks and business men and petulant, beauty-conscious girls going indifferently by. Pool rooms full of young men, Mexicans lounging in somber little groups. Then the tawdry lobby of the movie theatre.

As Mr. McCumber was getting the tickets, Rhoda noticed the younger and skimpier daughter of the washwoman from Arkansas stalk gawkily through the lobby accompanied by a spindling young man, her skinny legs resplendent in crude colored silk stockings. Then as she stood staring idly at a sanguinary picture, somebody came up from behind and called her by name. She turned and saw their former landlord, his hair as light and face as brick-red as ever.

"Say, awful glad to see you again. How's the ranch comin' on?"

"Oh pretty fair, considering everything. Of course you know since cotton dropped everything else is away down too; so it leaves us rather in the hole. How's the apartment house getting on?"

His face clouded.

"Tain't gettin' on, it's standin' still. Since cotton dropped the town's all thinned out. I wish I'd never put my money into it."

"That's just the way we feel about our ranch. But what can we do?"

"Not a damn thing. It's fierce, ain't it."

Mr. McCumber came up with the tickets and they passed through into the soul-satisfying fracas of a comedy: plates flying, flatirons falling, windowpanes crashing, a saucepan boiling over with a tremendous spill of brew and belch of steam, the roof finally caving in, a mass of heaped shingles and broken rafters emerging to view out of a cloud of dust. A glorious Saturnalia of destruction.

After the comedy the five-reeler. It had to do with the adventure of a little group of Americans in some out-of-the-way island off the coast of India. There was the lovely heroine and the dashing and intrepid hero, the pompous father and the fussy mother. A pot-bellied uncle furnished the comedy, an unwelcome suitor and a treacherous Indian prince the intrigue. Hordes of natives and Indian scenery filmed in Hollywood made up the background.

But the natives were real Hindus. Rhoda knew real Hindus when she saw them. Fascinated she gazed through the intervening darkness at the mild, fathomless eyes, the long hands, the lithe almost feline movements. She glanced sidewise at Mr. McCumber's plump, well-shaved cheek and took a certain pleasure in imagining what would be his astonishment, even horror, if he knew. She flattered herself that she could probably guess his past better than he could guess hers. If Andy Blake, on the other hand–. But no, she did not want to think about Andy Blake.

Of course in the end the Americans find themselves entrapped and besieged by the natives. The lovely heroine shows all kinds of heroinely courage. The acrobatic hero performs tremendous feats of strength, daring and agility. But all in vain. The hordes of natives by sheer force of numbers break down the outer gates, the inner gates, the doors, the windows, come swarming into the rooms and up the stairs with brandishing weapons. At sight of the thrilling conflict, the glorious havoc and wreckage, the audience throbs with joy and excitement quite untroubled by any misgivings; for they know that it is certain to come out all right.

Sure enough, the picture that follows the smashing of the last barricade shows an American battleship standing implacably in the harbor. The house bursts into applause. A boat is lowered from the side and manned by two rows of blue-jackets as alike as peas in a pod. Then a storm of cheers and clapping greets the chastely worded caption: "Just a few of the boys that have never been licked."

Rhoda looked on coldly. The whole thing seemed ridiculously distorted, false and silly. She shrank into herself, withdrew spiritually from the people about her with mingled feelings of cold contempt and burning resentment.

And now, alternately with the murderous hordes of natives pressing closer and closer upon the desperate little band of the besieged, the "boys that have never been licked" are seen pulling for the shore, disembarking, marching along the palm-bordered road, coming nearer and nearer. The excitement and joy are intense. At the last moment, when the athletic hero is securely bound and gagged, and the heroine, her hair still in perfect order, is being seized from behind by a gigantic Hindu with a big knife in his sash, the blue-jackets march into view, level their guns and send the natives scuttling for their lives like rabbits. The curtain goes down to the strains of "Yankee Doodle."

Mr. McCumber was too dignified to applaud—it was only the boys and the young mechanics who clapped and cheered —but glancing at his rather too-well-padded features Rhoda saw them overspread with a satisfaction at once genial and grim. She did not know why she should so utterly loathe that look, but it filled her with horror and repugnance. She felt herself the only person in the house who sympathized with the other side. She was right and they were wrong, hideously wrong, she told herself passionately. She was Ishmael with her hand against every man's hand and every man's hand against hers and she was glad of it. A hot rage swelled her breast and burned her cheeks.

"Pretty good picture, eh?" commented Mr. McCumber as he helped her on with her coat. "A thriller like that makes a man forget his worries for a few minutes anyway.—And now what's the good word? Shall we take a little run up to Imperial? Brawley? It's early yet."

"Oh no, we must go home now," Rhoda hastened to say. "You know we have to get up before four for the morning milking."

"Good Lord, you girls don't lead the life of a dog."

CHAPTER 15

THE DUST rose in choking swirls from the restless feet of the cattle in the corral, drifted on an imperceptible wind and settled upon the motley crowd that pressed about the two auctioneers, the recording clerk and the cattle in the selling ring. There were many kinds of people in the crowd: swarthy, heavy-set Portuguese, big bony Swedes with hair bleached white and skin burned brown by the Valley sun, sleek, well-formed men in business suits and clean collars, shaggy unkepts in greasy overalls, young men in cowboy hats, old men in battered derbys, men from most of the States of the Union, from many of the countries of Europe, from far-off India and Japan.

What divers pasts these minds might reach back into, Rhoda thought as she looked from Swede to Japanese, from Mexican to Hindu.

Through the crowd three young men ferreted in and out accosting the bidders and those who seemed as though they might be likely to bid. They were agile and plausible young fellows who buttonholed their men familiarly, looked them in the eye with engaging candor and did their best to carry them by storm.

On the outer fringe of the ring of bidders a few Mexicans lounged in that aura of somber repose that isolates them from all crowds and all excitements. Their women, wide-hipped and sad-eyed, held babies in their arms and stared impassively into vacancy. Nervous white women, some of them dressed in smart city fashion, some in sagging nondescript clothes, stood about bored and tired, chatted with each other to pass the time away, placated their fretting young ones with cookies, for lack of anything else to do craned their necks to see what was going on in the ring. Children with cups in their hands swarmed about the water faucet and muddied their feet in the soft puddle made by the continuous drip and spill. Nearby in the meager shade of one scraggy, dust-smothered palm tree an ice cream and soft drink wagon was doing a good business. Underfoot the bare ground, unwashed by any kindly rain was scattered with wind-blown rubbish and soft powdery dust. Over all the blue and stainless desert sky.

The auctioneer was a florid-faced man of tremendous belly girth who looked as if he might have stepped out of a page of Dickens. His vest was loud, his hat and top-boots horsey, he carried a rawhide whip and flicked it with a sporty flourish. The smell of the old-time livery stable, the savor of the race track clung about him. In the left corner of his lips he gripped a thick black cigar and held it there by means of that distortion of the mouth whose implication of sportiness and worldly wisdom is the envy of boys in their teens. He was unfortunate in not having been born at least a generation earlier. Perhaps he had drifted into the Valley because it was a place where horses and mules still counted for something. Even as it was he was reduced for the most part to handling mere cows. He looked at their thick necks, broad backs and ungainly hips with disdainful eyes, even when he was singing the praises of their parts and breeding, and when they were sold brought down the whip with a smart, sweeping crack too sporty and dashing for the transfer of mere bovine hulks.

He was auctioning off three cows at a time now. He had begun with one at a time but found the going too slow. And although the cattle were selling for little more than half of what they had been worth a year ago, the bidding was cautious and reluctant.

"Why hang it all if these three heifers ain't worth sixty dollars apiece they ain't worth a nickel," he bellowed in a tone of deep disgust. "What's wrong with you boys anyhow? Ain't you hep that now cattle's down's the time to buy up? Just because money's a little tight you boys ain't goin' to sit back an' miss the best bargains that's ever been offered in the Valley? You know well's I do these cows is sure to be worth twice the money a year from now. Don't hold back like a bunch o' tight-wadded Easterners that's never took a gamble in their lives. Come acrost now; who's startin' these three heifers at sixty apiece?"

"Sixty dollars," enunciated Mrs. Pruett in momentous solemn tones.

She had elbowed her way into the front row of the bidding ring, an incongruous figure in her prim black dress and Victorian-looking hat trimmed with jet and "tips" and anchored by the only hatpin left in the Valley to her unfrivolous twist of grizzled hair. Mr. Pruett accompanied by Kate and Rhoda had struggled to a place not far behind her. She scanned the cows with keen appraisive eyes.

"I'll get you good caows, never fear," she flung back to the girls behind her. "I was raised with milk caows an' if there's anything I don't know about a milk caow I'd like to hev somebody point it out to me. These smart young fellers won't be able to bullrag me into biddin' if I don't feel like biddin'; but when I see somethin' that's worth biddin' on I'll bid an' stick by it."

A woman standing beside Rhoda was trying to pacify a whimpering baby that had an ugly red sore on one little cheek.

"Seems likt he gets one risin' right after another," she complained to her companion. "I poultice 'em an' they go away, but more keeps comin'."

"They say risin's is healthy," reassured the other woman.

At noon there was a pause for lunch and the curiously diversified throng lined up in Indian file and passing a refreshment counter made of rough redwood planks laid upon trestles received beans, pickles and coarse slabs of barbecued beef. Coffee, too, in bright tin mugs. It was hot standing in the line under the January sun. The savory smell from the roasting pit and the aroma of the boiling coffee steamed up and titillated hungry nostrils. Rhoda found herself wedged between a silent little Jap and a pot-bellied man in corduroys who stentoriously proclaimed to the Swiss dairyman behind him that he was from "Missourah" and they'd have to show him that cattle were ever going to be worth anything again in the Valley.

Two men who had already been served were standing near Rhoda munching beef and beans from the paper plates that they held in their hands.

"Was you at Joneses' sale last Friday?"

"Nope."

"It was a crime the prices them fancy cattle sold for. Jones went around lookin' white as a piece o' chalk when he saw the way the biddin' was goin'. What with the drop in cattle an' havin' to give up his place he lost somethin' over six thousand in less'n a year. He said he wouldn't mind so much if he an' his wife hadn't worked so damn hard to lose it. All he hopes now is they'll let him keep his car so's he'll have somethin' to get outa the Valley with."

As the applicants received their loaded paper plates and brimming mugs of coffee they retired to their cars, for there was no place to sit: no grass, no shade, nothing but dust and sunshine.

Kate and Rhoda sat with the Pruetts in their car. It was drawn up near the milkhouse and the air was thick with that rancid sour smell that hangs dankly over places where much milk is handled. There was a steady buzz of blowflies over the empty skim milk cans. Houseflies swarmed everywhere and tried to attack the plates of food, settled in little black mounds on the crumbs that fell to the ground. In a mud-spattered Ford delivery near the Pruett car a girl and her lover, all unmindful of the stench and the flies, were having a hilarious banquet, eating from the same plate and drinking from the same glorified tin mug.

"You wouldn't see such carryin' on at a sale in my young days," barked Mrs. Pruett.

"Unsanitary too," contributed Kate with an indifferent shrug and grin.

Rhoda eyed the lovers furtively. The girl was an alluring young thing in all the warm exuberance of first youth. Spaniards had been her ancestors, and Indians too. Why, Rhoda asked herself, had she never had a lover when she was young like that? Or had she ever really been young? She could not remember that she had. For her there had never been any warm exuberance such as is the almost universal heritage of these dark-skinned people. She had always been pale, sedate, reserved. Why then had she denied her nature, laid aside all restraint and thrown herself into the arms of a stranger, a man of alien race of whom she knew nothing not even his name and who had treated her with the casualness that she deserved? What would Mrs. Pruett think of her, she wondered, if she knew the truth, Mrs. Pruett who seemed to be really fond of her, Mrs. Pruett who was buying cows for them to save them from losing their place, Mrs. Pruett who was not ashamed of any of her thoughts, feelings or opinions. How satisfying it must be to feel like that, to know for sure that you were always in the right, to feel no touch of shame for anything you thought or felt or did or desired, to be always just what people thought you were and take a pride in concealing nothing.

Her thoughts were interrupted by the plangent voice of the auctioneer recalling the sale to order. The bidding grew more lively now, for the cattle were going cheap beyond all

Valley precedents. Mrs. Pruett, back in her old station in the front rank, her hair a little scraggy, her queer Victorian-looking hat a little askew, stood staunch as Gibraltar. Impervious to the plaudits of the auctioneers and the exhortations of the boosters, she fixed her sharp, shrewd eyes upon the cows.

"Don't come 'round here botherin' me, young man," she said, waving away one of the boosters who had ventured to approach her. "I was judgin' caows when you was suckin' your mammy's tits. Like enough you can make some o' them frail an' weak men buy somethin' they don't want, but your blarney's wasted on me. I'm judgin' by what I see, not what I hear."

She was. Indomitable she stood in the place that she had elbowed for herself, her eyes focused to see just one thing, the points in milk cows. When she saw what she considered a good bargain she bid up to the limit that she had set for herself. When she had reached this limit she stopped short like a piece of arrested machinery. No leverage would budge her.

As the afternoon wore on and time became more precious, the bidding, artfully stimulated by the auctioneers and the active young boosters, grew hotter and faster. Five at a time the cattle were driven into the ring now. All or none. You could take 'em or leave 'em. When the big-bellied man's voice broke from strident bawling, his partner, a young fellow with a rapid accumulation of soft fat, took up the hue and cry. The boosters swaggered here and there through the crowd urging and exhorting the bidders. A little Jap in khaki riding breeches scurried about driving the cattle on and off. When he was not doing this he sat cross-legged on an overturned barrel and stared stoically before him. He was the owner of the cattle and knew that every time the whip cracked he lost money.

A man behind Rhoda was telling his neighbor about a sale that he had attended the day before.

"Say, you'd otta seen the way that Hindu stuff sold. All that expensive cotton machinery went for less'n the price o' junk. If a man had a barn now to store that stuff in he could make money holdin' it over."

Rhoda was dazed by the pushing crowds, the glare, the dust, the bellowing, the rapidity with which the bewildered cattle were driven in, appraised, sold and hurried out again. Her ankles ached with standing and she grew increasingly bored by what was for her a wearisome repetition of the same thing. In a moment when the others were not looking she slipped from her place and went back to the car.

Half reclining in the back seat, her head propped against her folded coat, she looked with uninterested eyes at the scene before her and wondered how much longer the sale would last. How tiresome and stupid it was and how tiresome and stupid her life, how tiresome and stupid this great, flat, bare Valley. Wherever you went always the same things: the same shanties, the same flat, rectangular fields, the same dirty ditches, the same long, dusty roads, so wide, so bleak and forbidding, the same tedious people talking always about crops, steak and money. Why had she come here to an unceasing round of toil, hopeless wakings, tasteless meals, dead evenings, tediously shared with another woman. What was there in this life for her?

A young man whom she recognized as the son of an El Centro butcher was examining an old runabout that stood near, testing the springs, shaking the wheels.

"Tain't such a bad old wreck," he said to the youth who was with him. "If the Jap don't want it I'll take it along. It 'ud make an elegant gut wagon."

A woman straggled past on her way to the faucet with three children trailing behind her. At the faucet she shook one of the children and slapped his ears smartly for stepping in the mud. For a moment Rhoda thought that it was Ruby Peterson. She had the same mud-colored wisps of hair, the same jerky movements and flat-chested slouch. But when she looked again she saw that it was not Ruby.

She fell to thinking of Ruby and wondering how she was getting on since she had had to give up her ranch and go to work as chambermaid in the Palace Hotel. Poor Ruby! She felt very sorry for her and yet she had to admit to herself that she despised her. How inconsistent she was. What right had she of all people to despise Ruby? And yet she did despise her and hated the implied bond of similarity of experience. How baffling it all was and how flat, empty and meaningless an existence like hers.

From time to time the hoarse bellowing of the auctioneer cut through her bitter thoughts.

"You all done? You all through? Ain't there nobody here with horse sense to know somethin' fer nothin' when he sees it? All right then, gone to the Jap at forty dollars apiece."

She heard the whip come down with its swish and crack. At the same time a hand touched her lightly on the arm. She started, turned and looked into a face that she had been trying to forget.

"Where did you spring from? I didn't know you were here."

"I've been here only a half hour or so, and about ten minutes of the bidding ring was enough for me; then I slid back among the Mexicans. I'm afraid I'm just a natural-born looker on."

"We haven't seen anything of you for a long time."

She thought she saw a shadow cross his face, a hint of something that he preferred to keep to himself.

"I've been quite busy lately, been helping to subsoil for old man Beasley—and one thing and another."

"These here five cows is all outa the same sire, Prince Regis Pontiac Leopold the Third, the best butterfat bull in Imperial Valley. I won't start 'em under sixty-five dollars."

A white turkey cock came strutting past the car, his harem of big bronze females trooping after him with subdued cheeps and gurgles. Andy Blake looked after him meditatively.

"He's handsome all right and you can hardly blame him

for feeling a little proud with such a large female following. But with his strutting he's scraped those beautiful wing feathers on the ground so much that he's got them all dirty and worn away at the ends. We men ought to take a lesson from him not to display too much manly pride for fear we make ourselves ridiculous."

"I don't think manly pride is one of your failings," she assured him. "You don't have to worry about repressing it."

"I'm not so sure of that. Men are all much alike at bottom, with the same basic smuggeries and asininities."

"What I say is buy a calf an' the first thing yuh know yuh got a cow. Who's startin' these five calves at twenty apiece?"

"What a gorgeous Indian red the flower of that castor bean. It makes a perfect harmony with the big bronze leaves."

It was a dwarfed and dusty castor bean bush straggling from the side of a ditch; but when she followed his eyes she saw it was indeed a beautiful harmony of terra cotta and bronze bound together with green.

"Now lookit here, boys, we ain't makin' yuh a present o' these cattle. Anybody that tries to start anything at less'n thirty dollars ain't startin' nothin'; an' the feller that tries to whoop the ante less'n a dollar musta shook down the baby's bank this mornin'. Lemme see yuh bid along here like western cattlemen, not like yuh made yer livin' out of a cow an' a hundred hens on a Vermont stone pile."

"I feel sorry for the eucalyptus trees these early spring days."

"Why do you feel sorry for them?"

"Because they look so sad and hopeless, like seedy old widows in rusty rags of mourning. But see how the young green of the cottonwoods comes peeping out there all along the line. That slim cottonwood behind the castor bean makes me think of a girl dressed for church on Easter morning."

"Do you ever go to church?"

"No, of course I never go to church."

"I thought so."

"Come on now men, get a little business sense into yer

beans an' don't pinch yer nickels too tight. Who'll gimme sixty-three apiece on these cows?"

"Doesn't that Mexican boy look like a gipsy? There by the water faucet. His eyes have that wild, shy look, like a deer's. They'll lose it I'm afraid when he gets to be a melon picker."

What power was in this man to make her see things that she had not seen before, to change this dull and tedious place into one full of variety and endless suggestion? A delicate pink flush began to tremble into her cheeks. Shadows of thoughts and fancies floated through her mind, too vague for words but alluring as flowers shining through twilight. She thought of that evening when he had come up behind her in the garden. Often and often she had said over to herself the little verse with which he had surprised her.

> "Not God, in Gardens when the eve is cool?
> Nay, but I have a sign,
> I'm very sure God walks in mine."

Dimly she sensed that in the mind of this man there lay a hidden labyrinth of thought, of beauty, of experience. Now if some day he should give her the clue to this labyrinth and let her wander there with him? She wanted to say something to show him that she understood, that she was not a clod, that she perceived, however dimly, that God was in the garden of his thoughts. But she did not know how to frame it; she was afraid that she might only make herself ridiculous.

"Now what d'yuh think o' this here bull? Some bull eh? He's half-brother to Prince Regis Pontiac Leopold the Third, an' I guess yuh all know what that means. Lookit the power in that animal's shoulders. Lookit the breadth between his eyes. An' he ain't no fancy bull just for looks; he's a butterfat bull. Yuh can ask anybody that has cows sired by him if they don't fill the milk bucket. Lotsa these pretty bulls that they ask big prices for ain't no better'n a common scrub bull when it comes to paddin' out the pocketbook. But this fella's bred for butterfat. Now somebody start him with a hundred an' fifty bones."

If he would only say something about Heine then she could let him know that she too knew "Du Schönes Fischermädchen," and it would be the beginning of a bond between them. Then she flushed, remembering the other woman, and wondered if she had told him.

Other lines drifted into her head.

> "Auf Flügeln des Gesanges,
> Herzliebchen trag'ich dich fort,
> Fort nach den Fluren des Ganges—"

Oh no, not to the meadows of the Ganges—not to India. That was all over and as if it had never been. But yet when they two flew away on wings of song it would be to some other place than India.

"It's getting cold; let me help you on with your coat. I like this desert chill and the way the long shadows crawl out over these flat fields when the sun drops. Do you have a fire in the evening at your place?"

"Yes, we have a little airtight heater."

"I've rigged up a fireplace in my shack out of some broken pieces of tile and brick, an old dishpan and a piece of flattened out stovepipe. Every time I light it I run grave risk of burning up my mansion and all my valuable possessions. But I do love to sit over a fire these chilly evenings."

> When winter comes I do retire
> Into an old room beside a bright fire.
> Oh pile a bright fire.

The sale was over; the people were dispersing. Kate appeared at the side of the car.

"Oh here's where you are. We've been looking for you everywhere. A fat lot of interest you've been taking in our new herd. Hello Andy, where've you been keeping yourself? What you doing these days?"

Before he could answer Mrs. Pruett came up beside Kate looking by this time a good deal the worse for wear.

"I've got you good caows, Rhody—fifteen of 'em an' a nice male. I hope you an' Kate does good with 'em. I'm most played out with the scramble an' hubbub.—What you doin' these days, Andy Blake?"

She fixed him with a look of sharp suspicion.

"Not a great deal of anything lately, Mrs. Pruett," he answered blandly. "I finished helping to subsoil the Beasley place last month. I haven't done anything since."

"Henry Crosby's bought most a whole string o' cows here today, an' he's alookin' around fer somebody to milk 'em. I reckon you could git the job if you'd a mind to it."

Frantically Kate drew Mrs. Pruett aside.

"What the dickens did you tell him that fer? We don't want him in our bunch. Rhoda's half soft on him already and the first thing we know she'll be wanting to run off and marry that good-for-nothing bum."

"Well the harm's done," snapped Mrs. Pruett tightening the thin line of her lips. "An' anyway I been judgin' folks for quite a lifetime an' I reckon Rhody's one that kin be trusted to do what's right an' look after herself without nobody's help."

The harm was done; when they turned back to the car Mr. Crosby had come up and was concluding a bargain with Andy Blake to milk eighteen cows morning and evening for the sum of eighty dollars a month.

The sun had dropped out of sight leaving a horizon of pure, cold apple green from which the amber edge was fast fading. Cattle were being sorted out and driven away. People were starting their cars and shivering into their coats and sweaters. The little Jap scuttled about turning the cattle over to their new owners. He had lost rather more than four thousand dollars, not counting the hundred and fifty that he had spent to feed the crowd.

CHAPTER 16

ANDY BLAKE was in the milking corral next morning.

For long, dead weeks Rhoda had been growing tired, oh so tired, of the drearily rigorous routine: tearing herself from sleep when the alarm clock rang in the black hour before the dawn, shivering with chattering teeth through the cold, damp darkness to the milking; then, in the sudden heat that seemed to drain and sap her strength like a million little greedy leeches, sitting at the cow's flank milking, milking, milking until all thought all sensation was numbed and she was nothing but a machine. In the afternoon wrenching herself from the all too short siesta, going back again, sitting at the cow's flank milking, milking, milking as though the strong white singing streams would never end. Then home to chores, cooking, dishwashing, and at last to bed and to sleep. The next day the same thing all over again.

Now from under the peak of her old milking cap covertly watching Andy Blake's movements as he passed from cow to cow or emptied his bucket into the big can or wheeled the rattling milk cart to the door of the dairy house, she felt herself powerfully shaken from her apathy, as if there had filtered into her veins something of his easy vigor, his lightness of heart.

Junie Doble, milking a little distance away, was singing as accompaniment to the rhythmic streams a song that she had learned at school.

Holà holà holà holà,
The world belongs to me.

In Junie's clear, piping soprano the little tune rose up into the sunny air like a bright gush of bubbles. A wild, gay, carefree little tune.

What was it about the tune that made it seem to fall like a garment about Andy Blake as he sat milking or moved from cow to cow or emptied his bucket into the big can?

And all the earth is filled with mirth
For me, a gipsy boy.

There was little of the gipsy in his appearance. Seen from a little distance he looked in his faded overalls and old sweater with burst out elbows and sagging pockets just like any other ranch hand. Yet she had a feeling that this was a man to whom in some way the world really belonged and for whom it was in very truth filled with mirth. An emanation from that lightly stepping figure stirred subtle vibrations on the crisp blue air that came to her with a tang, a zest, a heady stimulation.

Junie swept into the chorus, changing abruptly from a jaunty staccato to a long, swinging rhythm.

O how good just to be
Where the blue deeps of night
Give their peace to the woods
Where we live with delight.
When the fire sings its tune
And the sweet voices ring
In our hearts then 'tis June
And the gipsy boy's a king.

The long swing of the rhythm was like a cool wind in the face. She could smell the wood smoke and the burning leaves. Junie's childish treble had piped this song many times before and it had fallen upon deaf ears. Why did she hear it now?

He was there again in the evening. Every morning and every evening when she went to milk he was there. It was something to look forward to, something to live for. She drifted back into her old habit of daydreaming about him, speculating about his past, his habits, his thoughts and feelings, holding make-believe conversations with him, imagining lucky little accidents that would give them a chance to become known to each other. At milking time she watched him furtively from under the peak of her cap, listened for the sound of his voice. Sometimes when he happened near her he stopped to chat for a few moments, but only in the most casual way. She was satisfied. It was enough to see him twice every day and dream in the meantime her vague dreams. She was not tired any more. The dull veil lifted from before her eyes and the clear depth returned; the color crept back into her cheeks. Kate was not satisfied that it was a healthy color; to her it seemed somehow hectic, unnatural.

A week or so after Andy Blake joined the milkers they were further reinforced by two more. One was a tall fellow with large, calm features under a big western hat. The other was a slim sandy-haired youth whom Rhoda heard the others calling Thatch. They were both badly needed, for Mr. Crosby lured by bargain prices had bought still more cows and Mrs. Doble's hands had grown so stiff with rheumatism that she had had to give up milking altogether.

The first day that they worked the sandy-haired young fellow came up to Rhoda near the end of the milking. His hips and chest were so narrow that his clothes hung in folds about his skinny body.

"Want me to strip that caow for you? I'm a po'erful hard-fisted milker."

She looked up into a blunt-featured, freckled face from which beamed a pair of smiling, childlike eyes, as blue as the desert sky. She knew he must be Junie's brother. She smiled back at him.

"Why of course I don't want you to strip this cow for me. What makes you think I'm not a pretty hard-fisted milker myself?"

"Aw anybody with them slim hands an' wrists couldn't be a good milker—I mean a real sure 'nuf fust rate milker."

She smiled up at him quizzically.

"Then I'm only second class eh? Are you Mr. Doble's son?"

"Sure. My name's Thatcher Doble—Thatch fer short. I jes hopped off a freight at Calexico las' night with a feller I run into up in San Bernardino. We sidetracked the cops an' rode out here on the hind end of a empty lettuce truck. It was so dark the Jap drivin' it didn't even know he had a couple a passengers. I bin on a long trip up through Northern California an' Oregon. Ever been in Oregon?"

"No."

"Say, you'd otta see the big trees up there an' all the stuff that grows. Darn nice people too, most of 'em, an' not a bit stingy with their handouts. I like 'em a heap better'n these California folks that thinks about nothin' but money an' brags so everlastin' about their darn State. On'y in winter it gits too hateful cold an' rainy. I'd a been back here where the sun shines a long time ago if I hadn't a been in jail."

"In jail?"

"Sure. I been in jail lotsa times. But this here last one in this little Oregon town was the swellest jug I ever hit. Say we sure had it soft."

The big mild-featured man whom Thatch had picked up in San Bernardino passed at that moment on the way to the milk can with his brimming bucket and overheard the last few words.

"You had it soft in jail eh? By God, it was more than I did."

With these few words he was gone; but in the moment of his passing a black wave, powerful and sinister, engulfed Rhoda. She felt herself floundering helplessly in the strong suction of its seaward sweeping undertow.

Thatch was evidently not so susceptible to other people's auras.

"That guy's nuts," he said, nodding negligently in the direction of the receding figure. "A good feller—good as gold—but nutty as any lunatick. Well, as I was sayin', we had it soft in that jail: three good stiff meals an' the coffee pot boilin' on the stove the hull bloomin' day. We looked after our own fire, an' we was supposed to be allowed a scuttle o' coal a day, but we allus managed to git away with a extry scuttleful, an' we sure kep' that little old cast iron blow torch red hot. I wasn't cold onct all the time I was in that jug.—Then on the wall we had a cigar box nailed up an' in there we peeled our smokes. Everybody put whatever he had into the cigar box; pipe or chawin' terbaccer or tailor-mades or anything he happened to have in his clothes. An' when we run outa smokes whoever had any money sent out an' got more. Then if a feller come in that didn't have no money nor no terbaccer, why he was welcome to all his constitution 'ud stand outa the cigar box. An' with a fresh deck o' cards every few days say we did have some good times settin' around swappin' yarns. I'd a been there yet if they hadn't showed me the door an' told me to beat it. An' after I come outa that jail, say did I feel the cold? Oh baby!"

Andy Blake had sat down to milk a nearby cow and had been listening to Thatch's description of the idyllic jail. His presence disturbed Rhoda.

"You were in luck, Thatch," he called across the intervening space. "When I was in jail nobody ever showed me the door and offered to throw me out."

Could it be possible that he too, that all three of these men had really been in jail? Surely they were not the sort of people who get put in jail. Probably they had made it up among them to tease her. Then she remembered the black wave of rage that had engulfed her when Thatch's friend passed near.

"But I should think you'd have been glad to get out of jail for the sake of a change."

"A change! Say lemme tell you in winter time up north there ain't no change I kin think of that's equal to three squares a day, all the coffee you kin drink an' terbaccer you kin smoke, a game o' cards an' good comp'ny. You kin lay dollars to doughnuts any change off that's gonna be a change for the worse."

"How did you come to get put in jail?"

"Well this time it was makin' booze. You see I happened into a feller that was runnin' a little five-gallon can an' he put it up to me would I sell fer him an' go fifty-fifty on the profits, an' I didn't have nothin' else to do so I said sure I'd peddle the stuff. I done purty good for about a couple a weeks an' then a darn dirty stool pigeon that hung around the pool room there got a line on me an' trailed me down an' we was pinched an' that was the end o' that little money makin' scheme.—Say, did you ever see a abalone shell? I picked this one up over in the coast country alongside of a road where somebody'd been roundin' out postholes with it an' left it layin' by the fence. Over there they think they can't dig a good hole 'nerless they get a abalone shell to trim it out with. I thought this'n was purtier'n common so I fetched it along."

He pulled the shell out of his pocket and handed it to her.

She took it wonderingly, with a little gasp of pleased astonishment. As she turned it this way and that it changed like a wave of the sea with every play of light and shadow. The peacock greens and blues, the sun-flecks of yellow, the delicate pinks and deep purples flowed together and melted into each other, changed places with the changing light, so that its beauty was never the same. All the shifting color, all the depth and strangeness, all the miracle of the sea in the satin lining of that one shell but little larger than her hand. The marriage of water and sunlight. Looking at it a wave of delight passed over her face as if the rippling beauty of the shell were reflected in her features.

"Purty, ain't it?" said Thatch.

"Oh it's wonderful. I've never seen anything so lovely in my life."

"I bet if there wasn't but a dozen or so o' them shells in

the world they'd be worth a million dollars apiece. But 'cause there's plenty of 'em over there in the coast country you kin pick 'em up everywhere or buy all you want for a nickel apiece."

"A nickel apiece. Think of it."

She held it out to him.

"Put it in yer pocket, it's yourn."

"Oh thank you, I'll love to have it."

A flush suffused Thatch's freckles and he turned away with an abrupt movement.

Later in the morning Rhoda went into the Doble's dirt-floored shack to ask Mrs. Doble about her rheumatism. Mrs. Doble was making shift to peel potatoes with her numb and twisted fingers while her unimpaired jaws champed tirelessly on her wad of gum.

"Well I dunno, it don't seem hardly no worse nor no better," she answered dispassionately as if the disease belonged to somebody else. "The fingers don't ail me much—jes a creepin' stiffness—an' I wouldn't mind a hull lot if on'y I could keep on milkin'. I've milked caows ever since I was old enough to trip over a milk bucket, an' naow I ain't able to milk no more it jes seems like I can't take no int'rest."

"I suppose you're glad to have your boy back home again."

"Well I dunno. I dunno if he's better off home or not home. Thatch don't do much good no place he is. He ain't got his health like Cliff. When he was a little feller seven year old he like to died o' the diphtheria, an' we was off eleven miles from the nearest doctor an' didn't hev no money to pay doctors anyhaow an' o' course he didn't git much doctorin'. Then they took him away to the hospital an' he laid there for months an' months, an' when they brought him back they said he wouldn't never be real staout no more. An' since that he ain't never growed ner filled out like he'd otta; his backbone's allus scraped his belly. He's good hearted, Thatch, he'd take the shirt off his back for some other lazy bum he'd picked up somewheres; but he ain't to be depended on. He's a good milker too, but he ain't strong enough to do no real man's work an' that keeps him restless. He ain't no sooner home than he's gone again an' he ain't no sooner outa jail than he's in again an' that's haow it keeps a-goin' on."

She lifted her eyes from the potatoes, blank, washed-out eyes, and gazed apathetically through the open doorway at the deep green alfalfa fields and the blazing sapphire sky.

"I see they're puttin' the caows onto a new paster this mornin'. It's about high time too I reckon. They must a got them lands the other side o' the ditch ett off purty clean."

CHAPTER 17

ONE EVENING when Rhoda was emptying her last bucket of milk into the can she noticed Mr. Doble hand Junie a small pail and heard him say to her: "Here, Junie, take this gallon o' milk over to that woman 'tother side the ditch an' see to it you bring the bucket back. Don't leave 'em wash it neither, the dirty varmints."

"What woman?" asked Rhoda.

"Oh that Mexican woman over there. I heard she came down with a baby a day er two back an' she's got a swarm o' bigger uns runnin' araound. I reckon she could use a drop o' milk now an' then, an' old man Crosby ain't a-goin' to miss it on his porridge."

"Maybe we ought to go over and ask that Mexican woman if there's anything we can do for her," hesitated Rhoda, as Kate was about to crank the car.

"I don't know why, seeing we've never once laid eyes on the woman in our lives; but if you say so we'll go."

They crossed the road and the plank bridge over the ditch to a dingy cookhouse shack surrounded by the usual Mexican litter of old wagons, rags and firewood. They had scarcely noticed the place before, screened as it was from the road by the high ditch bank and the drooping boughs of eucalypti. Inside a young woman was lying under unspeakable rags of bedding with an infant by her side, a quaint, bright-eyed little thing with thick black fuzz all over its small head. In the thickening darkness the mother's face looked very pale against a tumbled mass of black hair. A girl about eight years old was stirring something over a small rusty cookstove, and two boys, barefoot, big-eyed of the strangers.

"How are you?" asked Kate, going up to the side of the bed, while Rhoda ventured to touch with her finger tips the soft fuzz on the baby's head.

"All right," answered the Mexican woman and continued to look at them with a wide stare.

"Where is your husband?" continued Kate in a tone that smacked of welfare work.

"He work on big ranch–pack lettuce–up near Brawley. He come home maybe at end of week."

"But who did you have to get the doctor for you?"

"Doctor? I not have no doctor."

"Who was with you, then, when the baby was born?"

"Nobody, only myself and those." She indicated the children with a movement of the hand. "I know what to do. I have five already before this one. Two die."

"For all the world like a wolf and her cubs in a cave," commented Kate as they drove homeward. "And a walking incubator. She doesn't look a day over twenty-three–and six young ones already."

The next morning when they went to milk they took the woman some soup and on several succeeding days went into the obscure clutter of the shack with some article of food for her and the big-eyed hungry looking children.

Then one day the little girl came running over to the milking corral, her mane of coarse black hair streaming out behind her.

"Mama says will you send for the priest?" she said, addressing Mr. Doble, who was the first person she came to.

"The priest? What for?" asked Chester Doble in a tone which suggested that he had been asked to summon the black plague.

"Cuz she thinks the baby's gonna die."

"The hell she does? How about sendin' for the doctor?"

"She didn't say nothin' about no doctor."

By this time the others had gathered around and after a short conference Andy Blake was dispatched in the Doble's old Ford truck to notify the nearest doctor—and a sky pilot if he happened to run into one. Mrs. Doble went across the ditch to see what she could do for the baby.

On the face of Dan Stoner, the big mild-featured man who had come with Thatch from San Bernardino, Rhoda noticed a strange expression, a convulsion of the features as of one in the grip of physical agony. When it had passed it left a look of deep sadness.

"Them Mexicans is folks, same as you an' me," she overheard him say to Kate who was milking near him.

"Well, aren't we doing what we can for them?"

"Yes maybe, but you talk about them like they was cattle. The world won't be no better a place to live in so long as some kinds o' people thinks the others is cattle."

And after Dan Stoner had got through his milking Rhoda noticed him over at the far edge of the eucalyptus grove by the side of the ditch walking up and down, up and down, his head under its big western hat sunk low on his chest.

In the evening when Kate and Rhoda went over to see how the baby was they found that it was dead. The mother was washing out some clothes on a bench beside the door. She was pale and heavy-eyed but there were no traces of tears on her face. The doctor had not come, but the priest had arrived in time to save the baby's soul. Inside, the dead baby lay on the bed wrapped in a ragged blanket, a crucifix hanging on the wall at its head. Without knowing, Rhoda crossed herself. It seemed to her that it was best for all concerned that the baby had died, and yet she could not help yearning over the stiff, cold little body. There was nothing soft about it any more but the thick black fuzz on its little head.

Next morning the county authorities had already come and taken the baby away for burial.

A few days later Rhoda noticed a man swearing at a lean horse in the cookhouse yard and she concluded that the husband had at last come back.

A strange man, Dan Stoner, nearly always preoccupied and silent. His big features had that quiet, self-contained, imperturbably mild look that one often sees in the rural districts of the South. Here in the Valley, which was full of poor cotton and tobacco raisers from the south eastern States, Rhoda had learned to know this type of face; but there was something almost uncannily mild and calm about this man's composed features. She found herself wondering if he had ever smiled and in spite of his mild look felt a little afraid of him. More and more he piqued her curiosity; she wondered what he was thinking about under that big western hat.

One day at the end of the milking she came upon him bending over a piece of wrapping paper which he had spread out on a corner of the long grease-soaked table that stood beside the milkhouse and held cans, buckets and strainers.

"What kind of sums are you doing there, Dan?" she asked.

"He's figgerin' up his income tax," informed Cliff who happened to pass by trundling the noisy milk cart.

He began to fold up the paper. "It's nothing," he said with a shy, self-conscious look that she had never seen on his face before, "on'y a little notion o' mine."

"Do tell me about it. I like to hear people talk about their ideas instead of always just how to make a living."

She felt him beginning to warm to her. His big hand smoothed out the paper for her inspection.

"Well it's a little idear I've kinder nursed for a good many years about a colony, a place you know where people that has the same notions about things could live together the way they want to an' be sep'rate from the rest o' the world. Now you see along this river is the power plant an' all around these factories is flower gardens, same's you'd have around your house. Then here's the farm land all cultivated with tractors an' the like, an' here's the public park an the community center or whatever you've a mind to call it, an' here's where the people live."

"But why would people want to live in a colony like that?"

He flashed her a quick, inquiring look that asked if she were indeed as uninformed as her question implied, then continued: "So's to get the benefit of what they earn. Like enough you haven't read Henry George an' Bellamy an' folks like that an' so the idear's new to you. Me, I've read a heap o' books about sech things. Fact is I ain't read much else. You see in a colony like this there wouldn't be one feller owin' the works an' the other fellers workin' for him. Everything 'ud be owned in common an' everything shared in common. Then there'd be no middlemen, no advertisin', no costs of distribution to speak of, no waste like there is in our present way o' doin' things. You see I was raised on a farm in Georgia an' I run away when I was fourteen cuz dad licked me for readin' when I'd otter been choppin' cotton. An' since that time I've worked in steel mills an' slaughter houses an' bakeries an' canning factories an' sech places an' then I've gone outa the towns an' worked in mines an' harvest fields an' loggin' camps an' I've seen a po'erful lot o' things anybody'd like to ferget. Then when I'd lay off I'd spend my time readin' books about what to do about it; an' once you begin to think about sech things you don't stop—not ever."

"I see. It would be a sort of Utopia where there was no

poverty nor sordidness, and people had time to think about something besides how to get a living."

"You bet." He warmed with the joy of having a sympathetic listener. "This here 'ud be the school. An' the kids wouldn't have to sit still five or six mortal hours an' learn rules an' lists of names an' dates, like they did when I was a young 'un. Lord, how I hated school! But on'y the people that wanted to teach 'ud be allowed to teach, an' the rest 'ud take care of itself. Then right here in the middle 'ud be the place where everybody lives—round you see to save space an' built o' solid concrete so's there'd be no fire. Once, an' I ain't never been able to ferget it, I saw the body of a little girl about like Junie brought out of a burnin' house all burnt an' charred an' since then I've thought how every house 'ud otter be made of concrete so's it won't burn."

"Round? Oh but I don't think I'd like that. And twelve stories high? Why it would look just like a gas tank with windows. And what queer shapes the rooms would be. And that deep well in the middle would be awfully dingy; it would hardly let in any light at these back windows. They'd be just like tenement rooms. Why not have little cottages scattered about?"

"Oh but this 'ud be a heap cheaper. I thought it all out by myself an' figgered it out careful. An' there'd be plenty of electric light in the shaft, an' up on top there'd be a roof garden an' on the ground floor all the cookin' an' laundry an' sech, so's the women 'ud have time for other things besides housework."

She saw by his look of pained bewilderment that the round monstrosity was very dear to his heart and she was sorry that she had said anything to hurt his feelings and shake his faith. Andy Blake came up with two foaming buckets of milk.

"Forget it, Dan, you couldn't make it work between now and doomsday, even if by some miracle you could get together the people and the money to start it," he said, pouring the milk through the strainer and displaying not a little of that zest with which men are wont to attack the pet theories of other men.

"Why wouldn't it work?" asked Rhoda.

"Because it never has. These things have been tried over and over again. They always die a-borning or shortly after."

"Then you think," said Dan, "that because a thing never has been it never will be. I'd rather be dead than go around with that notion under my hat."

To Rhoda's surprise Dan did not look at all pained by Andy's low opinion of his plan, but only argumentative. He folded up the paper and put it in his pocket.

"And even if the darned thing would work, you ought to be the last person on earth to be harboring a notion of shutting yourself up into a little private heaven in the midst of a big universal hell. After the way you stamped up and down last night and bellowed that nobody ought to rest until the whole world had a new social order I'm surprised to see you flirting with that colony idea again."

Dan's smile, a peculiar slow, dry smile, broke the calm of his big features.

"Well I reckon if it's any satisfaction to me to flirt a mite it ain't a-goin' to do no great harm. I ain't apt to be seriously involved, seein' it's all on paper an' like to stay there."

"And suppose you actually could get it to work, how long do you suppose it would be before it was infested with intrigues and squabbles and petty jealousies and honeycombed through and through with envy, malice and all uncharitableness?"

Rhoda did not hear Dan's reply, for the two men had turned and walked away, leaving her there as if she were an empty milk can. Looking after them she noticed that Andy's hand was on Dan's shoulder. A feeling of dreariness crept over her, then passed in a surge of indignation.

She felt very angry at Andy Blake for the cavalier manner in which he had flouted Dan's plan. To her it seemed a very nice plan indeed—all except the house where the people were to live—very interesting and intriguing. All the way home and all day as she went about her work she thought about it. Instead of that ugly round house twelve stories high, suppose they had little cottages nestled here and there among the trees and vines, such humble, charming little houses as one sometimes glimpses with delight in a little town or on the far outskirts of a city. A bright flower garden all around and at the back of the lot vegetables and chickens. Roses climbing by the door, hollyhocks against the wall, a big, shaggy dog asleep on the sun-steeped porch, a cat washing her face in the middle of the garden path. Birdsong and the busy cackle of hens. A little haven of order, beauty and peace. She would like a house like that if only she could share it with him. How nasty of him to put on superior airs and say Dan's plan was no good. How could he know that it wouldn't work? And she began to turn over again in her mind the details as the big, slow-spoken man had outlined them to her: the school where children would be taught in love and freedom, the factories set among lawns and flowers, the recreations, so easy of access, that one could turn to when the day's work was done. The idea had all the provocative allurement of novelty. Continually her thoughts circled about it. It was a lovely dream and what right had he to say that it might not come true?

Again and again she kept going back to the fascinating new idea, turning it over and over, looking at it from this angle and from that, as a woman might do with a bracelet that her lover had given her. At first she gloated over it in secret, then against her better judgment she could not resist showing it to Kate. She was scrubbing out the slimy inside of the olla under the ramada and Kate, bent over the washtub, was scouring with a scrub brush a pair of her grease-soaked milking overalls. Kate was never very good-humored or talkative when she washed overalls and she listened in silence, scrubbing with grim vigor.

"I always thought Dan was a little nutty," was all she said when Rhoda had finished.

Rhoda was not slow to notice that in spite of the fact that they did not always agree Dan Stoner and Andy Blake had discovered in each other something that they had not found in the other members of the milking group. She discerned in their easy casualness toward each other a freedom, an intimacy such as can exist only between two people who have much in common. What was this thing that they had in common? She wondered and watched.

Shortly after his arrival Dan had gone to live with Andy in the melon-crate house. Andy said he was a crack tortilla maker and a champion seasoner of beans and flapper of old-fashioned pancakes; but Rhoda knew that it was something more than Dan's culinary skill that had made him welcome there. Frequent discussions they must have over the evening bacon and tortillas, for they often continued them in the milking yard, reminding each other of what had been said the night before. They seemed to find everything to disagree about, and yet she felt that there must be something deeply fundamental about which they agreed. When the milking was over they would stroll away together deep in talk, deep sometimes, too, in intimate silence. Their very backs radiated companionship, Rhoda thought as she looked after them wistfully. As time passed and she continued to observe them she realized that these men had grown to love each other.

CHAPTER 18

MR. WILLIAM ROSS MCCUMBER had become a rather frequent visitor at the ranch. He called the girls by their first names now and insisted upon being addressed as "Bill." With a pair of Kate's overalls pulled over his business suit he helped with the milking and other chores so that they could all get away in time to take in a movie. In spite of or perhaps because of his cheerfulness and good humor Rhoda found him tiresome. She could think of nothing to talk to him about and was bored and disconcerted by his attentions. Again and again she regretted the foolish little flair of vanity that had prompted her to show him that she was not to be lightly disposed of as an "old maid." He got along better with Kate; but it was all too evident that it was not in Kate that he was emotionally interested. Why had she done such a silly thing and brought all this upon herself?

For a while she had rather enjoyed the movie shows—all but that first one with the Hindus in it; but she grew satiated with men dangling over cliffs and out of twentieth-story windows, with runaway trains and colliding automobiles, with wild horseback chases and daredevil leaps and hair-breadth escapes, and she could feel nothing but a bored contempt for the artificially prolonged suspense which was no suspense at all. She grew tired too of sumptuous interiors, of suave villains in evening clothes, of big-eyed ladies wearing costly, form-revealing gowns. And while the heroine bugged out her painted eyes and heaved her expensively draped bosom Rhoda's thoughts wandered to other things or she peered through the gloom at somber Mexicans, ranch hands in Sunday clothes, bulbous, double-chinned women, ruddy young mechanics, lovers holding hands, finding those people more interesting to watch than the stereotyped figures on the screen.

She fell into the habit of eyeing with especial interest the women about her: blowsy young ones champing their candy or gum, skimpy ones growing old in spinsterhood, stout ones with that settled, unexpectant, married-for-good-and-all expression; and the fancy took hold of her that these women were all there to see the lover that they would never get or had never had. It was only a fancy, she told herself; but she could not shake it off.

Mr. McCumber now came frequently to the Crosbys' Sunday dinners. They were hospitable folk and many people, including Kate and Rhoda, had a standing invitation to their table. Mrs. Crosby thought Rhoda wonderfully sweet, modest and sensible and Mr. Crosby stentoriously proclaimed Kate a "fine woman." The Crosbys, grown to be well-to-do farmers and further enriched by a substantial inheritance, had come to the Valley in its early days, homesteaded land and made money. Mr. Crosby had long ago ceased to work on his ranch and went every day to a real estate office in Calexico. Since his retirement from active farming he had developed a paunch, three chins, pouches under the eyes, a florid complexion, a sense of his own civic importance and a demeanor of weight and solidity. Withal he was playfully inclined and fond of a joke, especially if he made it himself.

Mrs. Crosby they found to be a good and kindly soul who in her lean, baby-ridden young days had been hard working and frugal. Now that her nest was well-feathered and empty, she had turned to other activities. She was still pretty in a plump, blonde way and had not lost all vanity. She wore a rubber reducing corset when the weather was not too hot and had spasmodic attacks of reducing exercises. She was a member of two women's clubs which occupied themselves with literature and local improvement. She read novels from the public library and also books and pamphlets on theosophy, spiritualism and astrology and believed everything that she wanted to believe along these lines. She had her feet, which were tender, cared for regularly by a chiropodist. She loved to hear on the phonograph old songs about such subjects as mother, home and heaven. The tears would well up into her eyes as she listened to

> It's oh for the days that are gone Maggie,
> When you and I were young.

She talked a great deal and very feelingly about food, declaring while spooning up a second helping of chocolate pudding that all of us without exception eat a great deal too much. She waxed eloquent over the difficulty of getting good meat in the Valley, the rapidity with which ice melted and bananas spoiled, the way she longed for fresh raspberries and could hardly ever get them. She hated to part with money but was generous with her food, her time, her advice, her sympathy.

"What you girls need to do," she said, drawing Rhoda aside one Sunday afternoon, "is to meet some really nice respectable people. The way you're situated you're thrown mostly with foreigners and Texans and people like Andy Blake and the Dobles. Come every Sunday that you can and I'll try to have some worth-while people to meet you. Mind you, Rhoda dear, this is for your special benefit because I have your best interests at heart."

She gave her a sly little dig in the ribs.

The Sunday guests were mostly well-to-do ranchers of the neighborhood or business people from Calexico or El Centro. They were for the most part decent, well-dressed not very well-mannered people who talked about food, money, crops and investments. The men, after a few preliminaries of polite banter with the ladies, monopolized the conversation, addressed themselves solely to the other men, tried to talk each other down and took no further notice of the women who had to sit in silence or be content with subdued overtones of twitter among themselves. It was better when the meal was over and they withdrew to the living room end of the big porch, for there the men at once gathered together in a tight group and tried to see which could bellow loudest about taxes and water assessments and date pollenizing and the Boulder Dam plan and the Japanese question and the menace of waterlogging and the best method of pruning grape vines, thus giving the women an opportunity to gather in a cosy little cluster and tell each other what length skirts were going to be next spring and what the Civic Improvement Club was planning to do and what make of oil stove was the best and what Christian Science had done for them and how to make delicious preserves of cantaloupe rinds and what the new clairvoyant in El Centro had told them about their past, present and future.

Mrs. Crosby, fine-tooth-combing her list of acquaintances for eligible men, had happened upon Mr. McCumber and was delighted to find him at once attentive to Rhoda.

"There isn't a better catch in the Valley, Rhoda dear," she confided. "He's working into a very good law practice and his reputation for honesty and integrity is absolutely unsmirched. Mr. Crosby has the highest opinion of him and aside from his business he's made several good investments that are sure to grow into money. I like you in that pink dress; it makes your cheeks look just the same color as the dress. I thought at dinner how pretty you were looking and I'm sure Mr. McCumber thought the same thing."

The segregation of the sexes, however, was so sharp and absolute and any departure from it so noticeable that Mr. McCumber had but few opportunities to improve his acquaintance with Rhoda at these Sunday dinners. Sometimes, to be sure, the mahogany phonograph was set going and under the cover of the music he had a chance to say a few words to her. But though general conversation lulled somewhat when music was started it was soon in full swing again and the record, whether it was of Caruso or Ed Simpson's jazz orchestra, spun round and round unheeded.

But when the piano was opened and Rhoda sang and played everybody kept still for the sake of politeness. She knew only a few simple old songs and her soprano though sweet was weak and vague; but she sang her old-time ballads with a tender grace. She was best in the gently mournful songs; the appealing plaintiveness of her voice enhanced the charm and melody of "Bendemer's Stream."

And I think is the nightingale singing there yet,
  Are the roses yet blooming by Bendemer's stream?

"That's the kind of music I like," Mr. McCumber would breathe enthusiastically under cover of the resumed buzz of conversation. "Something simple and sweet with a nice tune to it. I like to listen to a snappy jazz now and then, but a single one of these good old-fashioned songs is worth all the jazz in the world to my mind; and I don't think there's anybody could sing them better than you do."

His praise made her flush with pleasure. After all it was nice to be admired, and she rather fancied the singing herself.

But a few hours later in the cattle corral, dressed in her greasy old overalls, her sagging sweater and milking cap, she wondered that she could ever have had any enjoyment from the dull dinner table talk, the after-dinner twitter and the admiring glances of Mr. McCumber. How stodgy they had all been, herself included, there in the hot, food laden air stuffing themselves with Mrs. Crosby's over-rich cooking. How funny and pompous the men had looked with their bursting, well-tailored bodies, their beefy cheeks and comical, fat, self-important faces, each trying to bring the talk around to his pet grievance which was sure to be intimately connected with the leak in his pocket book. And the women in the after-dinner confidence circle, how shallow and tiresome most of them and with what silly airs and trivial concerns. How thick and stuffy the whole atmosphere.

Here in the corral nobody was polite to anybody else, nobody tried to pay compliments or be suave or affable. Here under the sky the air was cool and fresh, stimulating as a salt wave splashed in the face. The stars were beginning to twinkle into a blue almost as clear and luminous as themselves and the intense winter sunset was smouldering from flame to magenta beyond drooping black boughs that hung silent and motionless like sculptured fantasies. A somber tree, the eucalyptus, somber and self-contained, yet wayward withal and with a wild, dark spirit of its own. The big-shouldered Cliff moved about with lithe panther steps alternately singing and swearing as he marshalled the cows. Junie and Willetta quarreled vociferously about who should have the one three-legged stool or which should milk the roan cow and which the black. Andy Blake argued with Dan Stoner or swapped merry yarns with Thatch if Thatch happened to be nearer. Mr. Doble mumbled over and over to himself a monotonous chant that had to do with the adventures of the boll weevil that came out of Mexico into Texas looking for a home—and found it. It was his favorite song and always at milking time he crooned a few of its dozen or so stanzas.

I want a home. I want a home.

The plaintive need of the boll weevil as expressed by Chester Doble's resonant mumble in the over-recurring refrain was rich with a humorous folk song melancholy. It seemed to Rhoda a sign of rare philosophy that he could be thus drily jocular about the thing that had been the great tragedy of his life.

Through the cool of the darkly luminous twilight the streams of milk sang steady, purring songs. Everybody was milking, milking, milking; but with the milking everybody was doing also the thing that his spirit prompted. It came over her that it is only the poor and the unpretentious like these who are free to do the things their spirit prompts. At the table of the Crosbys she had felt self-conscious and alien. Here under the stars she belonged to her surroundings. The people about her belonged to their surroundings; their voices, their movements, their weathered old garments blended with the evening quiet and the subdued colors of the corral. Something of which they were unconsciously a part, something big, basic and powerful lapped them about, held them as in the hollow of the hand. The breathing and gentle movements of the cows, the purr of the streams of milk, the tinkle of the buckets, the voices of the milkers, the bass croon of Chester Doble sympathizing with the boll weevil mingled into a harmony that was one with the cool darkness, the pure sky, the sunset smouldering into magenta beyond black boughs motionless and fantastic. She felt that here she was at home, that these people were her people and this life her life.

CHAPTER 19

KATE AND Rhoda were rather late in arriving at the Crosbys' that Sunday and the other guests were already assembled on the spacious porch. It was hot and palm leaf fans were waving. Mrs. Crosby, arrayed in new summer silk and her best company manner introduced them to those of the guests with whom they were not yet acquainted and dwelt upon each individual's claim to distinction, such as hardware, cantaloupes, wet wash laundry and the like, with the unctuous satisfaction which respectable people display when they can name a proper social standing in connection with the person presented. The girls shook hands with ladies of soothing manners and men who looked freshly tubbed and smelt of shaving soap and cigars.

Mr. Crosby appeared in the doorway. Secure in his position as genial and generous host he could afford to dispense with a company manner.

"Hello there girls. I notice you always shed the pants on Sundays. How 'bout that? What I wanta know is when you're each gonna pick out a rich rancher an' shed the pants fer good? I can't see what's wrong with the fellas around here that they don't snap up a couple a husky, good-lookin' girls like you instead a some made-up chit from the ten-cent store. Reg'lar 'painted deserts' I call 'em."

Kate was in no way perturbed by Mr. Crosby's attempt to be humorous; but Rhoda, feeling Mr. McCumber's eyes upon her, flushed painfully.

"Mr. Pruett asked us that same question Sunday before last," she said to cover her embarrassment.

"An' well he might. He wants to see you girls come out on the big end o' the horn. Durn good fella, Pruett, an' the best heart in the world. Only thing wrong with him he's got no more business sense than a rabbit. Why if that man had taken my advice he'd a been worth a nice little fortune today instead a still drivin' his own mule team. It's queer how little foresight some men can have when it comes to a matter of business."

Rhoda did not tell Mr. Crosby that the Sunday before last Mr. Pruett had made exactly the same statement about himself. She could see him in her mind's eye trying to look impressive as he brandished the carving knife above the roast chicken.

"Crosby's a good fella, but he's got no head for business. Why that man's passed up some o' the best investments that's ever been offered in California—looked clean through 'em an' never saw 'em. With the capital he had to start with he might have been worth a cool million if he'd only taken my advice. It's nothing but sheer luck that's got him even as far as he is."

While they were waiting dinner somebody put a record on the phonograph. Mrs. Crosby's cousin from Los Angeles, a stoutish, amiable looking woman, was there on a visit.

"I intended to bring Milly some new records," she confided to Rhoda, "and then came away and forgot them. So I tried to get her some in El Centro, but I was surprised to find that they had hardly any of this year's things. However back here in the country I suppose one doesn't need to be right up-to-date in music."

The "Liebestraum" of Liszt, presented to Mrs. Crosby by a young Roumanian Jew, a blanket stiff who had worked for

Mr. Crosby, was spinning around unheeded by almost everybody.

"This is a very beautiful thing, don't you think?" said Rhoda.

"Oh yes, it's pretty. I have a lot of these old classical things that I might have brought along. Of course they must have been very popular when they first came out, but in the cities hardly anybody plays them any more."

When they went into the dining room Mr. Crosby, with a sly and wicked twinkle of the eye, beckoned the men into a corner where he produced from a wall cupboard a quart bottle with a big dimple in the bottom and an embossed and gleaming label.

"Have a little appetizer. This is no made-last-night stuff, but regular old bottled-in-bond Scotch. Fella that sold it to me knew the man that ran it all the way from the Canadian border."

"She sure slides down easy."

"I'll say she does. An' I bet she's got a good kick too."

They grinned with puerile satisfaction, like boys smoking behind the barn, wiped their mouths with their freshly laundered handkerchiefs and looked sly and prankish.

Mr. Crosby busied himself with mixing a somewhat weaker concoction.

"Come ladies," he invited gallantly, "just a little sip to give you strength to sit up and take nourishment."

"You men ought to be ashamed of yourselves, breaking laws the way you do," admonished Mrs. Catlidge the hardware merchant's wife; but she drained off her glass almost as quickly as Kate.

Rhoda tasted gingerly, hated the stuff, then took a brave swallow and got rid of it. The other ladies sipped, coughed, giggled, told each other confidentially how easily they were affected, swallowed part or all as they felt inclined and let their husbands drain the glasses.

Mrs. Crosby surreptitiously removed hers to the kitchen

and stirred it into the pudding sauce. The glasses were whisked out of sight and they sat down to the table.

"Where's those fellas that were working on the new garage and helping me fix the car this morning?" Mr. Crosby demanded to know as he picked up the serving fork. "I told them not to stir feet off the place till they'd had their dinner."

"They're washing up," Mrs. Crosby informed, coming in with an enormous platter of fried chicken. "They say they'd rather wait till we're through."

"Nonsense Milly, tell 'em to come on in. Nobody in this house waits till somebody else is through."

Justina the hired girl came in with two big vegetable dishes, followed by her sister who helped out on Sundays. They were thick, clumsy Mexican girls with neither necks nor ankles.

There was a shuffling and scraping of feet outside and the workmen filed in and sat down in constrained silence at the end of the table nearest the kitchen. There was Thatch Doble and Dan Stoner and Andy Blake and an old bony Mexican in patched and frayed overalls faded to a beautiful blue by many washings. The skin that drew tightly over his cheek bones was like burnished copper and from under white brows his eyes looked out somber and mournful like an autumn evening. Justina and her sister, when they had finished bringing in the food, came and sat down at the humble end of the table. Rhoda thought of descriptions she had read of old feudal banquets.

Soon every plate was heaped with fried chicken and three vegetables. Pickles, chili sauce, ripe olives and sliced tomatoes made the round of the table. It was a dinner to be proud of.

But Mrs. Crosby was not at all proud of it. She was thinking that if she had her way they would give up the ranch and go to live in Calexico where she could entertain decently like the other women of her class. There she could have a properly set table with a separate fork for each course and salads and desserts that looked pretty on the fine china and a trained maid in uniform who knew how to serve correctly instead of these raw girls who planked the vegetable dishes on the table and then sat down and helped themselves amid a lot of ragged, unshaven hangers-on. It was not that she bore these people any ill will or begrudged them the food that they were eating; but they made correct manners and interesting conversation impossible. Also she knew very well that they would much rather eat by themselves, and she was in favor of letting people have what they wanted. She wished that Mr. Crosby would not insist on benevolently inflicting on them what he considered they should have. But it was of no use to try to tell him anything. She sighed inwardly and resigned herself to making the best of it.

Rhoda too was made uneasy by the intruders. From time to time she glanced furtively at them and once she met Andy Blake's eyes. He winked deliberately and assumed an expression of great decency and refinement. She wanted to laugh and at the same time she felt like a simpleton and a booby sitting there with her muslin sleeve brushing Mr. McCumber's padded shoulder. A deep misgiving too, a sharp sense of something denied her made the food tasteless in her mouth.

There was little conversation until the second helping began. At this stage a thin vapor of talk began to rise above the heavy exhalations of the food. Mrs. Crosby and some of the ladies near her fell into a discussion of club activities.

"Every bit of the last musical program was classical," said Mrs. Catlidge, "but it was just as pretty and sweet as it could be."

"Next meeting Mrs. Williams is going to read a paper on Anatole France."

"Who is he?"

"Oh he's a writer who has sprung into fame just lately. I saw his name in the paper just the other day."

"I hope he hasn't got such terrible views as that man—

who was it—Shelly?—that Mrs. Gibbs read a paper on. Of course it does seem as if geniuses had to be allowed more freedom than most people; but when they back themselves up and say they're in the right I think that's going too far."

Mr. McCumber asked Mrs. Crosby's cousin who sat on his other side how she liked the Valley, how the roads were up through Indio and how real estate was selling in the vicinity of Los Angeles.

Somebody dropped a remark that started the Japanese question.

"Well I'm glad it doesn't have to be settled by a popular vote," sighed Mrs. Crosby. "I've got to admit that we've never had better neighbors than the Sumiyoshis. They mind their own business the best of any neighbors we ever had and we've never had a bit of trouble with them about the water or the fences or anything, and after all the vegetables they've given us and things they've done for us—not of course that we don't try to return the favors—I'd feel just terrible if I had to go to the polls and vote for Japanese exclusion."

"And they do have such darling little babies," breathed Mrs. Catlidge who was a childless woman.

"That's just it—too darn many of 'em," snorted her husband. "If we don't keep 'em out in another generation these 'darling little babies' 'll be taking away from our children what's theirs by rights. It's got to be done as a measure of self-protection."

The talk drifted to the relative merits of lettuce and cantaloupes as money makers, to the water question, to the farm bureau barbecue picnic, to the last shooting affair in Mexicali and the subsequent closing of the border.

"Nasty den 'o thieves that," observed Mr. Crosby. "What we otta do is to buy Lower California from Mexico, go down there and open up the mines and put water on the valleys and incidentally clean up these vicious border towns."

A smothered gurgle which might have been caused by a

chicken bone in the throat escaped from Thatch Doble. He put up his hand to further stifle it and muttered through his teeth to Andy Blake who sat next to him: "Saw the old boy down there not ten days ago—fuller'n a pin-cushion too."

Mr. Crosby's attention having been attracted to Thatch by the gurgle, he cleared his throat and addressed him in that extra hearty, good fellow, slap-you-on-the-back manner which he reserved for his dependents and inferiors.

"Well Thatch my boy, how's your mother's rheumatism? Did she try that liniment I told her about?"

"Yep, she's a-usin' it," returned Thatch, making innocent wide eyes, "but she says she don't seem to notice no p'tic'ler diff'rence."

"Well you tell her from me to keep on with it and don't get discouraged. A thing like that takes time."

"Paw says he don't look to see her git no better till we git outa here where the water's got so much alkali."

"What nonsense. Why there isn't a drier, healthier climate in the world, and I don't believe the water's got a thing to do with it," said Mr. Crosby whose household was regularly supplied with bottled water.

"I dunno. But anyway paw's all set on gittin' out."

"He surely doesn't want to go back to Texas where he worked for eleven years to pay for a place and then had to walk off and leave it?"

"No, paw ain't got no homesick hankerin' after Texas. But he's got a holt of a book lately that tells about a lota cheap farms up in the Ozarks an' he's all het up to go there."

"The Ozarks!" With a gesture of sheer amazement Mr. Crosby laid down his knife and fork. His guests smiled at each other and looked at Thatch with expressions of condescending pity. "What in Sam Hill does he want to go to the Ozarks for? Doesn't he know there's nothing there: no money, no land worth anything, no industries?"

"Yep, I reckon he knows that. But paw ain't mebbe so

dumb as you think. He's figgered it out that wherever a small rancher goes, rich country or poor country, he ain't goin' to git nothin' but his eats an' his shirt an' overalls anyways, an' he 'lows he'd rather have his eats an' his shirt an' overalls in some place where it ain't so flat an' so durn hot in summer an' where there comes rainy days an' winters when he don't hev to work, an' where he kin go huntin' an' fishin' an' kinder enjoy hisse'f."

"What a line of reasoning! Why Thatch, your family working for me earns in one month what you wouldn't make in a year in the Ozarks."

"Yep, paw knows that. But he says that fast as he gits it the storekeepers takes it away from him, so he might as well not git it."

A flush that was something more than the effect of over-eating suffused the features of Mr. Catlidge the hardware merchant and brought out the brick red of his neck in more colorful relief against his immaculate collar. He flashed at Thatch a violently indignant look, opened his mouth to speak but changed his mind and closed it again. Mrs. Catlidge's habitual expression of soothing amiability froze into a stern and formidable glower.

"That's the rankest kind of nonsense, Thatch," proclaimed Mr. Crosby. "In every farming community business keeps step with agriculture, the better the agriculture the better the business and the better off the farmer."

"Sounds good, but there must be a nigger in the woodpile somewheres," persisted Thatch, " 'cause it don't work out that way. When I was beatin' the trains here a while back I rid all over California an' up through Oregon an' Washington an' everywhere the towns looked mighty prosperous with lots o' fancy houses an' nice lawns an' big cars; but everywhere the small ranchers was so hard up they couldn't hardly pay their taxes an' the roads was jes crawlin' with bums that couldn't git a job even if they wanted one."

"The trouble as I see it," observed Mr. McCumber, clearing his throat with dignity and speaking in the measured platform tone with which he was accustomed to address the judge and jury, "the trouble as I see it is that nowadays the working class has so little thought for the future. Everything goes as fast as it's earned not only, as this young fellow says, because the cost of living is so high, but because of downright wasteful extravagance, especially among the younger men. If you young fellows here, for instance, instead of spending your money in pool halls and gambling places, save your money and take an interest in your own welfare and the welfare of your community you'd get somewhere in the long run."

"I'll say they would," assented Mr. Catlidge, helping himself from the plate of sliced tomatoes. "That's how we all got our start."

Rhoda noticed a queer sardonic smile pass over Andy Blake's lean features. There was amusement in it and bitterness and pity and despisal and a myriad of subtle shades of feeling that she felt but could not define.

"This new Ku Klux Klan is an excellent thing for young men," went on Mr. McCumber. "It takes them out of the pool halls and teaches them to have some public spirit and sense of their responsibilities as citizens. To my mind it's a mighty good organization."

"Well anything that does that I'm sure ought to have our support," breathed Mrs. Belton, the dentist's wife, a little woman with large, vague blue eyes, prominent teeth and a receding chin.

"Indeed it should," assented Mrs. Crosby.

"But don't you think, sir, that the Klan is likely to become a dangerous organization in this part of the country where we have such a mingling of races?"

There was a perceptible stir at the table and everybody looked toward Andy Blake. The women in particular turned their eyes curiously toward this workingman who spoke with such an accent of refinement. He was busy with a drumstick and took no apparent notice of the general scrutiny.

"Quite the reverse," returned Mr. McCumber with no abatement of dignity. "It seems to me that if there is any place that the Klan is needed it is here. I look to the Klan to see to it that the Valley remains a fit place for a white man to live in."

"You mean by keeping the other fellows so well under the thumb that the white man is always easily master of any situation."

"Not at all. I believe in giving everybody his just due. Nevertheless it seems to me that history has proved conclusively that the white race is the superior race."

The other people about the table looked impressed by the profundity of Mr. McCumber's argument and satisfied with his conclusion. The bony old Mexican and the two hired girls, quite unaware that anything was being said which concerned them, devoted themselves to the important business of eating.

"But it has always seemed to me that the Klan has no real basic principles, no firm and strong foundation."

Andy Blake's tone was still one of dignified argument; but with his off eye Rhoda saw him wink leeringly at Thatch and Dan Stoner.

"What, no basic principles? If the principles of adherence to law and order, of sound patriotism and pure Christianity aren't good enough principles I'd like to know what are? If Christianity is a myth and a fable, then the Klan has no basic principles."

"That's just it. Christianity *is* a myth and a fable."

A wave of astonished horror passed around the table. Nobody there had been inside a church for many years and nobody, with the exception of Mrs. Crosby and perhaps another lady or two who dabbled in newfangled cults, had ever given a single serious thought to the Christian religion or any other religion. Nevertheless they were horrified and genuinely so.

"Well of course if you take that attitude we have nothing to say to each other," said Mr. McCumber.

"Not a thing. We wouldn't convince each other in a million years," Andy assented with brisk cheerfulness as he helped himself liberally to the olives.

There was an awkward and resentful pause. A pompous solemnity sat upon the faces of the men, and the women were tight-lipped and stony-eyed. Mrs. Crosby flashed at her husband a look of rage. Now he had a chance to see what trouble he made by dragging people in who didn't belong. Everybody was ill at ease except Andy Blake and the three Mexicans, who still showed every sign of relishing their food.

Rhoda kept noticing that Dan Stoner had been growing more and more restless. Now he lifted his steady gray eyes and fixed them upon Mr. McCumber.

"The Ku Klux Klan keeps a-hollerin' that they want a better understandin' between capital an' labor," he said in his deliberate drawl, "but they don't say no single word about how to come by it. In the same breath they holler that they're opposed to strikes, the I.W.W. an' everything that ain't jes the way its always been. So it don't take a very sharp eye to see what side o' the fence they're on. Darn few workingmen belongs to the Klan, and the ones that do are the poor boobs that believes everything they read in the newspapers. I'll tell yuh, mister, who belongs to the Klan: it's storekeepers an' preachers an' lawyers an' undertakers an' real estate sharks an' the like, people that's livin' off the workers an' doin' good the way things is an' don't wanta see no change made."

"The Klan is opposed to strikes and the I.W.W. because it is opposed to every form of mob violence," said Mr. McCumber, swallowing an angry lump in his throat.

"Yep, that's what they holler, an' a course it has a mighty good sound. On'y thing wrong with it, it ain't true. What they really mean is that they're afraid the workers'll git together in dead earnest some day, an' they want to have a mob organized that'll be stronger than the workers' mob."

"You have entirely the wrong idea, young man. When did business men, clergymen, lawyers and such people ever resort to mob violence in this country?"

"When? On'y a few hundreds o' times this past few years. Like enough you haven't put much thought on it one way or 'tother an' so you don't know that most mobs is mainly made up o' white-collared fellers. They're the ones that does the lynchin's an' the tar an' featherin's an' all sech."

"Oh I don't believe that can be true," remonstrated Mrs. Crosby's cousin from Los Angeles.

"Yes ma'am, it is true, an' I'll tell you why. The fellers that works hard at manual labor, like farmers an' workingmen, ain't got no time an' energy left to mind other folks' business. If they kin keep the wife from grumblin' an put shoes on the young uns they're purty nigh satisfied. If you leave them be, they'll leave you be."

"Which is the same as to say they have no sense of honor," put in Andy Blake.

A wave of complacency relaxed the features of the assembled business men. They cleared their throats and looked as if about to speak.

"Well now I don't think I'd go so far as to say that," said Mr. McCumber in a mollified tone.

"It's the truth just the same," went on Andy. "They've hardly got any more sense of honor than a rabbit. To grow a real man-size sense of honor a man has to have time and money. If he hasn't got the time and the money he might as well give up hope. People with plenty of time and money make wars and lead mobs because they own things that they're afraid somebody is going to take away from them, and they call it defending their honor. The tenant farmer or the day laborer doesn't have to defend anything from anybody. All he's got is a wife and a few kids and it's a million chances to one nobody wants either his wife or his kids and so he doesn't have to work up any fine feelings or any fine frenzy, which means that he has no sense of honor."

"I wouldn't for the world subscribe to such a definition of a sense of honor," blurted Mr. McCumber. "To my mind a sense of honor is something very different from that."

"That's what I used to think too," returned Andy Blake, "till I got to going around the world and noticing how it worked. Then I found that a man is honorable as long as the rules of the game are definitely laid down and everybody is looking on, as when he fights in the ring or plays at cards or baseball or conducts some business where the conventions are so set and definite and everybody concerned is so well safeguarded by law that he can't cheat without getting into public hot water. He's honorable then and makes a brag about it. When he isn't honorable is when he can gain some advantage by being dishonorable and get away with it. And if he gets found out and there is the slightest room for a difference of opinion, he's sure to make a wonderful case for wronged honor. You see it happening all the time among politicians and business men. People who have anything to gain by it can always marry expediency to honor. If you don't believe me read the newspapers."

Mr. McCumber had cleared his throat to reply, but hesitated, not fully decided what to say, and in the moment of his hesitation Dan Stoner broke the astounded and resentful silence.

"You say it ain't white-collared men makes mobs. I'll tell yuh about a case that like enough yuh heard of when it happened, 'cause it was right here in the Imperial Valley. It was when the war was on an' I was workin' with a lot of other fellers balin' hay on a ranch out near Brawley. One night when we come into taown after work there was a bunch o' fellers in white collars had a rope drawn acrost the road stoppin' every car. We pulled up an' they asked us had we bought our liberty bonds. Some o' the fellers had bought bonds an' was wearin' their buttons. They didn't bother them but went after us fellers that didn't have buttons on. The boys stalled an' caged an' argued, but it didn't do no good; they saw it was gonna be up to them to buy liberty bonds whether they wanted to or not. So they signed the papers an' paid each man five dollars first payment on a liberty bond an' got their receipts an' their buttons. All but one feller. He said he didn't believe in the war nor any other war an' wasn't gonna do nothin' to he'p it along an' he'd see 'em in hell afore he'd buy one o' their damn bonds; an' to that a course they answered that he must be pro-German. Well they argued an' badgered an' bullied an' threatened, but he stuck it out. They let him pass that night, but the next mornin' they come out to the ranch where that feller was workin' an' grabbed him an' shoved him into a big automobile an' ran him over to a ranch where a man had a lota turkeys. They yanked off his shirt an' cut off his pants jus below the crotch an' smeared him all over with some tar they'd melted up an' then they poured them turkey feathers all over him. After that they run him to Brawley an' tied him to a palm tree in the park. I kin show you the very palm tree they tied him to, an' they nailed a big placard on the tree sayin' this was the feller that wouldn't buy liberty bonds. The thermometer went to a hundred an' twenty that day, like it does a good many August days, an' the tortures that feller suffered from the heat an' the flies an' mosquitoes nearly drove him mad. About four o'clock they come an' loaded him onto an automobile without no top an' drove him all the way down here to Calexico, a good thirty miles an' more, exhibitin' him to everybody on the way as the man that wouldn't buy liberty bonds. Then they tied him up on the main street of Calexico an kep' him there all evenin'. The feller was months gettin' over it. An' the men in that dirty mob that tarred an' feathered that feller? Was they workin'men an' ranch hands? No, there wasn't a workin'man or a ranch hand among them. They was storekeepers, clerks, real estate men, lawyers an' the like, every damn one of 'em."

"I never heard of such a thing occurring in the Valley and I don't believe it did either," pronounced Mr. Crosby in a manner that declared the whole thing disposed of.

A dark red wave of blood suffused Mr. McCumber's face. He opened his mouth to speak, but indignation choked him.

"Well then I reckon I must a dreamed it," said Dan Stoner, scratching his left temple. "I bin thinkin' all along that that feller they tarred an' feathered was me."

Mrs. Crosby came to the rescue by rising from the table.

CHAPTER 20

SHORTLY AFTER the baby's death Rhoda began to notice more Mexicans on the other side of the ditch: another young woman, slim and with a free, swinging step, who seemed vaguely familiar as if she had seen her somewhere before; a fat waddling young woman; an older one who always wore a black shawl over her head, a slouching, bronze-colored man with a big black mustache and more barefooted, big-eyed children.

"That's allus haow it is once Mexicans gits started in a place," commented Chester Doble. "A few fetches more, jes like flies. There'll be a whole village of 'em here afore they quit comin'. If I had a henhouse I'd buy me a padlock to put on it. What with the hens roostin' in trees an' the turkeys strayin' off Gawd knows where, a man 'ud better crate 'em all up an' take 'em in to the butcher once he gits Mexicans for neighbors. I dunno haow they all manage to squeeze into that there little cookhouse, but they don't aim to live no better'n hawgs. That's haow Mexicans is."

Rhoda could not help wondering how the six members of Chester's family managed to dispose themselves in their little two-room shack.

Chester was right in his prediction that there would be yet more of them. Another cookhouse came drawn by horses. A tent was put up, another tent. More copper-colored men came and black-shawled women and barefooted young ones. More old wagons came and skinny horses and long-eared, wise looking mules, more disreputable bedticks and torn quilts and dirty sheepskins and rags and bones and paper and tin cans and old lumber and packing boxes, until the corner behind the ditch was a tangled litter of rubbish. In the midst of this litter chickens pecked and roosters strutted and children scrambled. Above it hung clotheslines from which depended plaid shirts, overalls, whitish-gray diapers and the hard pinks, oranges and magentas that the Mexican women love to wear. Every day they had clothes on the line, yet they never looked clean.

"What a way to live," thought Rhoda, as she peered over the ditch bank at the accumulation of filth and rubble. Then she remembered Mr. McCumber's remark: "Good Lord, you girls don't lead the life of a dog," and she smiled thoughtfully to herself.

Andy Blake and Dan Stoner were always talking together. If only he would think her worth taking seriously and talk to her earnestly and absorbedly as he did to Dan Stoner how happy she would be. Now and then she caught snatches of their conversation.

"I used to think that way, Dan, but I've come to feel the uselessness of bucking things. I wish I didn't, but I do. Once that feeling gets hold of you, you have to take things as they come and let them go as they will."

"That feelin' won't never lay hold of me so long as I draw breath."

"Well for your sake I hope not, Dan."

What did he mean by "bucking things?" In a vague and general way she understood that they were both dissatisfied with the world as it was; but she longed to be invited into their discussions, to understand their points of difference, to be asked what she thought about it.

With the earnest and serious Dan Stoner he was almost always earnest and serious. But with Cliff and Thatch he was always laughing and telling yarns and talking about guns and dogs and places they had been. Often too she caught snatches of this talk; but sometimes it was carried on in suppressed tones broken by significant snickers and loud guffaws and then she knew that they were saying something which they did not want the women to overhear and her cheeks would burn with shame and indignation. Dan Stoner was only a poor tenant farmer's son and had been a workingman all his life, but he had some dignity and kept himself to himself. Andy Blake was plainly a man of education and refinement, a man who had had advantages. How then could he descend to telling dirty stories and making companions of Cliff and Thatch? What could they possibly be to him, she asked herself jealously.

"I used to think Andy was a kind of a freak and a nut," Cliff said to her one day. "But when you get to know him he's a hell of a good feller. Me an' Thatch likes him fine now."

Sometimes too he would lounge against the milkhouse wall and chat with Chester Doble about the tariff and the difference between the Republican and Democratic parties, which they amiably agreed was no difference, and the comparable value of Rhodes grass and Sudan grass as hay and as a choker-out of Bermuda and the chances of the cotton raiser's ever getting a square deal and the problem of ditch dredging and other subjects dear to the heart of Chester. He even played at ball and tag with Junie and Willetta, and with Mrs. Doble he was on friendly and sociable terms. He offered to make her a new wash bench, and one evening when Rhoda went over to the shack to ask Mrs. Doble about her rheumatism he was there at the door sawing briskly away and singing over and over to a ridiculous little tune of his own making,

Jesus was a carp, Jesus was a carp,
Jesus was a carpenter's son.

With everybody he had more to talk about than with her. Every day she grew more jealous of these conversations, these attentions to other people.

And then Thatch made it harder. Since his present of the abalone shell he had not ceased to give her things. He was always coming up after milking time and putting something into the back of her car or shamefacedly thrusting it into her hand: a crate of lettuce which he had adroitly filched from the back of a passing truck, a half-dozen or so big oranges or grapefruit or purple pomegranates procured only Thatch knew where. She hated to take the things and devoutly wished that he had selected some other recipient for his offerings. But though diffident Thatch was persistent and would listen to no refusals, and she could not fail to see in his desert blue eyes a devotion that pained and embarrassed her. As he continued to bring her things, she grew more and more awkward and self-conscious about accepting them, and Kate teased her without mercy about her mooncalf admirer.

If only it had been Andy Blake who had felt moved to give her things she would have stood all Kate's ridicule with equanimity.

While the open season was on—and indeed while it was not on—the young men often went duck hunting at night and bagged quantities of the wild ducks that came to feed on the freshly irrigated young barley that was planted in winter with the alfalfa. It was always Thatch who presented Rhoda with the finest of these, carefully dressed and drawn and all ready for the frying pan.

One morning just after she arrived at the corral he came up and tucked away a large parcel under the back seat of the car.

"I jes put some fine ducks in your car," he said, fixing Rhoda with his big childlike eyes of desert blue. "An' you kin bet yer one shirt there ain't no mudhens in 'em. Say, I have to laff every time I think about it, the way the folks in them fancy hotels eats mudhens an' thinks they're ducks is a crime. I took in a big mess las' week an' they was lousy with mudhens; but the cook he says, 'Oh that don't make no odds, ole hoss, I'll see you git yer money fer 'em jes the same as if they was all ducks. Once they're cooked an' seasoned them folks in the dinin' room'll eat mudhen till kingdom come an' talk pretty to each other about the d'licious wild duck.' I had to snigger to myse'f when I went past the dinin' room door on the way out an' saw all them slick guys with shaved necks an' them hoity-toity dames with paint on their faces an' thought haow they'd soon be eatin' my mudhens an' exclaimin' over the 'd'licious wild duck.' But mudhens ain't good 'nuf fer me an' I'm darn sure they ain't good 'nuf fer you."

Rhoda flushed painfully. "It's just awfully good of you, Thatch, to go to all that trouble for us. You oughtn't to do so much for us."

"Aw g'wan, what's dressin' a few ducks?"

Later in the morning when she was milking Grumpy, the black cow that always had to have her legs strapped together because she was an incurable kicker, she heard Thatch, around the corner of the milkhouse, say to Andy Blake: "Goin' to come to my weddin' tomorrer, Andy?"

"Wedding? Then you've really made up your mind to be a damn fool? You're honest to goodness going to get married, Thatch?"

"Sure I am. If I don't she'll nag me an' the relations'll nag me an' one of 'em'll like enough stick a knife into me, an' the best thing is to go an' have it over with same as gittin' a tooth out."

"Which one is she?"

"It's that fat bitch. Angie her name is, I think."

"You'd better beat it, Thatch. The world is quite a big place."

"No sir. I ain't ready to beat it."

There was a dogged stubbornness in the last answer.

Surely it must be a joke. But no it hadn't sounded altogether like a joke. She remembered too that fat girl on the other side of the ditch, a great shapeless lump of flesh. Could that be the one? And Thatch really be going to marry her?

A little later when she happened near Andy Blake she said to him: "I overheard you and Thatch talking a while ago. Who is Angie?"

"Angie is that fat girl on the other side of the ditch."

"And is Thatch really going to marry her?"

"He says he is."

"But why?"

"Well you see he's accidentally got her into a little trouble, or 'a peck o' trouble', if you want to look at it that way. Anyway, she says he has, and he thinks the easiest way out is to marry her. When he first told me about it I advised him against the Unholy Alliance. I tried to make it plain to him that he'd be sure to leave her sooner or later anyway and it would be kinder to leave her with one pledge of love than with several. But he wouldn't look far enough into the future to see my point."

She could think of no answer to make and went on milking in awkward silence. She was overcome with confusion and embarrassment all the more because Andy spoke of the matter with such casual offhandedness. Soon he moved on to another cow, humming to himself as he went:

> Oh I lost my love and I care not,
> He would come back but he dare not.

All day as she went about her work she kept thinking about it. What strange creatures people were and how strangely they acted, as if they could not help themselves but moved when some sinister influence pulled the string, like puppets controlled by the showman. Sinister surely the influence must be. In the old days the Indians had called this deep desert valley the hollow of God's hand; but now that people lived their tangled lives in it was it not rather the devil's hand and he with agile fingers pulling the strings that made them dance?

She lay awake thinking about it after she had gone to bed. It was a moonlight night and the roosters, perched in the cottonwoods and chinaberry trees, could not sleep. From her cot on the porch she looked out at the pale sky and the few dim stars, listening to the crowing of the roosters and wondering why that sound, so cheerful in the morning, is fraught at night with sadness and the thought of death. Somewhere in the near neighborhood a restless bird would lift his voice and crow. The sound would provoke an answer in a more distant barnyard and he in turn would awaken another still more distant, until the sounds, faint and very far, thin and very clear, trailed away into silence, like the voices of the departed choir after church. Far away beyond her range of hearing the crowing was still going on, she told herself; there was no knowing where the thread of song would end. And all because one rooster in the nearby chinaberry tree had been minded to raise his voice and crow. It was like that with people's actions; the merest accident, the most casual chance could prompt them to some deed that would influence drastically and for always their own lives and the lives of others. In what a hopelessly tangled mesh they were all caught. Surely they were in the devil's hand.

How dark too the net in which together they struggled and floundered; how little each knew of his fellows caught in the same meshes. It came over her that she was a stranger to everybody about her, more than all a stranger to the man she most desired to know.

Thatch got married the next day, "With a priest an' holy water an' all the fixin's," as he told his fellow milkers not without bravado the while he sedulously avoided Rhoda's eyes. Mr. Doble shook his head in a manner that proclaimed him a fatalist and Mrs. Doble back in her dirt-floored shack sighed with stoical resignation and said she never reckoned that Thatch would come to any good. But aside from these expressions of parental disapproval nobody seemed particularly excited or exercised about it and Thatch's habits remained unchanged. He continued to proffer his little gifts to Rhoda.

"But Thatch you ought to give these to your wife and not to me," she chided him when she came upon him one day slipping three big oranges under the back seat of her car.

He shot her a look of a puppy that has been whipped. "Aw shet up an' don't go to rubbin' nothin' in."

She was smitten with a sharp contrition and a feeling of acute pity for him. How could she have allowed herself to say such a cruel thing?

In February spring had come with a rush and covered the ditch banks with lush new Bermuda grass, thickened and darkened the feathery green of the cottonwoods and quickened to new life the gray-green desert woods in the abandoned fields. In the orchards it showered with pink the apricot and peach trees, unfolded scarlet blossoms on the delicate pomegranates and decked the grapefruit trees with waxy bloom. The chinaberry trees around the girls' shack sent forth long succulent shoots that swiftly unfolded to make the dense, dark growth of summer. Soon their purple blossoms opened and for a brief season the air hung heavy with a scent that sometimes reminded one of lilac, sometimes of heliotrope. The mornings were still full of freshness, but as March advanced it grew hot and languid when the sun struck squarely the backs of the milkers. It was hot too when the afternoon milking began, and now no desert chill fell with the twilight. Instead there slid from the wide, luminous horizons a gentle coolness that soothed and relaxed the flushed and tired milkers as they sat at the cows' flanks. It was soft, sweet, caressing like a breath from Heaven.

One day in April the word went out to fill up the horse-ponds and settling tanks in preparation for a three days' dearth of water. There were repairs to be made and dredging to be done and the ditches would be dry. Next day, instead of tawny water brimming from bank to bank there were deep, slimy-sided trenches with a trickle of water at the bottom. After the milking was over the young men and children went down into the ditch for fish. The Mexicans from the other side had already scrambled down the steep incline and were wading about in the deep bottom ooze. Kate and Rhoda lingered for a little while to watch the fun. It was a curious sight to see. No sooner were the fishers in the ditch than the mud was everywhere upon them, in their hair, down their backs, spattered over their faces. With trousers rolled to the crotch and sleeves to the shoulder they sprawled, slid, reeled, waded, wallowed and floundered through the deep, slippery silt making frantic grabs with their dripping arms at the elusive fish that were left gasping in the ooze or swimming about in fast-shrinking pools. Under the hot sun the ooze steamed and stunk. The grotesque fishermen dripped with sweat as well as mud.

Even Dan Stoner who rarely took part in the sports, was down there scrambling with the rest. Junie had begun to cry because she couldn't catch any fish and he had gone down to show her how to grab them. Andy Blake, as naked and dirty as the others, was having a glorious time. Rhoda could hear his laugh above all the babel and hubbub.

As she stood looking at the strange spectacle she was turning something over and over in her mind. This something was the fact that two days before, after the Crosbys' Sunday dinner, Mr. McCumber had managed to get her into the grape arbor by herself and had asked her to marry him. He had said that he wanted for his wife an old-fashioned girl, a gentle, pure and modest girl like her, and she had smiled demurely, whimsically, enigmatically. She had no slightest wish to marry Mr. McCumber and had told him so; but it was the first time that anybody had asked her to marry him and an offer of marriage even from an unwelcome wooer is a flattering thing and something not to be lightly dismissed from the mind. She had tried to be very definite in her refusal, but she knew that Mr. McCumber was not discouraged. She suspected too that he thought she had said no out of more coquettishness. If he only knew how little chance he had.

Thatch came scrambling up the steep, slippery bank, the bale of a bucket clenched firmly between his teeth, from crown to toe streaming with liquid mud.

"Rhody, jes lookit, ain't them a pair o' whoppers?" he exclaimed selecting two fish from the bucket and throwing them on the ground before Rhoda. "I bet nobody ain't took no better sammin outa the ditch today than them two. The rest is on'y small an' middlin' an' this here big feller's a bonyback. Nobody don't eat bonybacks on'y Mexicans an' swell folks in hotels, the same that eats the mudhens; but these here two big sammin'll make a dandy dinner for you an' Kate, Rhody."

Fat Angie, standing with arms akimbo and beetling stomach on the other side of the ditch, could not hear what Thatch said, but she could see enough to make her stare angrily at Rhoda. The handsome girl with the free, swinging step, whom Rhoda had noticed before on the other side of the ditch, was standing beside her. Again there seemed something vaguely familiar about her face and figure.

Down in the bottom of the ditch Andy Blake was still scrambling about as merry as a child. Rhoda thought how happy she would be if only he would clamber up the bank like Thatch, all dripping with mud, and lay his two best fish at her feet.

CHAPTER 21

UNDER THE delft blue sky in the before sunrise twilight the milkers were gathered together in a little knot discussing something.

"Who's dead?" asked Kate offhandedly, coming into the group.

"Nobody's dead," answered Thatch, "on'y Ma Crosby was born Gawd knows how many years ago tomorrer, an' old man Crosby's givin' us milkers a picnic to celebrate."

"A picnic? Where the devil can anybody go for a picnic in this flat hole that's the same every which way you turn? The only place I can think of to picnic is a ditch bank, and if there's any ditch bank that's any different from the one right beside us I'd like to have a look at it."

"Not so fast, Kate old hoss," came in Andy Blake's casual voice. "We're going to Mount Signal."

"Mount Signal!" Rhoda's face rippled into a smile as she lifted her eyes to where the big lonely mountain, as yet untouched by the sun, still wore its morning veils of blue and purple.

"Oh, that'll be a real treat," she cried, clasping her hands with pleasure.

Junie clutched her by the hand and bobbed up and down, delighted to find somebody who shared her joy and excitement, then darted over to Dan Stoner, who had just joined the group. Between these two, so opposed in size and demeanor, there had sprung up an odd friendship.

"Oh golly, we're goin' on a picnic, we're goin' on a picnic," she chanted ecstatically.

The man's mild, grave features relaxed and brightened. A slow smile lifted one corner of his mouth.

"A picnic eh?" he said as she slipped her hand into his. "Well if you've a mind to go, Junie, I recken I'll jes have to go along too."

"A course you're goin'. We're all goin'."

Chester Doble thoughtfully stroked his long, lean chin.

"I dunno as I'll know haow to act at a picnic," he said, smiling his dry smile which showed some of the places where his teeth were gone. "I'm fifty-seven naow, an' fur's I can think back I ain't been to no picnic since I was nineteen year old; so I reckon I'm a bit outa practice at the picnicin' job."

"Who's going to do the milking?" demanded the practical Kate.

"We'll milk in the mornin' same's usual," answered Chester, "an' Crosby's hired the Mexican bunch 'tother side the ditch to do up the night work. Don't leave nothin' lyin' around loose that you want to find agin."

Next morning the girls were up and milking their own cows while it was yet dark to get their work done before going to the Crosbys'. When after the milking they gathered at the Crosbys' house, Rhoda was disgusted to find there Mr. McCumber, spic and span in new corduroys and brisk with picnic jollity. Just what was needed to spoil her day, she told herself. Her vexation was further increased when she found herself railroaded to a seat beside him and the rest of the car so heaped up with picnic impedimenta that there was no room in it for anybody else. She cast regretful eyes at the dilapidated and uproarious Ford truck in which rode Cliff and Thatch, Dan Stoner and Andy Blake, the while she asked herself angrily why she should have to have this man's company foisted upon her. She was in no mood for agreeable picnic conversation.

Lifting its solitary peak in the middle distance Mount Signal did not seem far away. With its jutting surfaces standing out clear and clean-cut in the morning sunlight it looked almost like a place that one could walk to in an hour or so. They would soon be there, Rhoda promised herself, and she would see to it that she got rid of him. But the car travelled westward for miles before Mount Signal seemed even a little nearer. At length however it towered larger, the individual rocks stood out more boldly and Rhoda began to think that they were almost there. She sat nursing her anger, feeling vexed, nettled, frustrated, and to Mr. McCumber's well-meant attempts to be companionable answered only in tart monosyllables.

"Got a headache?" he asked solicitously.

"No."

"A penny for your thoughts."

"I was thinking," she answered, "how some people always manage to get whatever they go out after, whether it's a suit of clothes or an automobile or a position in life or a religion that fulfills their needs, while other people have to always do without, struggle, compromise and are never satisfied with what they get out of life."

"Well now I'll tell you," confided Mr. McCumber, "I'm inclined to think that people get out of life just about what they're willing to put into it."

It was just what she had expected him to say. Her lip curled in scorn and she disdained to answer.

"Take for instance those two birds that were at dinner the other Sunday," went on Mr. McCumber, "those fellows in your milking gang, Blake and Stoner. They seem to have pretty good domes both of 'em; but there must be somethin' very much the matter or they wouldn't be where they are. They couldn't a made a lower start than I did; I quit school when I was twelve an' went to work an' I bin workin' ever since. Trouble with fellas like them they got some loose wheels that keep 'em from fittin' in. They won't play the game the way it's played an' then they get sore an' want to take a battle axe an' bust up the whole works. They're dangerous fellas an' I wonder Crosby keeps 'em around. A couple a Mexicans 'ud do the work just as well an' let off no steam."

She made no answer, but after a few moments broke the silence with an explosive question.

"Why did you sell us that place when you knew we didn't have one chance in a hundred of paying for it?"

"Why—er—say, lookit here, I didn't misrepresent that place one single bit. The land's every bit as good as I said it was."

"I know the land's all right; but you knew that with our

small capital and ten per cent interest we had scarcely a chance of ever paying for it."

A flush passed over Mr. McCumber's distressed and bewildered face.

"But say, lookit here, I think that's awfully unreasonable of you; you were perfect strangers to me at the time and it wasn't up to me to butt in on your plans. If a fella's in the business of selling farms he can't last long goin' around advising people not to go into farming."

"That's just it," she answered with a dry note of finality. "Neither Andy Blake nor Dan Stoner would stoop to do that sort of thing, and so they have no good clothes and no big shiny car."

Eyeing him askance with cold disdain she saw his brow, his cheek, his neck flush a dark red, saw the crimson creep under the roots of his hair.

"Well for Pete's sake, if a woman can't put a mean interpretation on a perfectly straight and square business transaction! Why good Lord, Rhoda, if you had the faintest idea what arrant nonsense you're talking you'd turn around and laugh at yourself. These birds have been talking to you and filling your mind with notions; I've noticed that women have a way of falling for that sort of dope. I've got nothing against people expressing their opinions, whatever they are, but by golly when they go to making a knave out of an honest man that's always done the square thing—"

Again she saw the crimson wave suffuse his brow, his cheek, his neck, creep under the roots of his hair. Coldly she eyed him askance and felt a sense of cruel triumph at the sight of his bewilderment, his confusion and chagrin.

"Well say, lookit here," he blurted, "if you think I haven't done the right thing by you, let me take over the place, pay you what you've put into it and let you out on it entirely."

"You knew when you made that offer that I would not accept it," she said frigidly.

"I didn't know anything of the sort, and it's mighty unkind and uncalled for of you to suggest that I did. What sort of chance do you give a fella, I'd like to know? It seems to me you're acting like a little girl at a party who wants the biggest piece of cake, but you won't take it when it's offered to her and goes off and sulks in a corner."

"There isn't the least resemblance," she said icily. "I want nothing whatever from you and certainly wish to be under no obligation to you."

"Well then, what the devil—"

"I was merely trying to give you an instance to show you that being able to fit in and having good clothes and a fine car is not necessarily a matter for self-congratulation."

"Good God, if a woman can't wag a mean tongue—and twist a thing out of all relation to the truth."

He sat for a long time in gloomy and outraged silence, his eyes on the road along which he was steering.

They were approaching Mount Signal from the north now. It was strange how the mountain seemed to withdraw itself from them, stretching over and over long level spaces between them and its base. It seemed as if the more they travelled the more they had to travel and they would keep on going forever.

A gateway, the sun-steeped yard of an old adobe house set on the edge of the desert, a cursory inspection of their car and they were in Mexico.

Even when they came to the place where the straight green edges of the watered fields cut the sand as if God had reached down a great knife and divided the wet from the dry, Mount Signal still held itself aloof. On the other side of this last ditch crouched the desert and into it they plunged.

The ground was not flat now but heaped in mounds and hillocks of white sand scattered over with distorted evil dwarfs of vegetation: prickly thorn trees and spiny cacti and the strong, sharp bayonets of the Spanish dagger. Above the white sand the heat seethed and the fierce glare of sunlight dazzled the eyes. Inhospitable and barren, parched and distorted, the desert satisfied Rhoda's spirit. It looked as she felt, and she was glad that they had come into this stark and savage place.

Gradually the road dwindled to a trail across deep sand and Mr. McCumber had to steer carefully to keep in the ruts of cars that had gone before.

"What the dickens did they want to come here for?" he grumbled. "Lord help me if I ever get stuck in this sand. I can't see what there is here to attract anybody."

"I like it," said Rhoda.

They chugged along in estranged silence.

"Say look here Rhoda," Mr. McCumber blurted at last, "I don't suppose you really meant most of that stuff you said back there; and if I said anything that got your goat I'm sorry I said it, so what do you say to forgetting it?"

Before she could make the tart answer that was on the end of her tongue they found themselves in the midst of the picnic hubbub. They had reached the end of the trail and the occupants of the other cars were swarming about them talking, laughing, unpacking, dragging things out from under the seats, drinking great swigs of water from the canteens.

All about them stretched white dunes of sand scattered with cacti, thorn trees and greasewood; and at a little distance the mountain rose abruptly, a great unhewn pyramid.

They carried the canteens, the lunch baskets, the sofa pillows, all the picnic accessories across the hot, blinding sands to the shade of a desert tree, a low-spreading, gnarled tree of dark, fleshy leaves and wicked spines. Here, as is the way of picnickers, they were instantly filled with ravenous hunger, could hardly wait to build a fire and boil coffee; and the moment that Mrs. Crosby's beautiful lunch was spread out on tablecloths laid over the sand they fell upon it like starved refugees and proceeded to devour with enormous gusto three times the amount of food that would have satisfied them at home. The women, except for Kate who disdained such female activities, bustled about waiting on the men, dividing cakes and pies, passing sandwiches, pouring coffee, opening cans of olives and bottles of pickles. Mrs. Crosby had done herself proud. They were full of picnic mirth and jollity, full of squeals and giggles and guffaws and chatter about this and that.

When the edge of hunger was dulled Mr. Crosby and Mr. McCumber got into a discussion of some weighty male matter that had to do with stocks, shares and dividends. Their talk sounded earnest and wordy, but Rhoda noticed with malicious satisfaction that there was an absent look in Mr. McCumber's eyes and that he was not giving Mr. Crosby his whole attention. Dan Stoner told stories to Junie and Willetta about when he was a boy back in Georgia, about floods and forest fires and rattlesnakes and bears and bobcats. Mrs. Crosby talked earnestly with Mrs. Doble about rheumatism, its cause and cure. In the course of this conversation she discovered quite by accident that Mrs. Doble's family had once lived in the vicinity of the identical Missouri town in which her own youth had been passed.

"Well I declare, and so you belonged to the Wilkins family! Why I remember your father Tom Wilkins real well. Many and many a time he helped dad to butcher a hog. My sister Georgie and I used to run and hide under the bed so we wouldn't hear the squeals. Just think, Henry, Mrs. Doble was a Wilkins from Toddville. Well well, isn't it wonderful how small the world is after all. Do you remember that white house on the hill just as you went out of town on Belcher's Pike? That was where we lived. Well well, it does seem strange doesn't it?"

Of course Mrs. Doble thought it seemed strange. There was no end to their discussion of old times, old places and people.

Cliff and Thatch and Andy Blake sprawled on the sand and talked about guns, about dogs, about Ford cars, about the Mexican from the other side of the ditch who was jailed day before yesterday for getting drunk and trying to knife his wife. Junie and Willetta ran about picking up stones and pebbles that took their fancy and strange lava rocks perforated with holes, queer shaped things that made one think of skulls. The smoke of the campfire and the rattle of dishes, the idle laughter and talk, the litter of paper plates and tin cups and sandwiches and pickle bottles and orange peels made an impertinent little fleck on the silent and motionless bosom of the desert.

When they had eaten to repletion they dozed, stretched and smoked. Whenever Kate and Rhoda accepted cigarets Mrs. Crosby always looked a little uncomfortable and disapproving. She did not mind it so much in Kate, but she thought it a shame that Rhoda had been led astray. Rhoda caught a pained half glance from Mr. McCumber's eye and inhaled with deeper satisfaction. Dan Stoner lay down on his stomach and let Junie and Willetta cover him with sand. Mrs. Crosby and Mrs. Doble still talked about the good old days back in Toddville.

Rhoda took advantage of a moment when nobody was noticing to slip away by herself. She knew that soon they would begin to wander off in twos and threes to explore the strange neighborhood and she did not want Mr. McCumber as a companion. Peeping from behind a clump of desert shrubbery she saw them all wander away as she had expected, all except the two who had been born in Toddville. They were so deep in talk that they did not notice the departure of the others.

Rhoda followed in the wake of the explorers keeping at a distance and unseen, skirting about behind greasewood and cacti, then crossed the boulder-strewn stretch of ground to the base of the mountain and began to climb.

It was hard going. Again and again she careened and almost fell when loose stones turned beneath her feet or when she had miscalculated her balance on the tough surfaces. She clambered over boulders, picked her way perilously along ledges and the brinks of deep fissures, clung to the jutting surfaces to keep from slipping. When she was not watching her feet she was scanning the side of the mountain to see where the others were. From time to time she glimpsed Mr. McCumber scrambling vigorously over rocks and boulders and having a hard time to keep up with Thatch and Cliff. But she was attentively watching and carefully considering the movements of someone else. A little later her cunning was rewarded for quite as if by accident on rounding a big boulder she came face to face with Andy Blake alone.

"Hello Rhoda, what do you think of Mount Signal on close acquaintance?"

She felt her cheeks burning with something more than the exertion of the climb, and in her confusion her eyes failed to focus, making the rocks and the sky and Andy Blake's face flow together as if seen through running water.

"I think I've climbed about as far as I want to go," she panted, looking up at the rocks that now rose in precipitous and beetling walls.

"Me too for the easy downward path. I'm afraid I've got no more pride of muscle and agility than a mere female. Not so however your friend McCumber; he's bound he's going to show Cliff and Thatch and old man Doble that he can shake as limber a leg as any of 'em. He's most black in the face with the effort, but you've got to hand it to him that he's got pluck."

"He's got vanity, you mean—and don't call him a friend of mine."

"It's hot as hell up here. Let's go down and get under a tree."

They found the "easy downward path" much more difficult and hazardous than the ascent, and most of the way they went crab fashion, clinging for dear life to the rocks.

"Not so heroic, but a hell of a lot safer," gasped Andy.

The shade of the desert tree under which they sat breathing hard and mopping their faces after they reached the bottom seemed almost chilly by comparison with the bright seething heat of the bare mountainside.

"The sky is a great deal bluer here even than in the Valley," she said, fanning herself with her hat.

"Yes, of course it's much drier here—and then contrast of color has a lot to do with it."

How hot it was out there beyond the tent of shade. How blue the sky, how white the sand, how black the shadows, and what an immense and brooding silence everywhere.

Andy had stretched out face downward on the sand and found himself looking directly into a hill of red ants. He stirred the surface of the hill gently with a bit of sun-bleached twig.

"Did it ever occur to you, Rhoda, that there might be somewhere in the universe a race of beings to whom we are just as puny and insignificant as these ants are to us?"

"I hadn't thought anything about it."

"What a commotion I can stir up among the poor little devils with this bit of stick. They've completely lost their heads now and go chasing this way and that and bumping into each other and wringing their hands just as we'd do if we were overtaken by a flood or earthquake. Once I worked in a lumber camp up in Washington and my pal and I—Shorty we called him because he was six feet two in his socks—used to wage holy war on the bedbugs. Every so often when they got too thick we'd tote out the kerosene can and take everything off our bunks and pour the cracks full of kerosene. The bugs 'ud come swarming out of those cracks, big and little, scrambling for dear life to make their getaway, only to be drowned in a flood of kerosene when they thought they had reached a place of safety. It was tragic and piteous, come to look at it that way. Mothers running about seeking distractedly for their little ones, lovers annihilated in the very act of the first coy kiss, babies dead before they were born, the sick murdered in their beds, the newly married torn from each other's arms, families separated, plans frustrated, hopes brought to nothing, misery and anguish without end, eh?"

He turned his head and cocked his eye up at her with a look of waggish inquiry.

"You shouldn't talk that way. It's too serious a matter to joke about—for people I mean, not bedbugs."

"That's just the point I want to make. How do you know the bedbugs didn't feel the same way about it? It occurred to me when we were pouring in that kerosene that back away down in the small chinks where the stuff couldn't get and the survivors lived to painfully build up a new civilization all over again that the bedbug newspapers must be red with big headlines about the terrible disaster that had occurred, and the bedbug wrecking crews and policemen and mayors and city councils and club women and looters and social workers and clergymen and relief corps and ambulance drivers and Salvation Army captains must be busy as the devil clearing away the wreckage and succoring the wounded and getting away with what they could and shooting down the looters and telling somebody else what to do and quieting the mob and comforting the widows and binding up the wounds and rushing provisions and supplies to the spot and preaching sermons to the people about how it was a judgment of the Lord upon them for their evil ways. And I suppose among all the busy useful fellows there'd be sure to be some cynical, good-for-nothing old Diogenes of a bedbug that wouldn't lift a hand to help, but only shrug his shoulders and say, 'Oh hell, we multiply fast and it'll be all the same a week or two from now.' And all this because Shorty and I had scratched a little too much for perfect rest the night before."

A laugh and a shudder struggled for possession of her. The shudder stifled the laugh and she said: "I don't like to hear you talk so flippantly about things like that. It sounds—somehow—cruel and inhuman."

"Of course it's cruel and inhuman. It was a ghastly cruel and inhuman thing for Shorty and me to massacre those innocent bedbugs in their own homes, flood out their cities, their schools and colleges and art museums and demolish their civilization."

"You know I don't mean it that way."

"You don't mean it that way? Well then you're the one who is cruel and inhuman. Look here, supposing there is, as there well may be, a race of beings as superior to us as we are superior to bedbugs, and one of them by moving his little finger can cause an earthquake that kills thousands of us and horribly maims thousands more. And a woman among them, a fastidious, bedbug-hating Jane like you, says it doesn't matter, they're only pests and should be exterminated. But the man who did the deed—that's me—scratches his chin thoughtfully and says, 'poor devils, they've got feelings too and it looks as if the difference between us was only in degree, not kind, and it's a dirty shame they had to live if they can't live unmolested.' I put it to you, which of these two is the most cruel and inhuman?"

He glanced at her sidewise with a perversely prankish leer. She felt nettled and frustrated.

"You're trying to make fun of me because I haven't as much imagination as you. That isn't very kind of you, is it?"

A swift look of pained embarrassment passed across his face.

"Oh no, surely you wouldn't think that of me. The ideas just came into my head and I spat them forth. I won't say another word about bedbugs—or people either."

There was silence for a time while they sifted the clean, dry sand between their fingers, idly picked up and threw down rocks and pebbles of odd shapes and colors. She tried to pull a frond from a Spanish dagger plant that grew nearby, but the thing seemed made of iron. Andy took out his jack-knife and cut it away for her.

"They grew tough to stand the wear and tear, like little slum kids," he said, handing it to her.

She ran her finger thoughtfully along its smooth length

that ended in a point as long, strong and sharp as a big darning needle.

"What a cruel weapon. With this thing I could easily put out your eye or stab you in the heart or the stomach or anywhere I liked," she said with a whimsical little smile.

"Yes the desert seems cruel—and yet in a way kind too. See how beautifully clean it keeps everything, these stones and sands and lava rocks, how wonderfully and fearfully clean. A fierce purity like the purity of fire. If man had let the Imperial Valley alone it would still be all like this—only more so because it was a drier desert—fierce and pure and with a sort of savage nobility, and in it there would be no filth nor noise, no pain, no drudgery, no greed, no petty striving, no climbing over the bodies of others. I sometimes think it would have been better so."

"I've had thoughts sometimes like that myself. But it seems strange to hear you say a thing like that, you who are always whistling and laughing and seem to take everything so lightly."

"Do I whistle and laugh too much?"

"More than most people. You always seem so happy," she went on with a touch of wistfulness. "Don't you remember the other day I asked you how you felt and you said you were as brisk as a body louse and merry as a beggar."

"Did I say I was all that? One thing I'll have to admit, it wasn't original with me. A very great writer said it several hundred years ago."

"Well anyway that's what you said you were. And how can you say that and in the same breath wish the Valley had been left a desert?"

"But it wasn't in the same breath; I've breathed hundreds of thousands of times since I said that the other day. But fact is I *am* happy a good part of the time. I must have still a good deal of the kid in me, for when the sun comes up into this big sky and shoots the blue mist over the mountains full of pink and the morning air blows in my face and a little old meadow lark sits on a fence post and sings, why I'm born again, just like the earth, and all the reason in the world doesn't keep me from feeling as brisk as a body louse and as merry as a beggar."

"You're a very strange fellow."

"That's what everybody says."

There was a dryness in this last reply, something that shut her away from him, and she wished she had not said that he was strange.

He lay flat on his stomach building a pigpen out of small dry twigs, the kind of pen that children might make out of matches or clothespins. Then they put something in the middle to be the pig and then they put the roof on. She watched him wistfully and again she wished she had not made that silly remark about his being strange. She thought of the books on the shelf in his little shack. Perhaps she could reach him that way.

"Are you fond of reading?"

"I used to be, but I'm not any more," he answered indifferently.

He had demolished the pigpen and was drawing diagrams in the sand. She felt that he had no desire to continue the conversation. She sat in silence for a long time playing with the pebbles and lava rocks, sifting the sand through her fingers, gazing out abstractedly across the bright, blinding spaces beyond their sheltering tent of shadow. She felt baffled and lonely.

Glancing toward him she saw that he had drawn a notebook from his pocket and was scratching in it with a stub of pencil. At the risk of being again rebuffed she asked him what he was writing.

"A little flight of fancy that the desert suggested to me."

"Do let me look at it."

He handed her the notebook open at the page where he had been writing. She puzzled for a few moments over his illegible scrawl, then managed to make out:

If our bones were left to bleach on the blond sand
Under the deep sapphire brilliance of the sky
They would soon be clean and pure, as all things are clean and pure in the desert.
The sand slips through our fingers,
As through an hour glass;
But it is so quiet here that surely time is asleep.
Hush—let us not wake him.

A shiver crept over her and she felt suddenly cold in the midst of the heat and glare.

"What strange notions you have. Why should you think of such a thing?"

Again she had called him strange. Why had she done that?

"Why not think of it?" he asked. "When I see how beautifully the strong, dry sunlight purified everything I can imagine no better resting place for my bones."

"But why think of it at all?"

"Again why not? We're all going to die some time, and why not face the fact?

'Life is a feast and we have banqueted—
Shall not the worms as well?

And anyway what difference does it make in the scheme of the universe—what tiniest scrap of difference—whether you and I are sitting here talking together or have passed into the dry bone stage and are lying scattered on the sand? The big works go on without interruption in any case, just as they kept going on after Shorty and I cleaned our bunks. Do you remember those lines in Coventry Patmore's poem?

'The truth is great, and shall prevail
When none cares whether it prevail or not?'

A sense of dreary vastness, of being lost in a bleak and immeasurable solitude settled upon her and chilled her to the bone.

A great bird, an eagle probably, winged above them in the intense blue. Its purple shadow, silent as the hand of a ghost, flitted across the white sand and was gone. Andy followed it with his eyes.

"It should have come a little sooner so that I could have included it in the free verse. Perhaps I'll work it over and put in the eagle."

Then with a sudden change of mood he leapt to his feet.

"Come Rhoda, let's steal up stealthily upon what's left of the lunch. This desert air has filled me with a devastating urge to eat. There's something stimulating after all in the thought that we've made ourselves masters here, that we can eat and prance in this place where if the desert had its way we'd writhe and die. It inspires me with the thought of Mrs. Crosby's sandwiches and stuffed olives. Come on, let's eat and prance while the prancing's good."

But she could not change her mood with his; she could not shake off the heavy mantle of gloom that he had thrown upon her.

When they got back to the picnic place Mrs. Crosby and Mrs. Doble were still talking about old times in Toddville.

CHAPTER 22

ONE AFTERNOON when the girls went into the milking barn they found the others gathered in an excited knot by the dairy house. Junie was crying bitterly.

"I know damn well he'd never be able to pull off that stuff an' git away with it," Thatch was saying.

"It's Dan Stoner," said Cliff in answer to Rhoda's inquiry. "He's been pinched."

"Pinched? What for?"

"Search me. I'll be hanged if I kin git it through my noodle. Ask Andy."

"For criminal syndicalism," said Andy Blake.

His face was hard and set as if cast in bronze. It seemed like somebody else's face. It was unimaginable to Rhoda that these cold, stern features had ever relaxed to the play of fancy, to laughter and foolishness.

Criminal syndicalism! It sounded like something very terrible.

"But what did he do?" she asked, wide-eyed with amazement.

"Well ever since he came here he's been going around the Mexican workers all through the Valley, the fellows that cut corn and pick melons and crate lettuce and all that sort of thing, and talking to them about the things they're up against and giving them pamphlets printed in Spanish telling them they ought to organize to get better working conditions and more pay."

"And they put him in jail for that?"

"Yes."

"But how could they?"

"Because there's a law in California that says they can."

"Some darn dirty stool pigeon squealed on him," put in Thatch. "The same lousy breed that got me an' Dutch in bad up in Oregon for makin' the boys a little throat tickler. Say I wish I had—"

Thatch expressed a wish regarding stool pigeons that it is not seemly to set down in print.

"Mind you keep a decent tongue in your head, Thatch," admonished his father. "Remember there's wimmin standin' by."

"I don't give a damn. There ain't nothin' my tongue kin think of that kin tell half what I want to about them mangy, lickspittlin' curs, lettin' on they belong to yer gang an' slinkin' an' spyin' an' then runnin' an' tattlin' as soon as they git the goods on yuh. Gawd, anybody'd think there wa'n't a man breathed so low as to be a stool pigeon, an' yet the hull damn country's chuck full of 'em. Every place you step they're underfoot."

"Well Thatch," drawled his father, "you was goin' dead agin the law with the Volstead Act on the books. You had no kick comin' when they pinched you."

"I didn't say I had any kick comin'. I didn't hold nothin' agin the law. But by Gawd I sure did have it in fer that filthy skunk of a stool pigeon that asked me where could I git him a drink. Golly if I could right away sunk my fingers in his gullet he wouldn't a drawed no more dirty breaths."

Later when Rhoda found herself milking near Andy Blake she reopened the subject of Dan Stoner.

"How could there be such a law as that?"

"I'm afraid it's all too simple. The people who have things want to keep them—for themselves and their children—and the more they have the more they want. And as they have the money and hence the power they get the courts to decide that nobody must try to take anything away from them."

"But I thought the courts were supposed to administer justice."

"That's a pleasant little fiction."

He went on milking in silence and his face still wore the same set, cold look. She felt that he did not want to talk and asked no further questions. Only as he was moving away with his brimming bucket, she asked: "And will he have to stay in jail until his trial?"

"I'm going to ask Crosby if he'll do anything; but I haven't much hope."

The next morning she asked him if he had spoken to Mr. Crosby.

"Yes, and he's sitting tight. He said he liked Dan personally but his ideas were dangerous; and anyway he couldn't do anything in a case like this, it would hurt his business."

He walked away and left her. The expression on his face had not changed.

"Kate, why couldn't we go his bond?" she asked abruptly as they were driving home.

"Whose bond? Dan Stoner's? Why bless your heart we've

got no security to offer. With our place and our cows both mortgaged up to the hilt we'd look like thirty cents trying to go anybody's bail."

Rhoda sat silent, feeling like a rebuked child.

The following Sunday at the Crosbys' she watched for an opportunity to speak to Mr. McCumber in private. It was the first time that she had ever sought him out, and his face lit up with pleasure. It was apparent that he was ready and anxious to forgive her for the things she had said to him on the Mount Signal drive.

"Do you remember that fellow who was here to dinner a few Sundays ago, the one who told about being tarred and feathered here in the Valley? Dan Stoner his name is—he was arrested the other day."

Mr. McCumber's features showed a slight tendency to become rigid.

"Yes, I heard about his arrest."

"I wonder if you would be willing to go bail for him?"

A shadow crossed his face, the shadow that so often crosses the faces of people who own things. A hot wave of anger surged up in her.

"You don't need to say a single thing. I know you won't."

"Now lookit here, I didn't say I wouldn't. But it's this way—"

She deliberately turned her back and walked away from him. He came after her.

"But say, see here, what's the big idea in going off mad? I haven't said a word one way or the other."

"You don't need to."

"Say listen now, you're entirely mistaken about the way I feel about that fella. I don't bear him any personal grudge whatever even if he did as good as tell me the other Sunday that I was a fool and a liar. But what I want you to understand is that I know all about this man's sort; I know exactly where to place him and I know that he and his kind are dangerous enemies of society."

"I don't believe for a moment that he is a dangerous enemy of society."

"Of course you don't—and I don't blame you a bit. Those birds always do manage to line up the ladies on their side. They throw a spiel that the women all swallow hook, line and sinker. But I tell you I've been up and down and crossways on the old U.S.A. and I know what I'm talking about. Another thing, if I go bail for this fella it'll put me in Dutch with a lot of people that I have business dealings with. But I don't care a fig about that; all you have to do is to say the word and I'll do it."

He tried to fix her with his eyes.

"I certainly shall not say the word," she snapped and left him.

That same afternoon Mrs. Crosby drew Rhoda aside.

"Say I'm just terribly sorry about young Stoner; I hardly slept the night after I heard about his being arrested. I thought when he first came to work for us what a nice face he had and nice quiet way with him; but Henry says he has awfully inflammatory ideas that would simply wreck everything if they were put into practice. It's strange isn't it how many of those nice quiet young fellows have such wild ideas. I just hate to think of his having been put into jail, but I suppose he brought it on himself."

"How do you mean 'brought it on himself'?" asked Rhoda, still hot-cheeked from her encounter with Mr. McCumber.

"Well you see, in that case where he claims to have been tarred and feathered, it would have been so simple for him to have just bought the liberty bond like the other boys and saved himself all that. And of course if he hadn't been distributing inflammatory literature to the Mexicans he wouldn't have been arrested."

The next day there came for Rhoda in the mail one of those large, excessively ornate boxes of candy that women who are not being courted see only in the windows of confectionary and drug stores. She pushed the open box, paper lace, trailing ribbons and all, across the table to Kate.

"Isn't it kind and condescending of him? The baby can't have the slice off the moon, so we'll give it a stick of candy instead. You can have them all. I wouldn't eat one for a million dollars."

"This is one time when li'l Katy gets some good outa the ill wind," said Kate reaching for the chocolates.

Later, because she was very candy hungry, Rhoda surreptitiously ate three, then hated herself because she hadn't been as good as her word.

It turned out that such efforts were useless anyway. Andy Blake came back from a visit to Dan with the news that he would not accept any bail, he would remain in jail until his trial.

Thatch too went to see him and on his return was more communicative than Andy.

"It's gonna pan out all right about Dan," he assured Rhoda when he found himself near her at the milking. "After I left him in jail I was loafin' along the street an' I happened into a pool room an' there I run into the deputy sheriff. He's allus been a purty good friend o' mine, the deputy sheriff, an' I got to talkin' to him about Dan. He was purty well jagged at the time on some bootlegger's hooch, an' mebbe that's why he didn't keep his mouth as shet as he might a done. He gits me over in a corner an' he says, 'Doble,' says he, 'don't you worry about that pal o' yourn. He won't stay in jail. Ded gast it all' he says 'I didn't wanta pinch the man, but it was the law, an' a sheriff's gotta kinder look like he was tryin' to enforce the law. But Lord love you I know he ain't done nothin' to git jail fer, an' I ain't been handlin' men fer twenty years not to know with half a eye the feller's a better man than I am myself. Me an' the sheriff an' the warden was talkin' it over the other day. We don't want him in the jail no more'n we want a suckin' baby there, an' as soon as a good chanct shows up we'll jes quietly send him out to mow the lawn an' let him know we'll be lookin' the other way. It's dollars to doughnuts nobody won't make no fuss.' So I reckon, Rhody, Dan'll be outa the State before so very long."

But Dan did not go out of the State, nor even out of the El Centro jail.

"I allus thought he was bugs an' naow I know it," said Thatch disgustedly on return from a visit to his friend. "I like Dan fine, there ain't nobody I like better, but damn it all he's loony as a bedbug. There he sets an' fries in that hot hole—Gawd it's hotter'n hell inside them cement walls with on'y them little barred winders fer air—an' says he won't stir foot off the place till they've give him a trial. Kin yuh beat it?"

"Why doesn't he go?" Rhoda asked Andy Blake who she felt was better acquainted with Dan's psychology than Thatch.

"He says it would hurt his cause if he sneaked away and avoided the issue. He says that now they've arrested him, they've got to try him and find him guilty if they can. He's quite determined to stick it out."

"Do you think they'll find him guilty?"

"Probably."

The hard and stern expression that had frozen Andy Blake's features when Dan was arrested had relaxed with the passing of the days, leaving him more like his old careless self. He was sometimes heard to laugh now and to whistle as he went about his work. But often Rhoda noticed a listlessness in his step and a tired sagging of the shoulders. At such times a veil seemed to hang before his eyes, his face was sad and thoughtful and she noticed about the mouth wrinkles that she had not seen there before. He was like this on the day that she asked him about Dan. After he had finished with his cow he came, to her surprise and confusion, and stood by her side as she milked, leaning against the cow's shoulder.

"A present-day Jesus would be just such another as Dan,"

he said, looking down absently at the sharp streams of milk.

"What do you mean?"

"Just what I've said, that if Jesus were alive today he'd be just such a man as Dan, simple, without education, yet knowing a whole lot more than all the doctors of philosophy, and burning his heart out with the longing to regenerate mankind. And if Jesus were alive and here in the Valley today he'd be friends with just such people as Dan is friends with: children and work shattered women and Mexicans and bums, and milkers like you and me, and all the rest of the riff-raff. And he'd be despised by just the sort of people who despise Dan, by the politicians and preachers and educators and business men, by all such people as Crosby and that fat-necked McCumber fellow that Dan had the run-in with the other Sunday. Say that was a scream, wasn't it? I actually and literally nearly bust a gut trying to keep a sober face."

The melancholy look passed from his face and for a moment his old smile beamed forth like sunlight from behind clouds.

"The Crosbys and Mr. McCumber say that Dan is a dangerous character."

"Of course they do. The same sort of people said Jesus was a dangerous character, and they considered him so dangerous that they nailed him up on the Cross. They're likely to do much the same thing to Dan."

"I like Dan very much indeed and I don't think he's dangerous; but I've never been able to get really acquainted with him. He's always kept pretty much to himself."

"Yes, he's inclined to be solitary, and he's shy too; but he and I sort of took to each other from the start and in these few months that we've bunked together we've come to be damn good friends. I tell you, Rhoda, humanity doesn't deserve a man like Dan any more than it deserved a man like Jesus."

"I judge from a number of things you've said that you haven't a very high opinion of humanity in general."

"How can I? I'd give my eye teeth to be like Dan and believe that the human race was worth regenerating; but the facts as I see 'em won't let me. You know some of the scientists tell us that it was only by merest chance that the primates happened to develop beyond the other animals. The big lizards had a head start of them and by just such another mere chance were stopped before they got very far. Now somehow I can't help thinking that if some nice clean self-respecting animal that seems to have good and decent impulses and knows how to mind its own business, like the horse or the dog for instance, or even the remote ancestors of good old Spotty here, had been privileged to develop that we'd have today a saner, a kinder and a happier world."

She looked up at him with eyes full of pain and reproach.

"If you think the world is so bad and people so hopeless I don't think you ought to make a joke of it."

"My dear girl I'm not joking. I was never more serious in my life. All you need to do to convince yourself that the development of the human was a mistake is to visit the monkey cages of any zoo. There in the monkey cages among the descendants of those who they tell us were closely akin to our own ancestors you can see all the vicious traits that make our present-day society the mess it is. Vanity and libidinousness, jealousy and greed and petty knavery and the abuse of power and privilege are all on view in the monkey cage just as they are on view all over the world wherever you set your feet. Only among human beings these vices are vastly more complex and powerful and they are reinforced by hate and fear and cloaked by piety and self-righteousness, modesty, pride and duplicity, so that there is no fighting them in the open. That's the kind of world we have to put up with and the kind of passions we have to struggle with in ourselves all the days of our life. Whereas now supposing good old towser's ancestors—"

"Hey Andy, come on an' play ball."

It was Thatch's voice calling. The milking was over and

in the stimulating cool of the evening the young Dobles were spoiling for a game of ball. Already they were taking their positions in the nearly empty corral.

"All right Thatch, I'll be along in a minute," Andy called over his shoulder. Then to Rhoda: "Honest, I bet anything dogs or horses would have made a damn sight better job of governing the world. The Creator made an error of judgment and so here we are."

He lifted one shoulder in an unconcerned shrug and sauntered away. A few minutes later she heard his voice raised with the others in the game and saw him legging it from base to base apparently as happy and careless as little Junie. He seemed to have quite forgotten his somber and sardonic mood and all the things that he had said. She wished that she too had a life in which she could forget herself, shake off sad and evil moods and be gay and carefree. But for her there was no such soothing alternative. All the way home and all the rest of the evening until she fell asleep in her cot under the stars she pondered over his strange dark sayings.

CHAPTER 23

A STORM HAD come into the Valley, or what people called a storm; not one of the swirling windstorms that darkened the sun with dust and set the littered dooryards swirling, but the outer fringe of a coast rainfall that had seeped over the mountains and through the passes. For three days the sky was overcast and from time to time a few warm drops of rain fell. All day long through the soft gray stillness Rhoda heard the doves calling plaintively. On sunny days she did not hear them or did not notice their gentle croon; but now their soft insistent voices were continually afloat upon the quiet grayness. Released from the tension of the strong sunlight she moved as if in a dream world where the edges of everything were blurred. At the chores and at the milking she went about her work curiously shut in and folded down upon herself, conscious only of the soft enveloping grayness, of the softly crooning voices of the doves and with only one thought in her mind, that she loved him, that she loved him. Soft like gray velvet the atmosphere, soft like gray velvet the voices of the doves. All the sounds in the corral: the rattle of the cans, the purr of the streams of milk, the voices of the milkers seemed faint and far away and only the calling of the doves came to her through the brooding grayness. "I love him, I love him," the doves were saying. All day long through the soft quiet they kept saying it over and over with crooning melancholy voices.

In the afternoon of the third day it grew suddenly cooler and toward evening a wind tore the clouds apart, set them scudding in battalions along the horizon and rolled them into great fleecy masses with intense blue lakes between. The sun sank behind cloud mountain piled upon cloud mountain, all blazing with the sumptuous colors of the desert sky. From her cow's flank Rhoda watched the great fire burn ever brighter and hotter, then imperceptibly soften and fade. In the very heart of the sunset a single tall sentinel palm stood black and motionless like something that laughs at fire.

A little later when the milking was over and she stood by the car at the roadside waiting for Kate the whole world was suffused in a soft golden radiance. Two horsemen came cantering along the dusty road larger than life and aureoled in a cloud of glory, like angels on the last day. Then swiftly it began to grow dark.

Still Kate did not come. Only the black eucalyptus trees and the white tops of the Mexican tents showed above the ditch bank on the other side of the road, and over them a single blue line of smoke rose straight up into the clear air. Far away the bordering mountain range stretched its length along the sky line shadowy and vague; but in the middle distance the great cone of Mount Signal detached itself from the atmosphere in clear steel grays and rich, deep cobalt blues with unfathomable depths of purple shadow. Streaks of the fading sunset ran behind its northern side, but to the south the sky behind it was like a solid sheet of burnished steel. The thin blue line of smoke fluttered into shreds of vapor as it rose before Mount Signal, drifted lazily across the steel grays and cobalt blues, floated against the amber and saffron bars of sunset.

As Rhoda looked the column of smoke grew thicker, flames shot up quick tongues from behind the ditch and she knew that the people there were preparing to cook their meal under the sky as for untold ages their ancestors had done. One of their men was strumming on a stringed instrument and singing in his throaty native tongue a monotonous weird-sounding chant that was more like an incantation than a song. Out of the deep shadow beyond the ditch there came with his singing the rattle of harness, the braying of a mule, children calling to each other and a woman's laugh. All the dirt, the rags, the litter were out of sight and as if they had never been and there was left music, fire, the smell of wood smoke on cool, clean air, fantastic trees outlined in black against the flames, smoke veiling the blue and purple mountains, smoke mingling with the sunset, the kettle bubbling under faint stars, food and drink and love. A deep nostalgia for something that she felt she must have known somewhere, sometime, gnawed at her heart as she gazed across at the flames licking out of the black shadow and beyond to the cold grays and blues of Mount Signal and the fading streaks of sunset. If only she had been born to eat and sleep by a gipsy fire under the high tent of the sky with a great purple mountain standing guard, to sing when she was happy, to step forward and boldly wrest from the arms of her rival the man of her choice, to love gladly, carelessly, fiercely—

She turned her head with a swift, sharp movement to watch

a man cross the road from the milking corral and go down on the other side. His step was almost as free and panther-like as Cliff's, but his shoulders were not so heavy. Though it had grown almost dark she knew at a glance who it was and after the foolish little flutter that always assailed her at sight of him had passed away, a cold heaviness settled about her heart. Why was she always shut away from everything?

When he had passed out of sight she crossed over to the other side of the road with movements sly and lithe like a cat's and peered furtively down through the eucalyptus boughs. She saw him pick his way through the litter, saw him pause for a moment to speak to an old woman who was gathering sticks for the fire, then pass on and join the group about the blaze. Against the ruddy play of flames the people nearest her were silhouetted in black, like figures in a shadow play; but beyond the fire she could see colors and the play of expression on fire lighted faces. On the other side of the fire a girl in a yellow jacket and a purple skirt, coarse and crude colored rags enough, but picturesquely beautiful on her slim body, was frying tortillas over a bed of coals. She was the same girl whom Rhoda had seen standing beside Angie on the ditch bank. As Andy Blake joined the group that was outlined in black against the flames, this girl lifted her head and cast a look across the fire. In that moment the suspicion that Rhoda had been harboring for a long time was confirmed; she knew unmistakably now where she had seen the girl before. She had worn a salmon colored skirt that day when she had first seen her and a red handkerchief tied about her head.

A black wave of jealousy and hate engulfed her; she wished herself a tiger that she might spring down on them from her ambush and tear them to pieces. She was sorry that she had ever bathed his wounds. Why hadn't the two men killed him that night instead of letting him live to make her life wretched? What was he that he should be happy and careless in a life shut away from her while she pined in lonely misery? And she—a doltish Mexican girl with thick ankles—what right had she to have him?

"Rhoda for Pete's sake come on. Why are you hanging over the ditch there as if you were sick at your stomach? We'll be devilish late getting home as it is and I'm most starved. Just as I was pulling out Willetta came up to me with a bunch of decimal sums she wanted explained. I done my damnedest, but I don't think the kid knows a thing more than before I started; she's about as bright as a twenty-year-old penny."

There was water on that night and it was Kate's turn to attend to it.

"I'll go if you like," offered Rhoda. "I've got a stuffy headache and I think a little fresh air would do me good."

"Far be it from me to stop you. There isn't a thing interests me just now but sleep, so if I don't have to go out I'll turn in."

She began to discard her clothes as she spoke and before Rhoda left the house she was asleep.

Rhoda did not even look to see if the fields were watered to the ends. She turned off the water and slipped stealthily away.

The moon three-quarters-old was shedding a gray diffused light over the fields, but along the little bypath that led to Andy Blake's melon-crate house it was black with shadow from the eucalyptus trees with only here and there a patch of gray moonlight. As she hurried along she avoided the moonlit spots, slinking sidewise into the bordering shadow. Like a thief she trod softly, started at the crackle of a twig under her feet, skulked in the shadow and paused to listen and peer. Once a Johnny owl whizzed past her and uttered in her ear its harsh hysterical screech. To her taut nerves it was like an arresting hand and a blow in the face. She made a faint noise that was the beginning of a scream, then clapt her hands over her mouth.

A little further on she saw before her the melon-crate house dimly outlined in the gray moonlight. As if a ghost had reached out and seized her from behind she stood stock still.

Why had she come here, she asked herself like a sleep walker suddenly awakened, and why was she on her way to that place ahead of her?

All at once it seemed to her a terrible, an unspeakable thing that she should be where she was, that nothing so abandoned, so shameless had ever been done or even thought of before, that she was the first, the only woman who had ever rushed out into the night to thrust herself upon a man who did not want her. A panic fear like the instinct of a deer before hounds took hold of her, laid a tight and painful clutch upon her shrinking heart as she turned and fled backward the way she had come.

She had no more than started when she saw him coming toward her, first the light of his cigaret tip, then in a patch of moonlight the outline whose every detail she knew by heart. There was no time to hide, she too was in the middle of a patch of moonlight and he could not help seeing her. She stood paralyzed, her mouth dry. Her heart seemed to have stopped beating.

"Why Rhoda, is that you? I thought you girls always hit the hay long before this time of night. Nothing the matter I hope."

"Nothing of any account." Her parched tongue stuck to her parched palate, but she managed by a mighty effort to get out the words. "Only when we came to milk tonight one of our cows was missing and I thought she might have strayed in this direction. But I haven't seen any signs of her. Probably she's still in the pasture, just lain down somewhere, and she'll be with the rest in the morning."

"I hope so. With all the work you girls have to do, hunting for strayed cattle must be about the last straw. By the way, Dan's trial was today; Thatch and I have just come back from El Centro. They've sentenced him to ten years in the penitentiary."

"Ten years? In the penitentiary?" She repeated it after him in a dull, stunned way with a note of question.

"Yes, that's what they give you these days for loving your neighbor as yourself."

"But why didn't you go to the trial and testify for him?"

"He made me promise not to, said they'd like enough pinch me too after they heard what I had to say, the way they did with some fellows up the State a while back. Anyway I knew my testimony would do him more harm than good, so I didn't insist. Well goodnight, I'll try to sleep some of it off."

His voice had a flat, dead sound, like the voice of one who is very, very tired and as she looked after him she saw that his step dragged. Slunk back in the shadow she watched his retreating figure blur into the darkness, saw the glowing stub of his cigaret fall upon the path, then sank down at the foot of a eucalyptus tree huddled together in an agony of shame and self-despisal.

Later, skulking homeward through the shadows, the thought of the ten years in prison that stretched abysmally before Dan and the sorrowful preoccupation of Dan's friend made her shrivel into herself with a burning sense of her own pettiness and impertinence. Then she forgot Dan, forgot everything, in a mad desire to rush back, to tell him that she loved him, that she wanted him, that she had more to give him than a common Mexican girl. Then again with a leaden sinking of the heart she saw his listless step, heard the flat, hollow tones of his voice and was smitten once more with the full enormity of her impulse. Shame and self-contempt seared her more mercilessly than ever, but her cheeks would not burn anymore; they were cold, clammy to the touch.

A few days later Thatch observed to her off-handedly one morning that Andy Blake was going away that day.

She would not believe it. Sitting staring out at the horizon past the cow's bulging side, she told herself that it wasn't true, that it couldn't be true. Ever since that night she had kept away from him, had shrunk together with shame and humiliation whenever she had been forced to speak to him. Yet now she could not force herself to face the thought of the milking corral without him.

But at the end of the morning he came to her on his round of goodbyes.

"I'm beating it, Rhoda. Wish me a good journey."

For the first time she saw just a shade of embarrassment cross his face.

"You're really going away?"

"Yes. Since I took to the road I've never stayed so long in one place. I think it's on account of the mornings; they make you feel every day as if you were beginning life all over again. And as a fellow grows older it gets harder to come by that feeling. I've been over half the world and I've never been anywhere where the mornings were just like these. But now that Dan's gone I feel I've got to be hitting the trail again. I think I'll hike along up the State and then into Oregon and Washington."

"Tell me, are you always going to be a hobo?"

"I think so. The life suits me better than anything else I've tried so far. Of course a tramp has to forego many things; but on the whole I find I go lighter without worldly goods. I have a better time and make more friends."

"Of course you haven't always been a tramp."

"No. The accident of birth started me on a much duller and more respectable path; but I couldn't stick to it. I tried a number of 'walks of life' as they call them; but wherever I went I couldn't get away from the pious hypocrisy and the clutching greed. The more I saw of them the more they sickened me."

"And are you free from them now?"

"Fairly so. If people have nothing and are content with nothing they don't need to be hypocrites and they've nothing to be greedy about. I find I get along better with the fellows on the road than with any other sort of men. They're willing to live and let live. They take me for what I am and expect to be taken for what they are and no bones about it. I feel comfortable and at home with them. And really, Rhoda, the actual needs of a man are very simple needs and the world is a great place when you're footloose, heart whole and empty pocketed–anyway it is as long as you can keep out of the cop's clutches."

She was seized with a sudden access of temerity. He was going away and she would never see him again. Then why not say it? She lifted her eyes and looked him bravely in the face with only the faintest little quiver of the mouth.

"I want to ask you a question before you go. You'll think it's terribly impertinent of me, and of course you don't have to answer it unless you like. How was it that that Mexican girl could be–anything to you?"

"You mean Mercedes, Angie's sister?" He looked aside for just a moment, then met her eyes frankly. "Why–Mercedes is very beautiful–and–very approachable. Truly, Rhoda, it's just as simple as that. Three days after I'm gone Mercedes will be quite happy with somebody else. If she had been–not like that–not just as casual as myself–you wouldn't have needed to ask me anything."

"Then you don't ever want to have anything but casual love affairs."

"Of course. Life is full of uncertainties, but one thing I feel sure of and that is that I shall live and die a bachelor, and if I can manage it, a bachelor with a comparatively quiet conscience. Probably in my old age, when the process of disillusionment is quite complete, I'll be a hermit with a long gray beard away off on some lonely mountain slope or on the edge of some desert. Already I can see myself edging that way. What sort of a figure would I cut, a misfit, a ne'er-do-well, a vagabond, falling in love with somebody who would care for me too much? Look here Rhoda, now that I am never going to see you again, let me say one frank word. Do you remember that night when you were out in the garden among the chrysanthemums? Well that night I realized that I would have to pull myself up." A smile sad and whimsical flitted across his face. "Rhoda, if only you had been a man what great old pals we might have been."

"Come on Andy, I'm goin' your way an' I'll give you a lift."

Thatch at the wheel of the Doble's old Ford truck was calling to him.

With a sudden impulsive movement he took both her hands in his and looked intently into her eyes. All the things that he could not put into words, all his subtleties of apology and compassion, all their nearness, all their unbridgeable gulf of separation, all the pain and waste and pity and futility of the crossing of their lives he put into that one parting look.

"Goodbye, Rhoda dear."

She knew that he was glad and relieved to be gone and that she would soon become to him only a vague regret. If only she had known while there was yet time. And only by a hair she had lost him.

CHAPTER 24

THE JADED old car rattled and bumped over the dusty chuck holes leaving a thick cloud behind it. In the back was the empty egg crate and the groceries that they had just bought in El Centro. The eggs had taken another drop in price and had not brought enough to pay for the groceries. There was a heavy water assessment due and it would soon be time to pay the interest on their debt. Kate was in an evil temper; she drove gloomily, recklessly, and did not care how deep the chuck holes. Rhoda was thinking, as she had been thinking ever since he went away, about Andy Blake, wondering where he was, what he was doing, if he had found him a new Mercedes.

"What, another place empty? It looks like everybody's moving out. God I wish we'd never put our money into this damn hole. Now I suppose we're stuck here head over heels in debt to the end of time."

Kate slowed up in front of an oblong shanty that looked like a packing case dumped in the middle of a back yard. There was no tree near it nor shrub nor growing thing of any kind, only the powdery desert dust scattered over with rubbish left by people who had moved away.

"Let's go in and see if they've left anything."

It had become one of Kate's passions, this searching through and around empty houses for things that people had left behind. There was a certain alacrity in the way she got out of the car and a glitter of acquisitiveness in her eye as she picked her way among the scattered rubble, bending over to pick up and throw down again a broken washboard, a dishpan with the bottom eaten out, a chamber pot with a hole in it, a rust riddled toaster, the oil reservoir of a discarded stove.

"Damn little they've left that's any good to anybody," she said scornfully, throwing down a tin wash basin with two holes in the bottom. I thought we might be able to find something to feed calves out of. We're awfully short of calf buckets. Anyway we'll take along these packing boxes; they'll do for hens' nests."

She began to gather together the packing boxes and pile them inside each other, her eyes meanwhile roving over the ground in sharp search.

Rhoda had tried the door and finding it without a lock had gone inside.

"There's some stuff in here Kate," she called through the broken pane of a window.

A dozen or so of glass fruit jars, some of them merely

dusty, some caked inside with dried remains of jam, with turpentine, with cup grease, with all sorts of things that people put into fruit jars, were lying in a tumbled heap in one corner of the room. At sight of them Kate's eyes lit up.

"By George that's one lucky find anyway. That'll save us buying jars for our apricots and grapefruit marmalade. Let's see what else they've left."

She poked into the dark recesses of two cupboards that had been made by setting rough shelves into large packing cases. She got down on her hands and knees and peered underneath a lame and rusted cot. She pulled up a loose board in the floor and lay flat on her stomach to see what might be underneath. All she could see under the floor was a centipede and two pieces of broken brick; but from the cupboards she brought forth five more jars and from under the cot a pair of old shoes. She sat down on the floor and tried on the shoes, then walked about the room testing them out, her face overspread with satisfaction.

"They won't do so badly for milking shoes. There's just one little bust in the side and I can fix that with some of that whang leather I have home, that stuff you know that we found at the Jap's place after they moved away."

"But Kate they look awful; they're men's shoes and they're about three sizes too big for you."

"Well it's a darn sight better to have 'em too big than too small. And what's wrong with their being men's shoes? If I wear men's overalls why shouldn't I wear men's shoes? I tell you they'll come in mighty handy."

It was the look of satisfaction on Kate's face that brimmed Rhoda's cup of disgust. It came over her nauseatingly how low they had sunk, how despicable was this business of pawing over other people's leavings.

"I thought you said when you came here that farming in the West wasn't a penny pinching business," she said drily.

"Oh Lord, are you going to always keep throwing that up to me?"

"I didn't know that I'd ever mentioned it before."

Not another word was said. In silence they gathered up the jars and boxes, stowed them into the back of the car and rattled homeward. Of late there had been a constantly growing friction between the two women, a sense of strain, an increasing irritability on the part of both. More and more often at some remark of the one the other would take offense; instantly there would arise between them a prickly barrier of hostility and they would both sulk in silence for hours or even days.

It seemed to Rhoda as she sat staring blankly across the flat fields that she would rather be anywhere else in the world than here in the company of this bossy woman whose whole thought seemed to be of calf buckets and hens' nests. The whole Valley seemed a hateful jail. If only she were on the other side of the mountains.

All the way home they did not speak to each other, and they went about their afternoon chores and made the trip to the Crosbys' corral in stony silence. Rhoda had taken refuge in her thoughts of Andy Blake and did not know nor care what Kate was thinking about. But when the two women met again after the milking was over the tension had relaxed somewhat and Kate put into Rhoda's hands a bottle of sage honey that Mrs. Doble had given her and said that she would like to have pancakes for supper.

It was while Rhoda was frying the pancakes that evening that the devastating illumination came to her. So suddenly and sharply did it fall that the exact circumstances were engraved indelibly upon her memory. Kate was sitting at the table turning over under the lamp the pages of a farm journal.

"It gives some good pointers here, Rhoda, as to how to tell whether a hen is a good layer or not."

The crashing blow fell with that innocent remark. At that moment it came to Rhoda with sharp, decisive finality that it didn't matter in the least whether hens were good layers or not, whether hens existed or not, whether she herself existed or not, that nothing that had happened or could happen made any difference whatever, because it was all bound to end in nothing. As clearly as she had seen it through the train window there appeared before her eyes a dreary, sodden plain traversed by a deep-rutted road along which two sagging horses pulled a half-mired wagon, the driver a dark, shapeless hulk, his cap pulled down and collar turned up against the drizzle. He was cold, wet, miserable and doomed. When he got to that distant place where the gray sky bent to the gray earth he would fall off, horses, wagon and all, into an immensity of gray, vast and terrible, and that would be the end of him forever. It came to her with smitingly clear conviction that it was the same with herself, with Kate, with the Dobles. They would all flounder along, sapped and driven, until they came to the place where for them the world ended. Then they would fall off into that immensity of gray, vast and terrible, and that would be the end of them forever. Of what use then to plod and struggle forward, to keep up day after day and week after week and month after month and year after year the bitter and unremitting struggle for existence, seeing that existence would inevitably end at last and all the toil and worry and frantic endeavor would come to nothing.

In one instant, in the time that it took her to turn one pancake, these long thoughts took possession of her. In that moment everything that had ever seemed an excuse for living fell away leaving her stark, alone, poised on the sheer edge of the universe. She went on frying cakes, however, and when she had finished set them on the table. Kate looked at her across the redwood boards with sharp irritation.

"For God's sake, Rhoda, take a brace. Losing a few thousand dollars isn't the worst thing that ever happened; and that's all it means even if we do have to give up the place."

"It isn't that. I wasn't thinking anything about the money or the place." Her voice in her own ears sounded sepulchral.

"Well what the hell then? Surely you're not pining after

that good-for-nothing Handy Andy. You look as if somebody had just told you you had cancer or the world was coming to an end before morning. What business have you got to look like that? For the love of Mike don't do it, it gives me the creeps. Lord knows we have enough to put up with without borrowing trouble."

Rhoda made a visible but fruitless effort to change her expression. The piece of pancake that she was trying to swallow tasted like cotton wool and her mouth felt dry like scorched flannel. Her hands and feet had grown cold and numb. She felt as if all her functions as a living creature had ceased and her body was nothing but an empty shell.

When she opened her eyes the next morning she wondered for a moment whence came the strange inner feeling that was both an emptiness and a heaviness. Then she remembered that it was because nothing mattered and there was no use in living. A deadly coldness and oppression settled upon her; she felt starkly alone, isolated from everything about her.

When she went out into the chicken yard to feed the hens she could think only of how soon their silly cackling and singing would be put an end to and they would be simmering in the stew pot to become a few hours later only a few slivers of bones thrown to the dog. As she lagged through the dreary tedium of milking she was obsessed by the thought of the cows as poor suffering creatures doomed to pass every year through all the throes and emotions of maternity only to have their offspring immediately taken from them and after a few years of this meaningless existence to be knocked on the head and used as food to keep alive other creatures more unfortunate and unhappy than themselves because these latter knew beforehand the doom that awaited them. Everywhere she saw nothing but useless striving, futility, the grave. She found herself wondering how these people about her, sunk in such hopeless and abject misery, could still laugh, crack jokes and have no thought beyond the small happenings of their stagnant days. Milking is like plowing, it leaves the mind free to wander, whether on joyous flights or on long gloomy pilgrimages; and as she sat with busy hands and looked at Chester Doble turning his head to spit tobacco juice clear of the bucket, at the thick-legged Willetta vigorously chewing gum while she milked and at Thatch's long puny body sagging like a limp rag against the cow's side, she could see no meaning in nor reason at all for their existence any more than for her own and could think of nothing but the dark end that waited for them and for herself. How could Cliff bellow forth so exuberantly the latest song hit just heard in Mexicali?

Why she asked herself had she never realized all this before? And why had these people about her never realized it? And why had she thought of it at all; why had it come to her in a flash when she was turning that pancake? And why could she not shake it off and forget it as she had shaken off dark thoughts before?

She made a determined effort to shake it off, tried to chat with Thatch about duck hunting and the habits of ground squirrels and Johnny owls, listened to Cliff's account of his last fight in Mexicali, went in to see Mrs. Doble and talked to her about rheumatism and the making of lightbread. But through it all the old heaviness sat darkly upon her and as soon as she was alone again the black curtain of despair fell between her and the sun.

At home she could not lie down for her usual afternoon siesta but went plodding through the dust and the hot glare over to the Pruetts'.

Mrs. Pruett was ironing on the cool end of the porch. She unrolled a "fine shirt" belonging to Mr. Pruett and spread it out on the board.

"I don't never iron the back of a man's shirt," she informed Rhoda, spitting on a fresh iron to see if it was hot enough. "My mother allus used to say it itched a man's shoulder blades to iron the back of his shirt. But I like to do a nice job on the fronts an' cuffs. A course nowadays that folks don't use starch no more a person can't do much with 'em; but if I do say it that hadn't otta I did turn out a nice fine shirt in the days when they had stiff cuffs and bosoms. There was a pleasure too an' a satisfaction in a nice shirt bosom white as snow an' jes as hard an' smooth as glass. But land a mighty these days wimmin don't seem to take no pride in their housework, especially here in Californey where things is so lax. They don't hardly never go down on their knees to scrub a floor; they don't black a stove nor shine a tea kettle. They'll set around an' leave the dishes wait till it's near time fer the next meal, an' they're allus wantin' to be runnin' to taown—all of 'em jes the like o' Ruby Peterson."

"Have you heard anything about Ruby lately?"

"Yes, she's up an' married again—a man with eighty acres over near Brawley somewheres. It's queer haow these widders kin allus ketch another man, an' oftener than not a man with a good piece o' property. It's more than I'm able to explain, although a course I've allus known men ain't got much sense."

She slammed the iron down emphatically on the stand.

"Well it's a good thing for her and the children she's found somebody to provide for them all."

"That's one way o' lookin' at it. But it does seem to me a shame a widder woman like her that ain't lived right kin go out an' pick up a man with eighty acres all in nice thick alfalfa, an' a good quiet modest single girl that's a heap better lookin' than she is an' has a heap nicer ways gits to stay single. It ain't right to my mind."

Rhoda did not feel in the least flustered or embarrassed by Mrs. Pruett's allusion. While Mrs. Pruett was talking an insistent inner voice kept whispering to her that it was of no consequence whatever whether women were good housekeepers or not, whether they married or not, whether they were lax in their morals or not. It would all end the same way in any case, so what did it matter what anybody did?

Mrs. Pruett prattled on. She talked about bed sheets and dress patterns and turkey raising and the activities of the Home Missionary Society. Rhoda tried hard to interest herself in those things; but all the time Mrs. Pruett was vigorously speaking her mind she was thinking that soon even Mrs. Pruett's busy tongue would have no more to say, that they would put her into a hole in the graveyard and forget all about her and her convictions.

It was the same when they went to El Centro to sell their eggs and buy groceries. The place seemed no longer a bustling western town full of life and enterprise, but merely a hill of restless ants that swarmed aimlessly hither and thither, their feverish activity bound to end in nothing. She tried to talk to the grocer, to be chatty with the fat woman at the vegetable stand, to make a little conversation with the taciturn one-eyed man at the feed store who grimly hoisted their hundred pound sacks of feed into the back of the car. But always below the prattle about the weather and the scarcity of vegetables and the superiority of wheat over barley as an egg producer there boomed the heavy undertone of futility, emptiness, despair. The grocer and the vegetable woman and the feed store man were only three of the silly ants that swarmed over the pitiful anthill and she herself one of the puny and wretched insects hideously singled out to be blighted with the curse of seeing herself as she really was. Wherever she went or whatever she did, the same voice spoke to her. Even the snatches of songs and hymns that floated into her mind spoke of decay and death. She would find herself humming one of these things, then resolutely put it out of her mind only to make room for another to insidiously creep in.

All her attempts to think of other things only brought her mind around again to the one fixed idea. In its clutch she stood paralyzed with the heavy stagnation of despair. Nothing like this had ever smitten her before. To be sure there had been times when she had awakened in the middle of the night and thought dismally that she was growing old, that life was slipping away. She recalled too the dreary feeling that had taken hold of her that day at Mount Signal after reading Andy Blake's poem. But such things had passed away and been dismissed from memory. This refused to be dismissed.

The emptiness that Andy Blake had left behind him had been peopled for her by memories. Everywhere she had seen him, listened to his voice. But when there fell upon her the annihilating certainty that the world was a dead world all her cherished memories of Andy Blake were swept away and strive as she might she could not make her mind dwell upon him. The days passed and lengthened into weeks and still she could not bring him back into her life. Always the thought of him eluded her, slipped away like sand through the fingers, was overshadowed by the blackness of her despair.

And yet to the outward eye nothing was changed about her life. She went through the routine of the home chores and milked at the Crosbys' twice a day quite as usual. Only now she never quarreled with Kate, because nothing ever came up that seemed worth quarreling about. There was no room for anger or annoyance in the dead, cold calm of her profound sense of futility. Each morning when she opened her eyes it was to the same conviction of the utter uselessness of everything. Like an automaton she moved through the tasks of the day.

Often, standing over the deep, slow-moving yellow water of the big main ditch, she lingered and hesitated, telling herself how soon it would all be over if only she would make one plunge. No, she did not even need to make a plunge, but only let her feet slide on the slippery Bermuda grass of the bank. Yet always she turned away, wondering at and despising herself that she had no courage to let the water take her, she who was so sure that life held nothing more for her.

But as the weeks dragged on her obsession, like a disease which assumes chronic form, became blunted, though none the less ever present. Gradually, in place of an acute perception of the futility of all things, a dull lethargy settled upon her. As a prisoner grows resigned to a dungeon, her spirit began to fit into the groove of this dark bondage, to relinquish itself apathetically to its control.

CHAPTER 25

OF LATE Kate had been growing more and more irritable.

"I don't see how the devil we're ever going to make out on this place," she said one morning as they were gulping their hasty cups of coffee before going to the Crosbys'.

Rhoda made no answer.

"I said I don't see how the devil we're ever going to make out on this place."

Still no answer.

"Well say, if you don't care anything about the place or about anything else perhaps we'd better break up partnership and walk off and leave it. I'm willing to put up with my share of the loss if you are."

Still Rhoda said nothing.

"Don't you think you might condescend to open your mouth and say what you're willing to do about it?"

"I'm willing to do anything that you suggest," she answered indifferently.

"That's right. Pass the buck to me like you always do. I wish you'd climb down off that high horse you've been riding lately and if you've got anything on your chest spit it out. I don't mind how much anybody kicks if they think they've got anything to kick about; but doggone it this suffering in silence gets on my nerves."

"I haven't anything to complain about and I'm not suffering in silence, so you may as well leave me alone," said Rhoda, beginning to gather up the dishes.

"Well life with you these days is certainly one grand sweet song," Kate flung over her shoulder. She was bending down rubbing vaseline into her heels preparatory to putting on her milking shoes. In the dry hot air the skin of the heels just above the soles had calloused and broken into painful cracks in which the desert dirt clung obstinately. She took up one shoe, then instead of putting it on threw it to the floor with a bang.

"Damned if I haven't made up my mind to have a rest," she exclaimed fretfully. "I don't care if the bills get paid or not; you don't care and why the dickens should I care? You can drive over and tell Ma Crosby I'm sick and we'll be back when I get well or any other lie you like, it's all the same to me."

She went out and banged the door violently behind her.

A heavy lethargy settled upon the two women. For many days after they ceased going to the Crosbys' they could hardly rouse from this lethargy enough to milk their own few cows and separate the milk. They lived on bread and milk to avoid the trouble of cooking anything; they let the dishes pile up for days; they neither swept nor made the beds. They slept, and slept and slept.

"Darn it if I don't feel as weak as water all over," complained Kate. "I wish I hadn't quit the job; I feel a whole lot worse than if I'd kept on working. What's wrong with us anyway? By golly we seem to have the sleeping sickness."

They let the drinking water stand in the olla for days until a strong stench and a fetid taste of decay forced them to scrub out the jar. The water sank low in the settling tank and the horsepond and at night the slimy mud of their bottoms gave forth a dank and horrible odor. But sunk in the slumber of exhaustion they did not smell it. The weeds grew thick and tall among Rhoda's chrysanthemums.

But toward the end of the second week Kate began to grow restless, to poke about over the place and to work a little by fits and starts.

"Good Lord, it's discouraging," she complained one day at the table. "If you don't keep on the job every minute everything goes to hell here. I've been looking over the place this morning and doggone it there's everything the matter with it. The ditches are all choked up, the fences are breaking down, the alfalfa's getting full of Bermuda, the corrals need shovelling out. We'll simply have to get to work and clean things up."

Rhoda had made a chicken stew that day and a lemon pie. It was the first real meal she had cooked for weeks and she was surprised to find herself eating it with relish. Later she went out and dug the weeds out of her chrysanthemums, then helped Kate to clean the ditch that fed the settling tank. When she went to bed that night she found herself thinking of Andy Blake. She fell asleep and dreamed about him.

In the morning she was awakened by the blackbirds; and when she opened her eyes the thought of Andy Blake came to her and did not go away. A patch of sunlight banded the foot of her bed and in the thick dark foliage of the chinaberry trees that overhung the porch blackbirds in rich velvet coats and jaunty scarlet side-splashes were winging to and fro uttering their gossipy chirrs and twangs. An utter relaxation, an ineffable sense of peace possessed her as she lay looking through the heavy boughs at the deep blue sky and watching the saucy antics of the blackbirds. It came into her mind that this was a thing that Andy Blake would love to do, to lie relaxed and refreshed in bed and look up at the feathery boughs, the blue sky, the blackbirds winging to and fro.

She got up and dressed with a strange feeling of lightness and ease, agreeably conscious of the birds, the sky, the patch of sunlight. She thought of her old obsession; but it had no power over her now because she could dismiss it at will from her mind. Then something happened that amused her.

Snoopy the cat had climbed out on a chinaberry bough looking for a blackbird's nest and two blackbirds had descended on her back scolding noisily. Dozens of their kin took up the hue and cry in sympathy and fluttered about their enemy making a deafening clamor, until at last the cat leapt from the branch and made off toward the cattle corral, her ears laid back, her body a long gray streak close to the ground. Rhoda broke into a laugh.

"Look Kate, the blackbirds were too much for Snoopy."

Kate inwardly heaved a sigh of relief. Thank the Lord she's coming around to her oats, was the thought that passed through her mind. I was beginning to think she never would quit moping for that godforsaken son of a gun.

CHAPTER 26

"SAY DO you know how much money we've got on hand?" asked Kate one morning. "Seventeen dollars. And there's at least fifty due next week for water and one thing and another."

"Well we can go back to the Crosbys' at any time."

"Darned if I'll go back to the Crosbys' till week after next. Even at that we'll have more than our hands full getting this place halfway cleaned up by that time."

Rhoda was thoughtful for a moment. "We might sell some of our two-year-old hens," she suggested. "They're not laying much any more and we'll soon be wanting to get rid of them anyway."

"Mightn't be a bad idea," considered Kate. "But the commission men pay so little for them they're hardly worth selling. Why not try peddling them? We could get a lot more for them that way."

"Peddling? Carrying them around from door to door?"

"I don't see why not. We could get a much better price. We can try it anyway. I should think we could get rid of about forty and that ought to bring us in thirty dollars."

"Forty? Can we dress that many in one day?"

"Of course we can. And we may as well do it right away; we've got to have the money."

She drove over and borrowed a big iron kettle from the Pruetts, and early on the morning of the next day they set to work to dress the chickens, which they had caught and put into crates the night before. Kate cut their throats with a paring knife which she had sharpened for the purpose; and when they had stopped kicking and flopping soused them in the boiling water of the kettle, then hung them by the legs from a branch of the chinaberry tree under which they were working, pulled the rough of the feathers from them and passed them on to Rhoda to be finished.

Rhoda plucked away industriously, carefully stripping the undersides of the wings and pulling out the pinfeathers. She tried to keep her mind and eyes on her own work, for if she looked toward Kate she was filled with a sinking horror at the sight of the flopping hens all spattered with blood and the pool of thick gore that jellied on the ground. From time to time she edged a little further away, trying to avoid the nauseating smell of fresh blood and the stench of the scalded feathers.

From time to time a great flock of blackbirds came and settled on the cottonwood tree over the horsepond, hundreds and hundreds of them, filling the air with their deafening chatter. Then at some alarm they would take flight in a black cloud and the silence that they left behind bombarded the ears. Soon they would come back and do the same thing all over again.

At noon Rhoda could only drink a cup of tea, for the mere thought of eating anything turned her stomach. Kate laughed at her squeamishness and munched heartily.

As the afternoon wore on the pool of blood by the execution block grew horribly thick and began to stink in the intense heat. The block itself was a mass of clotted gore and blood-soaked feathers. Big iridescent blowflies crawled and buzzed over the pool and the block. The chickens had to be carried to the house as soon as they were finished to get them away from the flies. Kate's shirt and overalls were smeared with blood. Blood stiffened in her hair, streaked her face and ran red on her hands as on a butcher's. She grew cantankerous with exhaustion.

To Rhoda doggedly plucking away it seemed as if there was nothing left in the world but clotted and spattered blood, the smell of scalding feathers, the wings, legs, backs, breasts and rumps of half-plucked chickens, and worst of all the long limp necks horrible with clammy, blood-soaked feathers, and the gory head at the end from the open beak of which hung a dark blob of coagulated blood. Her knees trembled with weariness and she could hardly keep upon her feet, but she kept plucking away at the undersides of wings, at breasts, backs, rumps, legs, and at long, slimy, dangling necks with a bloody, open-beaked head at the end.

"Don't be so damn particular," snapped Kate. "We gotta get done before dark. Let the women that buy 'em pick out a few pinfeathers."

At five o'clock they had to stop to milk their cows and separate the milk. The sun had set and the swift darkness thickened almost to black before they at last finished the job by lantern light and wearily straggled to the house to wash and get something to eat.

The next morning they were up before the sun and by seven o'clock had the chickens packed and in the car and were ready to start. They had not gone a half mile however when they were met by one of those long processions so often encountered in the Valley, and had to pull up at the side of the road and wait till it had passed. First came cookshacks on wheels, trucks piled with farm machinery and swaying loads of baled hay. Then horses and mules, their ears up, eyes alert and necks arched forward in the excitement of the drive. Next the lumbering cattle, billow after billow of white-faced longhorns plunging and bellowing through a thick cloud of dust, breaking ranks here and there and being herded back into line by the ever-watchful outriders. On and on came the steers; it seemed as though the lurching red-and-white line would never end. But they did pass at last and the two horsemen in their wake. After them a plume of dust a quarter of a mile long kept pace with the herd. Some big landowner was moving his outfit from one ranch to another.

The women brushed and slapped the dust from their clothes as well as they could, wiped their faces and hands with their handkerchiefs and continued on their way. Halfway to town Rhoda heard a movement behind her and looking back saw that Rowdy according to his custom had crawled into the car when they were not looking. Now, feeling safe from being sent back, he was sitting on top of the box of chickens looking very wise, very alert and only a little apologetic.

"Drat that dog," said Kate. "Why didn't we make sure he wasn't in the car before we left?"

At her words the dog laid back his ears, made mild, please-forgive-me eyes and thumped his tail on the box propitiatingly.

"You're a bad dog, Rowdy," said Rhoda.

He assented and demurred with vigorous tail thumpings upon the top of the box, showed the whites of his eyes and lay down, his head between his paws, in what Kate called his watchful waiting attitude. There was nothing to do but let him come.

On the edge of town they debated as to where they should begin. Kate was in favor of attacking the most well-to-do quarter.

"But I just hate the idea of going up to those big fine houses," objected Rhoda. "Why not try the more middling ones?"

"We'll probably have to try 'em all before we're through," said Kate grimly, "and we may as well begin at the top."

She swung into the most exclusive street of the town.

"Here, you take that side of the street and I'll take this," she said, handing out two chickens to Rhoda.

Rhoda took the chickens and for a moment the power seemed to go out of her body. She stood with her arms hanging at her sides feeling as limp and flaccid as the dead fowl that dangled from her hands, their bleached combs dragging in the dust of the road at the end of their long, slimpsy necks. Then she saw that Kate was already disappearing around the corner of the first house. With a determined effort of will she summoned back her strength and her courage, took firm hold upon the legs of the chickens and went in the direction of the first back door.

A maid in uniform came to the door of the back porch.

"W–would you like to buy a chicken?" Rhoda tried to wrest her lips into the shape of a smile, but found that the muscles had frozen.

The maid stared at this apparition of a woman in soldier's clothes peddling chickens and gave a little half smothered giggle. "Nope, I guess not," she said and let the screen door swing to.

Rhoda went to the next house. There was nobody at home.

At the third back door the lady of the house answered her knock. She was a young, good looking woman. "No thank you, not today," she smiled with absolute suaveness and finality and let the screen door swing to.

At the next house a repetition of the absolutely suave and absolutely final smile.

At the next house there was no one at home.

On the front steps of the next house was nailed a sign that said in shiny blue letters against shiny white enamel, NO PEDDLERS OR AGENTS. Rhoda spied it just in time as she was going around to the back. She hurriedly retraced her steps and scurried past the formidable sign as fast as she could.

The stout middle-aged lady who opened the next door and said, "No, not today," was not exactly stern or repellent. But she had that calm, contained and inordinately self-possessed air so frequently found in women of her age and comfortable financial status. Looking at the set lines of this woman's face and rigorously corseted figure, Rhoda felt that she had no chance whatever of showing her the light about chickens or anything else.

When she had finished her side of the block she went back to the car where Kate was already waiting.

"How many did you sell?"

"None."

"None? Why what's the matter? I sold two. Listen, you can't just go up and hang the hens under their noses; you've got to make 'em understand that they're cheaper than anything they can get at the butcher's and a darn sight fresher and fatter. Don't be afraid to talk up to 'em."

She ran the car down to the next corner and they started out once more.

"These chickens are corn and milk fed. We raised them ourselves and killed and dressed them just yesterday and we're asking only twenty-five cents a pound for them," Rhoda explained all in one hurried breath to the woman who opened the door. The woman had a hatchet face, a beady eye and a hard mouth partly saved from collapse by the propping of a complete set of formidable false teeth. But she seemed an angel of light to Rhoda as she took the chickens, felt them over, chose the plumpest one and said she thought she'd take it. Rhoda ran joyfully to the car to get the spring balance. The chicken weighed three pounds and five ounces.

"Are you sure your scales are right?" asked the woman sharply.

"Well we'll call it an even three pounds," said Rhoda, smiling as engagingly as she knew how.

"All right," returned the woman and handed her seventy-five cents.

"These chickens are corn and milk fed. We raised them ourselves and killed and dressed them just–"

It was of no use to go any further for the door had been violently slammed in her face.

She had been so heartened by the success of her little sales speech that she had felt actually gay. With the slamming of the door her spirits ebbed like the gas from a pricked balloon and she felt more than ever forlorn, draggle-tailed, an incompetent, a failure, an outcast. She had not the heart to use the old formula again but made up a new one.

"Would you like to buy a nice fresh chicken, madam? Fattened on corn and milk and only twenty-five cents a pound."

"No."

It was a man who had come to the door. As she was hurrying away she heard him through the open window talking to someone inside.

"Something wrong with 'em I'll bet my shirt. Don't ever buy anything from these farmer-peddlers, Clara. When they get the roup or the pip or the cholera in their flock they kill 'em off and hawk 'em around town and try to undersell the butcher and the Lord only knows what kind of diseased meat we're eating. I know the game 'cause I was raised on a farm myself."

His voice mingled with the tinkle of a piano that came from the front of the house where some one was practicing finger exercises. She hurried away to get out of earshot of both hateful sounds.

In her retreat she almost ran into an alert, well-groomed young man carrying a neat leather suitcase. He rang the front doorbell of the house from whose back door she had just fled and in a trice had his suitcase laid open on the porch.

"Good morning, madam. I'm the Pugsley brush man, at your service. I want to make you right now a present of the best vegetable and general utility kitchen brush that's ever been put on the market. There, madam, that belongs to you. The little card attached will tell you the seventeen different uses to which the brush may be put, and I have no doubt you'll be ingenious enough to find out others for yourself. Do you ever have any trouble reaching the outsides of your windows madam? I see your house stands on a high foundation like most well-built houses, and your maid probably has to climb a stepladder every time she washes the windows. Now this window washer, madam, does away with all climbing, cleans and polishes at the same time. This long-handled brush is the finest thing in the world for ceilings, walls, both inside and out, screens and screen doors and everything that gets dusty these dry days. The bristles of this clothesbrush, madam, are from bears that live only on the high plateaus of Tibet. Positively none other are used in these brushes. This mop, of the best long staple cotton chemically treated, needs no oil. It needs to be washed no oftener than once a year, otherwise simply shake out the dust. It's guaranteed to last six years with ordinary care and more often it lasts eight and nine years."

Rhoda listened fascinated, peering through the grape trellis that screened her from sight. The lady of the house, who had not yet been allowed to say anything, was examining the brushes.

"Yes madam, we have a patent on this comb cleaner. We also have a patent on this removable toothbrush holder. You won't see these two things offered anywhere else for the next fifteen years anyway. Let me show you our toothbrush. It's the only brush that really reaches every portion of the teeth."

The lady said something which Rhoda's ear did not catch.

"Quite true, madam, our prices are a trifle higher than you have been accustomed to pay in the stores. But on the other hand we guarantee our brushes to outwear three of any similar kind offered by any other concern. You're looking for quality in the goods you buy, aren't you madam? I'm quite sure you wouldn't for a moment begrudge the slight additional expense if you were sure you were getting real quality. Well madam, that's what we're offering you in the Pugsley brushes."

Rhoda hung behind the grape trellis and watched and listened enviously while the triumphant salesman sold the lady nine dollars and thirty-five cents worth of Pugsley brushes. Then she sidled away, humble and downcast, to the next house with her chickens.

"Would you like–?"

"No."

When the two women met again at the car Kate had sold two more chickens and Rhoda only her one. What a good-for-nothing person she was, she reflected bitterly. Kate took no pains to conceal the fact that she was of the same opinion. They started out once more.

All morning long it was a repetition of the same thing: sidling timidly around to back doors, her chickens dangling from her hand, finding half the time that there was no one at home and the other half that they did not want to buy any chickens. Her sense of failure deepened till it became a sinking at the pit of her stomach, a deadly weariness and a nausea that grew more acute with every back door she approached. It was not that she received many rebuffs; only on rare occasions was the door slammed in her face and the cantankerous and hard-featured women were few and far between. Nor did she mind so much when she was turned away by staring, indifferent or giggling maids. What she came to dread and loathe was the kind and polite refusal, the cheerful condescension of smug and well-groomed women who had left their piano practice or novel or embroidery to answer her timid knock and who assured her with a pleasant and patronizing smile that they did not want any chickens today.

An old vegetable peddler with a rickety wagon and a raw-boned horse asked her how was business. The man collecting the garbage passed her the time of day as he dumped a big can of fermenting swill into his wagon. A little boy distributing handbills gave her one to deliver at the back door that she was approaching. A scissors grinder asked her if the people were home at the place that she had just left. She was one with the great backdoor fraternity, with the people who travel by lanes and alleys and crosscut paths from kitchen to kitchen. There was a certain cheer and comfort for her in the approaches of these people; they were genial and friendly. But they had no money to buy chickens.

Passing the Catholic church she hesitated. How long it was since she had been inside a church. How would it feel to pass up the steps into the cool dimness, to kneel in a pew and pay her devotions to the altar, to sit and rest a little while and let the calm, the quiet, the peace sink into her tired body and fretted spirit. The straight plain lines of the simple stuccoed structure were pleasing to the eye against the deep blue sky; the steps lay in a flood of sunlight. A pair of pigeons with iridescent necks and pink feet trod daintily over the bit of lawn.

A woman came out of the church and down the steps, an old Mexican woman with a black shawl framing her broad, leather-colored face that had for expression only a stolid glower of stupidity. A great hulk of a woman with coarse Irish features came waddling flat-footedly along the street, a rusty black sailor on her head, rusty black skirts sweeping the pavement. There was about her an atmosphere of stuffiness, of things old, stale and smelly. She'll go in, thought Rhoda—and she did.

Rhoda passed on. No she would not go in there to tawdry painted saints, gilt crucifixes and dusty paper flowers. There was nothing in there for her, she told herself. Whatever peace of spirit she had attained it was her own, intimately and peculiarly hers, bought for herself at the price of her own sweat and agony.

By noon she had sold only two chickens to Kate's seven. Only nine chickens sold and thirty-one still to dispose of. Sitting in the car under the shade of a pepper tree they ate the lunch they had brought with them in discouraged silence.

Through the hot, sleepy hours of the early afternoon, her body heavy and sluggish and the life of her spirit at its lowest ebb, she trailed leadenly from back door to back door, sunk in such a deep indifference of weariness that she forgot to feel degraded; and even when she occasionally sold a chicken she felt no stir of interest. Later in the day as the air began to cool her ignominy came back upon her and she shrank once more from approaching back doors. She was almost glad that there were so few people at home. Three fourths of the houses now were securely locked and deaf to rings and knocks. Their mistresses were out driving or shopping or attending teas or club meetings. Or they were out of town entirely, seeking in one or other of the coast cities the diversions which the Valley did not afford. Through the front windows of these closed houses Rhoda glimpsed pianos, cabinet phonographs, period furniture, Navajo rugs, Chinese and Persian rugs, if not real then very good-looking imitations; and through the back windows white enamelled kitchens, vacuum cleaners, electric washers and elaborate kitchen cabinets. What had these idle women done to deserve all these comforts and luxuries, she asked herself bitterly. They had got them, some way or other, out of the land, because there was nothing else in the Valley but the land: no industries no manufactures, no anything but the land. All these things to make these lazy women comfortable had come out of the land. And yet she and Kate who actually cultivated the land and worked so hard and such long hours got none of them. Neither did the Dobles nor any of the people who milked the cows and drove the tractors and stacked the hay and picked the melons and cut the corn and did all the carrying and lifting and bending and sweating, all the hard, tedious, body-breaking tasks that made the stingy land give up its richness. But the comforts and luxuries that the land afforded were for these people who lived only half the year in the Valley, who had lawns and leisure and music, who chugged about in big purring cars and spent the weekend in the mountains or at the seashore. What had they done to deserve all this? Especially what had these idle women done, these fashionably dressed women who drove big cars and read magazines and gave teas and attended silly clubs where they discussed the morals of the latest sensational novel or the ways and means of getting better telephone service, more shade trees and paved streets, so that they would be more comfortable still.

And it was these people who had put Dan Stoner in prison for ten years.

The nervous weariness that sends the blood to the head had for some time warmed her cheeks with a hectic glow. Now, as she meditated on these things, they flamed scarlet with her growing sense of injustice.

A smiling, buxom, middle-aged woman opened the door. Rhoda was deathly sick of smiling, buxom, middle-aged women.

"Would you like to buy a nice milk-fed chicken?" she asked indifferently, and stood ready to turn away as soon as the almost universal "No, not today," was spoken.

"Why I don't know," the woman reached out for the chickens. "They look like nice ones. How much are you asking a pound?"

"Twenty-five cents."

"Well that's reasonable enough. At the meat market I've been paying thirty-seven. I believe I'll take these two."

When Rhoda came back with the spring balance to weigh the chickens the woman was standing with a pair of shoes in her hand.

"You know," she hesitated, "I hope you won't be offended. I've been looking for somebody to give these shoes to and your feet look to me just about right for them. They pinch my corns and I'd be glad if you'd take them along."

Rhoda glanced at the shoes and at the kindly faced woman. She had an impulse to take them and throw them in her face. If they had been old shoes perhaps she might have yielded to the impulse. But they were new shoes, fine, pretty and dainty shoes, and Rhoda loved fine, pretty and dainty things. She needed a pair of shoes badly and these were much better than any she would be able to buy.

"Thank you, it's very kind of you," she said and took the shoes.

As she was scurrying along the street to the car with the shoes in her hand she noticed across the street a figure that had something familiar about it. Looking more closely she saw that it was Mr. McCumber. She flushed to the roots of her hair a shamefaced scarlet, hastily transferred the shoes to the other hand and quickened her steps, glancing furtively sidewise from time to time to see if she had been noticed. She managed to reach the car unobserved, but Mr. McCumber was still coming along the other side of the street and might see her at any moment. Kate was at the car to which she had just returned after an absolutely fruitless canvass of her side of the block.

"Kate, that's Bill McCumber coming along the other side of the street. Let's slip around the corner till he gets out of sight."

Kate fixed her with a stare of cold interrogation.

"What do we want to slip around the corner for?"

"Well we don't want him to see us peddling chickens, do we?"

"The hell we don't. Why in God's name should we give a quarter of a damn who sees us peddling chickens? All the crowned heads of Europe—if there's any left—can come and look on for all I care."

Kate was very tired and very cross. Just to be contrary she talked even louder than usual and flopped the chickens around noisily. But Mr. McCumber was evidently bent upon his own business. He did not turn his head and passed on without seeing them. Rhoda had dropped the shoes under the back seat of the car and said nothing about them.

They started out once more.

Up to this time Rowdy had been a good dog. All morning he had stayed in the car and guarded the chickens. At noon his mistresses had shared their lunch with him, complimenting him upon his good behavior. Through the heat of the early afternoon he had slept peacefully.

But with the first stirrings of coolness Rowdy awoke refreshed and restless with accumulated energy. He started to follow Kate, but she admonished him with such a firm tone of command that he slunk back and crawled under the car. He lay there for a few moments, his nose between his paws, his eyes furtively vigilant. Then he got up very quietly, sniffed out Rhoda's tracks and followed in the way that she had gone.

"Go back, Rowdy," she commanded as he came frisking at her heels. But the tone was not emphatic enough. He made humble eyes, but continued to come. Presently another dog came up and introduced himself to Rowdy, decided that he liked him and approved of him as a playfellow. When, having made the tour of her block without selling a single chicken, Rhoda went back to the car there were four dogs following her.

The two women tried to drive the dogs away and get Rowdy back into the car, but it was of no use. To their commands, threats and entreaties he would no longer even make humble eyes or flop an ingratiating tail. Instead he barked and curvetted defiance, his ears and tail up. Fortified by his companions, like a boy in a gang, he was entirely out of hand.

They started out again.

Rowdy chose to follow Rhoda and the dogs all chose to follow Rowdy. She tried to drive them back, but they only halted and came on again as soon as she began to walk. They sniffed at the dangling chicken heads, they circled yelping about her, they barked, snarled, frisked and fought among themselves, but always they were at her heels. The women who opened their doors and beheld this yelping pack stared, gasped and closed them again quickly. She was purple with confusion and shame.

Each time that she knocked at a door she drove the dogs off with all the determination that she could muster, so that they would be at some distance when the door was opened. But as soon as her back was turned they swarmed forward again. Their number grew to six, then seven, then nine. Their yelps and barking increased; they grew every moment more wild and turbulent. Every moment she became more confused and bewildered in her efforts to keep them at a distance.

She knocked at a door, drove the dogs away and turned about to proffer her chickens. Like a pack of wolves they swarmed back upon her and when the door was opened the leader, sniffling and yelping, darted past her into the aperture followed by the whole fry. Rhoda was too bewildered with dismay to try to stop them. She could hear them romping about in the inside of the house, pushing against chairs, jumping up and jumping down, snarling and snapping at each other. But she was powerless to do anything or to explain.

The woman who had opened the door gave a gurgle and a gasp, fixed Rhoda with a startled and questioning look, then a stare of stony and righteous indignation and made a dart for her broom. Rhoda fled.

She was sitting in the car when Kate returned, huddled in a shrinking heap in a corner of the back seat. All the hectic color had ebbed from her face and the pallor of extreme exhaustion had taken its place. The dogs, ejected from the sacred precincts into which they had so rudely broken, swarmed and yelped about the car; but she took no notice of them. Kate came back, still carrying the two chickens with which she had started out. She too was pale and her large, unmoble features were set in grim lines. Her gait was dragging and flat-footed.

"Hell," she said, and throwing the chickens into the car leaned wearily against the side.

Rhoda roused herself from her attitude of collapse.

"I won't stir feet to one more back door—not a single one," she snapped. "It's too disgustingly mean and degrading. I don't care if we have to throw them all away. I won't go near another kitchen door as long as I live."

Her voice rose in febrile, high-pitched tones.

"Well keep your shirt on and don't get so excited about it," Kate said in a manner deliberately intended to be insulting. "I can't say I'm all fired keen about battering any more back doors myself, but I'm not going to act like a baby about it."

She began to count the chickens with a self-contained and superior air. Rhoda huddled in her corner of the car feeling crushed, wretched and resentful.

"Twenty-five, twenty-six, twenty-seven. We've only sold thirteen. We'll have to try to get rid of them to some butcher or commission merchant and ten to one nobody'll want to buy them so late in the afternoon and if they don't get on ice tonight they'll be spoiled by tomorrow. It looks as if we're outa luck."

"We're always outa luck," wailed Rhoda dismally.

"Oh well it's no use going into mourning about it. If you'll move over and let me pack these chickens in there we'll get going and see what we can do."

Rhoda moved into the front seat and Kate started the car.

"Wait," exclaimed Rhoda when they had gone half a block, "how about Rowdy?"

"Oh let the damn dog go. He's given us so much trouble I don't want to lay eyes on him again."

"But Kate—"

Kate increased the speed of the car, her face rigid and implacable.

In a few moments they had reached the edge of the business part of the town and stopped before the warehouse of a dealer in eggs and chickens. He shook his head dubiously and looked at the chickens with a mixture of indifference and despisal.

"Killed yesterday, you say, and ain't been on ice? 'Twouldn't hardly pay me to try to handle 'em."

"You don't want them then?" asked Kate shortly.

"Well I can't say I do. But I'll take 'em off your hands at fourteen cents a pound. T'wouldn't pay me to give any more than that."

Kate answered never a word but cranked the car and sprang into the seat. The man opened his mouth to name another price, but she did not wait to hear it.

"I'll throw 'em in the ditch before I'll sell 'em for that," she barked grimly as they drove along.

Rowdy was with them again. He had run up panting when the car stopped and Rhoda had hurriedly opened the door to let him jump in behind.

"Drat the dog, I wish we'd left him for good," said Kate. But she could not repress a subtle softening of the features which showed that she was not speaking the strict truth.

She stopped in front of a butcher shop and was fishing out a sample chicken from the box in the back of the car when somebody came up from behind, tapped her on the shoulder and inquired: "Hello there, what are you girls up to now?"

Rhoda started, glanced up and looked straight into the eyes of Mr. McCumber.

He had never seemed so sleek and well-groomed, so tubbed, shaved, combed, brushed, shined and pressed. Her eyes fell upon the plump hand that lay on the top of the car door, immaculate and carefully manicured. By contrast with his groomed alertness she felt more than ever frowsy and wretched. Looking at him she was acutely conscious of the rusty and battered old car with its burst out upholstery and tag ends of string and baling wire and of her own dust-filled pores, grimy hands, straggling hair and down-at-heel shoes, worse than all, of her own lassitude and helplessness.

This man accomplished things and in accomplishing things kept clean, spruce, vigorous and good humored. She accomplished nothing and her expenditure of wasted effort left her looking and feeling like an old dishrag thrown out on top of the garbage heap. Shrivelled with a sense of her own scrubby ineptitude she shrank further into the corner and into herself.

But the more she shrank the more Mr. McCumber's eyes followed her, like ferrets after a rat. It was not that he had ferret eyes; they were clear, kindly, shrewd, domineering gray eyes; but they wouldn't leave her in peace. All the time that he was talking to Kate about chickens and butchers and commission men and state of the market, his eyes looked beyond Kate's face and over her shoulder persistently seeking her own evasive glance. He was the sort of man who went out to get whatever he wanted and travelled roughshod over everything until he had it. She loathed people like that. It was hideously mortifying. From the bottom of her heart she hated him.

Kate, afflicted with no sense of shame, but a very pronounced one of injury, was describing with a plentiful sprinkling of graphic and profane adjectives the trials of the day. Rowdy thumped his tail on the chicken box in his excitement at seeing a friend in a strange place.

"Well that's sure 'nuf hard luck all right; but maybe I can do a little something to lift the curse. I know a commission man, good friend o' mine. I helped him out of a little trouble a while back. We'll go around there and see if we can't get a decent price for the birds. Just straight ahead two blocks and a half block to the right.

He stood on the running board while Kate drove the car around to the place that he had indicated. It was the same commission merchant who had offered them fourteen cents a pound.

Mr. McCumber went inside, held a short conversation and came out smiling and triumphant.

"He'll take 'em at twenty-seven cents a pound."

"How did you manage it?" asked Kate, when the chickens had been weighed and the money paid.

"Well I did him a little favor that was worth quite a bit to him. It's a good thing to stand in well with the people who do business in your town you know. So I asked him to give me the best price he could and get out on 'em. But he admitted to me quite frankly that he'd make a decent profit on 'em even at twenty-seven cents. It isn't any charity money he's handing out; but he's a good fella."

"Well it's been mighty good of you and we're awfully obliged, aren't we Rhoda?"

"Indeed we are," said Rhoda, rousing herself and trying to look pleased and cordial. Yes, it was his policy to stand in well with everybody, everybody who had anything, everybody who could do anything for him. With the others it didn't matter. She thought of Andy Blake and of Dan Stoner and felt rising in her breast a seething hot rage against this man's smug good humor. If she had one of those Spanish dagger things that grew in the desert it would be a pleasure to thrust it in between his ribs.

Kate was out in front trying to crank the car.

"What in heck's name's the matter with this car?" she panted. Mr. McCumber hastened to her assistance.

He cranked and cranked. He adjusted the spark, changed the carburetor. He cranked and cranked again. He grew purple in the face. The engine gave not the slightest response. He lifted up the hood and looked thoughtfully and very wisely at what was underneath; but it was apparent that he did not know what to do about it.

"She acts as if she'd made up her mind not to go," he said, straightening up and looking meditatively at the disreputable old machine. "I tell you what we'd better do. I'll get my car and tow you around to a garage. I know a fella, friend o' mine—I got him out of a little trouble once—that'll fix it for you reasonably. That's what we'd better do. I'll be back in a minute."

"Drat the luck," said Kate when he was gone. "I suppose it'll take all the money we got for the chickens to pay for fixing the car." They sat in doleful silence waiting for him to come back.

He came in a few moments driving his big fawn-colored sports car and towed them around to the garage of the man whom he had gotten out of a little trouble. The mechanic spent a half hour or so examining the car, said she needed a good overhauling, but he could fix her so she'd run in an hour or perhaps an hour and a half.

"I tell you what we'll do," suggested Mr. McCumber. "I'm going to Calexico now and I'll take you girls along and leave you at your place. Then tomorrow I can call for you and bring you back to get the car. How's that?"

It sounded all right to Kate for a moment; then she changed her mind.

"No," she said, "I'd rather wait and bring the car back tonight. I don't want to take up time going for it tomorrow. You take Rhoda home now and she can be clawing together something to eat and I'll come later with the old bus."

Mr. McCumber's face beamed with animation and approval.

Aside to Rhoda Kate muttered: "He won't have the crust to charge so much if I stand over him and show him I know something about what he's doing. You go on ahead and fix up some dinner; I'm hungry enough to eat a dead cat."

Rhoda opened her mouth to protest, but she knew that it would be useless. Two wills both stronger than hers were arrayed against her. She seated herself on the yielding cushions of the big sports car. Mr. McCumber took the wheel with alacrity, backed, veered and rolled luxuriously down the street. How different it was from the rattle and bang and asthmatic gasp of the old Ford. How soft and smooth, how suave and yielding.

Mr. McCumber stopped before a butcher shop that had a vegetable stand in front. "I'll stand treat for the dinner," he suggested gaily, "and then if you don't hate my company too much you can ask me to stay and eat part of it."

"Oh no, I'd rather not," Rhoda began; but she got no further.

"Of course you'll let me buy it, whether I get to eat any of it or not. Come on in and help choose."

He led the way. He bought chops, thick porterhouse steaks, cauliflowers, egg plants, celery, olives, pickles, preserved ginger. She could not stop him. He bought dollars and dollars worth. The clerk who waited on them had never before sold her anything more expensive than a pound of hamburger or a scraggly slice of chuck steak, glanced at her with a knowing and congratulatory air and whispered something to one of the other clerks that made them both chortle. She wanted the earth to swallow her. The only thing she was thankful for was that Mr. McCumber had not noticed. She hurried him out with the packages and back into the car.

As they bowled along through the shanty-fringed outskirts of the town Rhoda called to mind the first time she had driven alone with Mr. McCumber. In this same car over this same road they had passed a year and a half ago through a blinding dust storm. It was his hands on the wheel that reminded her of it; she remembered that she had admired them because they were so firm, strong and capable. But at that time she had been for Mr. McCumber not a woman nor even a person, but merely a "prospect." She remembered too that brushing elbows with him and watching his capable hands she had allowed her fancy to wander and had been glad that he could not look into her mind and read her thoughts. A smile, sad and cynical, lifted one corner of her lips.

Thinking over the things that had happened since that day a year and a half ago, she was seized with an access of longing to turn back the clock, to begin again, to be given one more chance to win the man she loved. She could see again the corral under the first faint stars, Chester Doble rumbling about the boll weevil, Dan Stoner promising Junie to whittle her out an airplane when the milking was over, Andy Blake whistling toward the milkhouse with a foaming bucket in each hand. Now all that was changed. Chester Doble was preparing to take his family and go to end his days on an old run down farm in the Ozarks; Dan Stoner was in prison and Andy Blake a vagabond God knows where. The old life of the corral was over and gone and as if it had never been. But Mr. McCumber remained. He was stable, he fitted in, he was the sort of person who is allowed to have permanency and a secure hold on things. Nobody pushed him into the backwoods or into a jail or out onto the broad highways of the world.

Had she ever in all her life been so tired? Her body, weary in every nerve and bone, relaxed into the soft cushions, sensed gratefully the sustaining power of the strong velvet springs. She laid her head back remembering that she had never been able to lay her head back in the Ford. A drowsiness crept over her and her eyes closed. She seemed to be sliding away on soft, satiny billows over a gentle sea that bore her up, cradled her, sang to her.

Suddenly the soft shiny billows stopped moving.

She opened her eyes and saw Mr. McCumber's face very close to hers. It occurred to her passingly that if he should kiss her he would get a good taste of the grit and dust on her face.

He had pulled up the car by the side of the road. He was not a man to drive and make love at the same time.

"Rhoda."

She heard her name but it sounded faint and very far off. It was easier not to rouse from her padded lethargy.

"Rhoda, dear girl, you're going to marry me, aren't you?"

She sensed the meaning of the words, though they sounded as if they came from very far away. She was too tired to move, to rouse herself, but her mind began to work.

He was one of those people who always get along. If she married him she would always be safe, protected, taken care of, established in a secure and comfortable niche. She would have a piano, an electric stove, a vacuum cleaner, all the things that she had been begrudging to those women in town. Why not have them, seeing that she was denied all the things she really wanted?

His arm crept about her. His well-manicured hand closed about her grimy one with its dirty nails, callouses and hangnails. She was sure it must still smell of chicken legs.

If she married him that impertinent smart Aleck in the butcher shop would change his manner toward her. He would no longer be slapdash and indifferent or giggling and slily congratulatory. He would be polite, deferential; it would be Mrs. McCumber this and Mrs. McCumber that and "Boy, carry Mrs. McCumber's packages to her car."

"Rhoda, girl, this time I'm not going to take no for an answer. You're going to marry me of course, and pretty darn soon too."

If she married him she would never have to peddle chickens again.

He kissed her and she wondered if she tasted of grit and dust. But his arm about her was strong and protecting, his hand warm and full of comfort.

A car whizzed by leaving a trail of dust and laughter.

"Rhoda, kiss me."

She kissed him obediently on his shaven cheek faintly redolent of shaving soap and talcum powder. She was not able to put much warmth into the kiss, but it seemed to satisfy him. She reflected that he was the sort of man who likes his kisses modest—the first few anyway.

With a tightening of his right arm he drew her closer to him.

"Rhoda darling, you're just the girl I've always dreamed of—gentle, modest, pure."

A cynical smile flickered across her mouth. But as it

passed she lifted her eyes and looking into his saw in them the ecstatic glow, the exaltation and the dream that she knew would have been in hers if Andy Blake had ever made love to her. To keep from bursting into tears she smiled all at once her queer, crooked, perverse, bewitching little smile and hid her face on his shoulder.

Mr. McCumber, not a man to push things too fast, gave her a good squeeze and released her.

"C'mon sweets, let's get rolling."

The big car purred out of El Centro and headed south.

Again she leaned back against the soft upholstery and, closing her eyes, listened vaguely to the purr of the engine.

Suddenly the purr ceased and the car rolled to a stop. She opened her eyes and looked at Mr. McCumber.

He sat there for a moment looking straight ahead.

"Well, I guess yours is not the only car that can break down."

He got out, lifted the right side of the hood, and studied the engine for a moment.

"Turn on the key," he yelled.

Rhoda roused herself from her lethargy and examined the dashboard. It took her a few moments to find the key. Mr. McCumber just stood smiling and waiting patiently.

"Now turn it off," he said.

He came to her side of the car and leaned in the window.

"I think it's the coil; this is the second time the coil has gone out. The thing is mounted right on the block and gets too much heat."

He looked back down the road toward town. "It's over a mile to a garage that stocks coils. It'll take me about an hour to get there and back, but it won't take long to install it. I've got the tools."

Wouldn't you know he'd have the tools, thought Rhoda.

"Now Rhoda, I know you've had a long day. It's growing cool now, so just stretch out on the seat and have a nice rest. There's a pillow there; just relax and forget your troubles, and I'll take care of everything." He seemed genuinely solicitous.

Rhoda just nodded and closed her eyes. Her face bore no expression; it was the face of total physical and emotional exhaustion. But Mr. McCumber had scarcely departed when the billowy seats began to feel hot. She looked out the window to the west. The car was stopped next to a piece of uncultivated land, a remnant of the ancient desert, too high to be farmed. Wearily she got out of the car and walked slowly, head bowed, into the desert.

CHAPTER 27

SHE WALKED numbly, unthinking, unfeeling. Mr. McCumber's proposal, so recent in occurrence, didn't enter her mind. She sensed only a great heaviness and endless weariness.

The ground rose slightly and catching her shoe on a branch she began to notice vestiges of the original vegetation, gnarled, dwarfed shrubs, ancient cacti armored and waxed waiting for the rain that would someday come. At the top of the rise she stopped. The sun had gone down behind the coast range, but there were a few clouds in the eastern sky that caught the light and reflected it everywhere. She could see the coast range, Mount Signal, and the ranges to the east. The mountains cut a sharp outline against the light blue sky that darkened gradually as it left the horizon. She had never seen a blue so pure, so perfectly graduated. She turned slowly, inspecting the horizon. Everywhere on the horizon was light; it was impossible to tell where the sun had gone down.

I am standing in the palm of the Devil's hand, she thought, and I am standing here alone. I've always been alone. When I am humiliated, only I know the agony of it. My skin separates me from everything. I cannot even appreciate the sorrows of others. She thought of the Mexican woman with the dead child. There was no way to sense, to understand the poignancy of her tragedy.

She sat down on the edge of a little gully, first looking to see whether any of those fast-moving, hard-biting, red ants were present. She had hardly seated herself when she noticed, about three feet away, one of their trails, and coming up the side of the gully was one of them carrying something. She moved closer to get a better view. The object was large and flat, but she couldn't tell what it was in the dim light. The trail grew steeper as the ant progressed, and suddenly the ant stopped. She bent down to inspect the situation. The object he was carrying was caught between two tiny twigs. The ant struggled to force it through, but the sand rolled under its feet. It set the object down and, approaching it from the other side, tried vainly to pull it through. Other ants arrived. Each stopped and communicated with its unfortunate co-worker and went on. Then four ants arrived who stopped to offer help. They seized the object and tried to force it past the twigs—no luck. Then one ran in a circle around the scene of activity as though he were a straw boss surveying the problem. Again they seized the object, but this time they turned it on edge, and with much effort and slipping of sand made it to the top of the grade. The four assistants immediately returned down the trail, and the original ant again shouldered his burden.

Rhoda sat up. How can it be so important to those ants to transport that little piece of junk? And what are they going to do with it? Is it food? Something to build with? She found herself wishing she knew more about the habits of ants. But whatever they were going to do with it, it certainly mattered to them to get it moved.

Why is it that things matter more to these ants than they do to me; furthermore they are better organized than I am.

Suddenly the vision of Rowdy and his new found friends tearing into that woman's house appeared before her. Why did he do it? What did he hope to gain? Why, he had been confined to the Ford all day; he had found some new friends, and here was an opportunity to raise a little hell. It's precious little hell raising I've ever done. I wonder if Rowdy and the other dogs will laugh about their romp when they meet again. It's too bad dogs can't laugh. She saw herself standing there holding the chickens—the expression on that woman's face, the yelping and jumping of the dogs, the ridiculousness of the whole situation. She lifted her head and chortled, not her characteristic cynical curl of one corner of the mouth, but a belly filling laugh. And Rowdy knew he would get hell for that little excursion, yet the fun of it mattered enough to him.

She looked again at the bright horizon and the dark blues and purples of the mountains and clumps of eucalyptus trees. Funny, I didn't realize how tall those clumps of trees are; and how abrupt is the south side of Mount Signal. This is the first time since the first few days of my arrival that I have ever looked at things at a distance. I have been so involved with the present and the pressing that I have not been looking around.

She began to wonder what it was that made things matter. Why had the Hindu come back to tell her he was leaving? He didn't have to. Yet it mattered to him; it mattered to his sense of fairness in human relations. She saw him slouched in the old car, smoking a cigaret through his funnel-shaped hand, and watching the passers-by. Did he see more in those passers-by than she did? Yes, yes, I'm sure he did. He probably saw all kinds of things I didn't see.

And Dan Stoner—why didn't he take the opportunity to escape from jail? And why had he allowed himself to be tarred and feathered? Her memory ran over Dan Stoner, and gradually things seemed to jell in her mind. Dan Stoner was a man of principles, unwavering principles. Everything he did was based on these principles. Even when events brought him misfortune he stood by his principles. God, he's probably happier in jail than I am here free as a bird.

And Andy Blake; she tried to summarize him too in order to make some sense of him, but the parts didn't jell the way they did with Stoner. But there were things that mattered to him—the same things that mattered to Stoner and a few more such as carrying around a few battered books. All at once she realized that she actually didn't know him very well; she hardly knew him at all. But I might have known him; only I didn't have the courage to talk to him. She laughed silently. Love him? I never loved him—I could have loved him, no, might have loved him. Why did I allow myself to think I loved him? Why do I do anything? It was my family who decided I should go to work in an office. It was Kate who decided I should go West. It was the Hindu who decided to be my lover. I am like a pawn moved carelessly by any player. Why? Why? Again she thought of the ants and their singleness of purpose—and of Rowdy and his ability to take advantage of a situation. It matters to them, she thought, and they are not afraid. If Andy Blake had been interested in me, he would not have been afraid.

She stopped thinking about Andy Blake and thought about the Valley, its inhabitants, their struggles. She saw the picture of the downtrodden poor, the feeble efforts of their self-appointed leaders, the fear the members of the status quo had of these ineffectual leaders. But suppose the poor grew stronger and better organized? Suppose their leaders were more powerful, more influential?

What about me? Where do I fit into all this? She looked again at the sky; a faint light still silhouetted the mountains, but overhead stars were appearing in the dark blue. Hell, I don't have to stay here. I can go to San Diego or Los Angeles or even San Francisco. Or I could go home—no, I'll never go back, not to stay anyway. Or I could stay right here. Yes, the devil be damned, I could stay right here! She sat there, hands clasped, elbows on knees, ruminating, ruminating in the still desert night.

At last she stood up. She was amazed that she no longer felt tired. She took a couple of deep breaths and moved her arms as though doing exercises. I don't feel tired at all; I feel as vigorous as a colt. She walked back to the car and soon saw the figure of Mr. McCumber, coil in hand, peering about the landscape. As she approached he turned on a flashlight, carefully angled so that it would not shine in her eyes.

"Why Rhoda, you look like a million dollars; you must have had a good rest. There's nothing more refreshing than just turning off the mind."

Rhoda laughed. "Yes, most refreshing." She leaned on the fender as Mr. McCumber went to work changing the coil.

"Bill, what matters to you?"

He shot her a questioning glance. "What do ya mean, what matters to me? Everything matters to me."

"Well, I mean what are the things that matter most to you? Do you have some basic principles?"

He laughed. "Sure, I have principles, but you can't run your life on a few abstract principles."

"You can't?"

"Well, I suppose the principles govern a lot of what one does, but not everything—putting this coil on for instance. What has that got to do with principles? But it matters, because if I don't get it on we'll be in a bad fix. That's why everything matters; the tiniest details all matter. I've seen more than one business man go under because he didn't pay enough attention to details."

Rhoda thought of the ants.

Mr. McCumber's mind had just worked out a sly plan. "I'll tell you what matters most to me, Rhoda—making money, having friends, being influential, having a nice home —and you; you matter to me.

"Mm, you put me last."

"That's for emphasis–an old lawyer's trick."

Rhoda decided to direct the conversation away from this tack. "How about Dan Stoner; does he matter to you?"

Mr. McCumber stood up straight. "Now Rhoda, Dan Stoner was a man I had to respect; I admired his faith and his ability to stick to his faith. But there was no way I could get mixed up with him. I am operating in one aspect of society, and he in another. If I were to take up his cause I would be sacrificing the things I have worked for."

He paused a moment. "Look at it this way. I am not a criminal lawyer. But suppose some day I started taking cases such as Stoner's and became a lawyer for the social underdog. Then these things would matter to me; they would be part of my way of life. Right now they are in opposition to my way of life."

He plugged the distributor wire into the coil and, happy for the opportunity to change the subject, said, "Well, that ought to do it." He lowered the hood and cleaned his hands as best he could with a rag kept for that purpose. "Now for the supreme test." He got into the car, pressed the starter, and the engine responded instantly.

Rhoda got in. The big car surged smoothly forward under the expert guidance of Mr. McCumber.

"When shall we set the date, Rhoda?"

"I have not yet said that I would marry you," said Rhoda crisply.

Mr. McCumber glanced at her. He could see no indication of resistance, but he was astute enough to know that this was not the time to press the issue.

They rode for a few minutes in silence.

"Bill, how do you drive a gearshift car?"

He brightened. Glad to have conversation revived and pleased at being placed in the role of teacher, he explained the processes. He explained them carefully and logically.

"A few miles down the road there's a wide, straight stretch. Would you like to give it a try?"

He looked at her, uncertain what her reaction might be.

But her face was expressionless, and she continued to stare straight ahead. And in a voice that was clear, yet sounding to Mr. McCumber strange and distant—as though she was not talking to anyone in particular: "Yes, yes indeed, I'm certainly going to give it a try."

THE END

Afterword *by* Matthew J. Bruccoli

AFTER THE republication of *Weeds* by the Southern Illinois University Press in 1972 I received a letter from Patrick Kelley expressing pleasure at his mother's second chance for recognition. This letter was my first contact with the Kelley family, for the Press and I had failed to locate any of the Kelley children. I asked Mr. Kelley the mandatory question: Do you have your mother's unpublished work? He certainly did–stories, essays, poems, plays, a novelette ("The Heart of April") –and *The Devil's Hand.* With Mr. Kelley's help I have been able to piece together a chronology of his mother's career.

Edith Summers was born in 1884 in Ontario, Canada, and attended the University of Toronto where she won honors for language study, graduating in 1903 at the age of nineteen. She went to New York and worked for Funk & Wagnall's *Standard Dictionary,* incurring eye strain which bothered her for the rest of her life. In 1906–7 she was Upton Sinclair's secretary at his Helicon Hall experiment in communal living, where she met two Yale drop-outs, Alan Updegraff and Sinclair Lewis. She became engaged to Lewis, but married poet-novelist Updegraff by whom she had two children, Ivor and Barbara. While Updegraff courted the Muses, Edith taught night school in the Hell's Kitchen district of Manhattan. After her marriage broke up, she lived with sculptor C. Fred Kelley for more than fifty years. They never bothered with a marriage service.

Kelley had been raised on a farm and was good with his hands. In 1914–16 the Kelleys worked a tobacco farm in Kentucky, abandoning it to run a boardinghouse in New Jersey between 1916 and 1920, where their son Patrick was born. In November of 1920 they went to the Imperial Valley of southern California, near El Centro, and leased a 60-acre alfalfa ranch close to the Mexican border, just in time for the postwar land slump. During the summer of 1921 the Kelleys slaved in suffocating heat—losing money every day—and Edith began writing *Weeds*. In the fall of 1921 they moved to a chicken farm in the Mission Valley district on the edge of San Diego, where the novel was finished. At this time Fred Kelley had a nasty job in a meat-packing plant. The publication and failure—despite good reviews—of *Weeds* in 1923 is reported in the Southern Illinois University Press edition of that novel.

Upton Sinclair had tried to promote *Weeds,* and he urged Edith Summers Kelley to write the second novel she had in mind about the Imperial Valley. The chronology of the writing of *The Devil's Hand* can be reconstructed from Mrs. Kelley's letters to Sinclair.[1]

I haven't yet settled down to trying to start another book (2 April [1924])

I want to express my enthusiastic thanks for that letter which you sent to Mr. Baldwin. If eloquent persuasion can do anything to get me an award from the Garland Fund I am sure that your letter will have results. (27 February [1925]) [2]

[1] The Upton Sinclair Manuscripts, Lilly Library, Indiana University.

[2] Roger Baldwin of the American Fund for Public Service, which was also known as the Garland Fund. Mrs. Kelley's reference in the next letter to "the Civil Liberties award" may be a mistaken reference to AFPS, which was interested in civil liberties causes, or it may indicate that her grant was

Of course I was delighted to get the Civil Liberties award and shall start working on the new book at once. . . . I'm awfully grateful to you for thinking of this plan and taking the trouble to see it through, for without a little substantial encouragement I wouldn't have had the heart to tackle the book. (3 May [1925])

I've done nine chapters of the new book, which I have temporarily called "The Devil's Hand." That will be a third or rather more than a third of the book. I'm afraid it won't be in many respects so good a book as "Weeds". It seems inpossible [*sic*] to get into a portrayal of that new, raw and diversified life any such effect of depth and intensity as I managed to attain in "Weeds." Of course I have improved technically and I hope the new book will make up in color for what it may lack in some other things. I expect to introduce the I.W.W. They are quite active there and one of their number was tried in El Centro and sent up while we were in the Valley. I had intended to attend the trial but was prevented at the last moment. . . . However I found out a number of things about the case from different sources.

The Socialist Party seems in a bad way in this town. Out of a hundred thousand inhabitants there are only three hundred registered Socialists and they are nearly all tired old graybeards with one foot in the grave and their last shred of illusion and enthusiasm gone a generation ago. (29 July [1925])

As to my novel, I haven't made as rapid progress as I had hoped, but I think I shall have it finished in a few months. . . . I have had my last hundred dollars from Mrs. Davis and I hardly like to ask her for any more, especially as I can't write such direct propaganda as her committee would probably prefer. Of course the book will be a propaganda book, but I am afraid it will not be as direct as some of them might like. (17 January [1926])

---

made through the southern California branch of the American Civil Liberties Union, which Upton Sinclair helped organize in the early twenties. Sinclair's letters of support and Mrs. Kelley's application have not been found.

In spite of all the fine reviews it [*Weeds*] got it was a complete financial failure. According to a statement received the other day I still owe the publishers a hundred and thirty dollars of the five hundred that they advanced to me before publication.

I'm not quite through with the other book yet as my work was interrupted for some time by our moving [from North San Diego to Ocean Beach]. . . . While the house is building we are living in a shed which will afterward be a garage and I have a small tent in which to do my writing. (7 May [1926])

I'm afraid the publication of "The Devil's Hand", which I called my new book is indefinitely postponed. Harcourt Brace don't like it and I don't like it myself. So I am going to take it and throw away about half of it and make it over along rather different lines; and I think I can still make a worth while book out of it. One trouble was that I tried to work at it when conditions were so unfavorable that I simply couldn't give it my best efforts or even my second best. Another thing, some infernal inhibition seemed to descend upon me when writing the book and I couldn't get rid of it. Somehow or other I feel now as if the inhibition had lifted, and by attacking it from a different angle I think I can put new life into it. The thing went dead on me somehow. Perhaps it will go dead on me again when I go to work it over and if it does I may as well give up as far as that particular book is concerned. One thing I know, it's a whole lot easier to write a good book than a bad one. I sweat blood over this last book and all to very little purpose. (29 October [1926?])

You must wonder—if you ever think about it at all—why I don't get on the job and fix up that book and get it published and show some results for the help the Civil Liberties people gave me. I suppose I would have had it worked over by now if my eyes had not given out completely. . . . But now I am beginning to plan out a new novel. The one I wrote about Imperial Valley doesn't suit me a bit, although I think it can be made into a very good novel, and so I feel like laying it aside for quite a time and writing another book before working it over. (29 July [1927?])

I am anxious to get at my book "The Devil's Hand" and work it over. There are a great many changes that I want to make in it; but until I can read with ease it is impossible for me to work on it. (16 February [1928?])

An early admirer of Edith Summers Kelley's writing was Carey McWilliams—now editor of *The Nation*—who tried to place her stories and poems in the late twenties and early thirties. In an undated letter—probably written in 1929—she informed him:

I have another book almost written, but I had to stop work two years ago ancaunt [*sic*] of acute eye trouble. During that time I have not been able to read or write with any sort of ease. My eyes are now however greatly improved and I hope to be able to begin writing again soon. You wonder I suppose why I don't do magazine work and at least keep my husband out of the fish cannery. But really I can't do the stuff. I used to be able to but I have no heart for it any more and can't fool the editors. I've written a good deal of poetry during the past two years and maybe I'll get out a volume of that some time. Of course there's no money in it.

This is not so much a tale of woe as it sounds. My husband and I have had quite a bit of fun out of life even though all our moves have been financial failures. (10 April [1929?]) [3]

These letters raise a crucial question about *The Devil's Hand:* is the present version the original one that did not suit the author—or is it a revised version? We don't know. The only surviving complete text of the novel is the one that Fred Kelley had a typist prepare from her working draft after Edith's death in 1956. Patrick Kelley recalls that his father submitted this typescript to an agent who declined to handle the novel. It is only a hopeful guess that the re-typing was necessary because the original authorial type-

[3] Courtesy of Mr. McWilliams.

script had been reworked. If so, then this edition represents a revised—but not necessarily final—version.[4]

The moves from North San Diego to Ocean Beach in 1926 and then to Point Loma in 1928 were the result of Fred Kelley's modest success as a bootlegger, manufacturing and distributing home-brewed whiskey. All went well until he was trapped making a delivery, probably in 1929, and the authorities smashed his still. During the Great Depression, the Kelleys again experienced hardship and were compelled to leave their Point Loma home. They were land-poor. The banks holding the mortgages did not want to take over the property, so the Kelleys were able to hang on to their land. In 1937 Edith did some daywork as a charwoman, although she seems to have been motivated by curiosity as well as necessity.

During the early thirties Edith resumed writing fiction—she never stopped writing poetry—for a time; her material seems to have been short stories which were not published. There is no way to determine if she reworked *The Devil's Hand* at this time.[5] The Kelley story has a happy ending, at least in material terms. Fred and Edith Kelley moved to Pacific Grove in northern California in 1945 and then to Los Gatos in 1946, where they remained until her death in 1956. After the war Fred disposed of his real estate and invested the money. The Kelleys spent their last years in security: their income exceeded their expenditures. The story has a hero, Patrick Kelley, who preserved his mother's papers and who has generously cooperated with this editor and Southern Illinois University Press in our efforts to revive the work of Edith Summers Kelley.

[4] Sinclair Lewis read the early version of the novel, for on 19 August 1930 he wrote encouragingly to Edith Summers Kelley: "I hope that some day you will re-do the Imperial Valley novel. It has a wealth of magnificent material which I think would come into shape if you could go at it again afresh" (Lilly Library, Indiana University).

[5] It would seem not, for in a letter of 8 January 1940 to Carey McWilliams, Mrs. Kelley says she has been unable to revise *The Devil's Hand,* but still hopes to.

Now that *The Devil's Hand* has been rescued, I am being asked if it is as good as *Weeds*—or whether it is being published as a sentimental gesture. No; it is not as good as *Weeds*. Few novels are. But *The Devil's Hand* deserves publication on its own merits. There is a catchphrase in publishing, "worth publishing," which doesn't really mean much, for it implies no conviction. *The Devil's Hand* is better than "worth publishing." It is a successful novel that has the strengths of the author's first novel: emotional control and sharp observation. The reader of Edith Summers Kelley's novels is convinced that the author knows what she is doing, that she has disciplined her material and her attitudes toward it. Like *Weeds, The Devil's Hand* is a sociological novel that is not a problem novel or a protest novel. Mrs. Kelley resists blatant propagandizing—in contrast to her mentor Upton Sinclair—although the social messages of her second novel are strongly present. Her restraint is noteworthy in view of her deep social—and Socialist—convictions. Nevertheless her control is not perfect. Andy Blake and Dan Stoner are a bit too good to be true, and the novel is diminished when these two characters function as convenient spokesmen for the author.

The chief distinction of *The Devil's Hand* is that it is acutely observed social history. But it is fiction, not reportage, so Mrs. Kelley is able to—indeed, is required to—enforce the social history in terms of character. *The Devil's Hand* is of course Rhoda's novel, and it ultimately succeeds in terms of the authorial control over Rhoda's point of view. A rather simplified comparison between the technique of the two novels is that Judith is studied mostly from the outside in *Weeds*; but in *The Devil's Hand* nearly everything is seen from Rhoda's angle of vision, everything is filtered through her impressions—for example, the auction sequence in chapter 15. Moreover, Edith Summers Kelley elected to achieve this effect the hard way: not through a first-person narrator-protagonist, but by means of the authorial voice restricting itself to a central consciousness. In the perfectly controlled account of Rhoda peddling chickens we are utterly convinced of her defeat because we are involved in it. Her marriage of desperation follows with the inevitability of a syllogism.[6]

[6] I am grateful to the following people for generous help in researching the composition of *The Devil's Hand:* Mrs. Wanda Randall, Princeton University Library; William Cagle, Lilly Library, Indiana University; Alan Cohn, Morris Library, Southern Illinois University; Jean R. McNiece, New York Public Library; Carey McWilliams; Morris L. Ernst. Patrick Kelley made it all possible.

Edith Summers Kelley: *A Postscript*

by Patrick Kelley

SINCE THE republication of *Weeds* many people have asked me, "What was she like?—I mean what was she like as a day-to-day person?" or "What was she like philosophically?" or "What was she like as an artist?" These questions are easy to ask, but in the answering of them it soon becomes apparent that one cannot speak of one aspect without getting involved in the others. So we might just as well go back to—what was she like?

She was not five feet tall, had light golden hair and very pale blue eyes. She loved nature—animals, plants, the changes in the quality of the light as the day progresses, the changes in the seasons. Philosophically she was descended from Zeno, Epictetus, and Marcus Aurelius. Sorry to have to go back to Hellenic and Hellenized examples; but stoics, though they exist by the millions, do not ordinarily advertise themselves. So as a stoic she believed in moderation and did nothing in excess except write. She was even-tempered, undemonstrative, unsociable, and usually expressionless, except when laughing. In short, most of her activities were confined within her skull.

What were these activities? I think the most pressing question in her mind was: what in man is real, is firmly based in his constitution as man, and what are the variations, combinations and limitations of these attributes? Necessarily coupled with this question is its antithesis: what in man is epiphenomena, invented, imaginary, falsified? I'm afraid she came to the conclusion that most of the things that man worries about, fights about, kills his neighbors about, and strives for do not really exist. At least they didn't exist in her mind, but she was well aware that any kind of nonsense is real enough to the one who believes it. It was these ironies and discrepancies and conflicts created by man's absurdities that kept her laughing a good deal of the time.

She was kind, as courteous as taciturnity will allow, and unacquisitive. She believed in the simple life and followed it. Outwardly, a Puritan might have taken her for one of his own, but inwardly he would have been horrified to find her mind a collocation of skepticisms, disbeliefs, and heresies. Yet her curiosity ramified everywhere; though she gave no credence to the Bible as religious fact, she was interested in it as a social, historical, and literary document and could quote it by the yard.

Being curious, she loved to observe people to see how they acted and reacted in terms of pressures and motivation. Here she ran into a conflict because in order to observe people it is necessary to associate with them, and if there was one thing she hated it was to be bored by someone. She solved this problem partially by being an observer and not a participant. She watched and listened, didn't initiate conversation, fled when cornered by a bore. She was bored not only by nonsense but by small talk. The family (five of us) ate many a meal during which no one uttered one word.

In her lifetime she was acquainted with many extremists —anarchists, socialists, different varieties of communists, nihilists, and so forth. And though she was always interested in their points of view, she could never embrace any of their causes. She tried to see life as a whole, as a combination of forces shifting this way and that, but rarely deviating too far from the center.

Well, how did her point of view affect her writing? She was well aware that a bit of extremism helps sell a piece of writing. She was also aware that literary devices such as a clever stylistic technique and catering to the reader by building up to a climax or preparing the reader for a piece of pathos or humor also help sales. But she felt that life was not a series of climaxes, that one is rarely prepared for what is to come, and that cleverness in style was not suited to the subject matter of her novels. She holds up no signs saying: look at what a rascal this is—prepare yourself for this very funny sequence. She does not sit in judgment. She does not want to deprive the reader of his right to perceive relationships, derive inferences, mull over pathos mixed with humor.

How would she react today to learn that her work had been revived? I would guess that you would get a wry pensive smile with, "Fortune turns her wheel." But you would never know what she was thinking.

Textual Note: Setting-copy for this edition of *The Devil's Hand* is the typescript that C. Fred Kelley had prepared from her working draft after the death of Edith Summers Kelley. The draft was not preserved. Normal styling and correction of obvious typing errors have been imposed on this typescript. In addition, the following twenty-one substantive readings have been emended.

	(TS)	(Book)
5.33	she [	Rhoda
31.4	in [	on
35.1	men [	people
36.30	and irregular [	and at irregular
46.5	be interested [	be as interested
60.1	keep their [	keep in their
98.6	Do Kleines . . . Do [	Du Schönes . . . Du
.14	liebsten [	Schönsten
130.23	date [	time
157.25	having born [	having been born
166.6	Kleines [	Schönes
170.19	when [	whom
173.18	good 'nerless [	good hole 'nerless
192.24	decoction [	*stet*
198.18	myriad subtle [	myriad of subtle
207.9	so of big [	so big
215.13	in a new [	in new
219.25	and a [	and at a
252.29	existence be [	existence to
265.26	two complete sets [	a complete set
280.20	only other time on which she [	first time she